MARY RENAULT'S
EPIC NOVEL OF THE LAST
YEARS OF ALEXANDER THE GREAT!

"MARY RENAULT'S IS A SPECIAL BRAND OF HISTORICAL FICTION, at once imaginative, dramatic, seductive, and scrupulous . . . An interplay of passion and intelligence."
—Saturday Review

"SHE KNOWS THE TIME, AND SHE LOVES IT—IT SHOWS IN EVERY WORD SHE WRITES . . . The difficulty in dealing with Alexander in a work of fiction . . . is in this book superbly overcome: by using Bagoas, his lover, as the reader's eyes, she gets enough distance from Alexander to make him utterly real, human and superhuman at once, the incarnation of the spirit of the ancient world."

—Cecelia Holland

"A MASTER WRITER . . . RENAULT CREATES SEDUCTION SCENES THAT VIBRATE with sensuousness. She probes into emotional relationships with compassion and insight."

—Cleveland Plain Dealer

THE PERSIAN BOY

Other books by Mary Renault

THE BULL FROM THE SEA
THE CHARIOTEER
FIRE FROM HEAVEN
THE KING MUST DIE
THE MASK OF APOLLO
THE PERSIAN BOY

Published by Bantam Books, Inc.

The Persian Boy

MARY RENAULT

BANTAM BOOKS
TORONTO · NEW YORK · LONDON

RLI: $\dfrac{\text{VLM 6 (VLR 6–6)}}{\text{IL 8–adult}}$

THE PERSIAN BOY

*A Bantam Book / published by arrangement with
Pantheon Books, Inc.*

PRINTING HISTORY
Pantheon edition published 1972
Bantam edition published February 1974

*Bantam Books are published by Bantam Books, Inc. Its trade-
mark, consisting of the words "Bantam Books" and the portrayal of a bantam, is registered in the United States Patent
Office and in other countries. Marca Registrada. Bantam
Books, Inc., 666 Fifth Avenue, New York, New York 10019.*

PRINTED IN THE UNITED STATES OF AMERICA

If anyone has the right to be measured by the standards of his own time, it is Alexander.

Hermann Bengston,
THE GREEKS AND THE PERSIANS

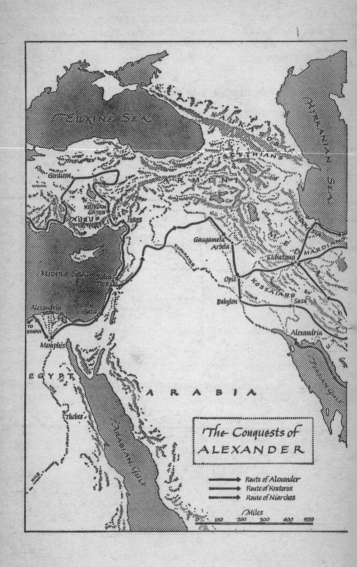

The Conquests of
ALEXANDER

→ Route of Alexander
→ Route of Krateros
→ Route of Niarchos

Miles
0   100   200   300   400   500

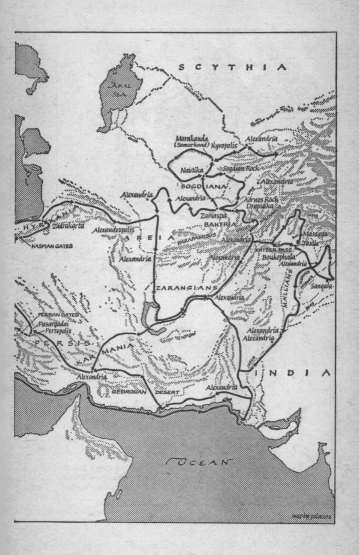

SCYTHIA

ARAL SEA

Marakanda
(Samarkand) Kyropolis
Alexandria

Nautika
Sogdian Rock

SOGDIANA

Alexandria

Alexandria

Alexandria

Aornos Rock
Drapsaka

Zariaspa
BAKTRIA

Zadrakarta

HY

KASPIAN GATES

Alexandropolis

AREIA

PARAPAMISOS

Massaga
Taxila

KHYBER PASS

Boukephala
Alexandria

Alexandria

Alexandria

ZARANGIANS

Alexandria

MALLIANS

Sangala

PERSIAN GATES

Pasargadai
Persepolis

PERSIS

KARMANIA

Alexandria
Alexandria

Alexandria

GEDROSIAN DESERT

Alexandria

INDIA

OCEAN

map in palacios

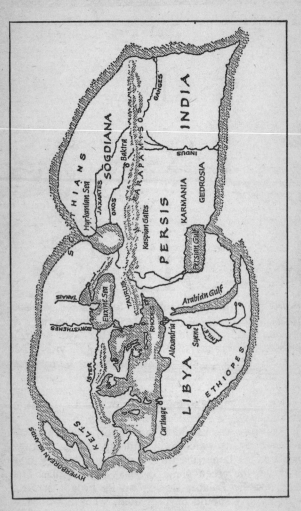

THE WORLD
as known in Alexander's day

1

L

EST ANYONE should suppose I am a son of nobody, sold off by some peasant father in a drought year, I may say our line is an old one, though it ends with me. My father was Artembares, son of Araxis, of the Pasargadai, Kyros' old royal tribe. Three of our family fought for him, when he set the Persians over the Medes. We held our land eight generations, in the hills west above Susa. I was ten years old, and learning a warrior's skills, when I was taken away.

Our hill-fort was as old as our family, weathered-in with the rocks, its watchtower built up against a crag. From there my father used to show me the river winding through the green plain to Susa, city of lilies. He pointed out the Palace, shining on its broad terrace, and promised I should be presented, when I was sixteen.

That was in King Ochos' day. We survived his reign, though he was a great killer. It was through keeping faith with his young son Arses, against Bagoas the Vizier, that my father died.

At my age, I might have overheard less of the business, if the Vizier had not borne my name. It is common enough in Persia; but being the only son and much beloved, I found it so strange to hear it pronounced with loathing, that each time my ears pricked up.

Court and country lords whom, as a rule, we hardly saw twice a year, were riding up the mountain track every few days. Our fort was well out of the way, a good place to meet. I enjoyed seeing these fine men on their tall horses, and felt an expectation of events, but not of danger, since none of them owned to fear. More than once they sacrificed at the fire-altar; the Magus would come, a strong old man who could scramble the rocks like a goatherd, killing snakes and scorpions. I loved the bright flames, and their light on the polished sword-hilts, gold buttons and jeweled hats. So it would all go on, I thought, till I could join them as a man.

After the prayer they would take the sacred drink together, and talk about honor.

In honor I had been instructed. Since I was five and had been brought out from among the women, I had been reared to ride and shoot and abhor the Lie. Fire was the soul of the Wise God. The dark Lie was faithlessness.

King Ochos was lately dead. If his sickness had killed him, few would have cried; but it was said that had been nothing much, it was his medicine he had died of. Bagoas had been highest in the kingdom, next the King, for many years; but young Arses had lately come of age and married. Ochos, with a grown heir and grandsons, had begun to trim Bagoas down. He died soon after this was seen.

"So now," said one of my father's guests, "the throne comes down by treachery, even though to the lawful heir. Myself, I acquit Arses; I never heard anything against the boy's honor. But his youth will double Bagoas' power; from now on, he might as well be King. No eunuch before has climbed so high."

"Not often," my father said. "But sometimes this lust for power will rule them. It is because they will see no sons." Finding me near him, he took me in his arm. Someone uttered a blessing.

The guest of highest rank, whose land was near Persepolis but who had followed the court to Susa, said, "We are all agreed that Bagoas shall never rule. But let us see how Arses deals with him. Young though he is, I think the Vizier has reckoned without his host."

I don't know what Arses would have done, if his brothers had not been poisoned. It was then he set out to count his friends.

The three princes had been much of an age. All three had been very close. Kings mostly change to their kin; Arses did not. The Vizier distrusted their private councils. Both the younger, without much time wasted between, got cramps in their bellies and died.

Soon after, a messenger came to our house; his letter bore the royal seal. I was the first person my father met, when the man had gone.

"My son," he said, "I shall soon have to go away; the King has called for me. A time may come—remember it—when one must stand for the Light against the Lie." He set his hand on my shoulder. "It's hard for you to be sharing your name just now with an evil man; you will not for long, God willing. And that monster can't hand it on. It is you who will carry it down in honor; you, and the sons of your sons." He lifted me up and kissed me.

He had the fort strengthened. It had a sheer cliff one side, and a gatehouse over the mountain track; but he had the walls raised a course or two, with better slits for the archers.

On the day before he was due to leave, a party of warriors rode up. Their letter carried the royal seal. We were not to know it came from a dead man's hand. Arses had gone his brothers' way; his infant sons were smothered; the male line of Ochos was wiped out. My father looked at the seal, and ordered the gates to be opened. The men rode in.

Having watched all this, I went back to some boy's

business in the orchard below the tower. There was some shouting; I came to see. Five or six men dragged through the door a man with a dreadful face. Its center was red and empty; blood streamed from it into his mouth and beard. He had been stripped of his coat; both shoulders dripped blood, for his ears had gone. I knew him by his boots; they were my father's.

Even now, sometimes I think how I let him go to his death without a word, struck dumb with horror. I suppose he understood; when he spoke it was to the purpose. As they led him on, he cried at me in a loud harsh voice, horribly changed by the wound where his nose had been, "Orxines betrayed us! Orxines, remember the name! Orxines!"

With the mouth open and shouting, the face looked more frightful than before. I did not know I heard the words it uttered. I stood like a post, while they pushed him to his knees, and pulled his head forward by the hair. It took them five or six sword-strokes, to cleave through his neck.

While they were about this, they forgot to watch my mother. She must have run straight up the tower; the moment he was dead she leaped from it, so they lost their sport with her. She screamed as she fell; but that, I think, was because she saw too late I was there below her. She struck the ground about a spear-length away, and her skull burst open.

I hope my father's spirit saw her quick death. They could just as well have taken his ears and nose when his head was off. The Vizier, when they brought it him, would never have known the difference.

My sisters were twelve years old and thirteen. There was another of about nine, by a second wife of my father's who had died of fever. I heard all three of them shrieking. I don't know if they were left for dead when the men had done, or taken away alive.

At last, the captain of the troop set me on his horse and rode with me down the hill. Slung to his saddle-cloth was the bloody bag with my father's head. I wondered, with what power of thought was left me, why he had had mercy on me alone. I learned the answer that same night.

He did not keep me long, being in need of money. In the dealer's courtyard at Susa, city of lilies, I stood stripped naked, while they drank date wine out of little cups, and haggled over my price. Greek boys are reared without shame and used to nakedness; we have more modesty. In my ignorance, I thought one could fall no lower.

Only a month before, my mother had scolded me for looking in her mirror, saying I was too young to be vain. I had no more than glimpsed my face in it. My new owner had more to tell. "A real thoroughbred, the antique Persian strain, the grace of a roebuck. See those delicate bones, the profile—turn round, boy—the hair shining like bronze, straight and fine as silk from Chin —come here, boy, let him feel it. Brows drawn with the fine brush. Those great eyes, smudged in with bister—aha, pools to drown love in! Those slender hands you won't sell cheap to sweep floors. Don't tell me you've been offered such goods in five years, or ten."

At his every pause, the dealer told him he did not buy at a loss. At last he reached his final offer; the captain said it was robbing an honest man; but the dealer said there was the risk to reckon for. "We lose one in five when we geld them."

Geld them, I thought, while the hand of fear closed the gate of understanding. But I had seen it done to an ox at home. I neither spoke nor moved. I begged for nothing. I had learned better than to hope there was pity in the world.

The dealer's house was strong as a prison, with courtyard walls fifteen feet high. On one side was a shed, where they did the gelding. They had purged and starved me first, which is thought to make it safer; I was led in cold and empty, to see the table with the knives, and the frame with splayed-out legs to which they bind you, with old black blood on it and dirty straps. Then at last I threw myself at the dealer's feet and clasped them crying. But they made no more of it than farmhands of the bawling bull-calf. They did not speak to me, just strapped me down, talking across me of some gossip in the market, till they began and I knew nothing, only the pain and my own screams.

They say women forget the pain of childbirth. Well, they are in nature's hand. No hand took mine. I was a body of pain in an earth and sky of darkness. It will take death to make me forget.

There was an old slave-woman who dressed my wounds. She was skillful and clean, for boys were merchandise, and, as she told me once, they thrashed her if they lost one. My cuts hardly festered; she used to tell me they'd made neat work of me, and later, she said giggling, I would be the gainer. I had no use for her words, and only knew she laughed when I was in pain.

When I was healed, I was sold at auction. Once more I stood stripped, this time before staring crowds. From the block I could see the bright glazes of the Palace, where my father had promised to present me to the King.

I was bought by a gem-stone dealer; though it was his wife who chose me, pointing a red-tipped finger from her curtained litter. The auctioneer had delayed and pleaded; the price had disappointed him. From pain and grief I had lost flesh, and no doubt most of my looks. They had stuffed me with food, but I had brought up most of it as if my body disdained to live; so they got me off their hands. The jeweler's wife wanted a pretty page, to set her above the concubines, and I was pretty enough for that. She had a monkey too, with green fur.

I grew fond of the monkey; it was my work to feed it. When I came it would fly through the air to me, and clasp my neck with its little hard black hands. But one day she wearied of it, and had it sold.

I was still young, living from day to day. But when she sold the monkey, I looked ahead. I would never be free; I would be bought and sold like the monkey; and I would never be a man. In the night I lay and thought of it; and in the morning, it seemed that without manhood I had grown old. She said I looked peaked, and gave me a dose that griped my belly. But she was not cruel, and never beat me unless I broke something she valued.

While I lay at the dealer's, the new King had been proclaimed. Ochos' line being extinguished, he was royal only by side descent; but the people seemed to think well of him. Datis, my master, brought no news to the harem, thinking the only concern of women was to please men, and of eunuchs to oversee them. But the chief eunuch would bring us all the gleanings of the bazaar, taking delight in this importance; and why not? It was all he had.

Darius the new King, he said, had both beauty and valor. When Ochos had been at war with the Kadousians, and their giant champion had challenged the King's warriors, only Darius had come forward. He stood six feet and a half himself, and had transfixed the man with a single javelin, living ever since in the renown. There had been consultations, and the Magi had scanned the skies; but no one in council had dared cross Bagoas' choice, he was too much dreaded. However, it seemed that so far the new King had murdered no one; his manners were reported gracious and mild.

As I heard this, waving my mistress's peacock fan, I recalled my father's birthday feast, the last of his life; the guests threading up the mountain and coming in through the gatehouse, the grooms taking their horses; my father with me beside him, welcoming them at the door. One man had towered over the others, and looked so much a warrior that even to me he did not seem old. He was handsome, with all his teeth still perfect, and had tossed me up like a baby, making me laugh. Had he not been called Darius? But one king or another, I thought as I waved the fan, what is that to me?

Soon all this was stale news, and they were talking about the west. There were barbarians there whom I had heard my father speak of, red-haired savages who painted themselves blue; they lived north of the

Greeks, a tribe called Macedonians. First they had come raiding; then they had had the impudence to declare war, and the coastal satraps were arming. But the news now was that not long after King Arses' death, their own King had been killed, at some public spectacle where, in their barbarous way, he had walked about unguarded. His heir was only a young lad, so there was no more need to be concerned about them.

My life went by in the small duties of the harem, making beds, carrying trays, mixing sorbets of mountain snow and citron, painting my mistress's fingerends, and being petted by the girls; Datis had only one wife, but three young concubines, who were kind to me, knowing the master had no taste for boys. But if ever I waited on them, my mistress would clip my ear.

Soon I was let out on little errands, to buy henna and kohl and herbs for the clothes-chests, and such things beneath the chief eunuch's dignity; and would see other eunuchs shopping too. Some were like him, soft and fat with breasts like women's, and after seeing one, though I was growing quickly, I would eat less. Others were shriveled and shrill like careworn crones. But a few stood tall and straight, with some look of pride in themselves; I used to wonder what their secret was.

It was summer; the orange trees in the women's court scented the air, mixed with perfumed sweat from the girls, as they sat dabbling their fingers at the rim of the fishpool. My mistress had bought me a little harp, to hold on the knee, and bade one of the girls teach me to tune it. I was singing, when the chief eunuch rushed in, wheezing with haste and quivering all over. He was bursting with news, but paused to mop his brow and complain about the heat, making them wait. One could see it was a great day.

"Madam," he said, "Bagoas the Vizier is dead!"

The courtyard twittered like a roost of starlings. My mistress waved her plump hand for quiet. "But how? Don't you know anything more?"

"Indeed, madam." He mopped his brow again, till she invited him to sit. He looked round from his cushion like a market storyteller. "It is common talk at the Palace, having been witnessed by many, as you shall hear. You are aware, madam, I know where to ask; if it can be known, it comes to me. It appears that yesterday the King received Bagoas in audience. With men of such rank, of course, only the choicest wine is offered. It was brought in, poured already into cups of inlaid gold. The King took the royal one, Bagoas the other, and the Vizier waited for the King to drink. For some time he held his wine-cup, speaking of some slight matter and watching Bagoas' face; then he made to drink; then he lowered the cup again, watching still. He then said thus: 'Bagoas, you have been the faithful servant of three kings. Such a man should be marked with honor. Here is my own cup for you to pledge me in; I will drink from yours.' The chamberlain brought it to Bagoas, and brought the other to the King.

"I was told, by one who did me the honor to confide in me, that the face of the Vizier changed to the color of pale river-mud. The King drank; and there was a stillness. 'Bagoas,' he said, 'I have drunk; I am waiting for you to pledge me.' At this, Bagoas laid hand on heart, fetched his breath short, and prayed the King to pardon him; he had been taken faint, and begged leave to withdraw. But the King said, 'Sit, Vizier; the wine is your best medicine.' He sat, for it seemed his knees failed beneath him; and the cup shook in his hand, so that the wine began to spill. Then the King leaned forward in his chair, raising his voice for all to hear. 'Drink your wine, Bagoas. For I tell you this and I do not lie; whatever is in that cup, it will be better for you to drink it.'

"At this he drank; and when he would have risen, the Royal Guard stood round him with pointed spears. The King waited till the poison had taken hold, before retiring and leaving them to watch him die. I am told he was an hour about it."

There was a great deal of exclaiming, like coins in the storyteller's hat. The mistress asked who it was that warned the King. The chief eunuch looked sly, and dropped his voice. "The Royal Cupbearer has been given a robe of honor. Madam, who knows? Some say

the King himself cast his eye on the fate of Ochos; that
when the cups were changed, the Vizier read his face,
but could do nothing. Let the hand of discretion cover
the wise mouth."

So, then, divine Mithra, Avenger of Honor, had
kept his day. The traitor had died by treachery, just as
he ought. But the time of gods is not like the time of
men. My namesake had died, as my father promised
me; but he had died too late for me, and for all the sons
of my sons.

2

TWO YEARS I served the harem, suffering nothing much worse than a tedium I wondered, sometimes, I did not die of. I grew taller, and twice had to have new clothes. Yet my growth had slowed. They had said at home I would be as tall as my father; but the gelding must have given some shock that changed me. I am a little better than small, and all my life have kept the shape of a boy.

Nonetheless, I used to hear in the bazaar praise of my beauty. Sometimes a man would speak to me, but I turned away; he would not speak, I thought, if he knew I was a slave. Such was still my simplicity. I was only glad to escape the women's chatter, see the life of the bazaar, and take the air.

Presently my master also gave me errands, taking notes to the jewelers of his new stock, and so on. I used to dread being sent to the royal workshops, though Datis seemed to think he was giving me a treat. The workmen were all slaves, chiefly Greeks, who were prized for skill. Of course they were all branded in the

11

face; but as punishment, or to stop their getting away, most of them had had a foot off, or sometimes both. Some needed both hands and feet, if they used a burin-wheel for carving gems; and these, lest they should slip off untraced, had had their noses taken. I would look anywhere but at them; till I saw the jeweler watching me, supposing me in search of something to steal.

I had been taught at home that after cowardice and the Lie, the worst disgrace for a gentleman was to trade. Selling was not to be thought of; one lost face even by buying, one should live off one's own land. Even my mother's mirror, which had a winged boy engraved on it and had come all the way from Ionia, had been in her dowry. No matter how often I fetched merchandise, I never ceased to feel the shame. It is a true saying, that men don't know till too late when they have been well off.

It was a bad year for the jewelers. The King had gone to war, leaving the Upper City dead as a tomb. The young King of Macedon had crossed to Asia, and was taking all the Greek cities there from Persian rule. He was not much more than twenty; it had seemed just a matter for the coastal satraps. But he had beaten their forces and crossed the Granikos, and was now thought as bad to reckon with as his father.

It was said he had no wife; that he took no household with him; only his men, like a mere robber or bandit. But thus he got about very fast, even through mountain land unknown to him. From pride he wore glittering arms, to be singled out in battle. Many tales were told of him, which I leave out, since those that were true are known by all the world, while of the false we have enough. At all events, he had already done all his father had intended, and still did not seem content.

The King, therefore, had mustered a royal army, and gone himself to meet him. Since the King of Kings did not travel naked to war like a young western raider, he had taken the court and Household, with its stewards and chamberlains and eunuchs; also the Harem, with the Queen Mother, the Queen, the princesses, and the little prince, and their own attendants, their eunuchs and hairdressers and women of the wardrobe and all the rest. The Queen, who was said to be of surpassing beauty, had always brought the jewelers good trade.

The King's attendant lords had also taken their women, their wives and often their concubines, lest the war should last some time. So, in Susa, only such people were buying jewelry as are content with chippings stuck in clay.

The mistress had no new dress that spring, and was sharp with us all for days; the prettiest of the concubines had a new veil, which for a week made life unbearable. The chief eunuch had less shopping-money; the mistress was skimped with sweets, the slaves with food. My only comfort was to feel my slim waist, and look at the chief eunuch.

If no thicker, I was growing taller. Though I had again outgrown my clothes, I expected to go on wearing them. But to my surprise, I got a new suit from the master; tunic, trousers and sash, and an outer coat with wide sleeves. The sash even had gold thread in it. They were so pretty that I stooped over the pool to see myself, and was not displeased.

The same day, soon after noon, the master summoned me to his business room. I remember finding it strange that he did not look at me. He wrote a few words and sealed the paper, saying, "Take this to Obares the master jeweler. Go straight there, don't loiter in the bazaar." He looked at his fingernails, then back to me. "He is my best customer; so take good care to be civil."

These words surprised me. "Sir," I said, "I have never been uncivil to a customer. Does anyone say I have?"

"Oh, tut, no," he said, fidgeting with a tray of loose turquoises. "I am only telling you to be civil to Obares."

Even then, I walked to the house thinking no more than that he had some worry about the man's goodwill. The captain who took me from my home, and what he did to me, was smothered up with other things in my mind; when I woke crying in the night, it was mostly from a dream of my father's noseless face, shouting aloud. Without thought of harm I went to the shop of Obares, a stocky Babylonian with a black bush of beard. He glanced at the note, and led me straight through to the inner room, as if I were expecting it.

I hardly remember the rest, except his stink, which I can recall today, and that, after, he gave me a bit of silver for myself. I gave it to a leper in the marketplace, who took it on a palm without thumb or fingers, and wished me the blessing of long life.

I thought of the monkey with green fur, carried away by a man with a cruel face, who'd said he was going to train it. It came to me that perhaps I had been sent on approval to a buyer. I went to the gutter and vomited my heart out. No one took notice. Damp with cold sweat, I returned to my master's house.

Whether or not Obares would have been a buyer, my master was not a seller. It suited him far better to be doing Obares favors. I was lent to him twice a week.

I doubt my master ever called himself what he was. He just obliged a good customer. Then a friend of Obares heard, and must be obliged for his sake. Not being in the trade, he paid in coin; and he passed the good word on. Before long, I was sent out most afternoons.

At twelve years old, it takes too perfect a despair to die alone. I thought of it often; I had dreamed of my father without his nose, and instead of the traitor's name he shouted mine. But Susa has not walls high enough to leap from; there was nothing else with which I could make sure. As for running away, I had for example the leg-stumps of the royal jeweler's slaves.

I went, therefore, to my clients as I was told. Some were better than Obares, some much worse. I can yet feel the cold sinking of my heart, as I walked to some house unknown before; and how, when one required of me something not fit to be described, I remembered my father, no longer a noseless mask, but standing on the night of his birthday feast while by torchlight our warriors did the sword-dance. To honor his spirit, I struck the man and called him what he deserved.

My master did not beat me with the leaded whip he used upon the Nubian porter, for fear of spoiling me; but the cane cut hard. While it still stung, I was sent back to beg pardon and make amends.

This life I led for rather more than a year, seeing no escape till I should be too old. My mistress did not know of it, and I conspired to deceive her; I had always some tale for her of my day's business. She had more decency than her husband, and would have been outraged, but she had no power to save me. If she knew the truth, the house would be in an uproar, till for the sake of peace he would sell me for the best price I'd fetch. When I thought of the bidders, I kept the hand of discretion before my mouth.

Whenever I passed through the bazaar, I imagined people saying, "There goes Datis' whore." Yet I had to bring back some news, to satisfy my mistress. The rumors were running, ahead of truth, that the King had fought a great battle with Alexander, at Issos by the sea, and lost, escaping with his bare life on horseback, leaving his chariot and his arms. Well, he got away, I thought; there are some of us would think that luck enough.

As proper news came in by the Royal Road, we learned that the Harem had been taken, with the Queen Mother, the Queen, her daughters and her son. I pitied them; I had good cause to know their fate. The girls' screams rang in my ears; I pictured the young boy flung upon the spears, as I would have been but for one man's greed. However, never having seen these ladies, and being bound for the house of someone I knew too well, I kept some pity for myself.

Later it was put about, by someone who swore it came straight from Kilikia, that Alexander had set up the royal women in their own pavilion, untouched by man, with their household to serve them, and that even the boy was still alive. This tale was laughed at, for everyone knew that no one behaves like that in war, let alone western barbarians.

The King had fallen back on Babylon, and wintered there. But it grows hot in spring; without much state he returned to Susa, to rest from his labors, while his satraps mustered another army. I was kept at work, and could not see the royal cavalcade, which, like the boy I still partly was, I had set some store by. It seemed that Alexander had not marched inland where he had been expected, but had had the folly to sit down before Tyre, an island stronghold which would not fall in ten years. While he kept up this pastime, the King could take his ease.

Now that the court was back, even though without the Queen, I hoped the jewel trade would prosper; then perhaps I might be let off *my* trade, to stay and serve the harem. Once I had thought it tedious; it beckoned now like a palm grove in the desert.

You might suppose by now I would be reconciled. But ten years are ten years, though one has left them behind for three. Far off on the mountain, I could still discern the ruins of my home.

There were clients from whom, if I had flattered them, I could have had good money I need not have shown my master. I could sooner have made a meal off camel-dung; yet some were drawn by my sullenness, and would court me to win a smile. Others would hurt me in various ways, but I divined they would do so in any case, and servility would encourage them. The worst, who left me covered in weals, my master denied me to, not from pity but because he damaged the goods. With others I learned resources. I did not refuse a small piece of silver, but used it to buy kif. Taking it seldom, I could smoke myself silly beforehand. That is why to this day the mere smell of it makes me sick.

Some, in their way, were kind. With these, it seemed that honor demanded a return. I would try to please them, since I had nothing else to give; and they were glad to teach me how to do it better. Thus I learned the beginnings of art.

There was a carpet-seller who, when he had done, would treat me like a guest, seat me by him on the divan, give me wine and talk to me. The wine I was glad of, since he sometimes put me in pain; not through his fault, for he was gentle and liked to please. I kept it to myself, from pride, or what modesty was left me.

One day he had a carpet of ten years' work hung on the wall, to take pleasure in, he said, before it went to the buyer; a friend of the King's, content with only the finest. "I expect," he said, "he may have known your father."

I could feel my face drain of blood and my hands grow cold. All this while, I had supposed my birth my secret, my father's name sheltered from my disgrace. Now I knew my master had had it from the dealer, and boasted of it. Why not? The Vizier, from whose vengeance I had been stolen, was disgraced and dead; it was no crime to have cheated him. I thought of our name in the mouths of all those who had had their hands on me.

A month's custom dulled me a little to it, but not much. There were some I would gladly have killed for knowing what they knew. When the carpet-seller sent for me again, I was thankful it was no one worse.

I was brought into the fountain court, where he sometimes sat on cushions under a blue awning, till we went indoors. But, this time, he was not alone; another man sat with him. I stood stock-still in the open doorway, my thought, I suppose, clear on my face.

"Come in, Bagoas," he said. "Don't look so startled, my dear boy. Today my friend and I ask nothing but the refreshment of beholding you, and the pleasure of hearing you sing. You have your harp, I am glad to see."

"Yes," I answered. "The master said you wished it." I had wondered if he had been charged extra.

"Come, then. We are both fretted with the day's business; you shall soothe our souls for us."

I sang to them, thinking all the while, They will be up to something later. The guest had not a merchant's look; he was almost like my father's friends, but smoother. Some patron of the host's, I thought; presently I shall be served to him on a platter, dressed with green leaves.

I was mistaken. I was asked for another song; then they chatted with me of nothings; then I was given a little present, and dismissed. No such thing had ever happened to me before. As the courtyard door closed behind me, I heard their low voices, and knew they spoke of me. Well, I thought, it had been an easy stint of work. I should hear from the other man later.

So I did. Next day he bought me.

I saw him come to the house. Wine was sent for; the Nubian, who had served it, said some hard bargaining was going on. He did not know what about; he had only simple Persian; but already I wondered. When afterwards the master sent for me, I knew before he spoke.

"Well, Bagoas." He was smiling from ear to ear. "You are a very fortunate boy; you are going to very good service." And for a very good price, I thought. "You will be sent for tomorrow morning."

He waved me off. I said, "What kind of service, sir?"

"That is your new master's business. Take care to show him respect. You have had good training here."

My mouth opened. But I said nothing after all. I just looked him in the face; his color changed, and his pig-eyes shifted. Then he told me to go; but it had done me good.

So, like the monkey, I was set for an unknown bourne. My mistress drenched me with tears; it was like being enfolded in wet cushions. Of course he had sold me without her leave. "You have been such a sweet good boy, so gentle. I know you still grieve for your parents, even now; I have seen it in your face. I do pray you have a kind master; you are still a child as the world goes, so quietly you have lived here."

We cried again, and all the girls embraced me in turn. Their scented freshness was pleasant, compared with certain memories. I was thirteen years old, and felt I could have no more to learn when I was fifty.

I was duly fetched next day, by a very grand eunuch, some forty years old, who had been handsome and still watched his figure. He was so civil, I ventured to ask the new master's name. He smiled discreetly. "We must first see you made fit for his household. But do not be anxious, boy; all that will be attended to."

I felt he was keeping something back, though not from malice. As we walked beyond the bazaar to the quiet streets where the big houses were, I hoped the new master's tastes were not too odd.

The house was like all such, shut off from the street by a high wall, with a great bronze-studded gate. The outer court had tall trees whose tops, even, had hardly showed from the street. It was all old and dignified. The eunuch took me to a little room in the servants' wing, with only one bed. For three years I had fallen asleep to the chief eunuch's whistling snores. On the bed were new clothes laid out. They were plainer than mine; only when they were on I saw their quality. The eunuch took my own clothes between finger and thumb, and sniffed. "Gaudy and shoddy. We can make no use of them here. However, no doubt some child of want will be glad of them."

I supposed I should now be brought before my master; but it seemed I was not accounted fit to see his face before my training, which began that day.

It was a huge old house, very cool, with a set of rambling rooms upon a court, long out of use it seemed, some with just an antique chest or an old divan with burst cushions. Through these we came to another, with good furniture, set out I supposed rather for store than use. At one end was a table with a fine carved chair; there was a sideboard, with good vessels of enameled copper; yet at the other end stood a stately bed beneath an embroidered canopy. Strangely, this was made up, and had its clothes-stool and its night-table. All was polished and clean, yet had no look of habitation. Creepers festooned the fretted windows; the light came in as green as water in a fishpool.

However, it soon appeared there was method in all this. This was my training-ground.

The eunuch sat in the carved chair enacting the master, instructing me in serving this dish or that, or pouring wine, setting down the cup or putting it in the master's hand. His manners were haughty enough for any lord's, but he never struck or cursed me, and I felt no ill-will to him; I saw the awe he inspired in me was part of my training too. For I perceived that indeed I had changed my state, and was growing scared.

My noon meal was brought here; I did not eat with the servants. I had seen no one but the eunuch, since I entered this house. It began to seem uncanny; I dreaded being told I must sleep here too in the great bed; I was sure there would be ghosts at night. But after my supper I slept in my little cell. Even the privy I went to had no one ever about, but was overgrown and full of spiders, as if not used anymore.

Next morning, the eunuch took me through all yesterday's lessons. As far as a man of his dignity could show it, he seemed a little keyed up. I thought, Of course, he expects the master; and growing anxious, at once let fall a plate.

Suddenly the door swung open, and, as if it had revealed a flower garden in full bloom, a young man came in. He strode forward, gay, handsome, assured, richly dressed and adorned with gold, smelling of costly essences. It took me some moments to reflect that, though more than twenty, he had no beard. He had seemed no more like a eunuch than a shaven Greek.

"Greeting, Gazelle-Eyes," he said, smiling and showing teeth like fresh-peeled almonds. "Well, indeed, they said no more than the truth for once." He turned to my mentor. "And how is he getting on?"

"Not badly, Oromedon, for one who has had no grounding. We shall make something of him in time." He spoke, not without respect, but not as one speaks to the master.

"Let us see." He beckoned to an Egyptian slave behind him to put some burden down, and withdraw. I was taken through all my table-work. As I made to pour wine, he said, "Your elbow is rather tight. Curve it like this." He flexed my arm in his hands. "You see? That makes a much prettier line."

I continued to the sweets, and stood awaiting censure. "Good. But now let us try with a proper service." From the slave's parcel, he unwrapped a treasure that made me stretch my eyes; cups, ewers and dishes of pure chased silver, inlaid with gold flowers. "Come," he said, pushing aside the copper. "There is a certain touch in the handling of precious things, which is only learned by touching them." He gave me a secret smile from his long dark eyes. When I took the things up, he said, "Ah! He has it. You see? He is not afraid of them, he feels how they should be cherished. I think we shall do well." He looked about. "But where are the cushions? And the low wine-table? He must learn how to serve the inner room." The other glanced up at him. "Oh, yes," he said, laughing softly, his gold earrings twinkling, "we can be sure of that. Just send the things, and I will show him all that myself. I shan't need to keep you."

When the cushions came, he sat, and showed me how to hold the tray to him kneeling. He was so friendly, even when correcting me, that I mastered this new work without nervousness. He got up, saying, "Excellent. Quick, deft and quiet. And now to the rites of the bedchamber."

I said, "I'm afraid, sir, I've learned none of that yet, either."

"You need not keep calling me sir. That was just to keep up your sense of ceremony. No, this is my part of your instruction. There is a great deal of ritual at bedtime, but we need do no more than run over it; most will be done by people of higher rank. However, it is important never to be at a loss. We will first prepare the bed, which should have been done already." We opened and turned it back; it had sheets of thread-drawn Egyptian linen. "No perfume? I don't know who got this room ready. Like an inn for camel-drivers. However, let us suppose the perfume scattered."

He stood by the bed and removed his fluted hat.

"That would be done by someone of very high rank indeed. Now there's a knack in taking off the sash; he will of course not turn around for you. Just slip your hands round and cross them; yes, that's right. And now the robe. Begin unbuttoning at the top. Now lift it off from behind, and slip it down; he will just move his arms from his sides enough for that." I removed the robe, baring his slender olive-colored shoulders, on which his black curls fell down, just touched with henna. He sat down on the bed. "For the slippers, go on both knees, sit back a little, and take each foot on your lap in turn, always beginning with the right. No, don't get up yet. He has loosened the waist of his trousers; you now draw them off, still kneeling, with your eyes cast down all the time." He lifted his weight a little, so that I could do this. It left him in his linen underdrawers. He was extremely graceful, with a flawless skin; the Median, not the Persian beauty.

"You have not folded them. The chamber-groom will take them away; but there must never be a moment when they lie about untidy. So, then, if this room were set out properly, you would put on the night-robe (my fault, however did I forget it?) under which he would slip off his drawers, in accordance with propriety." He covered himself modestly with the sheet, and tossed them onto the stool.

"And now, if nothing has been said beforehand, watch carefully for the sign that you are to remain when the rest retire. It will be nothing much; just a glance—like this—or a small movement of the hand. Don't stand about, but occupy yourself with something; I will show you, when all the right things are here. Then, when you are alone, he will motion you, like this, to undress. Go now to the foot of the bed, take off quickly and neatly, and lay them down there out of sight; he does not expect to see a pile of your clothes. That's right, take off everything. You may now allow yourself to walk up with a smile, but don't make it too familiar. That's perfect, perfect; try to keep that touch of shyness. And now—" He opened the bed, with a smile so gracious and commanding that I had got there before I knew it.

I started away, reproach and anger in my heart. I had liked and trusted him; he had tricked and mocked me. He was no better than the rest.

He reached out and caught my arm; his grasp was firm, but without anger or greed. "Gently, Gazelle-Eyes. Hush now, and listen to me." I had not said a word; but I sat still and ceased to struggle. "I have never, all this time, told you a word of a lie. I am just a teacher; all this is part of what I am here to do. If I like my work, so much the better for both of us. What you wish to forget, I know; soon you can do so forever. There is a pride in you, wounded but still unyielding; it is perhaps what shaped your prettiness into beauty. With such a nature, living as you have lived between your sordid master and his vulgar friends, you must have been holding back all the while. And very right. But those days are gone. There is a new existence before you. Now you must learn to give a little. I am here for that, to teach you the art of pleasure." He reached out his other hand, and gently pulled me down. "Come. I promise you, you will like it much more with me."

I did not resist persuasion. He might indeed possess some magic, by whose power all would be well. So at first it still appeared, for he was as skilled as he was charming, like a creature from another world than that I had been frequenting; it seemed one could linger forever in the outer courts of delight. I took all that was offered, neglecting my old defenses; and the pain, when it swooped on me with all its claws, was worse than ever before. For the first time I could not keep silent.

"I am sorry," I said as soon as I could. "I hope I did not spoil it for you. I couldn't help it."

"But what is it?" He bent over me as if it really concerned him. "I cannot have hurt you, surely?"

"No, of course." I turned my eyes to the sheet to blot my tears. "It always happens like that, if it does at all. As if they brought back the knives."

"But you should have told me this." He still spoke as if he cared, which to me was wonderful.

"I thought it must be the same with us all—with all people like me."

"No, indeed. How long ago were you cut?"

"Three years," I said, "and a little more."

"I don't understand it. Let me look again. But this is beautiful work; I never saw cleaner scars. It would surprise me, cutting a boy with your looks, if they took more than just enough to keep you beardless. Of course it can go wrong. The cuts can fester so deep that all the roots of feeling are eaten away. Or they can butcher you so that nothing is left for feeling, as they do with the Nubians, I suppose from fear of their strength. But with you, short of giving her fill to a woman— and few of us can do that, though one hears of it now and then—I can't see why you shouldn't enjoy it with the best. Do you tell me you have suffered this since you began?"

"What?" I cried. "Do you think I let myself be moved by those sons of pigs?" Here was one to whom I could speak at last. "There were one or two . . . But I used to think myself away from it, when I could."

"I see. Now I begin to guess the trouble." He lay in thought, as grave as a physician, then said, "Unless it is women. You don't think of women, do you?"

I remembered the three girls hugging me by the pool, and their round soft breasts; then my mother's brains spilled on the orchard pebbles, and my sisters screaming. I answered, "No."

"Never think of them." He looked at me earnestly, his lightness gone. "Don't imagine, if your beauty keeps its promise, that they won't be after you, sighing and whispering, and vowing to be content with anything you have. So they may believe; but they never will. No; in their discontent they will turn spiteful, and betray you. The surest way to end on a spike in the sun."

His face had turned somber. I saw there some dreadful recollection, and, to reassure him, told him again I never thought of them.

He caressed me consolingly, though the pain had left

me. "No, I don't know why I considered women. It is clear enough what it is. You have fine senses; for pleasure certainly, for pain therefore as much. Though gelding is bad enough for anyone, there are degrees of feeling. It has haunted you ever since, as if it could happen again. That's not so rare; you'd have got over it long ago, with me. But you have been going with men you despised. Outwardly you had to obey; within, your pride has conceded nothing. You have preferred pain to a pleasure by which you felt degraded. It comes of anger, and the soul's resistance."

"I didn't resist you," I said.

"I know. But it has bitten deep; it won't be cured in a day. Later we'll try again, it's too soon now. With any luck in your life, you will outgrow it. And I can tell you one thing more; where you're going now, I don't think it will much trouble you. I have been told to say no more, which is taking discretion to absurdity; but no matter, to hear is to obey."

"I wish," I said, "I might belong to you."

"I too, Gazelle-Eyes. But you are for my betters. So don't fall in love with me; we shall be parting all too soon. Put your clothes on; the getting-up ceremonial we'll do tomorrow. The lesson has been long enough for today."

My training took some time longer. He came earlier, dispensed with the haughty eunuch, and taught me himself the service of the table, the fountain court, the inner chamber, the bath; he even brought a fine horse, and in the weed-grown courtyard showed me how to mount and ride with grace; all I'd learned at home was how to stick on my mountain pony. Then we went back to the room with its green glimmering windows and great bed.

He still hoped to exorcise my demon, giving much patience to it; but the pain always returned, its strength increased by the pleasure it had fed on. "No more," he said. "It will be too much for you, and not enough for me. I am here to teach, and am in danger of forgetting it. We must accept that this is your lot just now."

I said in grief, "I'd be better off like those others, feeling nothing."

"Oh, no. Never suppose so. They put it all into eating; you can see what becomes of *them*. I'd have liked to cure you, just for your sake and mine; but as to your calling, that's to please, not be pleased. And it seems to me that in spite of this trouble—or maybe because of it, who can tell what makes the artist?—you have a gift. Your responses are very delicate; it is this which made your late employment so disgusting to you. You were a musician forced to hear howling street-singers. All you need is to know your instrument. That I will teach you, though I think you will excel me. This time, you need not fear being sent where your art will shame you; I can promise that."

"Can't you tell me yet who it is?"

"Haven't you guessed even yet? But no, how should you? One thing, though, I can say, and don't forget it. He loves perfection; in jewels and vessels, in hangings, carpets and swords; in horses, women and boys. No, don't look so scared; nothing dreadful will be done to you for falling short; but he might lose interest, which would be a pity. I wish to present you flawless; he will expect no less of me. But I doubt if your secret will come to light there. Let us think no more of it, and apply ourselves to useful knowledge."

Till now, as I found, he had been like the musician who takes up an unknown harp or lyre, testing its resonance. Now lessons began in earnest.

Already I hear the voice of one who has known no more of slavery than to clap his hands and give orders, crying out, "The shameless dog, to boast of how he was debauched in youth by one corrupted before him." To such I reply that I had been debauched for a year already, rolled in mire without help or hope; and now to be tended like something exquisite seemed not corruption but the glimpse of some blissful heaven. So too, after being the sport of rutting swine, seemed the subtle music of the senses. It came to me easily, as if by nature or remembrance. At home, I had sometimes had sensual dreams; if let alone, no doubt I should have been precocious. All this had been altered in me, yet not killed.

Like a poet who can sing of battles though not a warrior, I could conjure the images of desire, without suffering the sharpness of its wounds which I knew too well. I could make the music, its pauses and its cadenzas; Oromedon said I was like one who can play for the dancers, yet not dance. It was his own nature to take delight in the measure he gave it; yet I triumphed with him. Then he said, "I don't think, Gazelle-Eyes, you have very much more to learn."

His words dismayed me like news unknown before. I clung to him, saying, "Do you love me? You don't only want to teach me? Will you be sorry when I am gone?"

"Have you learned to break hearts already?" he said. "I never taught you that."

"But do you love me?" I had asked it of no one since my mother died.

"Never say that to *him*. It would be considered far too oncoming."

I looked into his face; relenting, he hugged me like a child, which did not seem strange to me. "Truly I love you, and when you go I shall be desolate." He spoke like one who reassures a child against ghosts and darkness. "But then comes tomorrow. I would be cruel to make you pledges; I may never see you again. If I do, maybe I cannot speak to you, and then you would think me false. I promised not to lie to you. When we serve the great, they are our destiny. Count upon nothing, but make your own nest against the storm . . . Do you see this?"

His brow had a scar, growing old and pale. I had thought it gave him distinction. Among my father's friends, anyone without a scar or two seemed scarcely like a man. "How did you get it?" I asked.

"I was thrown at the hunt, doing something that needed doing. It was that same horse you rode; it's still mine, you see; I have not been treated shabbily. But he can't bear flawed things. So try not to get yourself knocked about."

"I would love you," I said, "if you were covered with scars all over. Did he send you away?"

"Oh, no, I am very well provided for. Nothing is done unhandsomely. But I belong no more with the perfect vase and the polished gem. Don't build upon the wind, Gazelle-Eyes. That is the last of my lessons. May you not be too young to bear it, for you are not too young to need it. We had better get up. I shall see you again tomorrow."

"Do you mean," I said, "that tomorrow will be the last?"

"Perhaps. There is one more lesson after all. I have never told you the proper motions of the prostration."

"Prostration?" I said puzzled. "But they do that for the King."

"Just so," he said. "Well, that took you long enough."

I stared at him in a kind of stupor. Then I cried aloud, "I can't do it! I can't, I can't."

"Whatever is this, after all my trouble? Don't stare with those great eyes as if I'd brought you a death warrant, instead of your fortune."

"You never told me!" I grasped him in terror till my nails dug in. He loosened them gently.

"I dropped you hints enough; it was clear you'd do. But you see, till you are accepted in the Household, you are on probation. It is assumed you might fail, and be turned away. Then, if you had known whose service you were training for, it was thought you might know too much."

I threw myself on my face, convulsed with weeping. "Come," he said, and wiped my eyes on the sheet. "You have nothing, truly, to fear. He's had some hard times, and is in need of consolation. I am telling you, you will do very well indeed; and I ought to know."

3

I WAS SOME days in the Palace, before being presented. I thought I should never learn my way about this high maze of splendors; everywhere tall columns of marble or porphyry or malachite, with gilded capitals and twisted shafts; on every wall reliefs, colored and glazed brighter than life, of marching warriors, or tribute-bearers from the further empire, leading bulls or dromedaries, bearing bales or jars. When one lost one's direction, one seemed alone in a solemn crowd, with nobody to ask.

In the eunuchs' courtyard I was received without much warmth, as being destined for privilege; but for the same reason, none treated me ill, lest I should take my grudges with me.

It was on the fourth day, that I saw Darius.

He had been taking wine and hearing music. The room gave onto a small fountain court, sweet with the scent of lilies; in the flowering trees hung gold cages of bright birds. By the fountain the musicians were

putting up their instruments; but the water and the
birds made a soft murmuring concert. The court had
high walls, and was part of the room's seclusion.

He was on his cushions, looking into the courtyard;
by him on the low table were the wine-jug and empty
cup. I knew him at once for the man at my father's
birthday feast. But he had been dressed then for a long
ride up rough roads. Now he was robed in purple
worked with white, and wore the Mitra; the light kind
he used when at ease. His beard was combed like silk,
and he smelled of Arabian spices.

I walked with downcast eyes behind the chamberlain. One must not look up at the King; so I could not
tell if he remembered me, or whether I found favor.
When my name was pronounced, I prostrated myself
as I had been taught, and kissed the floor before him.
His slipper was of soft dyed kid, crimson, embroidered
with sequins and gold wire.

The eunuch took the wine-tray and placed it in my
hands. As I backed out of the Presence, I thought I
heard a faint stir among the cushions.

That night I was admitted to the Bedchamber, to
assist at the disrobing. Nothing happened, except that
I was given things to hold till the appointed person took
them away. I tried to show grace and be a credit to my
teacher. It seemed he had given me advanced instruction; in reality, some allowance was made for a be-
ginner. For the next night, while we waited for the
King to enter, an old eunuch, whose every wrinkle
spoke of vast experience, whispered in my ear, "If His
Majesty should beckon you, do not leave with the
others, but wait and see if he has any more commands
for you."

I remembered my training; watched under my eyelids for the beckoning; did not stand about, but oc-
cupied myself in a seemly way; and recognized, when
we were alone, the signal to undress. I laid my clothes
out of sight; I only failed in walking up with a smile.
I was so scared, I knew it would look like a sheepish
grin; so I approached grave and trustful, hoping for
the best, as the bed was folded back for me.

At first he kissed and dandled me like a doll. Later I divined what was required of me, for I had been well prepared; and it seemed I was acceptable. Certainly, as Oromedon had said, I was never betrayed into pain by pleasure. In all the time I was with him, he gave no sign of knowing a eunuch can feel anything. One does not tell such things to the King of Kings, if he does not ask.

I was to be enjoyed, like the flame and crimson birds, the fountain and the lutes; and this I soon learned to manage, without jarring his dignity. I was never insulted, never humiliated, never handled roughly. I was dismissed with a civil word, if he was still awake; and often next morning a gift would come. But I too had learned to understand pleasure. He was getting on for fifty, and in spite of the baths and the sprinkled perfume, already he began to smell rather old. For some time, in the royal bed, my one wish was to change this great tall bearded man for the supple body of Oromedon. But it is not for the perfect vase or the polished gem to choose their owners.

If I grew discontented, I had only to remember my former lot. The King was a man jaded with too much pleasure, but unwilling to put it by. I achieved for him what he needed; he was content and gracious. When I thought of those others, the greedy rough hands and stinking breath and nasty wishes, I was shocked that I had felt a moment's repining, and I showed my master the gratitude I felt.

Soon I waited on most of his leisure. He gave me a beautiful little horse, to ride in the royal park with him. No wonder Paradise was named after such a place. For generations, the kings had had rare trees and flowering shrubs brought from all over Asia; fullgrown trees sometimes, with their roots and soil, needing a train of oxcarts, and an army of gardeners to tend them on the way. The game, too, was choice; at the hunt, they would drive it towards the King to shoot at, and when he killed we would all applaud.

One day he remembered that I sang, and asked to hear me. My voice was never wonderful, like some eunuchs', which far surpass women's both in strength and sweetness; it was pretty and clear, when I was a boy. I fetched in the little harp my old mistress had bought in the bazaar. He was as shocked as if I had brought in some piece of offal. "Whatever is that thing? Why did you not ask someone for a proper instrument?" He saw my dismay and said kindly, "No, I understand your modesty prevented you. But take it away. When you have something fit to play on, then you shall sing."

I was given a harp of tortoise-shell and boxwood, with ivory keys, and had lessons with the Chief Musician. But one day, before I had learned his difficult pieces, I sat on the fountain-rim in the sunset light, and remembered it slanting far across the plain from our walls at home. When he asked me for a song, I gave one that my father's warriors used to sing at night by the watch-fire.

When I had done, he beckoned me over; I saw he had tears in his eyes. "That song," he said, "sets your poor father before me. What happy days gone by, when we were young together. He was a faithful friend to Arses, whose spirit may the Wise God receive; had he lived, he would have been welcomed here as a friend of mine. Be sure, my boy, I shall never forget you are his son."

He laid on my head his jeweled hand. Two of his friends were there, and the Chief Steward; from this moment, as he had meant, my standing at the court was changed. I was no longer a bought pleasure-boy, but a favorite of gentle birth, and they were all to know it. I was to know, too, that if my looks were damaged or went off, he would still look after me.

I was given a charming room in the Upper Household, with a window on the park, and my own slave; an Egyptian, who tended me like a prince. I was fourteen, my looks were changing from boy to youth. I heard the King tell friends that he had foreseen my promise, and I had fulfilled it; he did not believe that for beauty all Asia contained my equal. They would of course agree that I surpassed comparison. Certainly I learned to carry myself as if it were true.

His bed was canopied with a lattice, bearing a pure gold vine. Jeweled grape-clusters hung from it, and a great fretted lamp. Sometimes at night, when it threw on us its leaflike shadows, he would stand me by the bed, and turn me here and there to take the light. I thought this possession of the eyes would have contented him, but for his respect for his manhood.

However, on other nights he wanted entertainment. The world seems full of people who desire the same thing each time, not enduring the least change in it; this is tedious, but does not tax invention. The King liked variety and surprise; himself he was not inventive. I had run through all that Oromedon had taught me, and began wondering when the day would come for me, too, to start training my successor. There had been a boy before me, I had found out, who had been packed off after a week, because the King found him insipid.

In search of ideas, I visited the most famous whore in Susa, a Babylonian, who claimed to have trained at some temple of love in India. To prove it, she had a bronze in her room (bought I daresay, if truth were told, from a passing caravan) of two demons, with six or eight arms apiece, having intercourse while dancing. I doubted this would delight the King, but kept my hopes. Such women will always oblige a eunuch now and then; they get more men than enough; but her crude squirmings so disgusted me that without regard for good manners, I got up and dressed. As I put down my gold piece, I said I would pay for her time, since I had wasted it, but I could not stay to instruct her. She was so angry, I was halfway downstairs before she found her voice. So I was thrown on my own resource, since it seemed there was no one better.

It was then that I learned to dance.

As a child I had liked it, following the men, or prancing and spinning to some tune out of my head. I knew, if I were taught, I still had it in me. The King was glad for me to learn accomplishments (I did not mention the Babylonian) and hired me the best master in the city. It was not like my infant games; one had to train as hard as a soldier; but this I welcomed. It is idling makes eunuchs flabby; standing about, gossiping, waiting for something to do. It was good to get in a sweat and stir my blood.

So, when my tutor said I was ready, I danced in the fountain court for the King and his friends; an Indian dance with a turban and spangled loincloth; a Greek dance (so I believed) in a scarlet chiton; a Parthian dance with a little gilded scimitar. Even the Lord Oxathres, the King's brother, who had always looked down his nose at me because he liked only women, called out "Bravo!" and tossed me a piece of gold.

By day I danced in my finery; at night too I danced, wearing only the shadows of the fretted lamp that hung from the golden vine. I soon learned to slow down the pace towards the end; he never gave me time to get my breath.

I often wondered if he would have set such store by me if the Queen had not been captive. She was his half-sister, by a much younger wife of their father, and was of an age to have been his daughter. They said she was the loveliest woman in all Asia; of course he would be content with nothing less. Now he had lost her to a barbarian younger than she, and, from his deeds, it would seem hot-blooded. Of course he never spoke of such things to me. Indeed, once in bed he hardly spoke at all.

About this time, I caught a summer fever. Neshi, my slave from Egypt, nursed me with much kindness. The King sent me his own physician; but he never came himself.

I remembered Oromedon's scar. Since my mirror gave me bad news, it was better so. Yet, being young, I must have had something left in me that still looked for —I don't know what. I cried once in the night, when I was weak and silly; Neshi got up from his pallet to sponge my face. Soon after, the King sent me some gold darics, but still did not come. I gave the gold to Neshi.

It was when I was about again, and had been playing my harp in the fountain court with the King alone, that the Grand Vizier himself came in, panting with news. The Queen's Eunuch had escaped from Alexander's camp, and begged audience.

Had others been there, they would have been dismissed and I would have followed. But I was like the birds and the fountain, part of the appointments. Besides, when the man came in, for secrecy they spoke Greek.

No one had ever asked if I understood it. As it happened, there were several Greek jewelers in Susa, whom my old master traded with, in gems, or in me. So I had come to the Palace with a smattering, and had often passed idle time by listening to the Greek interpreter. He did all kinds of business in public, between court officials and suitors to the King; fugitive tyrants from Greek cities freed by Alexander, or envoys from states like Athens, which he had spared, as it seemed, to intrigue against him; generals of Greek mercenaries, shipmasters and spies. With all the Persian repeated in Greek, it was easy to learn by ear.

Impatient even through the prostration, the King asked if his family was alive. The eunuch said yes, and in good health; moreover, they were given their royal rank, and fitting quarters. This, he said (he was an oldish man and looked the worse for his long journey), was how he had escaped so easily; the guard on the royal women was posted more to keep intruders out, than anyone in.

On the ends of his chair-arms I could see the King's hands working. No wonder. What he had to ask should not be asked of a servant.

"Never, my lord!" The eunuch's gesture called God to witness. "My lord, he has not come even into her presence since the day after the battle, when he came to promise his safeguard. We were there all the time; he, also, brought a friend with him. I have heard that his companions, in their wine, recalled the fame of her beauty, and urged him to change his mind; and he too had been drinking, as all Macedonians do, yet he was angry, and forbade them to name her in his presence again. One who was there assured me of it."

The King was some time silent. Having given a long sigh, he said in Persian, "What a strange man." I thought he would go on to ask what he looked like, which I myself wished to know; but of course, he had seen him in the battle.

"And my mother?" He fell now into Persian. "She is too old for these hardships. Is she well cared for?"

"Great King, My Lady's health is excellent. Alexander always inquires for it. When I left, he was visiting her nearly every day."

"Visits my mother?" His face had changed suddenly. I thought that he looked pale. I could not think why; the Queen Mother was over seventy.

"Indeed, my lord. He gave her offense at first; but now, when he asks her to admit him, she always gives him leave."

"What insult did he offer her?" asked the King. He sounded eager.

"He gave her a parcel of wool for weaving."

"What? Like a slave?"

"So My Lady thought. But when she showed her affront, he begged her pardon. He said his mother and sister did such work, and he thought it would give her pastime. When My Lady perceived his ignorance, she accepted his apology. Sometimes they will be talking, through the interpreter, an hour together."

The King sat staring before him. Presently he gave the eunuch leave to go, and, remembering my presence, signed to me to play. I played softly, seeing him troubled. It was to be many years, before I understood the cause.

I gave the news to my friends at court; for I had friends by now, some in high places, some not, who were glad to hear things first. I took no presents for this; it would have been like selling my friendship. Of course I took bribes, to further suits with the King. To refuse would have been to proclaim enmity, and someone would have poisoned me. Needless to say, I did not bore the King with their tedious suits; it was not for such things he kept me. I would say sometimes, "So-and-so gave me this to get your favor"; it amused him, because the others did not tell. Now and then he would ask, "What did he want?" and say, "Well, we must keep you in credit. I daresay it can be arranged."

The strange conduct of the Macedonian King was much debated. Some said he liked to show himself a man of iron, above pleasure; some that he was impotent; some that he was keeping the Royal Family unharmed, to get good terms of surrender. Others, again, said he liked only boys.

The Queen's Eunuch said that, indeed, he was waited on by a band of highborn youths; but this was the custom of all their kings. In his own belief, it was in the young man's nature to be generous with suppliants. He quickly added that for beauty and presence he could not compare with our own King; he would scarcely stand higher than Darius' shoulder. "Indeed, when he visited the ladies to give his safeguard, the Queen Mother bowed to his friend instead. If you will believe it, they walked in together, side by side, and hardly distinguished in dress from one another. The friend was taller, and handsome for a Macedonian. I was distraught, having seen the King in the royal tent already. The friend drew back, and she saw my warning signs. She was of course distressed, and began her prostration again before the King. But he raised her in his hands, and was not even angry with this man; he said, as the interpreter assures me, 'Never mind, mother, you weren't far out; he is Alexander too.' "

Well, they are barbarians, I thought. Yet something sighed in my heart.

The eunuch said, "I never saw a king keep so little state; he lives worse than any general would with us. When he entered Darius' tent, he stared like a peasant at its appointments. He knew what the bath was, and used it, the first thing he did; but for the rest, one had hard work not to smile. In Darius' chair, his feet would not touch the ground, so he put them on the

wine-table, taking it for a footstool. However, he soon
moved in, like a poor man with a legacy. He looks like
a boy, till you see his eyes."

I asked what he had done with the royal concubines;
had he preferred them to the Queen? The eunuch said
they had all been presented to his friends; he had not
kept one. "It's boys then," I said laughing. "So now we
know."

The girls from the Harem, whom the King had
taken along, were of course the choicest, and a great
loss to him. However, he still had plenty; some only of
his nights were spent with me. Though it is true that, by
old custom, there were as many women as days in the
year, some were of course past youth; and it is an
absurdity such as only Greeks could invent, that they
were paraded nightly round his bed to choose from.
Now and then he would visit the Harem, look over the
girls, and learn from the Chief Eunuch there the
names of five or six he found most pleasing. Then at
night he would send for one; or sometimes for all the
group to play and sing to him, later beckoning one to
stay. He liked to conduct such matters gracefully.

When he went there he often took me with him. Of
course I should never have been brought in the Queen's
presence; but I ranked rather higher than the concubines. He liked to have his beautiful possessions admired, if only by one another. Some of the girls were
exquisite, with a fragile bloom like that of the palest
flowers. Even I could dream of desiring them. Perhaps
Oromedon had saved me from great danger; for already one or two had slid their eyes at me.

I met him once, crossing a courtyard in the sun,
gaily dressed as ever; it was strange to know my own
clothes were richer now. At first sight, I would have
run straight up to embrace him; but he smiled softly
and shook his head, and I now knew enough of courts
to understand. It would never do, to have it seen that
from the dish prepared for his master, he had kept a
portion back. So I returned his smile in secret, and
passed him by.

Sometimes, when the King had a girl at night, I

would lie in my pretty room, smelling the scented breezes from the park, looking at moonlight striking my silver mirror, and thinking, How pleasant and cool this is, to lie here alone. If I loved him, I should be grieving. It made me sad and ashamed. He had done me many kindnesses, raised me to honor, given me my horse and the gifts my room was full of. He had not asked love of me, not even to pretend it. Why should I think of such a thing?

The truth was, for ten years I had been beloved by parents who loved each other. I had learned to think well of love; having had none since, I had not learned to think worse. Now I was at the age when boys fumble about and make their first mistakes, laughed at by unkind girls before their elders, or tumbling some sweaty peasant and thinking, So this is all? To me none of this could happen; love was the image of lost happiness, and the stuff of fantasy.

My art had no more to do with love than a doctor's skill. I was good to look at, like the golden vine though less enduring; I knew how to wake appetite grown sluggish with satiety. My love was unspent, my dreams of it were more innocent than a homebred boy's. I would whisper to some shadow made of moonlight, "Am I beautiful? It is for you alone. Say that you love me, for without you I cannot live." It was true, at least, that youth cannot live without hope.

Summer grew hot in Susa; this time of year, the King should have been in the hills, at the summer palace of Ekbatana. But Alexander still sat before Tyre, stubbornly running out a mole to it; this was all I knew then of that great piece of siegecraft. Any time, they said, he might weary of the task, and turn inland; then Ekbatana would have been too far away. Indeed, it came to my ears that the captains thought the King should have stayed in Babylon. One said, "The Macedonian you would find nearer the action." Another answered, "Well, it's only a week from Susa down to Babylon; the generals there are doing well enough on their own. Or better." I slipped off unseen. It was no part of my duty to inform on men who meant no harm and were only speaking too freely, as my father had once done. To do the King justice, he never asked it of me. He did not mix business with pleasure.

Then Tyre fell.

Alexander had broken the wall and stormed the breach. There had been a great killing; the Tyrians had murdered Alexander's envoys before the siege, and then had flayed his men by pouring red-hot sand on them. The Tyrians who survived the sack had been enslaved, except those in Melkaart's sanctuary. It seemed Alexander revered this god, though he called him Herakles. What all this meant, was that Persian ships had no port of call in the Middle Sea north of Egypt, save Gaza, which could not hold out long.

Little as I knew of the western empire, the King's countenance told me how great the disaster was. Alexander's way was now clear to Egypt, where our rule was hated ever since Ochos put back our yoke on them. He had defiled their temples and killed their holy bull-god; now, if our satraps there were to shut gates against Alexander, the Egyptians would spear them in the back.

Soon we all knew that the King had sent an embassy, led by his brother Oxathres, suing for peace. The terms were not divulged. I had never been fool enough to coax the King for secrets. I'd been offered huge bribes to do it; but one learns as one goes along, and I found it policy to take small ones, saying he kept his counsel well, and though I would do my best for them, it would be cheating them to accept more. Thus they bore no grudges, and I could not come under the King's suspicion, for I never asked him anything.

Even though the embassy used the royal post-stages for fresh horses, lords do not ride like King's Messengers racing the wind. While we waited, life at the Palace was at pause, like dead air before a storm. My nights were spent alone. In those weeks, the King took a great turn for women. I think it gave him assurance he was a man.

When the embassy did return, its news was stale. Oxathres had thought Alexander's answer should go

quickly, and sent a copy by King's Messenger. Galloping the Royal Road with fresh horses and fresh men, it
arrived half a month ahead.

No need to ask questions. You could feel the thud
of it all through the Palace and on into the city. All the
world can quote it now, even from memory, as I do.

*You may keep your ten thousand talents; I am not in
want of money, I have taken enough. Why only the
half of your kingdom to the Euphrates? You offer me
the part in exchange for the whole. Your daughter
whom you speak of, I shall marry if I choose, whether
given by you or not. Your family is safe; no ransom is
required of you; come here yourself and make your
suit to me, you shall have them free. If you desire our
friendship, you have only to ask.*

There was a time, I forget how long, perhaps a day,
of still, stunned whisperings. Then suddenly all was
trumpeting and shouting. Heralds proclaimed the King
was marching west to Babylon, to ready his troops for
war.

4

WE STARTED in a week. It was without precedent, for the Household to move so fast. The Palace was in an uproar. All the chamberlains were clucking about like hens. The Chief Eunuch of the Harem was trying to make the King decide which girls to take; the Warden of the Silverware appealed to me to choose out his favorite pieces. He himself had no time for me; the men he now called to conference wanted no dancing with it, and at night, he was so tired that he even slept alone.

One day I took my horse along the riverbank where the lilies grow in spring. I could see clear to the hills. Our fort was going back to its native stones. I half thought of riding up to say farewell; but I remembered looking back there, from the captain's horse, the saddlebag with my father's head bouncing and dripping. The flames of the burning rafters had risen thirty feet high. I went back, and saw to my packing.

The eunuchs of the Household would travel like the women, in covered carts with cushions; but no one expected this of me. I saw my horse groomed, and had a try at an ass for Neshi; but he had to walk with the other followers.

I took my good clothes, and a change of clothes for the road, and some dancing-costumes. My money and my jewels were in my belt-wallet; there too, in case of mischance, I put my hand-mirror and combs, and my eye-paint with its brushes. I never used carmine. No one should, who has the true Persian looks. It is vulgar to color ivory.

I bought also a little dagger. I had never used weapons; but at least, for the dance, one is taught to hold them properly.

The older eunuchs were much distressed at it, and begged me to leave it behind. They meant that unarmed eunuchs taken in war count as women, but with weapons not. I replied that any time I liked I could throw it away.

The truth was, I had dreamed again of my father, the old frightful dream. Though I woke in a sweat, I knew he had the right to come to me, his only son, demanding vengeance. In the dream, I heard the name of the traitor who had betrayed him, as he cried it on his way to death. In the morning, as always, I forgot it. There seemed small chance I would ever give him his rights; but at least for his sake I would go armed. There are eunuchs who become women, and those who do not; we are something by ourselves, and must make of it what we can.

It is the custom for the King to start a march at sunrise; I don't know if it's to give him the blessing of the sacred fire, or to let him have his sleep out. The carts and carriages were drawn up overnight. Most of us were astir soon after midnight, getting ready for the road.

At daybreak, I could scarcely believe the real army was at Babylon, and that this horde, stretching a mile both ways, was no more than the Household.

The King's Guard, the Ten Thousand Immortals, who never left his person, took up a good deal of road. Then there were the Royal Kin. It is a title of honor, not of blood; there were fifteen thousand, though ten thousand had gone on to Babylon. They looked very fine; all their shields were worked with gold, and as they formed up by torchlight, the jewels in their helmets flashed.

Presently came the Magi with their silver carrying-altar, ready to kindle the holy fire and lead the march.

As I rode to and fro gaping at each new splendor, I wondered if I was working my horse too hard, with the march before him. Then I remembered that however many the horses and chariots were, the column would go at walking-pace, for the foot-men, and the Magi with their silver altar. I thought of the rashly spoken captain, who had said it was only a week from Susa down to Babylon. He was of course in cavalry. At this rate, we would take a month.

The transport alone seemed to stretch for miles. There were a dozen wagons for the King alone, for his tent, his furniture, his robes and tableware, his traveling bathroom and its appointments. There were the wagons for the Household eunuchs, and for their belongings; then the wagons for all the women. The King had taken all the younger concubines in the end, more than a hundred; they and their gear and their eunuchs were only the beginning. The lords at court, who'd not yet gone ahead to Babylon, had their wives and children with them, their harems, and all *their* luggage, as well. Then there were the store-wagons; such a host could not live off the country. The torches now stretched further than I could see. And behind the wagons and baggage train there were still the foot-followers: the army of slaves to set up camp and strike it, the cooks and smiths and grooms and harness-menders, and a great troop of personal servants, such as mine.

I rode back from the road to the Palace square, as the torches paled. Now they were bringing out the Chariot of the Sun. It was sheathed all over with gold; a sunburst emblem stood in it on a silver pole; the symbol of the god, its only rider. Not even the body of

its charioteer would sully it; its matched pair of great
white horses was led on foot.

Last came the King's battle chariot, nearly as
splendid as the god's. (I wondered if it was as good as
the one he had left for Alexander.) The charioteer was
putting in the King's weapons, javelins and bow and
arrows in their holsters. In front of it stood his litter
for the journey, with gold shafts, and a sun-canopy
fringed with bullion.

As the east began to glow, appeared the Sons of the
Kindred, elegant youths a little older than I, who
would march before and behind the King, dressed from
head to foot in purple.

All this order of the march was fixed by ancient
hierarchy. It was time to find my place alongside the
eunuchs' wagons; clearly there was none for me near
the King.

Suddenly, above the Sun Chariot shone a brilliant
point of light. The center of its sunburst was a globe of
crystal. It had caught the first shaft of sunrise. There
was a bray of horns and blare of trumpets. In the
distance a figure in white and purple, tall even from
so far, stepped into the royal litter.

Slowly, without at first any forward movement, the
vast train stirred into fidgeting and shuffling. Then,
sluggish as a winter snake, it began to crawl. We must
have been moving nearly an hour, before one felt to be
really marching.

We traveled the Royal Road, through the land of
rivers, low and green, with thick crops in rich black
earth. Shallow lakes mirrored the sky, spiky with
sedge. Sometimes great rough-rock causeways spanned
the swamps. Now they were mostly caked and dry, but
we never made camp there; they had a name for
fever.

I attended the King each evening when his tent was
pitched. There was room for most of his usual people.
He seemed to like the sight of familiar faces. Often he
kept me at night. He was harder to stir up than I had
ever known him, and I wished he would settle for sleep

instead. But I think the truth was that, if alone, he would lie awake.

Every few days, galloping to meet us, the last man and horse of the long relay as fresh and swift as a stag, a King's Messenger brought dispatches from the west.

Alexander had taken Gaza. It seemed he had nearly been put out of the way for good. He had been struck on the shoulder by a catapult bolt, and felled clean backward; it had pierced his armor, but he had got up and gone on fighting. Then he had fallen again, and been carried off like the dead. Our people had waited a while to see, he being known by now for a man who was hard to kill; and sure enough, though he had bled himself white, he was still alive. He would be laid up some time; but his advance guard was already on the march to Egypt.

When this was known, I thought to myself, Perhaps he's shamming, so that we take our time; then he could strike east like lightning and take us by surprise. Now if I were the King, I thought, I would be out of my litter into my chariot, and dash on ahead with all the cavalry to Babylon, just in case.

I longed for the trumpet calling us to ride. Each evening, reckoning that Neshi would have had enough with his footmarch, I curried my horse myself. I had called him Tiger. I had only seen the skin of one, but it was a good fierce name.

But when I went to the King at evening, he was playing draughts with one of the lords, in such abstraction that the man had hard work to lose. When the game was over, the King asked me to sing. I remembered the battle-song of my father's men which he had liked before; I hoped it would cheer his soul. After two verses, however, he called for something else.

I thought of his old combat with the Kadousian champion, which had won him his renown; I tried to picture him striding forward in arms, hurling his javelin, stripping the enemy of his weapons, returning to the warriors' cheers. He had been younger then; he had had no palaces, and fewer girls. And then again, a battle is different from such a combat, especially if one is in command; still more, if one is meeting the man from whom one fled last time.

My song drew to its end. I said to myself, Who am I to judge? What action shall I ever see? He has been a good master; that should be enough for me, who will never be a man.

Each morning, the Standard of the Sun was set up by the King's pavilion. Each morning, when the first sunbeam struck the crystal, the horns sounded, the King was escorted to his litter, the chariot was walked behind it. So we followed the Royal Road through the river country, and the night followed each day.

When I grew weary of the eunuchs' talk in the wagons, I would sometimes fall back to the harem train, to have a word with the girls. Each load, of course, was in charge of at least one reverend eunuch; if invited, I was safe enough to hitch my horse to the tailboard and clamber in. I found it instructive. This horde of women was nothing like my old master's little harem. The King was achieved once in a summer, or a year, or never; or he might send for a girl most nights in a month, then never notice her again. On the whole, it was each other they had to live with; they were full of factions, alliances and bitter feuds, few of which came of rivalry for the King, but simply of seeing each other day after day, with nothing to do but talk. It was amusing to visit such a world as this; I hoped never to be employed within it.

It was amazing how fast news flew along the column. People talked from tedium, to enliven the miles. Alexander was already getting about again, and was sending spies to learn where Darius was. From what I had heard by now, I could guess what was baffling the Macedonian. He would have thought of everything, except that his enemy could still be upon the road.

However, he must soon have found out; the next thing we heard, he was making south for Egypt. So there was no hurry after all.

We marched on, fifteen miles a day, till we came to the maze of canals and streams which lead the Euphrates into the Babylonian cornfields. The bridges are built high for the floods of winter. Sometimes the ricefields spread their tasseled lakes, off which the morning sun would glance to blind us. Then one noon, when the glare had shifted, we saw ahead the great black walls of Babylon, stretched on the low horizon against the heavy sky.

Not that its walls were near; it was their height that let us see them. When at last we passed between the wheatfields yellowing for the second harvest, which fringed the moat, and stood below, it was like being under mountain cliffs. One could see the bricks and bitumen; yet it seemed impossible this could be the work of human hands. Seventy-five feet stand the walls of Babylon; more than thirty thick; and each side of the square they form measures fifteen miles. We saw no sign of the royal army; there was room for it all to encamp within, some twenty thousand foot and fifty thousand horse.

The walls have a hundred gates of solid bronze. We went in by the Royal Way, lined with banners and standards, with Magi holding fire-altars, with trumpeters and praise-singers, with satraps and commanders. Further on was the army; the walls of Babylon enclose a whole countryside. All its parks can grow grain in case of siege; it is watered from the Euphrates. An impregnable city.

The King entered in his chariot. He made a fine figure, over-topping by half a head his charioteer, shining in white and purple. The Babylonians roared their acclamation, as he drove off with a train of lords and satraps to show himself to the army.

We of the Household were led through back ways along the straight high streets, to enter the Palace through doorways suited to our station, and make ready for the master.

Knowledge can alter memory. I see in my mind those glories; the fine-clay brick, polished, sculpted, enameled, glazed or gilded; the furniture of Nubian ebony inlaid with ivory; hangings of scarlet and purple, woven with gold and stitched with Indian pearls. I remember the cool, after the baking heat outside. And it seems that the coolness fell on me like the shadow of blinding grief; that the very walls oppressed me like a tomb. Yet I suppose I went in like any lad after a journey, wide-eyed for all the sights.

When they had laid out the King's own vessels for his food and wine, they made the bed, which was plated all over with gold, a winged deity at each bedpost. Then, for he would surely come back tired and dusty from his ride, they prepared the bath.

Because it is hot in Babylon, the bath is a pleasure-house, where one could spend all day; floored with marble from the west, with glazed walls, white flowers on blue. The bath is a spacious pool, whose lapis-blue tiles have gold fish impressed in them. There are pots with sweet shrubs and trees, changed at each season, jasmine and citron; the fretted screens give onto a bathing-place, let in from the Euphrates.

Everything had been prepared, everything shone; the water was clear as crystal, tepid, just right, the tank warmed with filtered sun. There was a couch with cushions of fine linen, to rest on after the bath.

Not a tile, not a golden fish, not a thread of linen there will ever leave my memory while I live. When I saw it that first time, I just thought it very pretty.

Soon we had settled in, the days turning as smoothly as the water-wheels below the Hanging Gardens; though our lot was lighter than the oxen's there. That beautiful man-made hill, with its shady trees and the cool groves within its terraces, needs a deal of watering, and it's a high haul to the top. Often amid its bird-song you can hear, if you listen, the cracking of whips below.

Fresh troops were still coming in from the distant satrapies, after months upon the march. All the city turned out to see the Baktrians. It was cooling down for autumn, but still they sweated, having put on their best for show; felt coats, quilted trousers, and fur-lined hats, all fine and warm for the Baktrian winters. You could tell their land was rich, by the lords' adornments, and the sturdy build of the men after so long a march. Each lord brought from his own stronghold his own warriors, as my father would have done if he'd been alive. But the Baktrian lords numbered hundreds. Their baggage was borne by a long train of their two-humped camels, long-bodied and thick-legged, shaggy, built for endurance.

At the head rode their satrap, Bessos, Darius' cousin. The King greeted him standing, in the Hall of Audience, and offered his cheek to kiss. He was the taller, but not much. Bessos was thickset like his camels, war-scarred, burnt almost black with sun and wind. They had not met since the defeat at Issos. Now I saw in Bessos' eyes, pale under black brows, a show of respect over a shadow of scorn; and in the King's, a shadow of mistrust. Baktria was the most powerful satrapy in the empire.

Meantime, news came that Egypt had opened its arms to Alexander, hailed him as liberator, and proclaimed him Pharaoh.

I knew little of Egypt then. I know it now; I live there. I have seen him carved on a temple wall, worshipping Ammon, made to look just like all the other Pharaohs, even to the little blue strip of ceremonial beard. Perhaps when they put on him the double crown, and set in his hands the crook and flail, he even wore it. He was courteous in such things. But it makes me smile.

He had been to Ammon's oracle, at green Siwah in the desert, where it seems he was told the god was there before the King his father, when he was conceived. So rumor ran; he went in alone, and said only, after, that he was satisfied.

I asked Neshi about this oracle, while he dressed me and combed my hair. He had been at a school for scribes, till Ochos conquered Egypt, when they had all been taken from their temple and sold. Even now, he still shaved his head.

He said the oracle was very old and revered. Long ago (and from an Egyptian that means at least a thousand years), the god used to speak in Thebes as he does at Siwah. In the days of the terrible Hatshepsut, the only woman Pharaoh, her stepson Tuthmosis was a young boy serving the shrine. The symbol of the god was carried by, as at Siwah now, in a boat enriched with gold and jewels and tinkling vessels. The bearers say that the carrying-poles press on their shoulders, when the god wants to speak; they feel the weight of him telling them where to go. He guided them to this young prince, who then was a nobody in the crowd, and made the boat bow before him; and they set him in the royal seat, knowing his destiny. Neshi had some very good tales like this.

I myself, when I made my pilgrimage (and a hard journey it is, though I have known a worse one), asked a question of the oracle. I was told it was enough for me to offer the proper sacrifice, and not be curious about one who had been received among the gods. Still, I could not be content never to have seen it.

Meantime at Babylon I had time on my hands, the King being always busy, and went about seeing the sights. I climbed the stair round Bel's temple-tower, though the top was ruinous where his concubine used to lie on his golden bed. I was much beset by bawds, my youth still being enough to explain my beardlessness. And I saw the temple of Mylitta with its famous courtyard.

Every girl in Babylon, once in her life, must offer herself to the goddess. The courtyard is one huge bazaar of women, sitting in rows marked off with scarlet cords. None may refuse the first man to toss in her lap a piece of silver. There were some as fine as princesses, on silk cushions, with slaves to fan them, next to hard-handed peasant girls from the fields. Along the rows strolled the men, as if at a horse fair; I half expected they'd start to look at their teeth. The pretty ladies don't have to wait long; but if a river bargee gets there before a lord, they must take him. Not a few stretched out their hands to me, hoping to pay their due with someone not too ill-favored. There was a grove nearby, where the rite was done.

Seeing some men stand laughing, I went to look. They were mocking the ugly girls, who sat day after day unchosen. That I might share the joke, they pointed one out to me who had been sitting there three years.

She had grown there from girl to woman. One shoulder was hunched; she had a great nose, and a birthmark on her cheek. The girls round her, plain as they were, seemed to look at her and take comfort. She just sat with folded hands, enduring the laughter, as an ox the whip and goad. Suddenly I was filled with anger at man's cruelty. I thought how the soldiers had cut off my father's nose alive instead of dead; how the men who gelded me had talked lightly across my pain. I took out a silver siglos from my pouch, and tossed it in her lap, saying the ritual words, "May Mylitta prosper you."

At first she seemed scarcely to take it in. Then the loafers gave a great bawdy cheer. She grasped the coin and looked up bewildered. I smiled and offered her my hand.

She got to her feet. Nothing could have made her anything but hideous; yet even a clay lamp is beautiful, when its light shines at dusk. I led her from her tormentors, saying, "Let them find some other pastime." She trotted along beside me, shorter by a head, though I was not yet full-grown. Low stature is despised in Babylon as in Persia. Everyone was staring, but I knew I must walk with her as far as the grove.

Inside, it was a disgusting spectacle. No Persian could well conceive it. The trees and bushes were not nearly enough for decency. In my worst days at Susa, I met no one so lost to shame as to do such things except in the inner room.

When we were just within the gate, I said to her, "You may be sure I won't put you to such disgrace as that. Farewell; live happy." She looked at me smiling, still too dazed to take in my words; then pointed into the grove, saying, "There is a good place."

That she could really expect such a thing had never entered my head. I could scarcely credit it. Though I had meant to keep my secret, I said unwillingly, "I can't go in the grove with you. I am one of the King's eunuchs. I was angry with them for mocking you, I wanted to set you free."

For a moment she stared at me, her mouth falling open. Then suddenly she screamed out, "Oh! Oh!" and struck me two great slaps in the face, one with each hand. I stood with singing ears, while she ran off down the street, crying out, "Oh! Oh! Oh!" and beating her breast.

I was astonished, and wounded by her ingratitude. It was no more my fault I was cut, than hers that she was ugly. But as, brooding on it, I walked home, it came to me that ever since I was born, somewhere I had been wanted, whether for good or ill. I tried to think how it would be, to have lived twenty years and never once have known it. It killed my anger; but I went home sad.

Babylon grew mild with winter. I turned fifteen, though no one knew but I. Our family, like all Persians, had always made much of birthdays. Even in five years, I had never quite grown used to waking on the day, knowing it would be just like any other. The King had never asked me when it was. It seemed childish to mind; he had been generous on many other days.

News came in piecemeal from Egypt. Alexander had been restoring the ancient laws; he had held a great feast, with contests for athletes and musicians. At Nile mouth he had laid out the plan for a city, marking the lines with meal, which flocks of birds had swooped down to feed on; this omen was held to mean that the city would come to nothing.

(I wonder how it looked when the birds came down. Flat green land, with papyrus growing; a few palms; some donkeys grazing; a cluster of fisher-huts. It is Alexandria now, a palace among cities. Though he never saw it, he has returned to it forever; and instead of birds it has taken in men from all quarters under heaven, as it has taken me.)

Next after the Baktrians, the Scythians came to Babylon, those who were Bessos' vassals; wild shaggy fair-haired savages, their faces tattooed blue. They wore pointed lynx-skin bonnets, loose blouses, and trousers tied at the ankle; oxcarts bore their black tents and their women. They are great bowmen. But they stink to heaven; if they are washed in their lives, it is by the midwife in mares' milk. They were hurried away into camp. No people could afford to be as shameless as the Babylonians, if they did not bathe every day.

News came that Alexander had left Egypt. He was marching north.

The King called a council in the great audience room. I hung about outside, to watch the great men leaving. A boy's curiosity took me there; but I learned something of use, which has stayed with me ever since. Only keep quiet at such a time and look like nothing, and you will see men reveal themselves. In the Presence, they have had to show respect and keep half their thoughts unspoken; outside, each will turn to whoever he felt to share his mind; and intrigue begins.

Thus I saw Bessos single out Nabarzanes, who had been in Babylon long before the King, for he was Commander in Chief of the cavalry. He had fought at Issos. His men thought well of him.

It was in the pleasure-houses, where I went to watch the dancing, that I heard them talk. They did not know who I was, as people did at Susa. Certainly, I was never tempted to carry their words to the King. They said that at Issos Nabarzanes had fought a great battle, though the King's choice of ground had been a blunder. The cavalry had charged when the rest were faltering, taken on the Macedonian horse, and hoped to turn the tide; then the King had fled, among the first to leave the battle. With that came rout. No one can fly and fight; but the pursuer can still strike. There had been a great slaughter; they blamed the King.

I had been long with soft-spoken men; I had not thought such words possible. They hurt me; one lives in one's master's name, and shares disgrace. The captain I'd overheard at Susa must have been one of Nabarzanes'.

He was tall and lean, Nabarzanes, with the pure-bred Persian face, clear-carved and proud. Yet he was easy-mannered, and could laugh, though not over often. At court he often greeted me very pleasantly, but it never went beyond that. I could not tell if he had a liking for boys, or not.

He and Bessos looked odd together, Nabarzanes sword-slim, in the plain good clothes of Persia; huge Bessos with his black bush of beard and chest as deep as a bear's, dressed in embroidered leather with chains of barbaric gold. But they were soldiers who had met upon campaign. They walked off quickly out of the press, as if impatient to talk in private.

Most people talked in public; and soon all Babylon knew what had passed in council. The King had proposed that the whole Persian army should retire to Baktria. There he could raise more troops from India and Kaukasos, fortify the eastern empire, or some such thing.

It was Nabarzanes who had stood forward, and quoted the words of Alexander's first defiance, when he had still been taken for a vaunting boy. "Come out and fight me. If you will not, I shall follow you wherever you may be."

So the army stayed in Babylon.

To fall back on Baktria! To surrender, without another blow, with all its people, Persis itself, the ancient land of Kyros, the heart and cradle of our race, even that with the rest. I, who had nothing left there but a memory and a roofless ruin, had been shocked to my soul; what Nabarzanes felt, his face had told me. That night, the King kept me with him. I tried to keep my mind on the kindness he had shown me, and forget the rest.

Soon after, I awaited him one morning in his inner room, when a white-haired, straight old man was shown into the anteroom. He was the satrap Artabazos, who had rebelled against Ochos, and lived an exile in Macedon in King Philip's day. I went in and asked if I could bring him anything while he waited. As I'd hoped, he began to talk to me; and I asked if he had ever seen Alexander.

"Seen him? I have sat him on my knee. A beautiful

child. Yes, even in Persia one would call him beautiful."
He sank into himself. He was very old. He could have
left it to his many sons, to follow the King to war. I
thought he was getting absent, as old men will; when
suddenly he opened a bright fierce eye under his thick
white brows. "And afraid of nothing. Nothing at all."

In spring, Alexander returned to Tyre. He sacrificed,
and held some more games and contests. It seemed he
was asking the gods' goodwill for a new campaign.
When spring turned to summer, the spies reported him
on the march for Babylon.

5

I<small>T</small> IS three hundred miles north up the Tigris valley, from Babylon to Arbela.

Alexander had turned northeast from Tyre, to skirt the Arabian deserts. From the north he would come down. The King marched north with the royal army; and the Household went with the King.

I had pictured an endless column of men, miles long. But the army was spread all over the plain, between the river and the hills. It was as if the land grew men instead of corn. They were wherever one looked, horse, foot and camels. The transport wound along in little trains, where the going was best. Apart, given as wide a berth as lepers, were the scythed chariots, with long curved blades standing out from their wheels and cars. One soldier, who was dim of sight and got in their way, had had a leg taken off, and died of it.

The Household had a fair passage; outriders went ahead to find us the smoothest ground.

Alexander had crossed the Euphrates. He had sent engineers ahead to bridge it; the King had sent Mazaios,

the satrap of Babylon, with his men to stop them. But
they pushed it out from their own side by sinking
piles; when Alexander came up with all his forces,
Mazaios' horse retired. The bridge was finished next
day.

Soon we heard he was across the Tigris. He
couldn't bridge that; not for nothing is it called The
Arrow. He had simply breasted through it, going first
himself to feel the way. They had lost some baggage,
but no men.

Then we lost him awhile. He had turned from the
river plain, to take his men round by the hills, where it
was cooler and would keep them fresh.

When his route was known, the King rode out to
choose the field of battle.

He had lost at Issos, his generals had told him, because he had been cramped for room and could not
use his numbers. There was a fine broad plain, about
sixty miles north of Arbela. I never saw it myself; the
Household was to be left in town with the gold and
stores, when the King took the field.

Arbela is a grey and ancient city, standing on its hill.
It is so old, it goes back to the Assyrians. This I believe,
for they still worship Ishtar without a consort. She stares
at you in the temple, horribly old, with huge eyes,
grasping her arrows.

We were all in turmoil, finding quarters for the
women; being shoved aside by soldiers who wanted
strong houses for the treasure and billets for the garrison; preparing a house for the King while he should
need it (the governor had to turn out for that). There
was hardly time to think we were on the eve of battle.

Just as we were settling down, there was crying and
wailing in the streets, and a rush of women to the
temple. I felt a strangeness, even before I saw the
omen. The moon had been eaten by darkness. I saw
her last curve vanish, somber and red.

I grew cold. The people were wailing. Then I heard
the brisk soldier's voice of Nabarzanes, telling his men
that the moon is a wanderer, so was the Macedonian,
and the omen was for him. All those around were

heartened. But from the old grey temple, where the women had served Ishtar a thousand years, I could still hear wailing, like a high wind in trees.

The King had sent a great troop of slaves to the battlefield, to level out broken ground for the chariots and the horse. His spies had told him the Macedonian horse were much fewer, and they had no chariots at all, let alone scythed ones.

The next news came not from spies but by envoy. He was Tyriotes, one of the eunuchs attendant on the Queen. Alexander had sent him, to bring word that she was dead.

We wailed as was proper, then the King sent us out. We could hear him shouting aloud, and Tyriotes crying out in fear. At length he came outside, shaking all over, disheveled from tearing his hair and clothes.

He had been captured before my time in the Household, but the older ones knew him well. They gave him cushions, and wine which he badly needed. We listened in case the King should summon us, but heard no sound. He put his hand to his throat; it looked bruised and red.

Boubakes the Egyptian, the Chief Eunuch of the Household, said, "It is never good to bring bad news to the great."

Tyriotes rubbed his throat. "Why are you not wailing? Mourn, mourn, for the love of God."

For some time we made the sounds of grief. The King did not call us. We took Tyriotes to a quiet corner. A house is safer for talking than a tent.

"Tell me," he asked, "has the King been distempered lately?"

We said, only a little out of spirits.

"He shouted at me that Alexander had killed the Queen trying to rape her. I embraced his feet, I repeated that she had died of sickness in the arms of the Queen Mother. I vowed Alexander had not set eyes on her, from that first day till she was on her bier. When she died, he held up his march for a day and mourned her fasting; that was my message, that she had had all her proper rites. What have the spies been doing? Is the King not informed of anything? Surely he knows Alexander does not care for women?"

We said that he had certainly heard as much.

"He should be thankful Alexander did not give the ladies to his generals, as most victors would. He has burdened himself with a royal harem, from which he is getting nothing. The Queen Mother . . . I don't know what ailed the King; he should be glad she is well cared for, at her age, by so young a man. It was only when I spoke of it, that he broke out. He said all this grief for the Queen was what a man shows his bedfellow. He took me by the throat. You know what huge hands he has; I am still hoarse from it, you can hear. He threatened me with torture unless I told the truth. To quiet him, I said I would submit to it if he wished." His teeth were chattering; I held the wine-cup for him, lest he spill it. "At last he believed me; God knows every word was true. But from the first, it seemed to me, he was not himself."

Still silence from the King. Well, I thought, the bad omen of the moon had been fulfilled. It would calm the people.

The Prince Oxathres had been sent for; now he came, and they lamented together. The Queen had been his full sister by the same mother; he was some twenty years younger than the King. After this, the King's grief having been released by weeping, we put him to bed; also Tyriotes, who looked ready to faint. His throat had turned black next day; he had to use a scarf to cover it, when the King summoned him again.

He went in terror, but was not kept for long. All the King asked him was, "Did my mother send any word to me?" He answered, "No, my lord; but she was much disordered with grief." The King then gave him leave to go.

Word came that the battleground was ready, as smooth to drive or ride on as a street. On one flank were the hills, on the other was the river. So the King put off his mourning, as not being proper for leading troops in war. All Persian kings lead the center, as all kings of Macedon lead the right. His chariot was brought up, equipped with all his weapons; he was dressed in his coat of mail.

Two or three eunuchs of the Bedchamber, who always saw to his clothes and toilet, went to attend him in camp. To the last I wondered if he would take me. It scared, yet drew me. I thought I could fight, if put to it, and it would be my father's wish. I hung about, but the King said nothing. With the rest I stood to see him mount his chariot, and withdrew from his escort's dust.

Now we were just the Household, women, eunuchs and slaves. The battleground was too far even to ride in sight of. We could only wait.

I went up to the walls, and looked to the north, and thought, I am fifteen years old. I would have my manhood, if it had not been taken away. If my father had lived, he would have brought me with him; he never held me back from anything I dared to do, not even for my mother. I would be with him now among our warriors, laughing together and making ready to die. That I was born to; this I am. I must make the best I can of it.

It came into my head to go round the yards where the women's wagons were, to make sure the horses were stabled near, the harness mended, the drivers ready and sober. I told them the King had ordered it, and they believed me.

While about this meddling, I ran, to my surprise, into Boubakes of Egypt, the Chief Eunuch; a tall and stately person, who had always been civil to me, but distant; I don't think he approved that the King should keep a boy. However, he asked me without reproof what I was doing. His own presence was more remarkable.

"I was thinking, sir," I said, "that the wagons should be ready. Supposing," I said, looking him in the eye, "the King should pursue the enemy. He would want the Household with him."

"My own thought also." He gave me a grave approving nod. It was no lie that our thoughts had been just the same. "The King has a far greater host than he had at Issos. Half as many again."

"Truly. And the scythed chariots, too." We looked at each other, and then away.

I hired Tiger, my horse, a private stable, with good strong doors, and took care to keep him exercised.

The King's Messengers had been set up with their relay-posts, to take dispatches between the King and Arbela. Most days, one came in. In a day or two, we heard the Macedonians had appeared on the hills above the plain of Gaugamela, where the King was awaiting them. Later again, that Alexander had been sighted, shown up by his flashing armor, riding with his scouts to survey the field.

That night there was a great play of summer lightning, which brought no rain. It was as if the north skies were burning. For hours it flickered and danced, without sound of thunder. The air was heavy and still.

Next day I waked in the dawn-dark. All Arbela was astir, the garrison were busy about the horse-lines. At sunup, the walls were full of people gazing north, though there was nothing to see.

I met Boubakes again, visiting the women's quarters, and guessed he was telling their eunuchs to look alive. Harem duties make such people fat and lazy. Still, these were faithful to their trust, as we were soon to learn.

Taking Tiger for his canter, I felt him on edge; he'd caught it from the other horses, who'd caught it from the men. Coming back I said to Neshi, "Keep a watch on the stable. See no one breaks in." He asked no questions, but was as twitchy as the horses. In war many chances can happen to a slave, both good and bad.

At noon came a King's Messenger. The battle had begun soon after sunup. Our army had stood by all night, the King thinking that Alexander, being out-numbered, might try for a surprise; but he had waited till the sky was bright, before engaging. The messenger was the sixth of the relay; he knew no more.

Night came. The soldiers lit watch-fires all along the walls.

Towards midnight, I stood up there near the north

gatehouse. It had been hot all day, but the night wind
blew cool, and I went back to get my coat. As I returned, suddenly Northgate Street was filled with
clamor; men heaving and crushing back from the
road, the halting drumbeat of half-foundered horses,
the crack of whips. The riders drove on like drunken
men who have forgotten where they are going. These
were not messengers; they were soldiers.

As they began to come to themselves and slow down
a little, people came up with torches. I saw the men
white with caked dust, streaked with dark blood; the
horses' nostrils flaring scarlet as they fought for breath,
their mouths all bloody foam. The men's first word
was "Water!" Some soldiers dipped their helmets in a
nearby fountain and brought them dripping. As if the
mere sight had given him strength, one of the riders
croaked, "All's lost . . . The King is coming."

I shoved forward and shouted, "When?" One who
had had a gulp to drink said, "Now." Their horses,
maddened by the smell of water, were dragging them
on, trying to get to the fountain.

The crowd engulfed me. Wailing began, and rose to
the night sky. It crawled and surged in my blood like
fever. I raised a voice which I hardly knew for mine, a
shrill crying like a girl's; it flowed from me, without
my will, without shame. I was a part of lamentation, as
a raindrop is part of rain. Yet as I cried, I was fighting
to get out through the press. I freed myself, and made
for the King's house.

Boubakes had only just come out upon the threshold,
and was calling a slave to go and learn the news. My
wailing ceased. I told him.

Our eyes spoke without more words. Mine, I suppose, said, "Again the first to run. But who am I to say
so? I shed no blood for him, and he has given me all
I have." And his answered, "Yes, keep your thoughts
to yourself. He is our master. That is the beginning
and the end." Then he cried out, "Alas! Alas!" and
beat his breast in duty. But next moment he was calling
all the servants to make ready for the King.

I said, "Shall I see the women put in the wagons?"

The wailing was washing all over the city, like a river risen in flood.

"Ride round to tell the wardens, but do not stay. Our duty is with the King." He might not approve of his master keeping a boy; but he would look after all his property and have it ready. "Have you your horse?"

"I hope so, if I can get to him fast enough."

Neshi was watching the stable door, without making a show of it. He had always had good sense.

I said, "The King's coming. I shall have to go with him. It looks like a hard journey, and worse for foot-followers. I don't know where he means to go. The Macedonians will soon be here. The gates will all be open; they might kill you, or you might get away, even to Egypt. Will you run with us, or take your freedom? Make your own choice."

He said he would take his freedom, and if they killed him he would still die blessing my name. He prostrated himself, though he was nearly trampled doing it, before he ran off.

(He did get back to Egypt. I found him quite lately, the letter-writer in a good village not far from Memphis. He almost knew me; I have good bones, and have looked after my figure. But he could not place me, and I kept quiet. I said to myself it would not be proper, now where he was respected, to remind him of his slavery. But the truth is, too, that though the wise man knows all beauty is born to perish, one does not care to be reminded of that either. So I thanked him for pointing me out my road, and went my way.)

As I took Tiger out from his stall, a man ran up, and offered to buy him for twice what he was worth. I had been just in time; soon horses would be fought over. I was glad my dagger was in my sash.

At all the harem houses, there was a great packing and harnessing up; you could hear from outside a chittering like a bird-seller's shop, and smell great drifts of scent from the stirred-up clothes. Each eunuch asked me where the King was going. I wished I knew, to set them on their way before their mules were stolen. I knew that some would be caught by the

Macedonians, and hated leaving them to their fate; I was less needed where I was going, and my heart was not in it. But Boubakes had been right. Faithfulness in disaster, as my father would have told me, is the only guide.

As I turned back into Northgate Street, my errand done, there was a pause in the wailing, like a storm-wind dropping to silence, and a sound of dead-beat horses. Through the stillness drove the King.

He was still in his chariot, with his armor on. A handful of cavalry came behind him. His face was empty, like a blind man's whose eyes can open.

There was dust on him, but no wound. I saw his escort, with faces slashed, or a limp arm, or a leg half blackened with clotted blood, gasping with thirst from their bleeding. These men had covered his flight.

On my fresh horse, in my clean clothes, with my whole skin, I had not the face to join this company. I made for the house by side-streets. This was the man who came forward to fight the Kadousian giant, when no other would. How long ago? Ten years—fifteen?

I thought of what he had come from now; the din, the dust-cloud; hurling of man on man and mass on mass; the heaving tide of battle; the sense of some plan reaching out for him, which was the mask for another plan; then the mask whipped off, the trap sprung; finding himself no more than a king of chaos. And then, the presence nearing him that he had seen and fled at Issos, that had haunted him all the way. Should I judge? I thought. On my own face there is not even dust.

It was the last time I could say so for many days. Within an hour, we were off towards the Armenian passes, making for Media.

6

F ROM THE hills we climbed to the mountains. We were on the road to Ekbatana. There was no pursuit.

By troops and single stragglers, the remnant of the army caught us up. Soon, if you had not seen what had taken the field, you could have called us a great force. Bessos' Baktrians were all there but for the dead. Being headed for their homeland, of course they had kept together. They were still nearly thirty thousand. The Immortals, and Royal Kin, and all the remnant of the Medes and Persians, both horse and foot, were now led by Nabarzanes.

We had, also, all the Greek mercenaries, about two thousand. It amazed me that, fighting only for hire, not one of them had deserted.

The most grievous loss was Mazaios, satrap of Babylon, and all his men. They had held their line, long after the center had broken with the flight of the King, whose life they may well have saved; Alexander, hot in chase of him, had had to turn back and deal with them. Not one of these brave warriors was with us now; they must all have perished.

Only about a third of the women's wagons had escaped from Arbela; two of the King's; the rest, the harems of lords who had stayed themselves to rescue them. But not one of the eunuchs had run off without his charges. What their fate was, I have never heard.

All the treasure was lost. But there were vaults of it at Ekbatana; the stewards had wisely loaded up with stores for the march, which we would need much more. Boubakes, I found, had had the King's baggage wagon all packed since morning. In his wisdom he had loaded a second tent, with a few small comforts for the royal eunuchs.

Even so, it was a hard rough journey. It was early autumn by now; still hot in the plains, but cool in the hills, and already cold in the mountains.

Boubakes and I had horses; three eunuchs rode in the baggage wagon. No more of us were left, except those of the women.

Each pass wound up higher and steeper; we looked down great clefts into stony gorges; wild goats gazed at us from the crags, and were shot for food by the Baktrian archers. At night, short of blankets in our little tent, the five of us huddled like birds for warmth. Boubakes, who had taken me into his grace and behaved to me as a father, shared blankets with me so that we had them double. He favored some scent with musk, but I was grateful. We were lucky to have a tent at all; nearly all the soldiers, their baggage lost, were sleeping under the sky.

From them, I pieced together the battle as best I could. Later on, I was to hear it gone over by men who knew; tactic by tactic, order by order, blow by blow. I have it by heart; I can't bring myself to go over it all again. To cut it short, our men all started tired, having stood to all night because the King expected surprise. Alexander, hoping for that very thing, gave his own men a good night's rest, and, when he'd finished his battle plan, turned in himself. He slept like a log; at sunrise they had to shake him. He told them it was because his mind had been at ease.

Darius leading the center, Alexander the right, he was expected to sweep centerwards at the onset. Instead, he wheeled round to outflank our left. The King sent troops to prevent this; Alexander lured more and more of them to the left, thinning out our center. Then he formed up the royal squadron, set himself at its head, gave the note for a deafening war-yell, and came thundering straight for the King.

Darius had fled early, but not, after all, the first. His charioteer had been shot with a flying javelin; when he fell, he had been taken for the King. The first flight began from this.

Perhaps he would have stood in a single fight, as long ago in Kadousia. If he had only seized the chariot reins, and given his war-cry, and dashed in among the enemy! It would have been quick, his name would have lived in honor. How often, before the end, he must have wished it too. But, caught in the panic like a leaf in storm, seeing Alexander on his black horse loom up through the dust towards him, he wheeled the chariot and joined the rout. From that, the plain of Gaugamela became a slaughterhouse.

One more thing I learned from the soldiers. Darius had detailed a troop to sortie behind the Macedonian lines, and rescue his captive family. They had reached the base-camp, shielded by the confusion; freed some captive Persians; and, getting to the ladies, called on them to fly. All had started up, except Sisygambis the Queen Mother. She neither rose, nor spoke, nor made any sign to the rescuers. They rescued no one; the Macedonians drove them off; but the last they saw of her, she was still sitting upright in her chair, her hands laid in her lap, looking before her.

I asked one captain why we were going to Ekbatana, instead of holding out in Babylon. "That whore of cities?" he said. "She'll open her legs to Alexander the moment he comes in sight. And hand the King over, if she had him there." Another said sourly, "When wolves are after your chariot, you either stay and fight them, or throw them something out, to keep them busy. The King's thrown Babylon. And with Babylon goes Susa."

I fell back to ride beside Boubakes, who did not think it proper I should talk too long with the men. As if he had read my thoughts, he said, "Did you say, once, you had never seen Persepolis?"

"The King never went there since I joined the Household. Is it better than Susa?"

He sighed and said, "There is no king's house more beautiful . . . Once Susa is gone, I doubt they can hold Persepolis."

We went on through the passes. The road was clear behind us. Alexander had chosen Babylon and Susa. When the column's pace grew tedious, I practiced archery. Some time before, I had picked up the bow of a dead Scythian, who had fled to the hills and then died of his wounds. He had been a smallish man and I could pull it easily. The first game I got was a sitting hare; but the King was pleased to have it for supper, as a change from goat.

He was quiet of an evening, and for some nights slept alone, till the air grew sharp, when he had a girl from the Harem. He never sent for me. Perhaps he remembered the song of my father's warriors, that I used to sing him. I do not know.

The high peaks were touched with white, when from the head of the last pass we saw Ekbatana.

It is, if you like, a palace and walled city. But it seemed more like some splendid sculpture wrought from the mountainside. The westering sun warmed the rich faded colors that crested its sevenfold walls, rising in tiers with the slope; the white, the black, the scarlet and blue and orange. The inmost two, which enclose the Palace and treasuries, had a fiery gleam. The outer was sheathed with silver, the innermost with gold.

To me, bred in the hills, it was lovelier than Susa a thousand times. I almost shed tears beholding it. I saw that Boubakes too seemed near to weeping. But what grieved him, he said, was that the King should be

driven to his summer palace with winter coming on,
and no other left for him.

We entered the city gate, and went up through the
sevenfold walls to the Palace above the golden battlements. It was all airy balconies, looking to the mountains. The soldiers, overflowing the town, built themselves huts of timber roofed with brush. Winter came
on.

The snow that had tipped the mountains crept lower and filled their clefts. My room (there were rooms to
spare, for so small a Household) was high in one of
the towers. Each day I could see the white descending;
till one morning, as in my childhood, I opened my eyes
to the snow-light. Snow lay on the city, on the thatched
huts of the soldiers, on the sevenfold walls. A raven
lighted on the nearest, loosing a little slide, and there
showed under his claws a patch of gold. I could have
gazed forever, except that I was freezing. I had to
break the ice in my water-ewer; and winter was only
starting.

I had no warm clothes, and told Boubakes I must
go to the bazaar. "Don't do that, my boy," he said. "I
have been going through the wardrobe. There are
things that have been lying there since King Ochos' day.
I have just the thing for you. No one will miss it."

It was a splendid coat, of lynx-skin lined with
scarlet; it must have belonged to one of the princes.
This was good of Boubakes. He may have noticed the
King had not lately sent for me, and wanted to make
me pretty.

The mountain air was like health after long sickness.
I daresay it did more for my looks than the coat; at all
events, the King sent for me before long. But he had
changed since the battle. He was restless and hard to
please; and I felt, as I never had before, that without
warning he might turn against me. It put me on edge;
I wanted only to get it over.

However, I could understand, and did not hold it
against him. He had just had news of how Babylon
the Whore had opened her bed to Alexander.

Even against him, I should think those great walls

could have held out a year. But the Royal Gate was opened. The Royal Way was strewn with flowers, and lined each side with altars and tripods burning precious incense. A procession met him bringing kingly gifts; purebred Nisaian horses, flower-wreathed oxen, gilded cars with leopards and lions in cages. The Magi and Chaldeans chanted praises, to the sound of harps and lutes. The cavalry of the garrison paraded without their weapons. Compared with this, the welcome to Darius had been like that for some third-rate governor.

Even this was not the worst. The envoy who met Alexander on his march, and put the keys of the citadel in his hands, had been the satrap, Mazaios, whom we had mourned for dead.

He had done his duty in the battle. No doubt in the dust and din he had not known at first that the King had fled. He had hoped for support, for victory. When he knew, he made his choice. He had led back his men at speed, lest he should be too late for Alexander. He had been in time; Alexander had reappointed him. He was still satrap of Babylon.

For all Mazaios' homage, Alexander had marched warily on the city, in battle order, leading the van himself. However, it was not too good to be true. He had Darius' gilded chariot brought, and entered in proper style.

I tried to picture this wild and strange young barbarian in the Palace I knew so well. For some reason, perhaps because the first thing he did in Darius' captured tent was to take a bath (by all accounts, he seemed as clean as a Persian) I saw him in the bathhouse, with its lapis tiles and gold fish, splashing in the sun-warmed water. It was an envious thought, at Ekbatana.

The servants fared well; their quarters had been unchanged for centuries, since the Median kings had lived there all through the year. It was only the royal rooms which, when the empire grew, had been made open and airy, to catch the mountain breezes in summer heats. Snow blew in at the windows.

We got shutters made, with fifty carpenters at it, and

filled the place with braziers. But nothing could really warm it. I could see how it irked the King, to think of Alexander basking in Babylon's mild air.

The Baktrians, who have hard winters at home, would have been well clad, had they not stripped down in the heat of Gaugamela and then lost their baggage. The Persians and the Greeks were no better off. The men from mountain satrapies went hunting their own furs; others bought in the bazaar, or rode into the country and robbed the peasants.

Prince Oxathres, and the lords and satraps, had quarters in the Palace. Bessos laughed at the cold through his black beard; but Nabarzanes noted we had tried to give him some comfort, and thanked us civilly. He was one of the antique school.

The soldiers had been paid from the Palace treasury. They brought the town trade; but being short of whores, caused much contention over honest women. When I went out riding, I soon learned to skirt the barracks of the Greeks. Their repute for liking boys is not unearned. Though they must have known I served the King, they would whistle and call, without any sense of propriety. However, it was their custom; and I respected their fidelity in disaster.

The last leaves fell from the lean and spiky trees, stripped by the wind even of snow. Drifts closed the roads. Each day passed like yesterday. I shot at a mark for pastime, and practiced my dancing, though it was hard to warm up and save myself from sprains.

The King's days passed heavily. Oxathres his brother was hardly thirty, unlike him in looks and mind, and would be gone for days on hunting-trips with other young lords. The King would entertain the satraps and nobility by turns to supper; but he would sink into his thoughts, and forget to invite their conversation. He got me to dance, I think, chiefly to relieve him of the need to talk. But the guests, who had few diversions, were gracious and made me gifts.

I thought it would not have been out of place to invite Patron, the Greek commander. But it never entered his head, to have such people indoors.

At last it thawed, and a messenger got through the half-flooded roads; a horse-coper from Susa, who came for the reward. We depended on such people now; they were always well paid, however bad their news was.

Alexander was in Susa. The city, though without the fulsomeness of Babylon, had opened its gates at once. He had taken entire the treasure, hoarded reign after reign; a sum so vast that, when I heard it, I could not believe there were such riches in all the world. Truly, enough to keep the wolf from the chariot.

As winter hardened, closing the roads again, shutting us up together week after week with only the muddy town or the barren hillsides, men grew prickly or dull or sour. The soldiers fell into tribal factions, reviving old feuds from home. Townsmen came up to complain that their wives, or daughters, or sons had been debauched. The King would not be troubled with such trifles; soon all petitioners sought Bessos or Nabarzanes. Yet idleness made him moodier; it fell on one man or another mostly by chance, but everyone was on edge from it. All that befell later, as I believe, was hatched in those long white empty days.

One night he sent for me, the first time in a long while. I saw Boubakes, as he withdrew from the Bedchamber, signal discreet congratulation. But from the first I was ill at ease with myself, uncertain of the King. I remembered the boy before me, packed off for being insipid. So I tried something which had amused him once at Susa. Suddenly he pushed me off, fetched me a great slap on the face, said I was insolent, and ordered me out of his sight.

My hands were shaking so, I could hardly get my clothes on. I stumbled down cold corridors, half blinded with tears of pain, anger and shock. Putting my sleeve to my eyes to wipe them, I ran clean into someone.

The feel of his clothes told me he was a lord. I stammered an apology. He put both hands on my shoulders, and looked at me by the light of the wall-sconce. It was Nabarzanes. I swallowed my weeping in shame. He had a biting turn of mockery when he chose.

"Why, Bagoas," he said with the greatest gentleness. "What is it? Has someone been ill-using you? That lovely face of yours will be bruised tomorrow."

He spoke as if to a woman. It was natural; yet, fresh from humiliation, I found it too much to bear. Without even dropping my voice, I said, "He struck me, for nothing. And if he is a man, then I reckon so am I."

He looked down at me in silence. It sobered me; I had put my life in his hands. Then he said gravely, "I have nothing to say to that." While I still stood rooted, feeling my words' enormity, he put his finger-tips to my stinging cheek. "It is forgotten," he said. "We must all learn to hold our tongues."

I would have prostrated myself, but he raised me up. "Go to bed, Bagoas. And don't lose sleep over your future, whatever may have been said. He will forget it, no doubt, tomorrow, or the day after."

All night I scarcely closed my eyes; but not from fear for myself. He would not betray me. At Susa, I had grown used to the petty court intrigues; to office-seeking, backbiting of rivals, the endless play for favor. Now I knew that I had looked into far deeper places. He had not hidden his contempt; and it was not for me.

When my bruise was gone, the King sent for me to dance and gave me ten gold darics. But it was not the bruise that hung about my memory.

7

WITH THE turn of winter, we had good news from the north. The Scythians, those in alliance with Bessos, were to send us ten thousand bowmen, as soon as spring cleared the passes. The Kadousians, who live by the Hyrkanian Sea, had answered the King's summons with a promise of five thousand foot.

The governor of Persis, Ariobarzanes, also got a message through. He had walled, clean across, the great gorge of the Persian Gates, the pass into Persepolis. It could be held forever; any army that went in would be destroyed from the heights above, with rocks and boulders. Alexander would, with any luck, be dead with his men before they reached the wall.

I overheard Bessos saying, as he passed me with a friend, "Ah, it's there we should be, not here." Happy for him, had some god fulfilled his wish.

It's a long hard ride from Persis to Ekbatana, with

only one spare horse. Before that news even reached us, if we had known it, Alexander was in Persepolis.

He had tried the Persian Gates; soon found them deadly, and withdrew his men. They had thought him gone. But he'd heard from a shepherd, whom he later made rich for life, of some dizzy goat-track, by which, if he did not break his neck, he could outflank the pass. Over this he led his men, through darkness and deep snow. He fell on the Persians from their rear, while the rest of his people forced the pass, now freed of its defenders. Our men were grain between the millstones. Meantime, we rejoiced at Ekbatana.

Days passed; the snow lay crisp, the sky was clear and windless. From the Palace windows I could see, between the orange battlements and the blue, the town lads throwing snowballs.

Long used to being with men, I had scarcely thought how it would be, to be a boy among others. I had just turned sixteen; now I would never know it. It came to me that I had no friends, as those boys down there would understand it. I had only patrons.

Well, I thought, no use lamenting; it won't put back what the slave-dealer cut away. There is the Light and the Dark, the Magus used to tell us, and all things that live have the power to choose.

So I rode out alone, to see the sevenfold walls with their colors and their metals, shining in the snow. On the hills a new air touched me, a scent of delight breaking through the whiteness. It was the first breath of spring.

The icicles melted from the waterspouts. Brown rusty grass showed through the snow; everyone went out riding. The King called a war council, to plan for when the roads were open and the new troops came. I took out my bow, and shot a fox in a gully. It had a beautiful pelt, with a silver sheen. When I had taken it to a furrier in the town, to have a hat made out of it, I went back to tell Boubakes. Some servant said he was in his room, he had taken the news hard.

From the passage I heard him weeping. Once, I would not have dared go in, but those days were done.

He lay prone on his bed, crying his heart out. I sat down by him and touched his shoulders. He lifted a face all blotched with tears.

"He has burned it. Burned it to the ground. Everything gone, ashes, cinders, dust." "Burned what?" I asked. He said, "The Palace of Persepolis."

He sat up and clutched a towel, fresh tears pouring down as soon as he had wiped his face. "Has the King asked for me? I can't lie here like this." I said, "Never mind, someone will attend to him." He went on, gasping and sobbing, about the lotus columns, the beautiful wall-carvings, the hangings, the gilded and coffered ceilings. It all sounded to me pretty much like Susa; but I grieved with him in his loss.

"What a barbarian!" I said. "And a fool, to burn it when it belonged to him." We had had that news some time.

"He was drunk, they say. You should not ride out so long, just because the King's in council. He would think it a liberty if he knew; it would do you harm."

"I am sorry. Here, give me your towel, you need cold water." I wrung it out for him, then ran down to the guard hall. I wanted to hear the messenger, before he was sick of telling his tale.

Those who had heard were still milling it over; but they had plied him with so much wine that he was now pretty near speechless, and was dozing on a pile of blankets. There was a crowd of Palace people, and some soldiers off duty.

A chamberlain told me, "They were at a feast, all roaring drunk. Some whore from Athens asked him to set the place alight, because Xerxes had burned their temples. Alexander threw the first torch himself."

"But he was living there!" I said.

"Where else? He sacked the city when first he took it."

This too I had heard. "But why? He never sacked Babylon. Or Susa." I had thought, to tell the truth, of some houses there I would gladly have seen in flames.

A grizzled soldier, a captain of a hundred, said, "Ah, there you have it. Babylon surrendered. So did Susa. Now in Persepolis, the garrison made a run for it, or started getting what they could out of the Palace for themselves. So no one surrendered, not in form. Well, now; Alexander gave out prize-money to his men at Babylon, and again at Susa. But it's not the same. Two great cities fallen, and never a chance to loot. No troops will stand that forever."

His loud voice had roused the messenger. He had stolen two horses from the stables, while the Palace burned, and had enjoyed his importance here, till the wine had quenched him. "No," he said thickly, "it was those Greeks. The King's slaves. They got free, they met him on the way, four thousand of them. Nobody knew there were so many, not till they came together." His voice droned off. The soldier said, "Never mind, I'll tell you later."

"He cried over them." The messenger gave a belch. "One of them told me so; they're all free now, free and rich. He said he'd send them all home with enough to live on; but they didn't want to be seen there, not as they are now. They asked for some land they could farm together, being used to the sight of each other. Well, then he was angry like nobody ever saw him, and marched straight up to the city and let loose his men. Just kept the Palace for himself, till he burned that too."

I remembered Susa, and the Greek slaves of the royal jeweler; their leg-stumps, their branded and nose-less faces. Four thousand! Most must have been there since King Ochos' day. Four thousand! I recalled Boubakes, bewailing the ravaged beauty. I don't suppose such people had come much in his way; or not more than two or three of them.

"So," said the soldier, "there's an end to the New Year festivals. I was posted there once, it was the sight of a lifetime. Well, it's war. I was with Ochos' force in Egypt . . ." He frowned to himself. Presently he looked up. "I don't know how drunk he was. He saved his bonfire, till he was ready to be leaving."

I understood him. Spring was breaking everywhere. But no soldier expects a eunuch to know anything.

"He's burned his quarters behind him. And you know where he'll be coming now? He'll be coming here."

8

I T WAS a day of late spring
rain, with brown torrents in the gullies, when the King
ordered the women to be sent north. They were to go
through the pass of the Kaspian Gates, to safekeeping
in Kadousia.

I helped load them into the wagons. You could see at
a glance the favorites; they looked worn out, with blue
streaks under their eyes. Even after these farewells,
there were figures lingering on the Palace roof, gazing
after them.

To the common soldiers it meant nothing, unless it
shortened their lords' tempers. Their own women
would trudge behind them, with the sacks that were
their households, as soldiers' women have done
since wars began. Being more used than the ladies to
shifting for themselves, not a few had scrambled off
from Gaugamela.

Alexander had set out for Media. He seemed in no
great haste, attending to this and that on his way. We
would soon be on the north road, where the Kadousian

and Scythian troops would march to meet us. With them, we would await him, and contest his passage to Hyrkania. So it was said. It was said also, though not so loudly, that if he were heard of within a hundred miles, we would be off through the passes ourselves, to Hyrkania and east to Baktria. "When we serve. the great, they are our destiny." I tried to live each day as it came.

On a clear day in early summer we started out. Where the road turned into the hills, I turned as I rode, to see the light of sunrise gleam on the golden battlements. Beautiful city, I thought, I shall never see you again. Had I only known!

As we passed mountain hamlets, I noticed how lean the peasants were, and how sullenly they watched us. It was a poor countryside for an army to have lived off. Yet, when the King passed by, they all did reverence. He was godlike to them, set above his servants' deeds. It has been in the blood of us Persians a thousand years. It was even still in mine, who knew what the god was made of.

We rode through bare open hills, under blue skies. The birds were singing. The cavalry sang as they rode; Baktrians mostly, on their stocky rough-coated mounts. Up here, it was hard to think one would not live forever.

But as we advanced, the singing fell silent. We were nearing the meeting-place appointed with the Scythians. They had sent no forerunners; nor had the Kadousians. Our own scouts had seen no signs of them.

The King retired early. Though the women were gone, he did not send for me. Perhaps what happened at Ekbatana had killed desire; or perhaps it had only happened because desire was waning. If so, I must prepare to be just a Household eunuch, with my little daily duties. Had we been at court, I might already have been allotted them.

If that happens, I thought, I will take a lover. I remembered Oromedon; he had had the sheen on him that, when I looked back, told its tale. I myself had had plenty of offers; discreet, of course, for fear of the King, but I had been let know where I was wanted.

With such follies the young, to whom each joy or trouble seems eternal, will concern themselves while the sky is about to fall.

Two days took us off the north road onto a country track. It led to the plain where the Scythians should be awaiting us.

We reached it about noon, a great space of upland grass and brush. Our camp had been pitched where a few starved trees leaned to the wind. There was a whining of curlews; conies bobbed off among the stones. For the rest, in all my life I had seen nothing look so empty.

The night came down. One grew used to the sounds of the camp; singing, the hum of talk, laughter or quarreling, an order, the rattle of cookpots. Tonight there was just a low muttering, like the sound of a torrent grinding its stones. It went on late. I fell asleep at last to the sound.

At daybreak, I woke to bad-news voices. Five hundred cavalry had slipped off in the night; and nearly a thousand foot, taking all their gear but their shields.

There was a voice outside speaking Greek to the interpreter. It was Patron, the Greek commander. He had come to report his men all present.

Long since, they could have deserted to Alexander, and helped him sack Persepolis. Here they had just their wages, while the treasury held out. Patron was a thickset grizzled man, with the square face not seen among Persians. He came from some part of Greece that had been beaten in war by Alexander's father, and had brought his men along with him; they had served in Asia since King Ochos' day. I was glad to see the King show him more warmth than usual. However, when at sunup he called a war council, Patron was not invited. He was a hired soldier and an outlander. He did not count.

The throne was set on its dais; the royal tent was

cleared and ready. The lords came straggling up, their coat-skirts flapping in the sharp wind, wearing the best clothes they had left; crowding outside, awaiting leave to enter. To one side, Bessos and Nabarzanes were talking eagerly. Some shock, which felt long expected, came to me from their faces.

I went in, and said softly to Boubakes, "Something dreadful is going to happen."

"What do you mean?" He grasped my arm till it hurt.

"I don't know. Something against the King."

"Why say such things, if you do not know?" He was cross because I had stirred his smothered fears.

The lords came in, did reverence, and took their stand in order of rank. We eunuchs, inside in the King's sleeping-place, listened through the leather curtains. This was mere custom; it was not a private audience. Though, if we could, we would listen to those as well.

The King spoke from the throne. It was soon too clear that he had composed the speech himself.

He praised his hearers' loyalty, reminding them— trusting man—how renegades like Mazaios of Babylon had been enriched by Alexander. He talked a good deal of past Persian glories, till I could feel the rising impatience with my skin. The pith came at last; he was for a last stand at the Kaspian Gates, victory or death.

There was a hush so thick, you could have stuck a knife in it upright. The Persian Gates, held by crack troops, had been forced in depth of winter. It was summer now; and as for our troops, could he not feel their temper?

But I, who had once been near him, thought I understood. He had not forgotten the song of my father's warriors. I felt his craving for lost honor. He had seen himself at the Kaspian Gates, gloriously redeeming Gaugamela. And not one man of all who were here had seen it with him. This was their answer, this dreadful silence.

On the toilet-table was the little knife we trimmed his nails with. I reached for it, jabbed it through the curtain, and put my eye to the slit. Boubakes looked shocked. I handed the knife to him. The King had his back to us; and for the rest of them, if we'd stuck our heads through the curtain, they'd not have noticed.

The King sat stiffly on his throne; I could see the peak of the Mitra, and a purple sleeve. And I saw what he saw—the faces. Though no one had dared a whisper in the Presence, they were all one glitter of moving eyes.

Someone stepped forward; old Artabazos, with his straight shrunk carriage and snow-white beard. When first I'd seen him, I had thought him in good shape for a man running up to eighty. In fact, he was ninety-five. As he approached, the King stepped down, and leaned him his cheek to kiss.

In his firm, high, ancient voice, Artabazos said that he and his sons would stand, to the last man, with all their people, in whatever field His Majesty should see fit to choose. The King embraced him. He withdrew to his place. For long moments, silence returned.

There was a movement, a low murmur. Nabarzanes came forward. I thought, It is now.

He was wearing the grey wool coat with embroidered sleeves, which he'd had on that night at Ekbatana. It was old and frayed. I daresay he had no better, so much had been lost. Power and danger hung about him, from his first words.

"My lord King. In this hour of so grave a choice, it seems to me we can look forward only by looking back. Firstly, our enemy. He has resource, great swiftness and resolution. He has good troops attached to his person. It is said, with what truth I cannot tell, that in hardships and in courage he is their example." He made a tiny pause. "At all events, he can now reward loyalty with Your Majesty's wealth. All this is said of him; but what else do we we hear wherever his name is spoken? That he is fortunate; that he has all the luck."

A longer pause. They hardly breathed, now. Something was coming; and some of them knew what.

"But is this so? If I find a stray blood-horse on my

land, you may call me fortunate. Or you may call its owner unlucky."

People at the back, who knew nothing, shifted about. The stillness in front was louder. I could see the purple sleeve stir on the chair-arm.

"Let godless men," said Nabarzanes smoothly, "speak of chance. We, surely, reared in our fathers' faith, believe all things are disposed by heaven. Why should we think the Wise God favors Alexander, an outland robber following other gods? Should we not rather, as I said, look back, seeking some past impiety for which we suffer punishment?"

The silence was now entire. Even the most ignorant had caught, like dogs, the scent of thunder.

"Lord King, the world knows with what blameless honor Your Majesty assumed the throne, after horrors you had no share in." His voice had sunk to a deep leopard-purr of irony. "Through your justice, a treacherous villian did not live to boast of them." (He might just as well have added, "or to accuse you.") "And yet, what has been our fortune since? We are the bowl Alexander's luck has emptied. My lord, it is said that curses can outlive the guilty dead. Is it not time to ask if Mithra, Protector of Honor, is yet appeased?"

Stillness. They had begun to see, but did not yet believe.

Nabarzanes' voice altered. Towering Bessos moved up towards him.

"My lord King, our peasants, when they are lost in their own hills, turn their coats, that the demon leading them astray may no longer know them. There is old wisdom in simple folk. We too, I now believe, must turn the unlucky garment, though it be of purple. Here is Bessos, who shares with yourself the blood of Artaxerxes. Let him wear the Hood, and command till this war is over. When the Macedonians are driven out, Your Majesty can return."

At last, they believed. In the lifetimes of us all, two kings had died by poison. But it was a thing unknown to man, that a Great King, robed and enthroned, should be told to get up and go.

The silence broke; loud cries of assent, prompt and prepared; shouts of dismay and outrage; mutterings of doubt. Suddenly a great shout of "Traitor!" drowned all the rest. It was the King, striding down from the dais in his purple robe, his scimitar drawn, making for Nabarzanes.

He was terrible in his size and fury. Even to me, in his royal state he was clothed with godhead. I looked to see Nabarzanes blasted at his feet.

Instead, there was a crowd about him, Nabarzanes and Bessos and the chief Baktrian lords, clinging in supplication. As they clung, begging mercy, they pulled down his sword-arm. His sword hung, uncertainly. They all prostrated themselves, bewailing their offense, saying they would withdraw from his displeasure, till he gave them leave to see his face.

They backed out. And all the lords of Baktria followed them.

Someone was panting beside me. Boubakes had made a slit in the curtain, about twice the size of mine. He was trembling from head to foot.

The tent now milled like a kicked anthill. Old Artabazos, his sons, and loyal Persian lords crowded round the King, protesting their sacred faith. He thanked them, and dismissed the council. We had hardly time to put ourselves in order, before he was inside.

In silence, he let Boubakes disrobe him and put on his leisure gown. He lay down on the bed. His face looked sunken, as if from a month-long sickbed. I slipped outside, without obeisance, without leave. It was an unheard-of thing to do. I simply knew that just now, there was no one he would not sooner see about him. Boubakes never reproved me.

I went out into the camp. My clothes were well-worn, and smelled of the stables now I had no servant. No one noticed me.

The Baktrians were busy about their quarters. They were starting to strike camp.

Quick work indeed! Had Bessos' fear of the King been real? Yet I could not see Nabarzanes giving up so easily. I pushed in among a crowd of Baktrians on their way; they were so full of their own concerns, I felt invisible. Mostly they were saying their lord ought to have his rights, it was time for a man to lead. But one said, "Well, no one can say, now, that the King didn't have his chance."

Separate and neat, as always, stood the Greek encampment. No one was striking tents there. They were just crowded together talking. Greeks are great talkers, but have often something to say. I walked over.

They were so engaged, I was in among them before anyone even spoke to me. Then one broke away and strode over. As he came, I'd taken him for forty, but now saw he was ten years younger; war and weather had done the rest.

"Beautiful stranger, do I see you here at last? Why do you never visit us?"

He still had real Greek clothes, though the stuff was threadbare. He was tanned as brown as cedarwood, and the sun had faded his short beard much lighter than his hair. His smile looked honest.

"My friend," I said, "this is no day for beauty. Bessos wants to be King. He's just told the King so." I did not see why I should keep from loyal men what every traitor knew.

"Yes," he said. "They wanted us to come over. They offered double pay."

"Some of us Persians keep faith too, though by now you must be doubting it. Tell me, what are the Baktrians up to? Why are they striking camp?"

"They won't go far." He was eating me with his eyes, quite frankly, yet without offense. "I doubt they'll even go out of sight. From what they told Patron, on the face of it they're withdrawing from the King's presence on account of having offended him. Of course, it's really to show their strength. We'll be thin on the ground without them. That's what they want us to see. Well, I've not served as long in Asia as Patron and his Phokians; but I know what good Persians feel about the

King. It's not our way in Athens; but our way's come to grief too, that's why I left. So I serve where I sign on, and where I serve I keep my bargain. A man must have something to put his pride in."

"You may well do that. All of us know it."

He looked at me wistfully with his bright-blue eyes, like a child asking for something it knows quite well it won't get. "Well, *our* camp will still be here at nightfall. What do you say to slipping out for a drink with me? I could tell you about Greece, since you speak the language so well."

I nearly laughed, and said I needed no telling. But I liked him; so I just said smiling, "You know I serve the King. And just now he needs his friends."

"Well, no harm in trying. My name's Doriskos. I found out yours."

"Goodbye, Doriskos. I daresay we'll meet again." I had no such expectation, but wanted to show goodwill. I gave him my hand, which I thought he'd never let go of, and returned to the King's tent.

He was shut up alone. Boubakes said he would see no one, or even eat. Nabarzanes had taken all his cavalry, and had made camp alongside Bessos. Thus far Boubakes got, and broke down in tears. It was dreadful to see him stuff his sash-end into his mouth, not to hide it from a young nobody like me (that was all I was, now) but lest the King should hear.

"The Greeks are loyal," I said. Once he would have scolded me for going anywhere near them. Now he just asked what were two thousand men, against more than thirty thousand Baktrians, and Nabarzanes' horsemen?

"There are the loyal Persians too. Who's commanding them now?"

He wiped his eyes on the other end of his sash and said, "Artabazos."

"What? I don't believe it."

It was true. The ancient was doing a general's round of the Persian camp, seeing the lords and captains, heartening them before their men. Such fidelity must have moved a stone. It was strange to think that when already old by most men's reckoning, he had been a rebel. But that was against Ochos, who I daresay gave him little choice between that and death.

Returning from his task, he came to the King, and got him to take food, which they ate together. We were told to withdraw, but overheard their talk. Since it was now unthinkable to lead the troops to battle, they would be marched tomorrow through the Kaspian Gates, starting at dawn.

While we were eating supper in our tent, I said what I could no longer contain in silence. "Why didn't the King go round the camp himself? He could be Artabazos' grandson; he's only fifty. He should make them *want* to fight for him."

They turned on me outraged, all together. Was I out of my mind? The King to bare his countenance to common soldiers, like a mere captain? Where would his royalty be, what reverence would they have for him? Far better he should bear adversity, as now, with the dignity of his sacred rank.

"But," I said, "Kyros the Great was a general in the field. I know, I come from his tribe. His men must have seen him every day."

"Those were ruder times," said Boubakes. "They cannot return."

"So we hope," I said. I put on my coat again.

By now it was full dark, but for the watch-fires, the torches spiked here and there into the ground, and the chinks of some lamplit tent. Passing a dead torch, I smeared some of its soot across my face, made my way to the nearest watch-fire, where I had heard a Baktrian accent, and squatted down with the crowd.

"You can tell God's curse is on him," the Baktrian captain was saying. "It's sent him mad. Marching us through the Gates, to be trapped like rats between the mountains and the Hyrkanian Sea. When Baktria could hold out forever." He went on about its countless strongpoints, each one impregnable except to the birds of heaven. "All we need, to finish the Macedonians there, is a king who knows the country. And how to fight."

"Baktria," said a Persian, "I know nothing of. But don't talk of God's curses, if you turn against the King. That's god-cursed, if anything ever was."

There were murmurs of agreement. I wiped my nose on my fingers in a vulgar way, looked stupid, and slid off out of the firelight.

Hearing talk in a tent ahead of me, I was about to slip round it, away from the bright torch outside, when a man came out, so briskly that we collided. He took me by the shoulder, not roughly, and turned me round to the light.

"My poor Bagoas. We seem always to meet like this. Your face is quite black. Has he taken to beating you every night?"

His teeth grinned white in the torchlight. I knew he was as dangerous as a hunting leopard, yet could not fear him, nor even hate him as I knew I ought.

"No, my lord Nabarzanes." By rights I should have bent my knee; I decided not to. "But if he did, the King is the King."

"Well, so. It would have disappointed me, if your loyalty had not matched your beauty. Do wipe that dirt off your face. I shan't harm you, my dear boy."

I found myself rubbing it with my sleeve, as if I owed him obedience. He means, I thought, that it is too late.

"That is better." He took off with one finger a smudge I had passed over. Then he laid his hands on my shoulders. His face was no longer mocking. "Your father died for the King, I've heard. But Arses was the trueborn heir, and fit to lead us. Yes, in Arses we would have had a warrior. Why do you think Alexander has not overtaken us? He could have done it long ago. I will tell you the reason; it is contempt. Your father died for our Persian honor. Remember that."

"I don't forget it, my lord. And I know where my honor lies."

"Yes, you are right." He pressed my shoulders and let them go. "Go back to him. You might lend him some of your manhood."

It was like the pat of a leopard, claws pricking through the soft paw. As he left, I found that, without thinking, I had bent my knee.

At the royal tent, I met Artabazos leaving. I made reverence and would have passed, but he put out his blue-veined hand. "You have come from the camp, my boy. What did you find?" I told him it was full of Baktrians, trying to subvert the loyal Persians. He clicked his tongue tetchily. "I shall have to see these men."

"Sir!" I said, careless of the impertinence, "you must sleep. You have had no rest all day and half the night."

"What I must do, my son, is see Bessos and Nabarzanes. At my age, we don't sleep as you young folk do." He did not even take a staff to lean on.

He was right. As soon as I'd told Boubakes the news, I lay down, and fell asleep like the dead.

The horns aroused me, with the call "Prepare to march." I opened my eyes, and found all the others gone. Something was happening. I scrambled my clothes on, and went out. The King, dressed for the march, was standing before his tent, his chariot already waiting. At his feet knelt Bessos and Nabarzanes. Old Artabazos stood by.

The King was saying how their disloyalty had grieved him. Both hung their heads, and beat their breasts. Bessos' voice, one could have sworn, had tears in it. His only wish, he cried, had been to ward off from the King a curse called down by others, as he would have lifted his shield in battle; he would have taken the curse on himself, and borne the wounds. Nabarzanes, touching the King's robe, said that they had withdrawn in awe of his displeasure; it would be their life's joy to be received in his grace again.

I looked with respect and wonder at Artabazos, whose work was thus rewarded; a soul beloved of Mithra, one to go straight to Paradise, whom the River of Ordeal would never scald. All was well again. Loyalty had returned. Light had conquered the dark Lie. I was still quite young.

The King, weeping, reached out his hands to them. They prostrated themselves and kissed the ground before him, declaring themselves the happiest of men and the most devoted. The King mounted his chariot. Artabazos' sons tried to get their father into a wagon, where he could rest. He scolded them soundly, and called for his horse. They withdrew abashed. The eldest was over seventy.

I went off towards the horse-lines. The soldiers, who had been milling and mixing and disputing through the night, were being shoved into marching order. The Persians were shaping best; but then, they were fewer. Fewer than last night, by far. So were the Baktrians; even with their numbers, it showed.

That came of the long night's trafficking. The Persians, knowing themselves outnumbered, had made off by hundreds; but they had put some Baktrians, too, in dread of vengeful Mithra. Between fear of him and Bessos, they had chosen the long walk home.

Riding back towards the Household wagons, I saw the Greeks lined up in column of march. They were all still there. Also, all armed.

On long marches when no action threatened, they had always piled their armor, helmets and weapons in their carts, keeping only their swords; wearing their short tunics (made from all kinds of stuff, they had been so long from home) and the wide straw hats Greeks travel in, their skins being tender to sun. Now they had on corselets or cuirasses, helmets, even greaves if they owned them, and their round shields hung at their backs.

Just then one fell out, and waved to me. It was Doriskos. What does he take me for, I thought; I will show him if he can make a fool of me in public. I was just going to kick my horse to a canter, when I saw his face. It did not look like dalliance. I rode up.

He grabbed my boot, and motioned me to lean over. No dalliance in that either. "Can you get word to the King?"

"I doubt it. He's on the road, I'm late. What is it?"

"Tell him not to be fooled. He's not seen the end of it."

"Oh," I said cheerfully, "that's over, they've sued for pardon."

"We know *that*. That's the thing; that's why Patron made us arm."

My belly closed on itself. I said, "What does it mean?"

"No one kept camp last night. It's common talk. They hoped to bring in the Persians; if they had, they'd have acted today. But the Persians said it was god-cursed; that's why so many made off. It'll be later now, when we're through the Gates; then they'll do it."

I remembered my life, and despised my faith in men. "Do what?"

"Take the King, and trade him to Alexander."

I had thought that I knew treachery. I had been an unborn child.

"Steady up, don't look so green." He reached up to keep me in the saddle. "Listen now; they're snakes, but they're not fools. The King's the King, but he's not the world's best general, let's admit. This one stroke would get him out of their way, and let them buy peace with Alexander. Then they'd go to Baktria, and make it ready for war."

"Don't hold me on, people are looking." I had quickly come to myself. "Alexander would never trust them, men who had done that."

"They say he's overtrusting, when faith's been pledged to him. On the other hand, God help you if you break it. I saw what he left of Thebes . . . No matter; just tell the King."

"But I haven't the rank to go up to him in public." This would have been true even when I was in favor. "It must be your general; no one less."

"Patron? The King hardly knows his face." He spoke not without bitterness.

"I know. But he must." None too soon, I had started thinking. "The King can speak Greek. Some of us do in the Household. But Bessos always asks for

the interpreter; so does Nabarzanes. If they're listening, Patron can still warn the King."

"That's worth knowing. I'll tell him that. We're a
handful to the Baktrians; but if the King trusts us,
we might still get him away."

I soon overtook the Household; it had not gone a
quarter-mile. The Sun Chariot had been lost at
Gaugamela; but two Magi with the altar still walked
in front. Behind that, all order was falling apart, all
precedence shattered. Men of both kinds were edging
each other to get near the King. Boubakes was riding
just behind his chariot, a thing unheard of. At his side,
on a great Nisaian charger as heavy-boned as a bull,
rode Bessos himself.

I fell in by Boubakes. He looked at me with dull
sleepless eyes, as if to say, "After all, what matter?"
We were too near the King to talk.

The shaded litter was left behind at Arbela; those
days were gone. He would be tired, after all day in
a chariot. Something I felt for him still, beyond mere
duty. I remembered him playful, kindly, amused, and
in the follies of pleasure. He knew himself despised.
Perhaps he had known it when he struck me.

The King was the King; he could not have believed
this sacred state could be altered, except by death.
Disaster after disaster, failure on failure, shame on
shame; friend after friend turned traitor; his troops,
to whom he should have been as a god, creeping off
like thieves every night; Alexander approaching, the
dreaded enemy; and, still unknown, the real peril at
his elbow. And to trust in, whom? We few, who for
the use of kings had been made into less than men;
and two thousand soldiers serving for hire, still loyal
not for love of him, but to keep their pride.

As we marched, the road rising through bare uplands, I suppose there was no one in the Household
who was not thinking, And what will become of *me*?
We were only human. Boubakes thought, perhaps, of
want, or a dreary life in some low-rank harem. But I
had only one skill, I had only known one employment.

I remembered slavery in Susa. I was no longer too young to find the means of dying. But I wished to live.

The road climbed higher. We were coming to the pass. Here was the barrier range of the Tapourians, great peaks, barren and harsh, so high that in summer they were still tipped with snow. Up the foothills wriggled our worm of road, and vanished in a cleft. In spite of all, my heart quickened. Beyond must be the sea, which I had never seen.

At each higher turn, rose a new wall of stark stone, weather-scoured, no living thing but a few cypresses bent like cripples. Here and there by a stream were poor fields and huts, whose wild people fled like rock-rabbits. But the air was like crystal. Ahead, plunging in shadow, was the steep gorge of the Gates.

Alexandria is a splendid city, with everything a sensible man can need. I daresay I shall end my life here, without ever again going far away. But when I remember the high hills, and a pass mounting to its unknown revelation, I will not think so. Even then, knowing the evil and the danger, knowing all I had known before, even then I felt it; ecstasy, prophecy, light.

A sheer cliff close above, a sheer drop below, far down the roar of water; we were in the Gates. Even so high, the rock-wall flung back the heat and the column labored. Surely, this pass could have been held. Just ahead, Bessos on his great horse still rode beside the King. No sign of Patron. Why should he heed my message, second-hand, and from the King's minion at that?

The road flattened and opened. We were at the pass-head; Hyrkania lay below us. It was another country. The mountains were clothed with forests, green fold after green fold. Then a narrow plain; and beyond, the sea.

From this height, the horizon stretched immense round its sheet of silver. I caught my breath with delight. The black shores puzzled me; I did not know they were covered with flocks of cormorants, millions and millions, fed by its endless shoals of fish.

The Tapourian range is a great parting of the waters. Truly, it was to be so for me.

Soon we were winding down among the trees. Streams plashed and trickled over red-stained boulders; the water was delicious, very cold with a tang of iron. We made halt in a pine grove, setting cushions for the King, and seeing to his retiring-tent.

When we set off again, the air grew closer and moister, tall trees held off the breezes that had tingled on the pass. We had halted late, because of its bleakness; now in the deep groves already the shadows darkened. Looking about, I was aware of someone new, riding just behind me. It was Patron.

He was a veteran. He had not labored his horse up hill when the going would soon be easier. I caught his eye, and fell back to give him my place. He dismounted, and led his horse; in sign of respect, or to be noticed. His eyes never left the King.

It was Bessos who saw first. His back stiffened; he came nearer the King, and started some kind of talk with him. Patron plodded along behind.

The road bent sharply. As the chariot turned, the King saw him, and showed surprise. No one should stare at the Great King's face, but Patron fixed his eyes on it. He made no gesture; just looked.

The King spoke to Boubakes, who fell back, and said to Patron, "His Majesty asks if there is anything you want of him."

"Yes. Tell His Majesty I would like a word, without interpreters. Say it is not for myself, but in his service. *Without interpreters.*"

Boubakes, his face changed, repeated the message. The chariot had its drags on for the slope, and was moving slowly. The King beckoned Patron up. I took his bridle, and led his horse for him.

He stepped up to the chariot, the other side from Bessos. His voice was low, I did not hear what he said; but Bessos could have heard it. Patron had taken the risk, on my bare word.

Soon he must have seen, from Bessos' look of baffled anger, that I'd not misled him. His voice grew louder. "My lord King, pitch your tent in our camp tonight. We have served you a long time. If you ever trusted us, believe me, you need to now."

The King was quite quiet. His countenance hardly altered. I was the better for his fortitude; one needs some pride in one's master. "Why do you say this?" He spoke haltingly; his Greek was no better than mine. "What do you fear for me?"

"Sire—it is your cavalry commander, and that one there beside you. You see why I can't speak names."

"Yes," said the King. "Go on."

"Sire, they lied this morning. It will be tonight."

The King said, "If it is ordained, so it will be."

I understood his quiet. My heart sank like a stone. He had despaired.

Patron came nearer, leaning to the chariot. He was an old soldier, he knew what he had heard. He put out his strength, as if to hearten a flagging battle-line. "You come over to us, sire. What men can do, every one of us will do it. Look at all this woodland. When night comes, we'll get you away."

"To what, my friend?" With despair, he had recovered dignity. "I live too long already, if my own people wish me dead." I don't know what he read in Patron's face, which I could not see. "Be assured, I trust you. But if what you say is true, you are outnumbered ten to one, you and the faithful Persians. I will not buy a few hours more of breath, at the cost of all your lives; that would be poor thanks to you. Go back to your men; and tell them that I value them."

He saluted, and fell back behind the chariot. As he took back his horse, his eye said, "Well done, boy. No fault of yours." I turned to look at Bessos.

Dark blood engorged his dark face. He looked like a demon. He could not tell what Patron had revealed. For one moment I thought he would draw his sword upon the King, and butcher him out of hand. However, a dead king was spoiled merchandise. He took time to master himself; then he said to Darius, "That man means treachery. No need to know his tongue, it was in his face." He paused, hoping to draw some answer; but the King was silent. "The scum of the earth. No stake in any country, on sale to the highest bidder. Alexander must have outbid you."

Even from a kinsman, this was insolence. The King said only, "I trust not. His suit was refused in any case."

"Sire, I am happy for it. I hope you trust my good faith as you did this morning; may the gods witness it."

The King said, "May they be my witnesses also."

"Then I am happier still."

"But if Patron is the man you think, he will be foolish to count upon Alexander. He rewards surrender; but he is very harsh to treachery."

Bessos looked sidelong under his black brows, and said no more. We wound downhill through the darkling forests. The high peaks, where we could glimpse them, still glittered golden. Here it would soon be night.

We made camp in a broad open glade. Long fading bars of red sunlight crossed it. It felt close and hot. I daresay at sunrise it would have looked delightful. None of us saw the sun rise on it, so I cannot say.

There was a village somewhere near. The Persian soldiers went off to forage in the usual way. When they were gone into the trees, the place was still full of men. The Baktrians had all remained, and were building watch-fires. They were still all under arms. We knew what it meant. It was like the last turn in a long fever.

Oxathres came to the King, and said that when the loyal Persians came back, they would make a fight of it. The King, embracing him, told him to do nothing without orders. He was a brave soldier, but none of that kin had the makings of a general. Patron could have done more with two thousand men than he with twenty thousand; I daresay the King knew it. When he had gone, he sent for Artabazos.

I found him, a little stiff from his ride but still alert. As I led him to the King, I saw the Greek camp by itself among the trees. They were still all armed, and had set outposts.

Round the royal tent stood the Royal Bodyguard; there were still some Immortals left, armed with their spears of honor. The gold pomegranates caught the firelight; and their eyes, staring somberly before them.

From within, we heard the King give Artabazos Patron's news. He was some time silent, thinking no doubt of his long night's labors. Then he besought the King to make camp among the Greeks; the Persians, for whom he himself would answer, would rally in strength to the Greeks, if the King were with them. I was thinking, Poor good old man, you have lived too long for your peace, when he added briskly, "These Greeks are soldiers by trade. The Baktrians are only called out on levy. I saw discipline in Macedon. The difference between a blood-horse and an ox. Trust to the Greeks."

How often we had listened like this from mere curiosity, or to be abreast of some small intrigue. We listened now for our lives.

"It is finished," said the King. "All my life I have hoped too willingly. Lately it has cost too much, to too many men. Now I have put hope away, do not wish it back to me."

There was a smothered sound. It was Artabazos weeping.

"Dear friend," said the King, "you have lost many years with me. The rest are yours; go with the Wise God's blessing."

The weeping went on. The King raised his voice and called to us. Artabazos was clinging to him, small against his height, the old face buried in his robe. He embraced him, saying, "This faithful servant will not lay down his charge; but I have released him. Lead him away."

He loosed the old man's hands, which clung like a child's; it took all of us to ease him out without roughness. The King hid his face from it. We saw Artabazos to his people; when we returned, and looked for the King, at first we did not see him. He lay prone on the ground, his head upon his arms.

One thought was in all our minds. But no weapon

was near him, his shoulders moved with his breath. He lay like the run-down hare, coursed to its limit, awaiting the hounds or spear.

He had not dismissed us. We did not know what to do, but gazed at this painful sight in silence, feeling our own despair. After a while, a thought came to me; I fetched his sword from within, and laid it on the table where he could find it easily. Boubakes saw what I was about, but looked aside.

For my master, I had done this last thing. I could not feel, There lies the one who was my lover. I was in his service, and had served as I was called to do. He was the King.

After a while he moved his head, and gave us leave to go.

Our sleeping-tent had been half put up and left; one end sagging from a loose pole, the other end on the ground. No slaves were to be seen. From all around came a discord of quarreling, arguing, orders shouted in vain. It was no longer an army, only a great confused crowd of tribes and factions. For a while we sat together on the slack tent-hides, whispering. Then I looked up and said, "The Bodyguard has gone."

I went to make sure. Nothing, not so much as one gold-hafted spear. The Immortals had put off their immortality. We were alone.

After a time of silence, I said, "I think he spoke. I'll see if he wants anything."

He was lying as before. I stepped up softly, and knelt by him. I had heard nothing; but old days had come back to me. The very perfume I was wearing had been his gift. When all was said, I was not just like the others.

He lay, his head on one arm, the other flung forward. I dared not take his hand unbidden. He was the King.

He moved, aware of me, and said, "Send me Boubakes."

"Yes, sire." I was someone to take a message. He had forgotten.

Boubakes went in. Suddenly he gave a great wail, such as is only heard at a death. All three of us ran inside. The sword still lay on the table, the King upon the ground. Boubakes knelt there, beating his breast, tearing his hair and clothes. We cried, "What is it?" as if the King had not been there. All things we knew were breaking.

Boubakes sobbed, "His Majesty bids us go."

The King leaned up on one arm. "You have all done your duty well. You can do no more for me. I acquit you of your service. Save yourselves while you can. This is my last command to you; you will all obey it."

A vast horror overwhelmed us: the doomed King, the forsaken tent, the black strange forest full of wild beasts and enemies. I hope it was for him we wept; it is easy now to think so. We cried aloud in the night, drunk with fear and grief; like mourners at a bier, each threw his voice into the outcry, no longer knowing which of its sounds was his.

As I flung my hair back from my eyes, I saw someone at the entry. Even in my distraction, I remembered there was no guard. I went over just as I was. It was Bessos and Nabarzanes, with men behind them.

Bessos looked at the prone King, struck his fist into his palm, and said to Nabarzanes, "Too late! I warned you." He ground his teeth together.

Nabarzanes said, "I never thought he could do it." His face had no anger; only respect, and perhaps relief. He caught my eyes, and gravely nodded.

Bessos seized my shoulder in his huge paw and shook me. It lifted me off my feet. "Did he finish it? Is he gone?"

Boubakes answered for me. "I rejoice, my lord, His Majesty is in good health."

Nabarzanes' face set hard as a wall-carving. He said to Bessos, "So, then. Come."

The King rose to his feet as they came inside. He said only, "Why are you here?"

"I am here," Bessos said, "as King."

The King was quite quiet. "What kingdom has God given you?"

"I have obeyed the people's wishes. You should have done the same."

The King said, "As you see, I am no longer able to punish traitors. But I know who will."

Bessos lifted his head. "I am ready to abide the judgment of Mithra."

"So I suppose, since you do these things. But I was speaking of Alexander."

Nabarzanes, silent till now before him, said, "Don't name the enemy to whom you have given our people. We do this to set them free."

"Come with us," said Bessos.

I thought, Shall I put his sword in his hand? But he was in reach of it. It was no right of mine, to tell my master when to die.

He stepped back; I think he meant to take it. But he was never swift in act, or certain in mind. As he moved they closed on him. He was a big man; but his muscles had grown slack. When their men came in, he ceased resistance. He stood with dignity; he could suffer like a king, at least. Perhaps Bessos felt it. He said, "Well, if we must bind him, let his fetters match his rank." He took off his massive gold neck-chain, and, while two Baktrians held the King's arms behind him, wound it round them like a rope.

They led him out between them, their hands on his shoulders as if he were a felon. From the Baktrians outside came low muttering, confused shouts, and laughter that was half fear.

Nearby stood a common transport cart, roofed with hides. The tents had been brought in it. Towards this they led him. We stared after him, unbelieving, helpless, dumb. Boubakes, rousing himself, cried out, "At least let him have some cushions!" We ran back and fetched them. The King was already inside, two camp slaves with him; guards or attendants, I never knew. We threw in the cushions; then the soldiers shoved us away. The horses were hitched up, the driver mounted. We seemed to stand for an eternity while all this was done, and the cavalry mustered. The infantry was more a crowd than a column. Bessos gave an order; the cart began to jolt over the clearing towards the road.

A soldier ran past, carrying something I knew. It was the King's water-ewer. The tent was overrun with Baktrians, who had stayed to plunder it. Some were fighting outside over the best things. It was like a sack.

Boubakes looked at me with desperate eyes, cried, "Let us go to Artabazos!" and ran off towards the Persian camp. The others followed. The soldiers let them go. They were just eunuchs, empty-handed, of no account.

I stood pressed to a tree. It looked a long way across the clearing. I remembered Susa. I was not like the others; I was loot.

The wagon had vanished. Close by was our sagging, half-set tent. I ran inside, pulled down the unsteady pole, and let the whole mass sink down on me.

The stiff folds let in some air. I should not smother. I lay there in pitch darkness, as if I were in my grave. Indeed, my life was buried here. When my sepulcher yielded me up, it would be to some fate unknown to me as to the child closed in the womb.

9

I LAY IN my lair. The cured leather was heavy, and stank, but I dared not stir. Sounds of commotion came through muffled, then lessened as the King's tent was picked clean. Once two men approached and I was in terror; but they thought, as I'd hoped, that if the tent had not been put up it must be empty. After that, there was nothing to do but wait.

I waited long, too muffled to trust my ears. At last, I squirmed till I could put my head out. The glade was empty but for smoldering campfires. After the darkness, even starlight seemed bright; but, beyond, the trees hid everything. There were sounds there of men, going away; loyal troops surely, Artabazos' men, who had left the rebels, being too few to fight them. I had better catch up.

Burrowing about in the tent, I gathered my belongings. Now for my horse. I had only to think it, to know the answer. All the same, I had to go stumbling over to the picket-lines. Of course nothing on four legs was left.

My poor beautiful little Tiger, the gift of a king; he was not bred to carry weight. I grieved for him, flogged along by some heavy oaf of a Baktrian, in what time I had for it before I felt the truth of my own plight.

The enemy was gone. So were all those who would befriend me. Night must be far spent. I had no notion where they would be making for.

I would need food. In the King's tent, all that had been in his supper dishes had been tossed out on the floor. Poor man, he had eaten nothing. I filled a napkin, and dipped my water-flask in the stream.

The sounds were now distant. I followed them, praying these were not Baktrians who had just deserted. They seemed to go along the mountain flank; they had left a well-beaten track. It crossed streams; I was wet to the knees, and my riding-boots oozed water. I had not gone cross-country since I was a child, with a scolding and dry clothes awaiting me.

There was no sign yet of dawn. I began to hear women's voices, and hastened on. They were camp-followers with their baggage, Persians. At this rate, I would soon be abreast of the column. A half-moon was giving a little light, I could go faster now.

Soon I saw a man ahead. He had stopped to make water; I turned away till he had done, and then approached him. He was a Greek; it was them I had overtaken. The women had misled me; of course, they would all be Persian. Hired men brought none from home.

He was a thick man, rather squat, black-bearded. It seemed I knew him, though of course this was impossible. He came and peered at me. His sweat stank. "Why, by the dog!" he said. "It's Darius' boy."

"I am Bagoas, from the Household. I am trying to find Artabazos' Persians. Am I far out of my way?"

He paused, looking me over. Then he said, "No, not too far. Just follow me, I'll put you on the path." He led off into the wood. He was without his armor, as their custom was on the march.

No sign of a path appeared. The wood seemed to get thicker. We were not far in, when he faced about. One look was enough. There was no need of words, and he wasted none. He merely fell on me.

As he bore me to the ground, memory returned to me. He was indeed like someone I'd known: Obares, the jeweler at Susa. In an instant I lived it all again. But I was no longer twelve years old.

He was twice my weight; but I never felt a doubt that I would kill him. I struggled rather feebly, to hide what I was doing, till I had my dagger out; then I drove it between his ribs, up to the hilt. There was a dance I'd practiced, a favorite of the King's at bedtime, which ends with a slow back-somersault off the hands. It is wonderful how strong it makes your arms.

He threshed about, choking blood. I dragged out the knife and thrust it into his heart. I knew where that was; I had heard it often enough, thudding away, along with heavy breathing in my ear. He yawned then, and died; but still I stabbed in the dagger, wherever I thought good. I was back at Susa, killing twenty men in one. It was not a pleasure I wish to know again; but I know it was one. I can feel it to this day.

Above me a voice said, "Stop!" I had been aware of nothing, but the body by which I knelt. Doriskos stood beside me. "I heard your voice," he said.

I stood up, my knife-hand bloody to the wrist. He did not ask why I had done it; my clothes had been pulled half off me. As if to himself, he said, "I thought you were like a child."

"Those days are long past," I answered. We looked at each other in the dim light. He had his sword. If he wanted to avenge his comrade, he could kill me like a newborn pup. It was too dark to see his eyes.

Suddenly he said, "Quick, get him out of sight. He has a kinsman here. Come on, take his feet. There in the thicket, down that gully."

We parted the bushes. It was a winter watercourse, deep and steep. The body tumbled, the bushes closed again.

"He told me," I said, "that he would lead me towards the Persians."

"He was lying, they're marching ahead of us. Clean your hand, and that dagger. There's water here." He showed me a trickle down the rocks. "There are leopards in this forest. We were warned not to straggle. He should have remembered."

"You are giving me my life," I said.

"I don't reckon you owe it. What do you mean to do with it, now?"

"I'll try Artabazos. For the King's sake, he might take me in."

"We must move, we'll lose the column." We scrambled through the rocky woods; when we came to anything steep, he helped me over it. I was wondering how Artabazos had really felt about the King's keeping a boy. And he was so old, a ride like this could kill him. About his sons, I knew next to nothing.

"I daresay," said Doriskos, "the old man will do what he can. But you know where he's going now? To surrender to Alexander."

God knows why I had not thought of it. A friend of the young man's childhood could count on mercy. Oppression of spirit kept me silent.

"In the end," said Doriskos, "it will come to that with us. No way out of it. None of us will trust Bessos; at least Alexander has a name for keeping his word."

"But where *is* Alexander?"

"He'll be through the pass by now. Two of the Persian lords went pelting off to meet him. They said the King would be better off with him than with the traitors. They won't lose by it, of course."

"Pray God they won't be too late."

"When Alexander hurries, he hurries. We'd no wish to be in his way. The Persians are well ahead of us; they want to make terms, not be ridden down. Ah, there's the column." They were threading through the trees like shadows, keeping their voices low. He did not lead me across to them, but kept alongside. By now I was bruised and sore from the hard going, and glad of his helping hand. When I stumbled, he took my bag for me. A glimmer in open places proclaimed the first of dawn. He sat down on a fallen tree-bole. I was ready to rest.

"So the upshot is," he said, "we're skirting the hills, lying low, making for Hyrkania; and after that who knows? If you press on, I daresay you might overtake the Persians at the noon halt. It'll be a sweat for you, you're not used to going on foot." He paused; the dim light now showed me his blue eyes. "Or you could march with me, and let me give you a hand. However we get along, you won't need to use your knife on me."

I remembered his smile from our first meeting. It was less wistful now, and more hopeful. With surprise I thought, I can say yes or no for myself. The first time in my life. I said, "I'll come with you."

So we joined the column. Even after daylight, I did not cause much stir. Several of the men had boys who marched beside them. There were many more with women; but they all had to keep behind.

When we halted to rest, I shared the last of my food with him; the only time, he said, he was likely to eat from a king's table.

He was the kindest of companions. When my feet grew sore, he searched all through the troop for some soldiers' salve, took off my boots, and dressed my feet himself, saying how slender and beautiful they were, though they were in such a state I was ashamed to have them seen. Once, when no one was looking, he even kissed them. It was lucky that when I fought in the thicket, my bow had fallen free, and the quiver had saved my arrows; so I was able to offer something —besides what would have contented him—by shooting for the pot.

From him I learned something of Athens, where, he said, his father had been well off, till some enemy brought a lawsuit against him unjustly; hiring a famous speechmaker to blacken his name with lies. The jury found against him; he was ruined, and Doriskos, the younger son, had to hire out his sword. He said this same speechmaker used to exhort the people how to vote, on the laws, and even on peace or war. This was called democracy, he told me, and had been a fine thing in the good old days, when speechmakers told the truth.

I said we were all brought up to speak the truth in Persia; it was our greatest proverb. No doubt Bessos and Nabarzanes had been taught it too.

It was sad that, with all this goodwill between us, I found his love-making quite without interest. I always pretended pleasure; he set store by this, and one could do no less for a friend. That was the only art I used with him. The Greeks, as it seems, are artless in these matters.

I remembered how, when I fell from the King's favor, I had said to myself that I would take a lover. I had pictured stolen meetings by moonlight in the park; the whisper of silk at a window; a jewel tied to a rose. Now here I was with a foreign foot-soldier, in a shelter made of brush.

One night he told me of a boy he'd loved in Athens, though his beauty was a pale star to the moon of mine. "He hardly had the first down on his face, when I found he was spending my money on women. I thought it would break my heart."

"But," I said, "that is nature, surely, if you take a boy up so young."

"Beautiful stranger, it would never happen with you."

I answered, "No. That is why they do it."

He was some time quiet, then asked if I was very angry. He had been good to me, so I said not. In Greece, he assured me, it was never done. But so long as they sold boys young into the brothels, I did not think the Greeks had so much to boast of.

Living among these was easier, from their having been in Persia so long, and knowing the customs. Though without modesty before each other, they understood it in me. They respected the sanctity of rivers, drawing off water for washing, not defiling the stream. Their own bodies they strangely cleaned by smearing them with oil, which they scraped off with blunt knives, exposing themselves so carelessly that from shame I used to go away. The smell of the oil was disagreeable close to; I never quite got used to it.

At night, the women would make a shelter for their men (some had children too) and cook them supper; they never saw them all day. As for the boys, pretty peasants bought from poor homes for a little silver, led leagues away, and losing all their Persian decencies, I did not like to think what their fate would be. The soldiers who bore the fewest burdens, and laid none on others, were those who had come already lovers from Greece.

In this manner we journeyed, with adventures which then seemed great, for more than half a month, till we came to the eastern hills which end the snow-range, and look down on Hyrkania. Here the Greeks made camp, solid shelters in a wood; they would lie low till they knew where Alexander was. They planned to send him envoys under safe-conduct, not stumble into his hands.

Before long, some hunters told us he was moving along the mountainsides, beating the coverts, since these heights commanded his flank. They could not say if he knew that the Greeks were there.

It was only I who, when all these questions ceased, asked for news of the King. They said he was dead; they supposed Alexander killed him.

The time had come for me to be on my way. Somewhere, Artabazos must have left a camp, when he himself went to Alexander. I asked the hunters. They said a Persian lord was camped in the forest, a day's journey eastward; who, they did not know. He and his people were all strangers to those parts.

Doriskos and I said our farewells that night; I must start at dawn. No one else on earth cared if I lived or died, and now I felt it.

"I never had a boy like you," he said, "and I never shall have. You've spoiled me for all the rest. Henceforth I shall stick to women."

All day I went through the forest by hunters' trails, fearful of snakes at my feet and leopards in the branches,

wondering what I should do if the Persians had moved
their camp. But before the sun was low I came to it,
tucked away by a mountain stream; a thorn-hedge
round it, and a guard at the gate who looked like a well-
trained soldier. When he saw I was a eunuch, he
lowered his spear and asked my business. I became
aware I was almost in rags, my clothes worn out and
filthy. I told him who I was, and begged for a night's
shelter. After the forest, I did not care who they were,
if they took me in.

He sent in the message. Presently a civil man, like a
soldier-servant, brought me inside. It was a camp for
no more than a few hundred men; there had been thousands with Artabazos. Huts had been run up from
timber and thatch; no tents. It seemed these people
had come traveling light; but there was a corral of
splendid Nisaian horses. I inquired the name of my
host.

"Never mind. He offers you hospitality. These days,
least said is best."

His dwelling was built like the rest, but much bigger,
with several rooms. To my astonishment, the servant
led me to a well-furnished bathroom, which could only
be the master's. "You will like to bathe after your
journey. The water will not be long."

I was ashamed to soil the couch with my dirty
clothes. Two Scythian slaves filled the bath with hot
water and cold; there was scented oil in it. It was
pleasure beyond words. I washed myself and my hair;
scarcely noticing when the well-trained servant came
in, his eyes politely downcast, and took away all my
garments.

While, drowsy with contentment, I reclined in the
warm water, the inner door-curtain moved a little.
Well, I thought, what of it? That fight in the thicket
has made me nervous as a girl. A man like that would
have come in. Must I take everyone for an enemy? I
got out and dried myself, and put on the fine wool
robe that had been left ready.

Instead of my clothes, came a tray of excellent
food; suckling kid with sauce, wheat bread, a fragrant

wine. Wondering at all this in so rude a setting, I remembered glimpsing, below, the city of Zadrakarta. It seemed my host had arrived with nothing much, except a good deal of money.

I sat full of well-being, combing my hair, when the servant brought in a suit of clothes, saying, "The master hopes you will find these fit."

They were of fine cloth, a loose coat of dark red, blue trousers and embroidered slippers. They had been stitched here and there, to make them smaller; they must have been measured against mine. I felt like myself again. To honor the event, I touched up my eyes and put on my earrings.

The servant, returning, said, "My master will see you now."

It was only as I settled my sash, that I remembered my dagger. It had been taken with my clothes, and not brought back.

In the master's room, a filigree lamp hung from the rafters; bright hangings of local work relieved the timbered walls. My host reclined on the divan, a wine-table before him. He smiled, and raised a hand in greeting.

It was Nabarzanes.

I stood dumb as an ox, my mind in turmoil. Rather than come under this man's roof who had sold away my master's life, I ought to have slept out in the forest. Now, bathed, fed, clothed and sheltered, I could not help what I felt; it was gratitude that he had not told me.

"Come in, Bagoas." He seemed not at all put out by my lack of manners. "Come, sit down. I hope that they looked after you."

I collected myself and bowed, the least I could do now, and said, speaking the bare truth, "My lord, I am greatly in your debt."

"By no means. Sit here and let us talk. It is rarely I have a guest here; I am grateful for your company." I sat down on the divan, and took the wine he offered me. "But," he said, "whom did you expect to find?"

I told him Artabazos, or his people.

"A fine old man, a pattern of antique virtue. Alexander will welcome him with open arms; it is the kind of thing that delights him."

He must keep himself well informed here. But I was thinking how far he had gone beyond the duty of host to wayfarer, and how the curtain had moved. As far back as Babylon, I had sometimes wondered.

"You are anxious," he said in the friendliest way. "I understand it; you can have had no easy journey, your dagger has had use. Set your mind at rest; I do not take guests under my roof and then abuse them."

My thoughts rebuked, I said that I was sure of it. His person had never been displeasing to me. I would have requited kindness gladly, but for what he had done. It was a matter of honor.

"I know your loyalty to the King." He must have read my face. "In one thing he was happy; he had devotion from his betters. There must have been something in him, though it was never my luck to find it."

"He raised me from nothing, and gave me all I had. Not even a dog would have turned against him."

"No. Even the beaten dog is true. Yet the master dies, and the faithful hound runs stray."

"He is truly dead, then?" I thought of the cart and the golden bonds, and my heart was angry.

"Yes, truly dead."

Of a sudden I wondered why, after making this good bargain, he was lurking here in the woods with so small a following. And where was Bessos?

I said, "I hear Alexander killed him."

"Peasant rumor, my dear boy." He shook his head with a sad smile. "Alexander would never have killed him. He would have entertained him graciously; set his son on his knee; given him some minor palace to retire to; married his daughter, and courteously required to be named his lawful successor. If later he had rebelled, he would have been stamped on without pity; but of course he would never have done so. He could have lived quite peacefully into old age. All this he began to think of, while Alexander was overtaking us. He came like a Scythian wind; the pass must be strewn with

foundered horses. The King's conveyance was too slow;
we freed him and brought a horse. He refused to
mount, saying he put more faith in Alexander than
in us; he would remain, and make his own terms. By
then Alexander was cutting up our rear guard. Each
moment was life or death. The King would not be
moved. That was why we were forced to kill him with
our own hands. Believe me, I regretted it."

I was silent, gazing into the shadows beyond the
lamplight.

"I know," he said, "what you would be saying, if
the laws of hospitality did not restrain you. Take it as
understood between us. He was the King, such as he
was. But I am a Persian; for me, the second out-
weighed the first . . . I did not seek, as the Vizier
your namesake did, for a King who would be my
creature; but for one who would lead us to honor,
whom I could serve with pride. Well, Mithra has had
the laugh of me. After all's done, I am a Persian without a King."

Wine-softened I might be, but not yet stupid. Why
was he telling me all this, why own he had killed the
King? Why was he brushing off the difference of rank
between us? I could make no sense of it. "But my lord,"
I said, "you were all for proclaiming Bessos. Is he
dead too?"

"Not yet. He has put on the Mitra and gone to
Baktria. He will be dead whenever Alexander gets to
him. I am punished, my dear boy, much more for my
folly than my treason. I thought I had found a King
for Persia. I had found a mountain bandit."

He topped my wine-cup. "I had supposed he could
put on kingship, when it was laid in his lap. Not so.
As soon as Darius was in bonds, the Baktrians became
a rabble. He could not keep them from sacking the
King's tent, which was now his own. They would even
have had the treasure-chest, had I not arranged to
secure it."

He spoke with his leopard-purr. Much was now made
clear.

"That was a mere beginning. They rioted along as if

in enemy country, plundering, raping, killing. Why
not? They were not in Baktria. I reminded Bessos he
was now Great King; they were violating his subjects.
He thought it a fit reward for good service. I urged
the need for haste; if Alexander overtook us, we would
lose our whole enterprise. He made light of it. I saw the
truth; he did not get them in hand because he could not.
They had been good soldiers, serving in the old order
they understood. Now they knew only that there was
no King. And they were right. There was none indeed."

His dark eyes stared beyond me. Since he holed-
up here, maybe I was the first comer to whom he
could tell the tale. "So, when Alexander came storming
down on us, with the handful who could keep up with
him, he found our rear guard strolling like drunk
peasants on market day. His hundreds rounded up
thousands, like cattle. I had had enough. I had spent
myself, my rank, my fortunes—my good faith too, you
would tell me if you could—to change a useless
coward for a useless bully. Even Issos was not so bitter.
I took my own riders, who had still some discipline
left, and led them cross-country to where you find us."

There was nothing to say; but I remembered my
debt to him. "My lord, you are in danger here.
Alexander is moving east."

"Yes, I have heard so. I am planning as best I can.
But, my dear boy, enough of my business. Let us think
of yours. It distresses me, to think of you living hand
to mouth like this. But what prospect can I offer you?
Even should God permit me to see my home again, I
should be at a loss. I must own to having wished often
that you were a girl; or that I could find a girl with
your face. But that is as far as my nature takes me. Indeed, you look far less girlish than you did in Babylon.
It improves you, it has given you distinction. I would
be out of my mind, to put you anywhere in my
harem." He grinned at me; yet I felt something behind
this play.

"And yet," he said, "you are without doubt the most
lovely creature my eyes have rested on; woman, girl
or boy. There can be only a few more years of it; it

would be a crime to waste them. The truth is, you should serve only kings."

Since he chose to amuse himself, I waited in patience.

"How I wish I could put some future in your way. But I have none myself. In fact, it is clear to me that I must go the way of Artabazos, with none of his fair prospects."

"Do you mean," I said startled, "to Alexander?"

"Where else? He is the only Great King we have, or shall have now. Had he been a Persian, and what he is, we should all long since have followed him. All I hope for, at the best, is to be let live in quiet on my own estates. Kings are always affronted by king-killing, and yet . . . He is a soldier. He has fought Darius twice. I think he may understand me."

In honor I could not answer.

"He has given me, at least, a safe-conduct to know his terms. If he is set against me, I shall have safe-conduct back here. From then, I shall be driven game."

"I hope not, my lord." It was true. He smiled at me kindly.

"Did you see my gift-horses outside? They will be caparisoned, of course, with gold and silver. But he will have plenty just as good."

In courtesy, I said he could have none finer.

"No, they are nothing much; not for Alexander. After all, he is now the richest man in the world. What can one give to such a man? If he wants it, he already has it. There is only one real gift for a man like that; something he has been wanting a long time, without being aware of it."

"That would be hard to find, my lord, when you do not know him."

"And yet, I believe I have seen the very thing."

"I am glad, my lord. What is it?"

He answered, "You."

10

W<small>E PERSIANS</small> have a saying
that one should deliberate serious matters first drunk,
then sober.

I woke next morning on my pallet in Nabarzanes'
room, where I had slept unmolested as with a kinsman.
My head scarcely ached; it had been good wine. Dawn
bird-song filled the forest. Trying to remember where
I was, I saw across the room my host still sleeping.
Memory stirred, together with the sense of some frightful thing impending.

We had talked and drunk, drunk and talked. I remembered saying, "Is it true they paint themselves
blue?" Yet at some much later time, it seemed to me
he had taken me in a chaste but warm embrace, invoked the gods for me, and kissed me. I must have
consented.

In the camp a hound bayed deeply. Men were stirring; I must think before he woke. Some of the talk was
coming back to me. "It is for you to choose. I have
used no deceit with you. You would learn the truth

when I had gone, and, if you prosper, might be a dangerous enemy. But you showed loyalty to Darius, in the presence of me who killed him. I trust you to keep as good faith with me. You will speak of me as you have found."

He had said also, "When I had my command, I made it my business to learn about Alexander. One should know one's enemy. Among matters of more use, I found that his pride extends into the bedchamber. He has never lain either with slave or captive. I daresay the first thing he will ask is whether you are free, and have come there willingly."

"Well," I had answered, "then I shall know what to tell him."

A little bird perched on the timbered window, singing so loudly its throat beat like a heart. Nabarzanes slept on, as peacefully as if his head had no price upon it. He had said, as I remembered, "Twice to my knowledge, men seeking favor have offered to buy him Greek boys famed for beauty. He refused with indignation. But, my dear Bagoas, it appears that none of these eager sycophants took the trouble to offer him women."

I seemed to recall his taking a lock of my hair still damp from the bath, and winding it round his fingers. We were fairly drunk by then. "It takes no great fortitude," he said, "to resist a name in a letter, joined to the word beautiful. But the living presence, ah! that is another thing."

What had my life been, I thought, since the King had died? There was no trade I knew to live by, but what I had. Only one thing had been wanted of me; even by Nabarzanes, though for another man. If I went tramping on with nothing, I should soon end where I began when I was twelve years old.

Yet it was terrible, to part from all I knew and make my life among barbarians. Who could say what this Macedonian was like in the inner room? I had learned at Susa that the outward man could be a mask for horrors. And then again, supposing I did not please him?

Well, I thought, better the unknown danger than

creeping miseries, coming slow like leprosy, till one bears at last a life whose mere thought would once have made one end it. One throw, win or lose; so be it.

Nabarzanes stirred, yawned and smiled at me. It was not till we were at breakfast that he said, "Does sober agree with drunk?"

"Yes, my lord, I'll go. On one condition, that you give me a horse. I've had enough of walking. And if you're presenting me to the richest man in the world, I should look as if I were worth something."

He laughed aloud. "Well begun! Never cheapen yourself with Alexander. You shall have clothes too, not those makeshifts; I am sending to Zadrakarta. In any case, we must give those scratches time to heal. Now I see you by daylight, you have certainly traveled rough." He turned my face in his hand. "Skin-deep. A few days merely."

Four days later, our cavalcade rode down to Alexander's camp.

Nabarzanes had been generous. My horse, a chestnut with blond mane and tail, was even prettier than poor Tiger; I had two fine suits, the best one, which I was wearing, with real gold buttons and embroidered sleeves. "I am sorry, my dear boy," he'd said, "that I can't give you your dagger back. Alexander would think I was sending him an assassin."

Behind us came the string of Nisaian horses, with sparkling cheek-rosettes and bridles, and saddlecloths fringed with bullion. Nabarzanes rode beside me, dressed as a noble suppliant; somberly but becomingly, looking as well-bred as his horses. I hoped Mithra would forgive my kindly thoughts of him.

In front rode the guide, a Macedonian officer who spoke a few words of Persian. He pointed out the camp in the plain below, at the foot of the hills, beside a river. It was not very big; Alexander had divided his forces to search the mountains and man their strongpoints, and had only his own troops with him. We could see his tent. It was imposing, and had a Persian look.

Nabarzanes said, "He took it at Issos. That was

Darius' tent. I would know it anywhere." He never spoke of Issos without bitterness. I remembered his men in Babylon, saying how well he'd fought till the King had fled.

We rode into camp through staring Macedonians, till we came to the open space before the tent. Grooms took our horses. Nabarzanes was announced to Alexander, who presently came out.

How clearly, even now, I remember him a stranger. He was not so small as I had expected. Of course he would have measured like a boy against Darius; the young Macedonian who had come out behind him was taller, too. He was of middle height; but I suppose people had expected his stature to match his deeds.

Artabazos had said that even in Persia he would have been called beautiful. Just now, he had been riding about for days in an open helmet instead of a hat, and had been caught with sunburn. Being fair-skinned, he had gone rather red, a tint not much admired among us, recalling the northern savages. But he had not their rufous hair; his was bright gold. He wore it rough-cut, in a length between neck and shoulders; it was neither straight nor curling, but fell like a shining mane. When he turned to the interpreter, I perceived his features were very fine, though marred by a sword-cut on the cheekbone.

After a time, Nabarzanes bowed, and pointed to his train of gifts; then looked towards me. I was too far to hear his words; but Alexander looked, and for the first time I saw his eyes. Them I remember like yesterday; my own mind less clearly; a kind of shock, a sense that one should have been more prepared.

I came up with lowered gaze, and made the prostration. He said in Persian, "You may rise." At this time he scarcely knew any of our language, but had learned this off along with the words of greeting. He was unused to being bowed to down to the ground; you could tell it made him uneasy. One gets up in any case, without command; but no one had liked to tell him so.

I stood before him, my eyes cast down as is proper

before a king. He said suddenly, "Bagoas!" and I was
startled into looking up, as he had intended.

As one might smile at the child of a stranger seeing
it scared, so he did at me, and said to the interpreter,
"Ask the boy if he is here of his own free will."

I said, "My lord, I speak Greek a little."

"You speak it quite well." He looked surprised. "Did
Darius speak it, then?"

"Yes, my lord King."

"Then you know what I just asked."

I replied that I had come freely, hoping for the
honor of serving him.

"But you come with the man who killed your master. How is this?" His eyes had changed. He was not
trying to frighten me; but they had grown cold, and
that was enough.

Nabarzanes had withdrawn to a decent distance.
Alexander just glanced towards him. I felt myself being reminded that he knew no Greek.

"Lord King," I said, "Darius loaded me with kindness. I shall always grieve for him. But Lord Nabarzanes is a soldier. He thought that it was necessary." I
saw his eyes change as if at something he understood.
I said, "He repents it truly; that I know."

He paused; then said abruptly, "Has he been your
lover?"

"No, my lord. Only my host."

"Then that is not why you plead for him?"

"No, my lord." I think it was his eyes, rather than
Nabarzanes' counsel, which told me not to cheapen myself. I said, "If he were my lover, I would not leave
him."

He raised his brows; then he turned with a smile to
the young man behind him. "You hear that, Hephaistion? An advocate worth having."

The young man, without as much as a bow or a
My Lord, said, "All the same, they might at least
have finished him off."

To my surprise, Alexander did not notice the dis-
respect. "We were treading on their tails," he said.

"They were in a hurry. I'd no notion he spoke Greek. If only I'd been in time!"

He had a look at the horses, commended them through the interpreter, and invited Nabarzanes inside his tent.

I waited by the fidgeting horses, while the Macedonians looked at me. Among Persians, the eunuch knows himself marked out at sight by his lack of beard; it was most strange to be in a crowd where no young man had one. Alexander had shaved from his youth, and liked his fashion followed. Persian soldiers would have had any man's blood, who told them to make themselves like eunuchs; but I don't think this had even occurred to the Macedonians. They had no eunuchs. I was the only one.

No one molested me. There was discipline, but not the reverence one expects to surround a king. They stood about and stared, and discussed my looks as if I had been a horse, not knowing I could understand them. The lower ranks I could not; but though they spoke Macedonian, which is barely Greek, I knew what they meant. I fought back the tears of wretchedness. What would become of me, among such people?

The tent-flaps opened. Alexander came out, with the interpreter and Nabarzanes. The King said something, and offered his right hand. I saw from Nabarzanes' face it was the sign of pardon.

He made a graceful speech of loyalty, and was given leave to depart. Turning to me, he said very solemnly (the interpreter was in hearing), "Bagoas, serve your new master as well as you did your former one." As he turned towards his horse, he winked at me.

He returned to his ancestral lands and his harem, and must have lived there, as he had said, in quiet. I never saw him again.

Alexander ordered the horses led away, then turned to me, as if he had only just remembered me. I have seen it better done. For an instant, I could have sworn I saw a look that one can't mistake. When it is hard and smug it is a bad lookout; but sometimes it is a softening. It vanished utterly, before I could be sure of it; there was only a soldier's briskness.

"Well, Bagoas, you are welcome to my service. See Chares, my chief steward, and he will find you quarters. I will see you again later."

Well, I thought, that is plain enough.

The sun was sinking; my spirits also. I wondered what time he went to bed.

I ate with the clerks who kept his records. They looked surprised. There was no other place for people like me, except with soldiers or servants. The food was coarse and rough, but they seemed used to nothing better. After a while, one of them asked me how the archives were kept at Susa; as I knew this, they became more friendly; but they offered me no advice about my duties. I did not like to ask what sign the King gave, for one to stay when the rest retired. Eunuchs anywhere would have been more helpful.

The King was already at dinner with his chief officers. I returned to Chares, the chamberlain, a Macedonian of good rank. I did not think much of his service; even for a camp it was rough-and-ready to a Persian eye. When I appeared, he seemed not to know where to put me; but looking at my good clothes (I was deep in my host's debt, there) he gave me a damp towel and a dry, for the King to wipe his hands on. I stood by his chair, and he used the towels; yet I felt even he had not expected me.

I had heard already of their barbarous way with wine, bringing it in with the meat. But nobody had prepared me for the freedom of speech the King permitted. They called him Alexander, without title, like one of themselves; they laughed aloud in his presence, and far from rebuking them he joined in. The best you could say was that when he spoke, nobody interrupted him. They fought over their campaign like soldiers with their officer; once, one said, "No, Alexander, that was the day before," and even for this received no punishment, they just argued it out. However, I thought, does he get them to obey in battle?

When they had eaten (food like a peasants' feast-day, with no sweets at all) the servers left, but for the wine-pourers. So I went into the King's sleeping-place, to prepare his bed. It amazed me to find it not much better than a common captain's, with scarcely room for two. There were a few fine gold vessels, I daresay from Persepolis; but the furniture was just the bed and clothes-stool, the washstand, a writing-table and chair, a rack of scrolls, and a fine bath of inlaid silver, which must have been Darius's, taken with the tent.

I looked about for the perfume-sprinkler, but could not find it. Just then a Macedonian boy of about my age came in and said, "What are *you* doing here?"

One would have supposed he had surprised a thief. I did not return his rudeness, but said I had been taken into service that day. "It's the first I've heard of it," he said. "Who are you, to sneak in here without leave? I'm on guard here. For all I know, you've come to poison him."

He bawled out to another youth, who came in from outside, and they were about to lay hands on me, when a young man entered. The boys looked crestfallen before he had even spoken. "In the name of Zeus!" he said. "Can't you take guard, Antikles, without shouting and brawling like a market porter? I could hear you outside; you'll be lucky if the King didn't. What's this about?"

The youth jerked his thumb at me. "I found him in here, handling the King's things."

The young man lifted his brows. "You could have asked one of us, before you made this uproar. We're all sick of dry-nursing you. How the King manages with such raw oafs about him, I can't think."

The boy, suddenly very angry, said, "And how much longer did you want to do squire service, that you can't let go of it? I'm on duty. Am I meant to let in any spayed catamite some barbarian leaves behind?"

The young man stared at him till he flushed. "For a start, don't be foul-mouthed, Alexander doesn't like it. For the rest, just take my word that the boy has leave to be here. I heard Alexander speak to him. I won't tax your understanding with more than that. By the dog of Egypt! If I were half such a fool as you, I'd hang myself."

The boy muttered and went out. The young man gave me a long look over, smiled pleasantly, and departed also. I could make out none of it.

In fact, along with fresh troops from Macedon, the King had had fresh body-squires. By Macedonian custom, lords' sons did this duty, part of which was to guard his person at night. Two or three years was the usual time of service; but in four years of war, the squires he set out with had become grown men. He had chosen them himself in Macedon; they knew all his ways, and he was used to things running smoothly. Now, promoted to the cavalry, they were supposed to be training the new boys, whom they held in the greatest scorn. All this I found out later.

I was now alone in the tent. No one seemed to be waiting to help the King disrobe; but no doubt they would be there presently. I kindled the night-lamp from the hanging one, and set it by the bed; then went to an empty corner, and sat cross-legged in the shadow, thinking about my fate.

There were voices outside; the King came in with two officers. It was clear they had just walked over engaged in talk; they would not be putting him to bed. This was awkward; he might not wish them to know he'd sent for me; so I stayed quiet in my dark corner.

When they went, I was about to rise and disrobe him; but he began to pace about as if he were alone. It seemed he wished his thoughts to be undisturbed. One learns when to be quiet.

He walked to and fro, his head tilted sideways, his eyes looking, as it seemed, out through the tent. After a while he sat down at the table, opened a wax diptych, and began to write. It seemed a strange task for a king. He had clerks to write whatever he wanted. In all my time with Darius, I had never once seen him touch a writing-tool.

Suddenly, without a word with the guards outside, without a pause at the entry, without asking leave, a young man came in. I knew him; he had been with the King when Nabarzanes brought me. The King, his back to the entry, went on writing. The man came straight up behind him, and took him by the hair.

I was too terrified even to scream. In an instant I thought a thousand horrors. I must get to the forest before the body was found. The killer planned to accuse me, knowing the King had sent for me. I would be three days dying.

Then, just as I rose to run for it, I perceived no blow had been struck; the newcomer had no weapon; and the King, a quick-moving man, had made no resistance. His head had not been pulled back, nor his throat cut. Simply, the other was ruffling his hair with his fingers, as a man does with a boy.

Astonishment held me rooted. I had understood. The man—I remembered his name, Hephaistion—now leaned his head beside the King's, to read his writing. Coming a little to myself, I moved softly back to the concealing shadows. They both turned, and saw me.

My heart almost ceased to beat. I prostrated myself and kissed the floor. As I rose, Hephaistion was looking at the King with lifted brows, half laughing. The King, however, looked straight at me, and did not laugh at all.

He said, "Why are you here?" but all Greek had failed me. He beckoned me up, felt me over with hard firm hands, and said, "No weapon. How long have you been here?"

"My lord King, since after dinner." I dared not remind him he had sent for me; no doubt he wished it forgotten. "I am sorry, indeed, my lord. I—I thought I was to wait on you."

"You heard me say I would tell you your duties later."

At these words, I felt a blush of shame flood my whole body and scald my face. Gladly I would have been swallowed by the earth. I could say nothing.

He saw my confusion. His harshness gone, he said quite gently, "Don't distress yourself. I see you misunderstood me. I am not angry with you, Bagoas. You have leave to go."

I made reverence and went out. The night guard stood facing outwards. I paused on the dark side of the tent. I had no friend here, no one to advise me. I must learn whatever I could.

The King said, "Since after dinner! And not a sound. He creeps about like a cat."

"He was stiff with fright," Hephaistion answered. "What have you been doing with him, Alexander? Eh?" He was laughing.

"At a guess," said the King, "I should say he thought you meant to murder me. Remember he's used to Persian manners, and court manners at that. Poor little wretch! He was Darius' boy. I told him I'd see him later; of course he thought I wanted him for the night. I have put him to shame; all my fault; his Greek seemed good. I should have used the interpreter. One should have some Persian oneself, for things like this."

"That would be worse. It took you long enough to learn Greek. Well, there's your teacher. You might as well find some use for him; as it is, you've bought yourself talk enough."

One of the guards moved; I had to slip away without hearing more.

My bed was in the clerks' tent. A torch outside lit it dimly through the entry. Two were sleeping; the third, who had seemed to be, peeped out as I took off my clothes. It was a fit end to a dreadful day. I pulled up my blanket, bit on the pillow, and soaked it with silent tears.

I remembered Nabarzanes' promises. What perfidy! How could he not have known this, knowing so much? The whole Macedonian army must know. How long must those two have been lovers, to behave like that, to talk like that? "It took you long enough to learn Greek!" Ten years?

The Queen's Eunuch had told us how they had visited the royal tent together, and the Queen Mother had not known which to bow to. "Never mind, mother, you weren't far out; he too is Alexander." Not even from her had he troubled to hide it.

Why, I thought, did he ever accept my service? What does he want with a boy? He is somebody's boy himself. And he must be twenty-five at least.

One of the clerks was snoring. For all my anger, I thought with longing of Nabarzanes' house. Tomorrow it would be forsaken; by next year, rotting back into the forest. So all that was Persian in me would rot away, as I trailed through strange lands, a servitor in this barbarian army.

I recalled Nabarzanes saying, in a haze of lamplight and wine, "What can one give to a man like that? Something he has been wanting a long time, without being aware of it . . ." Well, he had fooled me as he did Darius; I should have expected it. And yet, he brought me here to win favor for himself; he never pretended otherwise. I am unjust, I thought. He must have acted in ignorance.

Soon after, worn out with trouble, I fell asleep.

11

Wʜᴇɴ ᴏɴᴇ is young, morning light does wonders. In the picket-lines, my horse (I had called him Lion) had been well cared for. Though the faces of the Thracian grooms seemed at first hardly human—these were the men who really painted themselves blue—one of them told me with grins and gestures what a fine horse he was. As I cantered up river in first light, my heart revived; till I saw a sight so shocking, I hardly believed my eyes.

A dozen young men were in the river itself, their whole bodies in the sacred waters, washing themselves; and, as if delighting in this impious pollution, splashing about or swimming. Among them was a mane of golden hair, which, wet as it was, could be nobody's but the King's. I thought that he looked my way, and galloped off in horror.

Barbarians! I thought. What vengeance will Anahita of the Waters take on them? It was a beautiful morning, fresh but turning warm. Truly, I had left all civilized things behind me. All the same . . . if one

128

knew no better, what pleasure to slide through the sparkling river, bare as a fish.

But where it flowed past the camp, I saw there was no insult these people would not offer the deity of the stream. They were not only washing themselves; they were scouring pots, watering horses. All my disgust returned. No wonder I had had trouble finding a vessel to draw water for my toilet!

Still worse a misery was the indecency of the privies. Just a trench, even for the Household, and people walking in, which was bad enough. But the squires, and other mannerless people, would try to take a look at me. Any Persian boy has satisfied his curiosity about eunuchs before he is six years old; but here, grown men supposed one had been cut down to the shape of a woman. The squires had had a bet on it. For some days, exposed to these immodesties, I had to get to the woods before nature would obey me.

I had heard no more about my duties, and dreaded presenting myself at the King's supper table. However, instead of dismissing me, he gave me some promotion. During the day, a number of noble Persians had come in, to surrender and swear allegiance. Nabarzanes had been let go with a bare pardon, because he had killed his King; but these others had been received as guests of honor. More than once, when something choice had been put before Alexander, he would direct a server to take a portion, and say to me, "Go to So-and-so, and tell him I hope he will enjoy this dish with me." Though used to better food, the guests were pleased with this Persian compliment. I wondered he had learned so quickly; little knowing how.

Quite often, as he sent these delicacies away, I would warn him there would be nothing left for him; but he only smiled, and ate what everyone had. His sunburn had healed. One had to own that he was comely, even in Persia.

He never made me carry anything myself. He remembered last night, and was trying to heal my pride. It seemed that for someone reared in the wilds, he had much natural courtesy. One could not say as much for his Macedonians. His friends followed his lead; Hephaistion kept his eye on him all the time; but some (mostly those who had kept their beards) made it clear enough what they thought of eating with Persians. At any difference of manners, they would laugh or even point. There were lords here, whose forebears had been kings before Kyros' time; but I was sure these uncouth westerners would have wished to see them carrying in the dishes. More than once, Alexander turned a cold eye on these boors; a few took notice, others pretended not to see.

He has himself to blame, I thought. He lets them go on in his presence like untrained dogs who will not come to heel. He is feared in war, but not at his own table. What must my people think of him?

One or two of the Persians glanced at me. Not all knew who I was; Darius had never dreamed of showing me at his side in public. Yet Alexander, whom I was nothing to, seemed quite pleased to have me seen. Of course, I thought. I am spoils of war, like Darius' chariot. I am Darius' boy.

On the third day Chares the chamberlain gave me a written message, and sent me to find the King, saying, "I daresay he is in the ball-court."

Inquiring for this place, I found a square of canvas walls, and heard shouting within, and the sound of thudding feet. The entry was a doorless overlap, without a guard. I went in; and paused frozen where I stood. Eight or ten young men were running about there, and every one stark naked.

It was beyond belief. The only grown men I had ever seen in such a state were the slaves who had been sold along with me, and criminals at the place of execution, whose offenses had merited such disgrace. What sort of people had I come among? I was about to escape, when a big hairy young man came bounding up and asked me what I wanted. Averting my eyes, I said I had come here by mistake, having been sent by Chares to the King.

"Yes, he's here," the young man said, and bounded a few steps off. "Alexander! It's a message from

Chares." Next moment, there stood the King, as naked as all the rest.

From his lack of shame, you might have supposed he had never worn clothes nor felt the want of them. I cast down my eyes, too shocked even to speak, till he said, "Well, what is this message from Chares?"

I begged his pardon, my confusion now complete. He took the note and read it. While the first young man's sweat had smelled as strong as a horse, the King seemed as fresh as if straight from the bath, though he was flushed with exercise. It was said of him that the ardor of his nature burned up the humors. Just then my only concern was to hide my own flush of shame.

"Tell Chares—" he said, and paused. I felt him look at me. "No, tell him I'll send for him shortly." Clearly he did not trust me with the simplest message; I could not wonder. "That's all then," he said; and then, "Bagoas." "Yes, my lord?" I answered, looking at my feet. "Cheer up, boy. You'll soon get used to it."

I went off in a daze. Even though the Greeks were a byword for immodesty, I had never thought a king could sink so low. Why, I myself, trained in my calling to strip off in the inner room, would have been ashamed, outside of that, to be less decent than anyone else. It is something, I thought, when a king can put a courtesan to the blush. Has he no sense of his dignity at all?

We moved camp soon after. The speed of it amazed me. When the trumpet sounded, everyone seemed to know his task without orders. I was the last to get my horse, and the Horse-Master cursed me; when I rode back the tent was gone, and my things were sitting in the open. We were on the march, an hour before Darius would have been wakened.

I looked to see where Alexander would take his place; there was no sign of him, and I asked the clerk who rode beside me. He pointed outwards; some way off was a chariot, going at a fair pace; a man was jumping off it, running alongside without its slowing down for him, and jumping on again. I asked, "Why

does he make the man do that? Is it a punishment?"
He threw back his head and laughed. "But that's the
King." Seeing me bewildered, he added, "He's taking
exercise. He can't bear to dawdle at foot-pace. Often
he hunts, when the game is good."

I thought of the shaded litter, the Magi with their
altar, the miles-long train of eunuchs and women and
baggage. It seemed like another life.

We were moving northeast into Hyrkania. At the
next camp, Artabazos came in to surrender.

He had been resting awhile after his long march,
and getting his sons together. Besides the elder ones,
he brought in nine handsome young men I had never
seen before. He must have begotten them all between
seventy and eighty.

Alexander met him outside the tent; came forward,
took both his hands, and offered his cheek to kiss.
These courtesies done, he embraced him as a son
might do a father.

He of course spoke Greek, from his years of exile.
Alexander put him at his right hand at supper. Standing
by his chair, I heard him laughing with the old man
over his childish scrapes, and recalling the tales of
Persia he had heard upon his knee. "Ah," said
Artabazos, "but even then, my lord, you used to ask
me what weapons King Ochos used." Alexander
smiled, and helped him to meat himself from his own
dish. Even the rudest of the Macedonians held their
peace.

Just after, an envoy came in from the Greek troops,
asking for terms of surrender.

I was thankful for Artabazos, who I knew would
speak for them, as indeed he did. But, taking it ill that
Greek should fight against Greek, Alexander sent word
they could come in to learn his terms, or stay away.

They came in two days later, the greater part of
them. Some had gone off through the pass to try their
fortunes; one Athenian had killed himself, being well
known in Greece as an enemy of Macedon. The rest
were in good discipline, though rather lean. I could not
get near, but thought I could glimpse Doriskos, and

wondered how I could rescue him, if he was condemned to die.

But Alexander's only vengeance was the fright he gave them by refusing terms. Patron and his veterans, who had been serving before he declared war, he sent back to Greece with safe-conduct. Those like Doriskos, who had joined up after that, he reprimanded, said they did not deserve release, and simply hired them, at the wage they had had before (his own men were paid higher). They were marched straight off to their camp, and I had no chance to bid Doriskos farewell.

It was shortly after this, that Alexander went off to fight the Mardians.

They lived in thick mountain forest, west in the range, and had sent no envoys. They were known for their fierceness; but as they had nothing worth taxing, Persian kings for generations had let them be. They were also famous robbers; Alexander did not mean to leave them in arms behind him, nor to have it said they were more than he could handle.

He went traveling light, for rough campaigning. Left in the base-camp, I tried to find my feet; helped in this by his having taken his squires along. These boys, who seemed to think I had chosen my own condition, felt for me contempt, mingled with envy they did not own to. They could do their duties, in a rude and simple way, but knew nothing of such manners as I'd been trained in. It irked them that Alexander did not mock what they called my fawning barbarian ways, but chose me to compliment his guests of honor. They were forever plaguing me behind his back.

Chares, who had always treated me well, used to consult me about fine points of Persian etiquette, there being no one else from the court. I had time for riding, though the plain was humid and close. My having a good horse of my own was a great grievance with the squires, who thought it should have been taken from me. They themselves had army mounts, issued them by the Horse-Master.

The King was back in a half-month. He had chased

the Mardians up the mountains, where they'd thought to sit him out; but finding him clamber after them, they gave up, and acknowledged him King.

That night at dinner, I heard him say to Ptolemy, his bastard half-brother, "He'll be back tomorrow!" So joyful did he sound, I thought he must mean Hephaistion; but the man was there at table.

Next morning there was a stir of expectation in the camp. I joined the crowd near the royal tent, though I had wakened with a headache. Seeing that the old Macedonian near me had a kindly face, I asked who was arriving. He said smiling, "Boukephalos. The Mardians are bringing him back."

"Boukephalos?" Surely this meant Oxhead; an odd name. "Who is he, please?"

"You have never heard of Oxhead? Why, Alexander's horse."

Remembering how satrap after satrap had brought him steeds matchless in their kinds, I asked why the Mardians were bringing this one. He answered, "Because they stole him."

"In that horse-thief country," I said, "the King was lucky to get him back so soon."

"It had to be soon," said the old man calmly. "Alexander sent word that if he were not returned, he would fire the forests and put them all to the sword."

"For a *horse?*" I cried, remembering his kindness to Artabazos, his mercy to the Greeks. "But he would never really have done it?"

The old man considered. "For Oxhead? Oh, yes, I think so. Not all at once. He would have begun, and gone on till they brought him back."

The King had come out, and was standing before his tent, as he'd done to welcome Artabazos. Hephaistion and Ptolemy stood by him. Ptolemy was a bony-faced warrior with a broken nose, some ten years older than Alexander. Most Persian kings would have had such a person put out of the way when they assumed the throne; but these two seemed the best of friends. At the sound of approaching horns, all three were smiling.

A Mardian chief came first, in an ancient robe which looked as if it had been stolen in Artaxerxes' day. Behind was the string of horses. I saw at once there was not a Nisaian among them; but size is not everything.

I craned over all the shoulders, to glimpse this peerless pearl, this arrow of fire, that was worth a province and its people. He must be such, for the King even to have missed him, among so many. Darius had always been superbly mounted, and would soon have noticed a falling off; but it was the Master of the Stables who knew which was which.

The cavalcade approached. The Mardians, in token of repentance, had adorned all the horses with their barbaric finery, plumes on their heads, on their foreheads nets of scarlet wool, glittering with beads and sequins. For some reason, they had made gaudiest of all an old black horse that was plodding along in front, looking dead-beat. The King took a few steps forward.

The old beast threw up its head and whinnied loudly; you could see, then, it had been a good horse once. Suddenly Ptolemy, running like a boy, took its bridle from the Mardian, and loosed it. It broke into a stiff-legged canter, all its foolish fripperies jingling; made straight for the King, and nuzzled against his shoulder.

The King stroked its nose a time or two. He had been standing, it seemed, all this time grasping an apple, and with this he fed it. Then he turned round with his face pressed to its neck. I saw that he was crying.

There seemed nothing, now, with which he could still astonish me. I looked round at the soldiers, to see how they would take it. Beside me, two weathered Macedonians were blinking and wiping their noses.

The horse had been pushing at the King's ear, as if to confide in him. Now it sank creaking on its haunches. This done, it sat like one who has achieved something, and expects reward.

The King, his cheeks still wet, said, "He's too stiff for this. He will keep it up. I'll never get him out of it." He bestrode the saddlecloth. The horse heaved itself up quite briskly. They trotted off towards the stables. The assembled army gave a cheer; the King turned and waved.

The old man by me turned to me with a smile. I said, "I don't understand, sir. Why, that horse looks to be well past twenty."

"Oh, yes. It is twenty-five; a year younger than Alexander. It was meant to be sold to his father, when he was thirteen. It had been mistreated on the way, and would let no one near it. King Philip would have none of it. It was Alexander who cried out that a great horse was being thrown away. His father thought him too forward, and gave him leave to try, thinking it would humble him. But it trusted him, as soon as it felt his hand. Yes, that was the first time he did what his father could not . . . He had his first command at sixteen, and before that he was at war; all that time, he has ridden Oxhead. Even at Gaugamela, he saved him up for the charge, though he changed horses soon after. Well, Oxhead has fought his last battle. But as you see, he is still beloved."

"That is rare," I said, "in kings."

"In anyone. Well, I don't doubt he would do as much for me, seeing he has risked his life for me, though I am no more use to him now than that old horse. Once I told him tales of heroes, now he could better them himself. But though he was no more than a child when I stood between him and his tutor's harshness, he never forgets. In the hills behind Tyre, he got himself benighted with me, nearly alone, because I outwalked my strength and he would not leave me on anyone else's arm. My own fault too, I would go along. We were lying up in the rocks; winter, and a bitter wind, and the enemy watch-fires too near. He felt at me and said, "Phoinix, you're freezing. This won't do. Wait here." He was off like a flash; I heard shouts and cries from a watch-fire; back he came like a torch-racer, with a burning brand. Alone, with just his sword, and he put the fear of death in them. We kindled our blaze, and they all went running, they never looked to see what troops he had. So we sat warm for the night."

I would have liked to hear more from this old man, who seemed fond of talking. But just then I felt sick, and had to run away and vomit. My head burned; I shivered. I told Chares I had fever, and he sent me to the hospital tents.

They were pretty well full of wounded from the Mardian war. The doctor put me in a corner, telling me not to walk among the others, in case my fever was catching. One thing it did for me, was break me in to Macedonian privies. My only thought was to get there fast enough.

I lay weak as a babe, keeping nothing down but water, hearing the men brag of the campaign, of women they had raped, or of Alexander. "They were stoning us from up the cliff, rocks that could break your arm through your shield. Up he comes, strolling through it. 'Well, men, what are we waiting for, enough stones to build a sheep-pen? This way up.' And he's up the gully like a cat into a tree. We clawed up after him; they couldn't hit us there, we took them in flank. Some of them jumped off the cliff, but we got the rest."

There were some whom pain kept quiet. One man near me had an arrowhead in his shoulder. They had cut down for it in the field, but could not draw it out; the wound was festering, and was to be searched that day. He had been dead silent a long while, before the surgeon came with his tools and servant. The others called awkward words of cheer, and fell silent too.

He bore it well at first, but soon began to groan, then to cry out; before long he struggled, and the servant had to hold him down. Just then a shadow crossed the doorway; someone came in and knelt beside the bed. At once the man was quiet, but for a hissing of his breath between his teeth. "Hold on, Straton, it'll be quicker then. Hold on." I knew the voice; it was the King's.

He stayed down there, taking the place of the doctor's servant. The man never cried again, though the probe was deep in the wound. The arrowhead came out; he gave a deep sigh, between relief and triumph. The King said, "Look what you had in you. I never saw a man bear it better." The wounded man said, "We've seen one, Alexander." There was a murmur of assent around the tent.

He laid a hand on the good shoulder, and stood up, his fresh white tunic all dirtied with blood and matter which the wound had spirted. I thought he would go to make himself presentable, but he just said to the surgeon, who was dressing the wound, "Don't trouble with me." A tall hunting-dog, which had sat quiet by the entry, got up and padded at his heel. He looked about him, and came towards my corner. I saw great red fingerweals on his upper arm. The wounded man must have been clutching at him— the sacred person of a king!

There was a common, wooden stool, used by the wound-dressers. He picked it up, himself, with his own hand, and came to sit beside me. The dog started to nose me over. "Down, Peritas. Sit," he said. "I hope dogs are not a pollution in your part of the world, as they are among the Jews?"

"No, my lord," I said, trying to believe all this was happening. "We honor them in Persia. They neither break faith, we say, nor do they lie."

"A good saying. You hear that, Peritas? But how are you, boy? You look clapped-out. Have you been drinking bad water?"

"I don't know, my lord."

"Always ask about the water. Mostly, down in the plains, it's better in wine. Worse water, more wine. I've had your trouble. Sicker than a dog, and then a flux. You, too, I can see from the way your eyes are sunken. How many times today?"

I recovered my speech and told him; he was fast making me proof against any shock. "That's no joke," he said. "Drink plenty, we've good water here. Nothing to eat but slops. I know a good infusion, but the herbs don't grow here; I must find out what the natives use. Look after yourself, boy, I'm missing you at dinner." He stood up, the dog doing so too. "I'll be here awhile; take no notice if you want to go outside. None of your Persian formality. I know what it is to be kept about, when you're doubled up for a crap."

He strolled on to another bed with his wooden stool. I was so stunned that I had to go out almost at once.

When he had left, I slid my hand-mirror from the purse under my pillow, and peered at it behind the blanket. I look dreadful, I thought, and he said so too. Did he truly mean he was missing me at dinner? No, he had a good word for everyone. You look clapped-out, he said.

I became aware of a youngish veteran, tough and big-boned, growling at me. Had he seen the mirror? "Please speak Greek," I said. "I don't understand Macedonian."

"Now, maybe, you know how he felt about the hospital at Issos."

"Issos?" I must have been thirteen. "I know nothing about a hospital."

"Then I'll tell you now. Your people cut in at Issos when the King had marched beyond it; he turned back there to fight the battle. Meantime, he'd left the sick there, in a tent like this. And your royal whoremaster, who ran like a goat before Alexander's spear, was so brave with men too weak to stand on their feet, he had them cut up in bed alive. They . . . well, I suppose *you* know all about such things. I was there when we found them. If they'd been only barbarians, it would still have made me sick. There were one or two left living; both hands off at the wrists and the stumps seared. I saw Alexander's face. We all thought he'd do the same the first chance he had, and we'd all have helped. But no, he had too much pride. Now my anger's cooled, I'm glad of it. So you can lie there safe, snugged up with your bowl of gruel."

I said, "I did not know. I am sorry." Then I lay down, and pulled up the blanket. Your royal whoremaster. Each time he had run away, I had thought,

Who am I to judge? But now I judged him. Had it been coward's cruelty, or was he taking his ease, uncaring? Small odds. I was sad already with sickness; now this shame. I, who had given myself consequence because a king had chosen me! He had not done even that; some pander had done it for him. I covered myself like a corpse, and gave myself up to grief.

Through the blanket and my sobs, I heard someone saying, "See there what you've done. The boy's half dead; now you've put him in a convulsion. They're not made like us, you fool. You'll be sorry if he dies of it. The King fancies that boy, I could see it with half an eye."

The next thing I knew, a heavy hand grasped my shoulder, and the first man (who should never have left his bed) told me not to take it so much to heart, it was no fault of mine. He pressed a fig into my hand, which I had sense enough not to eat; but I pretended to. The fever rose and burned in me. It scorched up even my tears.

It was sharp, but short. Even after we had been carted on wagons to the next camp, I mended, though most of the wounded had setbacks. The man with the arrow wound died on the way. His shoulder mortified. In his delirium he called upon the King; the man beside me murmured that even Alexander had not yet conquered death.

The young heal quickly. Next time we moved camp, I was fit to ride.

There had been changes in my short absence. From a group of the Companion Cavalry, the cream of the highborn Macedonians, a voice called to me in Persian, "Here, Bagoas! Say something for me in Greek." I could not credit my senses. It was Prince Oxathres, Darius' brother.

Being one of the fair Persians, he did not look strange among Macedonians, though taller and handsomer than any of them. He was not with the Companions by chance. Alexander had enrolled him.

At Issos, they had fought hand to hand before the royal chariot. They had met too over Darius' embassy, when Tyre had fallen. They had felt each other's quality. And now that Bessos had put on the Hood, rather than see his brother's murderer on his throne, Oxathres preferred Alexander, who would help him with his blood-feud.

Well might he be angry at that wretched death. It was only now that I learned all the story. Nabarzanes had told me only the truth he knew. They had stabbed Darius with their javelins, killed his two slaves, maimed the horses, left him for dead; but with Alexander hot on their heels they had struck clumsily. The cart dragged on, the wounded beasts sought water. The dying King heard them drink, while he lay covered with blood and flies, his mouth cracked dry. At last came a Macedonian soldier, puzzled that the horses should be slashed instead of stolen; pausing, he heard a groan. He was a decent man; so Darius got a drink before he died.

Alexander, coming too late, threw his own cloak over the body. He had sent it to Persepolis, to be buried with kingly honors; giving it to the Queen Mother first for tending.

I had now to think of my future. Since the King had no use for me in my calling, I must seek favor in other ways, if I was not to sink to a mere camp-follower. I could guess where that would end. So I looked for opportunity.

Since the capture of his old horse Oxhead, the King was displeased with his squires. His horses were their charge; they had been leading them through the forests, when the Mardians fell on them. They had reported themselves vastly outnumbered; but Alexander, who spoke Thracian, had had a word with the grooms. They, being unarmed, had had no face to save. He was still nursing Oxhead like a favorite child, taking him out each day in case he should be pining. He had pictured him, no doubt, ending his days as a half-starved beast of burden, beaten, and full of harness sores.

These youths, though wellborn, were new to courts, and were already tiresome to Alexander, coming after their well-trained elders. He had had patience with them at first, but now had less; and from ignorance, they did not know how to bear themselves under displeasure. Some were sullen, others nervous and clumsy.

Errands would often take me to his tent. I would take notice of any small service he was about to need —his wants were simple enough—and do it without fuss. Soon he would employ me for this or that; before long, he would keep me there to be at hand. I would hear him say to the squires, impatiently, "Oh, leave it; Bagoas will see to it."

Sometimes when I was there Persians came for audience. I would admit them with the right degree of respect for each man's rank; now and then I saw that he took a hint from me.

He was curt with the squires, as an officer to raw cadets. To me he was always civil, even when I showed ignorance. Indeed, I thought it his misfortune to have been born among barbarians. Such a man deserved to have been a Persian.

It seemed to me I might well be better where I was, than where Nabarzanes had meant for me. Who knows how long a king's fancy will endure? But a useful servant is not put away so lightly.

Yet he never called me to attend to his bath or bedtime. I didn't doubt it was because of that first night; and whenever Hephaistion came, I was gone beforehand. I had warning from Peritas, who knew his step, and would thump the floor with his tail.

My preferment so displeased the squires, that only in the King's presence was I safe from insults. I had been prepared for envy, but not for so much coarseness. I was not established enough to tell the King. Besides, he might have thought me soft.

Our next march was to the city of Zadrakarta, near the sea. It has a royal palace. I don't know when a king had last put up there. Darius had meant to make for it; it was swept and garnished, though rude and quaintly antique, its moth-holed rugs replaced with crude stuff from Scythia. A band of old eunuchs flocked about me, asking how the King liked things done. Though they had been mildewing here for forty years, it was something to hear my native speech from my own kind. They begged to know if they should stock up the harem. I said it would be better to await the King's commands. They looked at me slyly, and said no more.

He meant to rest his troops a half-month at Zadrakarta, give them games and shows, and sacrifice to his gods for victory. Meantime the men made holiday, and the streets were best left before dark.

The squires too had time on their hands, as I learned the very first day.

I was looking about the palace, doing no harm to anyone, and had come out among old courtyards, when I heard spears thudding on wood. They saw me, and ran out. "Come along, lily-boy. We'll make a soldier of you." There were eight or ten of them, and nobody else in sight. Their target was a great battered piece of planking, with a Scythian drawn life-size in the middle. They pulled out the javelins and made me throw. I had not handled a spear since my child's toy one, and could not even hit point-first. They roared with laughter; one, from bravado, stood up before the Scythian, while another lodged a spear each side of him. "Your turn next!" someone shouted. "Over there, No-Balls, and don't wet your pretty trousers."

I stood before the board; a spear struck on my left and on my right. I thought they had done; but they all yelled out that they had hardly started.

Just then a young cavalryman, one of the former squires, looked in and asked them what they were doing. They called out that they had no more need of nursemaids, and he went away.

This last hope gone, I gave myself up to death. I was sure they meant to kill me, and put it down to mischance. But first of all, they wanted to see the soft Persian eunuch crawling to their feet, entreating mercy. Oh, no, I thought. That's one thing they shall not have. I will die as I was born, Bagoas, son of Artembares, son of Araxis. No one shall say that I died Darius' boy.

So I held myself straight, while the best shot of them clowned about, pretending to be drunk, and threw his

spear so close I could feel the whiffle. They had their
backs to the courtyard gateway. Of a sudden I saw a
movement there. A man had come in behind them; it
was the King.

He opened his mouth; then saw one of them poised
to throw, and waited, his breath drawn in, till the spear
had landed safely. Then he shouted.

I had never before heard him use the uncouth tongue
of Macedon. No one had yet told me it was a sign of
danger. No one needed to tell me now.

Whatever he said caused them all to drop their
javelins, and stand with crimsoning faces. Then he
changed to Greek. "You ran fast enough from the
Mardians. But I see you can all be warriors, against
one boy untrained to arms. And I tell you this—as I
see him now, he looks more like a man to me than any
of you do. Once and for all, I expect to be served by
gentlemen. You will refrain from insulting the members
of my Household. Anyone disobeying this order will
return his horse and join the column on foot. Second
offense, twenty lashes. Have you heard me? Then get
out."

They saluted, stacked their arms, and left. The King
walked towards me. I would have prostrated myself.
But the closest javelin had pierced my sleeve, pinning
me to the target. He strode forward, looked to be sure
it had not gone through flesh, wrenched it out and
flung it away. I stepped from among the shafts, and
again began the prostration.

"No, get up," he said. "You need not keep doing
that, it is not our custom. A good coat spoiled. You
shall have the price of a new one." He touched the
rent with his fingers. "I am ashamed of what I have
seen. They are raw; we have had no time to train
them; but I am ashamed they are Macedonians. Nothing like that will ever happen again, that I can promise
you." He put his arm across my shoulders, patted me
lightly, and, smiling into my eyes, said, "You behaved
yourself very well."

I don't know what I had felt till then. Perhaps just
awe of his splendid anger.

The living chick in the shell has known no other world. Through the wall comes a whiteness, but he does not know it is light. Yet he taps at the white wall, not knowing why. Lightning strikes his heart; the shell breaks open.

I thought, There goes my lord, whom I was born to follow. I have found a King.

And, I said to myself, looking after him as he walked away, I will have him, if I die for it.

12

THE ROYAL rooms were above the banquet hall, looking towards the sea. He was pleased with the sea, being used to it near in boyhood. Here I waited on him, as in his tent before; but, as before, never at nighttime.

In a half-month he would be at war again. It did not give me long.

I had thought myself skilled, at Susa, never having seen what my training lacked. I knew what to do when I was sent for. In all my life, I had never seduced anyone at all.

Not that he was indifferent. First love had not bereft me of all sense; something had been there when his eyes met mine. In his presence I felt more beautiful, a sign that one can't mistake. It was his pride I feared. I was his dependent; he thought I could not say no. How right he was! Yet if I offered myself, having been what I had been, what would he think? I might lose even what I had. He did not buy at market.

The squires were my unwilling friends. He kept me

closer about him; to rebuke their spite, or so he let it seem. For my spoiled coat, he never even counted out the gold, just gave me a handful. I had something becoming made, and, you may be sure, put it on for his approval. He smiled; emboldened, I asked him to feel how fine the cloth was. For a moment, it seemed something might come of that. But no.

He was fond of reading, when he had the time. I knew when to be quiet; we all learned that at Susa. I would sit cross-legged by the wall, looking at the sky with its wheeling gulls that came for the palace offal, stealing a glance at him; one must not stare at a king. He did not read aloud to himself, like other people; one scarcely heard a murmur. But I knew when the murmur stopped.

He was aware of me. I felt it like a touch. I lifted my eyes, but he kept his on the book. I dared not come forward, or say, "My lord, here am I."

On the third day was the victory sacrifice and procession. He lived so simply, I had never guessed he had a love of spectacle. He rode in the cavalcade, in Darius' chariot (I found he had had the floor raised up a handspan), his gold hair crowned with gold laurel, his purple cloak clasped with jewels. He loved every moment; but I was nowhere near, and at night there was a feast at which he stayed till dawn. I lost half next day, too, for he did not rise till noon.

Yet Eros, whom I had not yet learned to worship, did not forsake me. The next day he said, "Bagoas, what did you think of the dancer last night at supper?"

"Excellent, my lord, for someone trained at Zadrakarta."

He laughed. "He claims it was Babylon. But Oxathres says he's nothing compared with you. Why have you never told me?"

I did not say I'd been racking my brains for a chance. "My lord, I have had no practice since I left Ekbatana. I would be ashamed you should see me now."

"Why, you could have used the ball-court any day. There must be somewhere here." He strode out, attended only by me, through the ancient maze of rooms, till we found one with space and a good floor, which he had cleared and scoured before nightfall.

I could have exercised without music, but I hired a piper, in case it should be forgotten where I was. I got out my spangled loincloth, and let my hair hang free.

After a while the piper faltered, and glanced towards the door; but I, of course, was too intent on my dance to see. I finished with my slow back-somersault off the hands. By the time I came right side up, no one was there.

Later that day, I sat again in the King's room, while he read his book. His soft voice ceased. There was a silence like a note of music. I said, "Your sandal-string is loose, my lord," and knelt beside him.

I felt him look down; I would have looked up, in another instant. But then the dog Peritas thumped the floor with his tail.

Having undone the string, I had to do it up again; so Hephaistion was in the room before I could get away. I bowed; he greeted me cheerfully, patting the dog which had come to fawn on him.

So ended the fifth day of fifteen.

Next morning, the King went out fowling, in the marshlands beside the sea. I thought he'd be gone all day; but he was back well before sundown. When he came from the bath (where still he had never sent for me) he said, "Bagoas, I shan't sit late at dinner. I want you to teach me a little Persian. Will you wait up?"

I bathed, and put on my best suit, and tried to eat. He was dining with a few friends, and did not need me there. I went up and waited.

When he came, he paused at the door, making me fear he had forgotten to expect me. Then he smiled and came in. "Good; you are here." (Where else? As a rule he never said such things.) "Bring up that chair to the table, while I find the book."

These words dismayed me. "My lord King, could we do without a book?" He raised an eyebrow at me.

"I am very sorry, my lord, but I cannot read. Not even Persian."

"Oh, that's no matter. I never thought you could. The book's for me." He fetched it, and said, "Come, sit here." There was about a yard between us. The chairs quite put me out. There one is, trapped, and can get no nearer. I looked with regret at the divan.

"We'll work like this," he said, setting out tablet and stylos. "I shall read out a Greek word and write it down; you will tell me the Persian, and I shall write the sound as it seems to me. It's what Xenophon did, the man who wrote this book."

It was an old book, much used, the split edges patched with glue. He opened it tenderly. "I chose this for your sake; it's the life of Kyros. Is it true you come from his tribe?"

"Yes, my lord. My father was Artembares, son of Araxis. He was killed when King Arses died."

"I heard so," he said, and looked at me with pity. Only Oxathres, I thought, could have told him that. He must have asked about me.

The big old lamp-cluster, a ring of lamplets, hung over the table, its many flames making double and treble shadows under his hands, the light touching his cheekbones but not his eyes. He was a little flushed, though I could tell he had drunk no more at dinner than they always did. I looked down at the book with its unknown markings, to let him look at me.

What can I do? I thought. Why ever did he get us into these stupid chairs, which is not at all what he wants, and how can I get us out of them? Things told me by Nabarzanes were coming back. I thought, Has *he* ever seduced anyone, either?

He said, "Since I was a boy, Kyros has seemed to me the pattern for all kings, as Achilles—whom you won't know—is for all heroes. I have passed through your country, you know, and seen his tomb. When you were a child there, did you hear any tales of him?"

His arm rested quite near me. I wanted to grasp it,

and say, "Won't Kyros keep?" He is in two minds, I thought, or we would not be sitting like this. If I lose him now, perhaps it will be forever.

"My father told me," I said, "that once upon a time there was a cruel king, called Astyages; and the Magi predicted that the son of his daughter would take his throne. So he gave the baby to a lord called Harpagos, to do away with. But the babe was beautiful and he could not kill it; so he gave it to a herdsman, to leave it on the mountain and be sure it died. The man went home first, and his wife's own baby was dead, and she was crying, 'We are growing old, and who will feed us?' So the herdsman said, 'Here is a son. But you must keep it secret forever.' He gave her the child, and put the dead one on the mountain in the royal clothes; and when jackals had gnawed it so that no one could know it again, he brought it to Harpagos. And Kyros grew up the herdsman's son; but he was brave as a lion and beautiful as morning, and the other boys made him their King. When he was about twelve, King Astyages came to hear of him, and sent to see him. By then he had the family looks; and Astyages made the herdsman tell. The King meant to kill the boy; but the Magi said that his being King in play had discharged the prophecy; so he was sent back to his parents. It was on Harpagos that the King took vengeance." I dropped my voice to a whisper, just as my father had done. "He took and killed his son, and roasted his flesh, and gave it Harpagos to eat at dinner. When he had eaten, he showed him the boy's head. It was in a basket."

I had nothing near finished; but something made me stop. His eyes were on me. I almost swallowed my heart.

I said, I will love you forever, though what my tongue said was, "Is that in your book, my lord?"

"No. But it's in Herodotos." He pushed back his chair, and walked towards the window that faced the sea.

Thankfully I got up too. Would he make me sit down again? The clerks who wrote out his letters had to sit while he walked about. But he said nothing. He turned and came back to where I stood under the lamp, with my back against my chair.

Presently he said, "You must tell me when I say the Persian wrongly. Don't be afraid to correct me, or I shall never learn." I took a step towards him. My hair had fallen forward over my shoulder. He put up his hand and touched it.

I said softly, "My lord knows well that he only has to ask."

Eros had gathered his net in the strong grip of a god, and pulled in his catch, no longer to be defied. The hand that had touched my hair slid under it; he said, "You are here under my protection." At this, without respect for the sacred person of a king, I put both arms round his neck.

That was the end of his pretenses. Now here I stood, in the sole embrace which, out of so many, I had ever worked to get.

I did not speak. I had gone far enough above my place already. All I wished to tell him was, I have only one thing in the world to give you, but that is going to be the best you ever had. Just take it, that is all.

He still seemed hesitant; not from reluctance that was sure; but from something; a kind of awkwardness. The thought broke in on me, Where has he lived, and he a soldier? He knows no more than a boy.

I thought of his famous continence, which I had supposed to mean only that he did not rape his captives. I thought of it when he went to the outer door, to tell the guard he was going to bed and needed no attendance (I expect they had had a bet on whether I would come out). As we went through the Bedchamber, I thought, Everyone else has always known what he wanted. Shall I have to find it out for him? I do not know his customs, I may offend against what is permitted. He must love me, or I shall die.

Peritas, who had heaved himself up from his corner and strolled in after us, curled up at the bed's foot where I had been taught to lay my clothes, lest the sight of them offend the King. But the King said, "How

does all this come off?" and in the end they were all
in a heap with his own upon the clothes-stool.

The bed was ancient but grand, of painted and gilded
cedarwood. And now it was time to serve him the
royal Persian banquet he must be expecting from
Darius' boy. I had it ready, with all the seasonings.
But though in my calling I felt as old as time, my
heart, which no one had trained, was young, and suddenly it mastered me. Instead of offering spices, I
simply clutched him, like the soldier with the arrow
wound; uttering such follies as I blush even now to
think of, and, when I remembered I was speaking
Persian, repeating them in Greek. I said I had thought
he would never love me. I did not beg him to take me
with him wherever he was going; I did not think so far.
I was like a traveler in the desert, who comes to water.

The last thing he could ever have looked for was to
be eaten alive like this. I doubt he understood a word
of it, smothered upon his shoulder. "What is the trouble?" he asked. "What is it, then, tell me, don't be
afraid." I lifted my face and said, "Oh, I am sorry,
my lord. It is nothing. It is love." He said, "Is that
all?" and laid his hand on my head.

How foolish my plans had been! I should have
learned better from seeing him at table, giving away the
best though he was left with none. He distrusted taking
pleasures for himself, from pride, and jealousy of his
freedom; and I, who had seen what I had seen, was not
one to blame him. Yet he did have something from
those empty dishes. He was in love with giving, almost
to folly.

"Only love?" he said. "Don't fret, then; we have
enough to go round, between us."

I should have seen at table too that he never
snatched. Except for Oromedon, which did not count,
he was the youngest man I had ever been to bed with;
yet his embrace had changed to comfort, as soon as
he'd thought I was in trouble; he would have heard out
the whole tale, if there had been one. Indeed, one
learned soon enough, and some learned to his cost, that
he would do anything in return for love.

He really wanted love from me. I could not credit such fortune; nobody ever had before. In the past, I had taken pride in giving pleasure, since it was my skill; never had I known what it was to take delight in it. He was not quite so ignorant as I had supposed; it was just that what he knew had been very simple. He was a quick learner, though. All I taught him that night, he thought that by some happy harmony of our souls, we were discovering together. So, indeed, it seemed at last even to me.

Afterwards, he lay a long time stretched out as if he were dead. I knew he was not asleep, and began to wonder if I was meant to go. But he drew me back, though he did not speak. I lay quiet. My body echoed like a harp-string after the note. The pleasure had been as piercing as the pain used to be before.

At last he turned, and speaking gently, as if he had been a long time alone, said, "So they did not take that from you." I murmured something, I don't know what. "And after," he said, "does it bring you grief?"

I whispered, "No, my lord. It never happened to me till now."

"Truly?" He took my face in his hand to look at by the nightlamp, then kissed me, saying, "May the omen be happy."

"And my lord?" I said, gathering courage. "Does my lord feel grief?"

"Always for a time. Take no account of it. All good things must be paid for, either before or after."

"You will see, my lord, I shall learn how to keep grief from you."

He half laughed under his breath. "Your wine is too strong, my dear, to drink it often."

I was amazed; all other men I'd known had pretended to more than they had. I said, "My lord is as strong as a young lion. This is not the body's weariness."

He raised his brows, and I feared he was displeased; but he only said, "Well, learned physician, then tell me what it is."

"It is like the bow, my lord; it is the strongest that

wearies, if it is not unstrung. The bow must rest. So too the warrior's spirit."

"Ah, so they say." He ran a strand of my hair slowly between his fingers. "How soft it is. I never felt hair so fine. Do you worship fire?"

"We did, my lord, at home."

"You are right," he said, "for it is divine."

He paused, seeking words; but there was no need. I had understood him. I laid down my head in submission, saying, "For me let my lord never turn aside out of his way; let me be like a cup of water drunk down in haste at noon, and I am content."

He reached out to my closed eyes, and touched my lashes. "Ah, no. Is this how I repay you? No more, or we shall both be weeping. Who is talking about noon? The moon is only rising. There is no need of haste tonight."

Later, when the moon stood high, and he lay sleeping, I leaned to look at him. Exaltation of spirit had kept me wakeful. His face was smoothed and beautiful; he was satisfied, and in sleep he was at peace with it. Though the wine is strong, I thought, you will come back for more.

What had Nabarzanes said? "Something he has wanted a long time, without being aware of it." That subtle serpent; how had he known?

His arm, darkened by sun, lay bare, and his shoulder, milk-white, but for the deep pitted wound from the catapult bolt at Gaza. The stain was fading; it was the color of watered wine. Softly I touched my lips to it. He slept soundly, and did not stir.

My art would not have been worth much, if I could not lead him, once I had understood. A light cloud crossed the moon. I remembered that first night in his tent; and how Hephaistion came and went just as he chose, pleasant with me as with the dog. Was he too secure to spare a thought for me? Too secure even to care? "You can't guess what I did last night." "Of course I can. You slept with Darius' boy. I knew you would before long. And was he good?"

He was seemly in sleep, his mouth closed, his breathing silent, his body fresh and sweet. The room smelled of sex and cedarwood, with a tang of salt from the sea. Autumn drew on, the night wind blew from the north. I drew the blanket over him: without waking, he moved to me in the great bed, seeking warmth.

As I slid into his arm, I thought, We shall see who wins, tall Macedonian. All these years you have made a boy of him. But with me, he shall be a man.

13

AT ONCE the news was everywhere. Alexander took this with calm. He could be secret at need; he was never furtive. He did not conceal that my presence pleased him, but offered no foolishness to mockers. I was proud of his behavior, coming so new to it, whereas I had been trained in the right deportment. It was I, now, who attended him at the bath; he used to send out the rest.

Once or twice, while I stood by his chair at table, I saw Hephaistion's eye on me; but he gave no other sign, coming and going as freely as before. I had no means of knowing what he said when I left the room. The walls are four feet thick, at Zadrakarta.

To me Alexander never spoke of him. I did not deceive myself with this. He was not forgotten; he was unassailable.

I thought of the King's old war-horse, for whose sake he would have sacked a province, though it would never carry him in the charge again. It is like that, I thought; he never turns love away, it is not in him. I thought

Hephaistion had not done so badly. If the beautiful boy you caught in a haystack gets to be a general of cavalry at eighteen, and is still your boy, you have not much to complain of. And if he goes on to be Pharaoh and Great King, with the treasures of Babylon, Susa and Persepolis poured at his feet, and the world's fiercest troops adoring him, is it wonderful if he finds he is a boy no longer, and wants a boy of his own? How long, I wondered, since they'd done more than just think of themselves as lovers? Since last he rode the black horse to war? And yet . . .

But with the night my troubles left me. He knew what he wanted now, but I knew better. Sometimes in the dance one is lifted beyond oneself, and cannot fail; it was like that.

Once when through the deep window the moonlight glinted on gold, I was put in mind of my old room at Susa, and uttered the invocation of my dreams. "Am I beautiful? It is for you alone. Say that you love me, for without you I cannot live." Rightly I had believed it magical.

I doubt he'd ever in his life lain down with anyone for whom he had not felt some kind of fondness. He needed love as a palm tree needs water, all his life long: from armies, from cities, from conquered enemies, nothing was enough. It laid him open to false friends, as anyone will tell you. Well, for all that, no man is made a god when he is dead and can do no harm, without love. He needed love and never forgave its betrayal, which he had no understanding of. For he himself, if it was given him with a whole heart, never misused it, nor despised the giver. He took it gratefully, and felt bound by it. I should know.

It pleased him to think he'd given me what Darius could not; so I never told him Darius hadn't thought of such a thing. He always liked to surpass his rivals.

But still, when desire was spent, he fell back into heaviness of soul, so that I feared to break his solitude. Yet I wished to repay his gift of healing. I would draw a finger-tip from his eyebrow to his throat, and he would smile to show me he was not sullen nor ungrateful. One night, remembering the book he had shown me, and that he had set store by it, I said softly in his ear, "Did you know, my lord, that Kyros the Great once loved a Median boy?"

At the name his face lightened a little, and he opened his eyes. "Truly? How did they meet?"

"He had won a great battle, my lord, against the Medes, and was going over the field to view the slain. He saw the boy, who was wounded almost to death, lying by his dead father. Seeing the King, he said, 'Do what you choose with me, but do not deface my father's body; he kept his faith.'

"Kyros said, 'I do not do such things. Your father shall be buried with honor.' For even as the boy lay in his blood, he loved him. And the boy looked up at Kyros, whom before he had seen only far off, flashing in arms, and thought, This is my King. Kyros had him taken up from the field and tended, and honored him with love; and he was faithful forever. And peace was made between the Medes and the Persians."

I now had all his attention. His melancholy was gone. "I never knew of this. Which was the battle? What was the boy's name?"

I told him; love gave my invention wings. "Of course, my lord, in our part of the world people are full of these old stories. I can't say if they are all true." I had made up every word of it, and could have done it better if I had had more Greek. For all I know, Kyros never loved a boy in all his life.

My spell had worked. I found a few more tales which, true or false, were really told in Anshan country. A little later, he said that not even Kyros' boy was more beautiful than Alexander's; and afterwards he did not grieve, but slept.

The very next day, he got out the book again, and started to read it me. I had him to myself for a full hour. He said he had read it at home while still a boy, and it had shown him the portrait of a true ruler's soul.

Well, so it might; but if it was meant to be a portrait of Kyros, Kyros would have been surprised. It had been written, not by some learned Persian who had read the records and talked to old men of the tribe, but by a hired Greek soldier of Artaxerxes' day, who had fought for Kyros the Younger against the King. After he had led his men safe out of that and back to Greece, I suppose it was no wonder they believed any tale he told there.

Of course, Alexander only read me his favorite pieces. As it was, with anyone else I don't know how I could have kept my eyes open. We were both rather short of sleep. Since I could have looked at his face forever, he never knew when I stopped listening. I could always tell when something he liked was coming.

"Not all of this," he said, "is history, as I've found since I was here. Your boys are not trained up in public barracks?"

"No, my lord. Our fathers train us for war."

"And the young men too?"

"Yes, my lord. They fight with their fathers' tribesmen."

"So I thought. He is far too fond of the Spartans. But it's true, I think, that Kyros liked to share his cooks' best dishes with his friends?"

"Oh, yes, my lord. It has been an honor ever since, from the King's table." So *this* was where he had found it! The man Xenophon must have been in Persia just long enough for that. I was so touched, I nearly cried.

He read me a tale about how his lords chose for Kyros, from the spoils of battle, the loveliest of the noble ladies, who was weeping for her dead lord. But Kyros, who knew he was alive, would not even see her face, but kept her in honor among her own household, and sent the husband word of it. When he came in to surrender and swear loyalty, the King led her out and joined their hands. As Alexander read it me, I knew suddenly that this was what he had planned for Darius and his Queen. It was why he had mourned her fasting. I saw how he had pictured it, just like the book; and thought of the hide-roofed cart with its cushions dripping blood.

He had no harem with him anymore. Before I came, he had settled the Queen Mother at Susa with the young princesses.

A king, the book said somewhere, *should not only prove himself better than those he rules; he should cast a kind of spell on them.* I said to him, "Let me say that in Persian," and we smiled at one another.

"You must learn to read Greek," he said. "It's a great loss to you, not to read. I will find you a gentle teacher. Not Kallisthenes, he thinks himself too grand."

For some days we read the book together, and he would ask me if this or that was true. He was so fond of it, I never liked to say that this Greek storyteller, coming from Athens where they had no kings, had dreamed of one and given him the name of Kyros. Where the book was wrong about Persian customs, I always told him, so that he should lose no face before my people. But when he read aloud some precept that had shaped his soul, I always said it had been handed down from Kyros' mouth in Anshan. There is nothing like giving joy to the one you love.

"I was mistaught as a boy," he said. "I won't insult you with what I was told to think about the Persians. The old man, I suppose, is saying the same things still in his school at Athens. It was Kyros who opened my eyes, in this book when I was fifteen. The truth is that all men are God's children. The excellent ones, he makes more his own than the rest; but one can find them anywhere." He laid his hand on mine.

"Now tell me," he said, "is it really true that Kyros allied with the Medes to fight the Assyrians, as it says here? Herodotos says, and you were saying, that he beat the Medes in war."

"He did, my lord. Any Persian will tell you so."

He read from the book, *"He ruled over these nations, even though they did not speak the same tongues as he, nor one nation the same as another's; yet he was able to spread the awe of him so far that all feared to withstand him; and he could rouse so eager a wish to please him, that they all desired to be guided by his will."*

"That is true," I said. "And will be again."

"Yet he never made the Persians overlords of the Medes; he ruled over both as King?"

"Yes, my lord." As I'd heard it, some of the chief Median lords had joined in revolt against Astyages, because of his cruelty. No doubt they made terms for this, and Kyros kept them like a man of honor. I said, "It is true, Kyros made us all one kingdom."

"So it should be. He did not make subject peoples; he made a greater empire. He chose men for what each man was in himself, not from hearsay and old wives' tales . . . Well, I don't suppose he found it hard to persuade the conquered. To persuade the victors, that's the thing."

I was seized with wonder. Why, I thought, he wants to follow Kyros even in this. No, to go before him; for Kyros was pledged, but he is free . . . And I was the first Persian he had told.

It was long since I had remembered my father clearly. Now his face returned to me, blessing my sons to be. Maybe, after all, his words were not empty wind.

Alexander said, "Yes, tell me your thought, what is it?"

I answered, "That the sons of dreams outlive the sons of seed."

"You are a seer. I have thought so often."

I did not say, "No, I am just a eunuch making the best of it," but told him all about the New Year festivals, which Kyros began as a feast of friendship; and how he led the peoples to conquer Babylon, the Medes and Persians vying to show valor before him. Sometimes from eagerness I stumbled in my Greek, and he would say, "Never mind. I understood you."

All day there was a shine on him; and at night, it was as if I'd come to him Kyros' boy, instead of Darius'. He fell without grief into smiling sleep; and I said to myself, That's one thing I've done for him that Hephaistion couldn't.

How perverse is the heart. Darius had neither offered love nor asked it; yet I had felt it right I should
be grateful for all he gave me, a horse, a mirror, a
bracelet. Now in my riches I scorched my soul because
another came before me; I must have him all.

In all but words, he showed he had more pleasure
with me than with anyone before me; he was too
generous to belittle it. But the words were never spoken,
and I well knew why. That would have violated loyalty.

"Never be importunate," Oromedon had said to me
long' ago. "Never, never, never, never. The quickest
way to the dusty street outside. *Never.*" And he, who
was always gentle as silk, had given my hair a twitch
that made me yelp. "I did that for your sake," he
said, "to make you remember."

Nobody owns the gods. But there are some they
choose to make more their own than the rest. I remembered.

There were times when I could have grasped him in
both hands, crying aloud, "Love me best! Say that you
love me best! Say that you love me best of all!" But I
remembered.

Standing by the wall in the audience room at
Zadrakarta, I watched him giving audience to Macedonians. He had these people in without formality,
walking about among them.

"You are a musician," Oromedon had said. "All you
need is to know your instrument." He had simpler
ones in mind; this harp had many strings, some never
for my sounding. And yet, we had made harmony.

So I was thinking, when a courier came in with a
batch of letters from Macedon. The King took them
from him, and sat down with them on the nearest
divan he saw, like a common man. He would do these
things. I longed to tell him they did him injury.

As he turned the letters over, Hephaistion strolled
across, and sat down beside him. I gasped aloud; this
passed all other effronteries. But Alexander just gave
him some of the rolls to hold.

They were not very far away from me. I heard

Alexander, as he picked up the thickest letter, say, "From Mother," and give a sigh.

"Read it first and get it over," Hephaistion said.

Though I hated him, I could see how Darius' ladies had done him royal honors in their grief's confusion. By our Persian canons, I suppose he was the more beautiful; taller, with features regular to perfection. When his face was still, it was grave almost to sadness. His hair was a shining bronze, though much coarser than mine.

Meantime, Alexander had opened Queen Olympias' letter. And Hephaistion, leaning easily on his shoulder, was reading it with him.

Through my own bitterness, I perceived this had shocked even the Macedonians. Their murmurs reached me. "Who does he think he is?" "Well, we all know that. But he need not shout it."

One of those veterans who stood out by their beards and their uncouth manners said, "If he can read it, why can't all of us hear?" He spoke aloud.

Alexander looked up. He did not call his guards to arrest the man. He did not even rebuke him. He just drew off his signet ring, turned to Hephaistion smiling, and laid on his lips the royal seal. They both returned to the letter.

I could always move smoothly, even if blind with tears. No one noticed me going. I ran to the stables, and rode off out of town, along by the sea-swamps, where clouds of black birds rose up wailing and screaming, like the thoughts of my heart. As I turned for home, my black thoughts settled, like crows upon a gibbet. I cannot bear my life while this man lives. He will have to die.

Walking my horse through sandy scrub, I thought it over. As boys they were vowed together, and while this man is faithful, Alexander feels himself bound. He will acknowledge him before all the world, though he loves me best in his heart, and my heart is scalding in fire. No! For Hephaistion, only one thing will do. I am going to kill him.

Tomorrow, then, I will go to the beggars' market and buy old clothes. Somewhere out here I will change, and hide my own clothes in the sand. I will wrap my head in a clout to hide my beardless face, and go to the little streets under the wall. I shall find a druggist there who will ask no questions. It cannot be long before I have the chance to get at his wine or food.

In the stables I called a groom to my lathered horse, and went back to the audience room, to look at him and think, You will soon be dead.

Quiet by the wall, I went over my plan. I would buy the poison; so far, good. Would it be in a phial, or a bag? I would keep it—where? In my clothes? Round my neck? How long would I have to hide it?

As my hot blood cooled, I began to think of a thousand mischances that could discover me, before I could use the drug; milling over these little things, till like a lightning-flash I saw the great one. If I were found with poison, who would ever doubt it was for the King? I had been brought to him by a man who had killed one king already.

So, then, Nabarzanes would be dragged from his home, and crucified beside me. I would be long remembered; the Persian boy, Darius' whore who fooled the great Alexander. So he too would remember me. Rather than that, I myself would take the poison, though it turned my entrails to shriveling fire.

The Macedonians had had their audience. It was Persians now. Their presence reminded me whose son I was. What had been in my mind? To murder a faithful man, because he was in my way. So had King Arses' brothers been faithful, and in the way. So had my father.

Next time I saw Hephaistion near the King, I said in myself, Well, I could kill you if I chose; you are lucky I will not stoop to it. I was young enough for this to make me feel better; too young, and too full of my own troubles, to think of his.

What he had had, would never again be anyone's. His claim was honored; how could he ask for more? Well, he might have asked that his beloved should not become a lover, or have from a dark-eyed Persian boy what he'd never been thought to need. Maybe, since their youth, desire had faded (if so, I could guess whose had faded first); but the love was there, public as marriage. Lying alone in those nights at Zadrakarta, Hephaistion could not have slept at ease. I should have seen in his arrogance with the letter a plea for a proof of love. Alexander had seen; and given it in the face of everyone.

That night, between grief and guilt, I lost my sense of harmony, was strained and silly, and tried a trick I had learned at Susa, the kind of thing he had never guessed I knew. I felt my blunder. I feared disgust, not reckoning on his innocence. He exclaimed, "Don't tell me you did that with Darius!" and laughed so much he nearly fell out of bed. I was so put out, I hid my face and would not look at him. "What is it?" he asked. I said, "I have displeased you. I will go." He pulled me back. "Don't sulk at me. What is it?" Then his voice altered, and he said, "Do you miss Darius still?"

He was jealous; yes, even he! I flung myself on him, embracing him with a fury more like war than love. He was some time calming me down, before we could begin. Even then I was still strung up, and at the end felt pain, almost like early days. Though I kept quiet, I suppose he felt some difference. I lay silent, doing nothing to divert his sadness. It was he who said, "Come, tell."

I answered, "I love you too much, that's all."

He drew me over, and ran my hair softly between his fingers. "Never too much," he said. "Too much is not enough." In sleep he did not toss himself free of me as he sometimes did; he let me stay in his side all night.

Next morning, as I got up, he said, "How is your dancing?" I told him I was practicing every day. "Good. Today we are giving out the list of contests for the victory games. There will be one for dancers."

I turned a cartwheel across the room, and a back-somersault after.

He laughed, then said seriously, "One thing you

must know; I never direct the judges. It's bound to
make bad feeling. At the games at Tyre, I'd have given
anything to see Thettalos crowned. For me, no tragedian
touches him; he has been my envoy too, and done
me very good service. But they chose Athenodoros,
and I had to put up with it. So I can only say, win
for me."

"If it kills me," I said, doing a handstand.

"Oh, hush." He made the Greeks' sign against bad
luck.

Later he gave me a fistful of gold for ·my costumes,
and sent me the best flautist in Zadrakarta. If he had
divined my trouble, and could not cure it, he knew
how to make me forget.

I was tired of my old dances; for him I composed a
new one. It began fast, Kaukasian style; then turned
slow, with the bends that show one's balance and
strength. The last part would have the sparks in it;
not too many since I was a dancer and not an acrobat;
but enough. For my costume, I ordered a Greek-style
tunic, made all of scarlet ribbons, caught together just
at the neck and waist. My sides were bare. I had
anklets sewn with round tinkling rattles of beaten gold.
For the first part, I would use the hand-clappers.

I practiced for my life. The first day, when I'd done
and sent off the flautist, Alexander came in and found
me toweling down, still out of breath. He took my
shoulders between his hands. "From now on till the
games, you sleep in here. One thing at a time."

He had a bed sent in for me. I knew he was right,
but grieved he could do without me; still knowing less
than the least of his soldiers what he could do without. I thought I could not bear a night away from him,
but had worked so hard I slept as I lay down, and did
not stir till morning.

On the day of the games, I went early to his room,
where a squire was dressing him. As soon as he saw
me he said, "Oh, Bagoas will see to it; you can go."
Some of the squires had improved and the King
had warmed to them, but this one was awkward. He
went out sulkily; the King said, "In all this time he

can't hang a cloak." I put in the brooches properly, saying, "Next time, ask me." He drew me by the hands and kissed me. "We shall see each other when you dance."

In the morning were the athletic events, running, jumping, throwing the disk and javelin, boxing, jumping, wrestling. This being the first time I had seen Greek games, I daresay I felt some interest, though they have bored me ever since. After the noon break came the dancing.

For this and for the music, the army carpenters had run up a theater, with a stage and backdrop facing a gentle slope, benches for the important people, and a dais for the King's chair. The backdrops were painted with real-looking columns and curtains. We have no such art in Persia. I had never seen such a place before, but had been over it, and found that the floor was good.

The slopes were filling, the generals were taking their seats upon the benches. I went where I was shown, and joined the other dancers, on the grass near to the stage. We glanced sideways at each other; three Greeks, two Macedonians, and one other Persian. The King came in to the sound of trumpets. The other dancers all looked at me with hatred, knowing who I was.

But I don't think that, by the end, even they would have disputed my win. I knew it must be a good one, for his sake as well as mine. True enough, he never interfered with the judges; but judges are only human. Those at Tyre might have known he thought well of Thettalos; but this was not quite the same as being his lover. A near thing would not do.

At Susa, I had danced for favor, from the fear of being turned off, from conceit of myself. I danced now for the honor of our love.

Turns were settled by drawing lots; I came on fourth. And I was not halfway through my first quick dance with the hand-clappers, before the applause began. It was new to me. My biggest audience had been a handful of Darius' guests, who offered praise as courtesy. This roar was different; it carried me on wings. When

I came to my somersaults at the end, I could hardly hear the music.

The judges made their choice in no time at all. I was sent to get my crown.

With the din following me all the way, I went up to the dais, and set my knee on its edge. Someone passed him the glittering wreath. I looked up, and met his smile.

He put the crown on my head, his touch caressing me. If happiness could overfill one like food or drink, I should have burst asunder. Hephaistion never did that for him, I thought.

The next contest was for kitharists. If the Wise God had sent his angels down to play, I would never have known the difference.

I remember nothing, between this paradise and standing by his chair at the evening feast. It was a grand banquet, quite well done for Macedonians, in the great hall of the palace, blazing with lamps; too many guests to use Greek couches. He had asked more Persian lords than ever before. All through the meal I was busy with gifts and messages. They all had something to say about my dance. I said to myself, He is honoring my people for what he finds in them; but a little, too, for me. And I thought with ecstasy of the coming night.

I went up before him. Instead of the bath-robe and towels, there were fresh clothes laid out. If I had not been living in a dream, I would have expected it; this I saw, in time not to make a fool of myself.

He came up, embraced me—the attendant squire had withdrawn when he saw me coming—and said, "Today I was envied by all Zadrakarta, and not for being King." I undid his cloak for him and helped him change. "Don't wait up for me, my dear. It's all old friends, we shall be drinking until daylight. Go to bed and keep warm, or you'll be stiff tomorrow."

A Macedonian night, I thought as I laid his purple cloak away. Well, he has given me warning. Never mind; however drunk he is, it shall be I who'll put him to bed, not that loutish squire. It's little enough to do for him.

I took a spare blanket from the chest, and rolled myself up in a corner. The hard floor did not keep me long awake.

I heard his voice. The birds were astir, but dawn had not yet broken.

"Every step on my feet. It took four of them to shift Philotas."

"And they won't get far," said Hephaistion. "Now, can you get to bed?"

"Yes, but come in." A pause. "Oh, come in. No one is here."

I felt very stiff. He'd been right about keeping warm. I drew up my blanket, lest my face should catch the light.

Hephaistion had Alexander's arm across his shoulders, not quite carrying him. He sat him down, took off his sandals and girdle, pulled his chiton over his head and eased him into bed. He placed the table, set there the water-pitcher and the cup, looked about for the chamber-pot and put it in easy reach. He wrung out a towel from the ewer, and wiped Alexander's forehead. Though unsteady on his feet, he did all this quite neatly. Alexander sighed, and said, "That's good."

"You'd better sleep it well off. Look, here's the water and there's the pot."

"I'll sleep it off. Ah, that's good. You always think of everything."

"I ought, by now." He bent and kissed Alexander's forehead. "Sleep well, my love." He went, closing the door softly.

Alexander turned on his side. I waited a good while, to be sure he was fast asleep, then put back the blanket stealthily. I stole off to my cold bed, as dawn came with the squalling of the gulls.

14

AT SIXTEEN, in Zadra-
karta, my youth began. Before, I had passed from
childhood into some middle state, where youth was
permitted only to my body. Now for seven years of my
life it was given me back. All that long wandering has
the taste of it.

There are places stamped on my memory; and long
months when the face of the earth swims past me, as
the shipping does when one sits beside the Nile. Mountain passes, wastes of snow, springtime forests, black
lakes in upland moors, flatlands of pebbles or parched
grass; rocks eaten into shapes of dragons; heavenly
valleys full of fruit-blossom; mountains without end,
spearing the sky, white and deadly; foothills with banks
of unknown flowers; and rain—rain streaming down as
if the heavens were dissolving, turning earth to mud,
rivers to torrents, weapons to rust, men into helpless
children. And the red-hot sandhills, day after day, by
the glaring sea.

So we marched east from Zadrakarta, when I was

sixteen and mad with love. We skirted the mountains that stretched on from Hyrkania, and entered wide empty land. Yet we lived in a moving city.

The King's train was now no less. He had crossed from Greece with a regent to rule his kingdom, free as a bird, just a general with the rank of King. Then the great cities fell, and Darius died. Now he was Great King in his own empire, and all its business traveled with him.

We were in a land without towns, like ancient Persis before Kyros' day. Hundreds of miles apart were forts like my childhood home; bigger, because they had been seats of kings, but not really different; a strong house on a crag, a tribal village round it. They had passed from kings down to chiefs and satraps; but, ancient and rude as they were, were still called king-houses. For the rest, there were nomad herdsmen seeking pasture, or hamlets where there was water all year round. For league after league, our camp was the only town.

It held the army, and the second army that served it, of armorers, engineers, carpenters, tentmakers, sutlers, leather-workers, grooms; the womenfolk and children of all these; the slaves. There were a score of clerks by now. And these were only the army in Alexander's pay. A third army followed us for trade; horse-copers, cloth-sellers, jewelers, actors, musicians, jugglers, panders and bawds, whores of each sex or none. For even troopers were rich; as for the great generals, they lived like minor kings.

They had households of their own in wagon trains, with chamberlains and stewards. Their courtesans lived as fine as Darius' women. They themselves after exercise were rubbed down by masseurs with oil of myrrh. Alexander only laughed at them, as at the foibles of friends. I could not bear to see how he let them surpass him in state and pride. I knew what Persians would make of it.

He himself had no time for show; or, often, for me. At the end of every march there would be a day's business waiting; envoys and scouts and engineers and petitioners, and the common soldiers who brought him their troubles as of right. After all that, he wanted his bed only for sleep.

Darius, when he found desire to fail him, would feel wronged by nature, and send for someone, such as me, whose skill was to put things right. Alexander, his eyes upon tomorrow, thought nature meant him to get a good night's rest.

There are things one can't explain to a whole man. With people like me, sex is a pleasure but not a need. Much more I loved his body just to be near it, like a dog or a child. There was life in his warmth, and sweetness. But I never said to him, "Let me in, I'll be no trouble." Never be importunate, never, never. There were other things for which he needed me every day; and the nights of reward would come.

On one of these, he said to me, "Were you angry that I burned Persepolis?"

"No, my lord; I was never there. But why did you burn it down?"

"Up. We burned it up. The god inspired us." By the night-lamp, I saw his face like a rapt singer's. "Curtains of fire, hangings of fire; tables, spread with great feasts of fire. And the ceilings were all of cedarwood. When we had done throwing on the torches, and the heat drove us outside, it was going up like a torrent into the black sky, a great fire-fall pouring upward with sparks for spray; roaring and blazing right up to heaven. And I thought, No wonder they worship it. What is there on earth more godlike?"

He liked to be talked to after the act of love; there was still something in him that rebuked desire as weakness. At these times I would speak to him of serious things; laughter and play were for beforehand.

Once he said, "Here we lie like this, and still you call me My Lord. Why do you do it?"

"It is what you are; in my heart, in everything."

"Keep it in your heart, my dear, before the Macedonians. I have seen some looks."

"You will always be my lord, whatever I call you. What must it be?"

"Alexander, of course. Any Macedonian trooper can call me that."

"Iskander," I said. My Greek accent was not very good yet.

He laughed and told me to try again. "That's better. When they hear you lording me, they think, 'So he's setting up as Great King.' "

He had given me my chance at last. "But my lord, my lord Iskander, you *are* the Great King of Persia. I know my people; they're not like the Macedonians. I know the Greeks say that the gods envy great men, that they punish hu—" I had been working hard at my books, but the word escaped me.

"Hubris," he said. "And they are watching me for that already."

"Not the Persians, my lord. In a great man they look for grandeur. If he seems to hold himself cheap, they withhold respect."

"Cheap?" he said from the bottom of his chest. It was too late to go back.

"My lord, courage and victory we honor. But the King . . . he must be apart; great satraps must approach him like a god. For him they make the prostration, which only peasants would make for them."

He was silent. I waited fearfully. At last he said, "Darius' brother wanted to tell me that. But he did not dare."

"Now my lord is angry?"

"Never, at counsel given in love." He pulled me closer to prove it. "But remember, Darius lost, and I'll tell you why. One can rule satraps that way; but never soldiers. They don't want to follow some royal image they have to approach on their bellies. They want to know you remember them in some action a year ago, and whether they've a brother serving; they like a word if he dies. If they're snowed on, they like to see the general snowed on too. And if rations are short, or water, and you keep ahead of the column, they want to know you're doing it on the army issue; *then* they'll follow you. And they like to laugh. I learned what they laugh at in my father's guardhouse when I was six years old.

They made me Great King of Persia, remember. . . . No, I'm not angry; you were right to speak. You know, I have the blood both of Greeks and Trojans in me."

I knew nothing of it, but devoutly kissed his shoulder.

"Never mind. Say I like your people; or find something of myself in them. Why say yours or mine? They should all be ours. Kyros did not rest till he had achieved it. Now it's time to make a new thing again. The god does not lead us all this way for nothing."

I said, "I have talked too much. Now you are wide awake again."

Last time I'd said this, he had replied, "Why not?" Tonight he said, "Yes," and went on thinking. I fell asleep beside his open eyes.

We were coming into Baktria, over huge rough uplands already touched with autumn, cut by harsh winds from the freezing mountains. I bought myself a coat of scarlet cloth lined with marten-skins, having lost my lynx-skin one at the Kaspian Gates. Camp-followers and soldiers bundled on extra warmth with sheep and goat skins; the officers had cloaks of good woolen cloth; but it was only the sleeved and trousered Persians who looked really warm. Sometimes Macedonians gave me a glance of envy; but they would have died before they put on the garb of the defeated, the soft and rotten Mede. They'd as soon have eaten their mothers.

The first rains fell; the wet ground made heavy going, streams were in spate; we seemed now to move as cumbrously as Darius' train. I learned the difference, when news came in that Satibarzanes, satrap of Areia, had rebelled behind us. He had given himself up freely at Zadrakarta; Alexander had offered him his right hand, asked him to dine, confirmed his satrapy, and given him a guard of forty Macedonians to help man his strongpoint. All these he'd murdered, once Alexander was gone; and was calling his tribesmen out to fight for Bessos.

Over our vast straggling horde, a trumpet sounded. The horse-train trampled and whinnied; orders barked in the snapping air; in less time than one could believe, the cavalry came out in column. Alexander mounted his war-horse; they plunged off into the weather, the ground shuddering under them. It was as if a slow giant had opened his cloak, and hurled a javelin.

We made camp and waited among all the winds of heaven; men and women were scratching the plain for firewood. I went to my Greek lessons with Philostratos, a grave young Ephesian, who did not despair of me. (To him I owe it that King Ptolemy lets me use his library, and I have read most Greek authors worth mentioning, though I cannot to this day make out the simplest inscription in my native tongue.)

The clerks kept up the records, so I got the news. The tribesmen had fled at the mere rumor of Alexander; the satrap had escaped to Bessos. Alexander had marked him down for death; he could never abide treachery. Nonetheless, the new satrap he had appointed for Areia was another Persian. He rode back in a snowstorm, and settled to his load of business.

The returning troops made a great rush for women, or whatever their fancy was. I knew better than to await any such summons. When he poured out his strength in war, he kept nothing back; and there was a half-month's work of government saved up for him. He got through it in five days. Then he asked in some friends, and they sat up all night drinking. He grew talkative, and fought over the whole war again. Then he slept all day, and on through the next night.

It was not the wine, though he had had a lot of it; he could have slept that off in half the time. Wine was what he used, to bring his mind to a stop when it had forgotten rest. Drunk as he was, he managed to take a bath, which he liked at bedtime. He never laid a hand on me, except to steady his steps. Wine brings out hidden things, and it did with him; but coarseness in the bedchamber was never one of them.

The day after, he woke as fresh as a foal; got through another mountain of work; and said to me at bedtime, "How can it have been so long?"

I made him welcome in every way I knew, and

some I had only just thought of. It was a joke of his
that I was making a Persian of him; the truth was that
I was forgetting already how to please anyone else. A
gentle subtlety was better for him than passion. Though
I had the art to draw men into violent pleasures, and
had done it also with him, it left a cloud on him; and
for me it was only a taught skill. I should have obeyed
my heart from the first; but no one before him had
ever let me have one. Now I had shown him his way
about the garden of delight, or as much of it as ever
would delight him, he wanted a companion there, not
an entertainer. He was never clumsy; it was his nature
to be a giver, here as elsewhere. And, here as elsewhere, if he was vain it was never about nothing.

Prince Oxathres had been promoted into the King's
Bodyguard. Alexander liked handsome men there, and
thought it due to his rank. He was within a thumb-
breadth of Darius for height; Alexander said to me
laughing that it was a change for Philotas, to have
someone look down at him. I replied with constraint,
which I hoped he noticed. This Philotas had been
on my mind.

He was the grandest of the generals, Commander of
the Companions, thought handsome, though too red
for a Persian taste. Of all those who put on more state
and luxury than the King, he was the chief. I swear he
went hunting with more gear and attendance than
Darius had, and the inside of his tent was like a palace.
I had taken a message there, and he had looked at me
with contempt. It did him no good with me, even that
Hephaistion disliked him too.

When one knows the ways of courts, one knows
what to look for. Sometimes I would post myself outside the audience room, as I'd done at Babylon, to
watch faces as men came out. There would be the
usual run of relief, disappointment, pleasure, familiar
ease; but Philotas' smile used to drop off his face too
quickly, and once I could have sworn I saw a sneer.

I kept it in my heart. I dared say nothing. Alexander
had known him all his life; with boyhood friends, he

was loyal beyond sense. Not only that; the man's father, Parmenion, outranked every other general, even Krateros who outranked all others here. Parmenion had been King Philip's chief commander. I had never seen him, because his army was guarding the western roads behind us, a trust on which all our lives depended. So I held my peace; only praising Oxathres' Nisaian chargers and their splendid trappings, and adding, "But of course, my lord, even at Darius' court he was never as rich as Philotas."

"No?" he said, and I could see it had made him think; so I clasped him laughing, and went on, "But now not you yourself are as rich as I."

The only upshot of this, that I could see, was his looking at Oxathres' horse-trappings, and liking them so much that he had them copied for old Oxhead. No Greek horse looks wonderful to a Persian; but now he was fed, tended and fresh, you could believe he had carried Alexander in battle for ten years and never once shown fear. Most horses would have been bothered by the new finery, the headstall with the cockade, the silver cheekpieces and the hanging plaques on the collar; but Oxhead thought very well of himself, and paced along making the most of them. There was a good deal in him of Alexander.

I was thinking this, as I sponged him down before dinner. He liked that as well as his bath at bedtime; he was the cleanest man I ever knew, when his wars allowed it. I used to wonder at first what faint pleasant scent he used, and would look about for the phial; but there was none, it was the gift of nature.

I praised the horse-trappings, and Oxhead's looks in them, and he said he was having more made as gifts for his friends. I toweled him down; all muscle, not overbuilt as those clumsy Greek wrestlers are. I said, "How well, my lord, you would wear the clothes that match the trappings."

He looked round quickly. "What put that in your head?"

"Only seeing you now."

"Oh, no. You are a seer, I told you so. I have been thinking, in one's own kingdom one should look less like a stranger."

His words delighted me. The wind was whistling round the tent. "I can tell you, my lord, in this weather you'll be much warmer in trousers."

"Trousers?" he said, staring at me in horror, as if I had proposed he should paint himself blue all over. Then he laughed. "My dear boy, on you they are enchanting; on Oxathres, they decorate the Guard. But to a Macedonian, there is something about trousers . . . Don't ask me why. I'm as bad as all the rest."

"We'll think of something, my lord. Something more like Persian court dress." I longed to make him beautiful in the fashion of my people.

He sent for a bolt of fine wool, for me to drape on him. But I had hardly started, when it turned out that not only would he not wear trousers; he would not have long sleeves either. He said they would fidget him, but I could tell it was just a pretext. I told him it was Kyros himself who'd put the Persians into Median dress; what's more, it was true; but even this magic name had no power upon him. So I had to resort to the antique Persian robe, so terribly old-fashioned that no one had worn it in a hundred years, except the King at festivals. If I'd not seen Darius being put into it, I'd never have known how it was made. It has a long skirt, stitched in folds on a waistband; a kind of cape, with a hole for the head to go through, covers the upper part and hangs over the arms to the wrists. I cut it all out and tacked the skirt together, put it on him, and moved the mirror about for him to see.

"I remember this," he said, "in the wall-reliefs at Persepolis. What do you think?" He moved sideways to the mirror. He was like a woman for dressing up, whenever he got a good excuse.

"It has great dignity," I said. He could carry it off, though it really called for height. "But do you like it to move in?"

He paced about. "If one doesn't need to do anything. Yes, I'll have it made up. In white, with purple borders."

So I found the best robe-maker (there were so many Persians in camp, that craftsmen followed them) and he made it with the real elaborate drapings. The King wore it, with a low open tiara, when entertaining Persians. I could see it increased respect. There are ways and ways of doing the prostration, which he did not see as I did. I had never told him, not wishing to betray my people; it hurt their pride, to see lower-born Macedonians make no reverence at all.

I told him now that they were well pleased with the robe. I did not say, though I longed to, that Philotas had looked down the length of the table and caught some crony's eye.

As I expected, Alexander soon found the robe tiresome; he said one could not stride out in it. I could have told him no one strode out at a Persian court. He had another made, pretty much like a long Greek chiton, except that the top overhung the arms. He wore a broad Median sash with it; purple on white. It suited him; but as far as the Macedonians were concerned, it might as well have had sleeves. He was so sure he had struck a happy mean, I hadn't the heart to tell him.

Hephaistion, as always, was on his side, and had taken to Persian horse-trappings. I heard murmurs about sycophancy as he passed; but I knew them mean. I had had time to consider Hephaistion. How easily he could have had me poisoned, or accused me through false witnesses, or had jewels hidden in my pack and charged me with their theft; something like that would have happened long ago at the Persian court, if I'd displeased a powerful favorite. He had a rough tongue among fellow soldiers, yet had never used it on me. If we had to meet, he would just speak to me as if to some wellborn page, civil and brisk. In return I offered respect without servility. Often I wished him dead, as, no doubt, so he did me; but we had reached an unspoken understanding. Neither of us would have robbed Alexander of anything he valued; so we had no choice.

Marching east over bare dun upland, and through rich valleys on which we fed, we halted at the king-house of the Zarangians. It was a rude old castle, rambling about over massive rocks with crazy rough-hewn steps, the windows mostly arrow-slits. The local chief moved out of the tower rooms; they smelled of his horses which had been stabled below. Alexander moved in, knowing he would lose face with the tribesmen if he did not. The squires had a guardroom halfway up; above were the King's chamber and an anteroom; a sort of closet, used by the squire who had the care of his weapons; and another closet for me. Outside of that, the other rooms, where his friends were lodged, were reached by going outdoors.

I had a brazier brought up for him to take his bath by; the place had a whistling draft, and after the march, he wanted a good clean-up before supper. The water was good and hot; I was rubbing down his back with ground pumice, when with a groaning creak the crude door flew open, and one of the squires burst in.

Alexander, sitting in the bath, said, "Whatever is it, Metron?"

The youth stood breathless. This one had made efforts, and shaped quite well; if only from respect for Alexander, he was civil even to me. But he now stood white as a bed-sheet, trying to find his voice. Alexander told him to take a hold of himself, and speak up. He swallowed.

"Alexander. There's a man here says he knows of a plot to kill you."

I rinsed the pumice off Alexander's back. He stood up. "Where is he?"

"In the armory, Alexander. There was nowhere else to put him."

"His name?"

"Kebalinos, sir. Leonnatos' squadron. Sir, I brought your sword."

"Good. You put a guard on him?"

"Yes, Alexander."

"Good boy. Now tell me what he said."

I was still drying and dressing him. Perceiving I was not to be sent out, Metron said, "He's here for his brother, sir, young Nikomachos. He didn't dare come himself, they'd have guessed why. That's why he told Kebalinos."

"Yes?" said Alexander, very patiently. "Told Kebalinos what?"

"About Dymnos, sir. He's the one."

Alexander's brows went up a moment. Metron buckled his sword-belt on.

"He's—well, a friend of young Nikomachos, sir. He wanted him to join in, but Nikomachos said no. Dymnos had counted on his saying yes to anything; so he lost his head, and told Nikomachos they'd kill him if he didn't join. So then he pretended he would, and told his brother."

"They? Who are the others?"

The youth strained his face. "Alexander, I'm sorry. He told me, but I can't remember."

"Honest at least. If you want to make a soldier, it's when taken by surprise you have to keep your wits. Never mind; go and fetch me the Captain of the Guard."

He started pacing the room. He looked stern-faced, but hardly shocked at all. I'd learned already that more kings had been murdered in Macedon even than in Persia. There, they used the dagger. It was said his father had been struck down before his eyes.

When the Captain of the Guard came in, he said, "Arrest Dymnos of Chalestra. He's quartered in the camp, not the palace. Bring him here." Then he went with Metron to the armory.

From the anteroom, I heard the man inside cry, "Oh, King! I thought I'd never get word to you in time." Being scared he gabbled, so I missed some of his story. There was something about Dymnos feeling slighted by the King, then, "But that's only what he told my brother. He couldn't account to me for the others being in it"; and he gave their names, which like Metron I have forgotten, even though I saw them die.

Alexander let him run on, never checking him when he rambled; then said, "How long did your brother know this, before he told you?"

"Just till he could find me, Alexander. No time at all."

"Today, then, while we were making camp, this happened."

"Oh, no, Alexander. That's why I came like this. It was two days ago."

"Two *days?*" His voice had altered. "I've never been out of camp. How long were you in this, before you changed your mind? Arrest him."

They pulled him out, a young soldier, gaping with fright. "But Alexander," he called, between a croak and a shout, "I went the moment I heard. I swear it, I went straight to your tent. Didn't he tell you, then? He said he'd tell you as soon as you were free. And again next day. I swear it, King, by undying Zeus. Did he never tell you at all?"

There was a silence. Alexander searched the man with his deep eyes.

"Release him, but stand by. Now let me understand you. You are saying you told all this to someone at my headquarters, who undertook to report it?"

"Yes, Alexander!" He had nearly sunk down, when the soldiers let him go. "I swear it, only ask him, King. He said I'd done right, and he'd report it as soon as he had the chance. Then yesterday he said you'd had too much business, but he'd do it before night. And then today, when we could see Dymnos and the rest still going free, my brother said I must see you somehow myself."

"It seems your brother's no fool. To whom had you given this message?"

"To General Philotas, King. He—"

"*What?*"

The man repeated it, stammering in terror. But what I saw in Alexander's face was not disbelief. It was recollection.

Presently he said, "Very well, Kebalinos. You and

your brother will now be held as witnesses. You have nothing to fear if you speak the truth. So prepare your evidence, and be ready to give it clearly."

The guards removed him. Alexander sent everyone else to summon men he needed. Meantime we were alone. I tidied the bath-things, stupidly concerned that all these people would be here before I could get hold of the slaves to carry the heavy bath away. I was not leaving him by himself till someone came.

Striding about the room, he came face to face with me. Words burst out of him. "He was with me an hour that day. The last part of it, he was talking horses. Too much business? . . . We have been friends, Bagoas, we've been friends since I was a child." He took another turn, and came back. "He changed after I went to Siwah. He mocked it to my face, but he has always mocked the gods, and I forgave it him. I was warned of him in Egypt; but he was my friend; what was I, Ochos? Yet he has never been the same; he changed when I had the oracle."

Before I could reply, the men he'd sent for began arriving, and I had to withdraw. The first was General Krateros, who had his lodging close by. As I went, I heard Alexander say, "Krateros, I want a guard put on every road out of here; every track and riding-path. No one at all, for any reason, is to leave this place. Do that, it can't wait; then come back and I'll tell you why."

The other friends he'd sent for, Hephaistion and Ptolemy and Perdikkas and the rest, were shut with him in his room, and I could hear nothing. Then came trudging feet upon the stairs. Young Metron, running ahead, now over his fright and full of self-importance, scraped at the door. "Alexander, they're bringing Dymnos. Sir, he resisted arrest."

Four soldiers brought on an army stretcher a youngish, fair-bearded Macedonian, with blood over his side and trickling from his mouth. His breath was rattling. Alexander said, "Which of you did this?" and they all turned as white-faced as their burden. The leader, finding a voice of sorts, said, "He did, King. I'd not even arrested him. He did it as soon as he saw us coming."

Alexander stood by the stretcher. The man knew him, though his eyes were glazing. The King put a hand on his shoulder; meaning, I supposed, to shake out of him the names of his confederates while there was time. But he just said, "How have I wronged you, Dymnos? What was it?"

The man's lips moved. I saw on his face a last shred of anger. His eyes rolled round and lighted on my Persian clothes; and his voice, half clotted, began to say "Barbar—" Then the blood came up, and his eyes fixed in his head.

Alexander said, "Cover him. Put him somewhere out of sight and set a guard." The soldier of lowest rank spread, unwillingly, his cloak over the corpse.

Soon after, Krateros returned to say the guard-posts were being manned; then someone announced that the King's supper was ready.

As they all passed my closet, to which I had withdrawn, Alexander said, "The outpost guards must still be on their way. He must know nothing, at all costs, till the roads are closed. We shall have to break bread with him, however little we like it." Hephaistion answered, "He has broken it with you, without any shame."

It was a Macedonian supper; I was not needed. I should have liked to watch the faces. People like me are blamed for curiosity; having lost part of our lives, we are apt to fill the gap from the lives of others. In this I am like the rest, and make no pretenses.

The royal hall was a stone barn, with a rock floor that stubbed one's toes. Not much of a place for his life's last feast; but I wished him nothing better.

I got rid of the bath, made the room fit for company, had supper, and came back to warm my hands at the brazier, and think about the closing of the roads. After a while it came to me. Philotas was son to Parmenion, the greatest man in Asia next the King. It was he who secured our rear. He was warden of the Ekbatana treasury; and had his own army, which from that hoard he could pay forever. Many were hired men, who had only fought under him. Philotas was his one son left living; two others had died upon campaign. I understood.

The King's supper finished early. He came back with his friends, and sent for young Nikomachos to hear his story. He was young, girlish and scared; the King treated him gently. After that, at about midnight, the conspirators he had named were all arrested. Philotas was taken last.

He was led in stumbling and blinking; he had drunk hard at supper, and been fast asleep. Now everyone was secured, they did not trouble closing doors for secrecy. I heard it all. Till now, the King had been like iron; now, for a moment, I seemed to hear the voice of a hurt angry boy, to an elder he once looked up to. Why had he hidden Kebalinos' warning? How could he do it? And, in the madness which, say the Greeks, the gods inspire in their chosen victims, Philotas answered the boy, and not the King.

With a blustering laugh, a little off the note, he said, "Why, I thought nothing of it, who would? My dear Alexander, you don't want to hear of every spiteful little fancy-piece who has a tiff with his keeper."

He was a great one for women, and boastful of it. The scorn in his voice was carelessness, and I daresay the drink. But it did his business. Fifteen years older in an instant, the King said, "Dymnos has killed himself, rather than face his trial. But you will stand yours tomorrow. Guard! Confined to quarters under close arrest."

The trials were held next day, on the heath outside the camp. It was cold, with grey scudding clouds threatening rain, but the whole army turned out, more than could get in hearing; the Macedonians in front, as was their right. Amazing to tell, the King could put no Macedonian to death without their vote. At home, any common peasant could have come and voted.

There being no place for me, I watched from the tower the small figures stand in the open square.

Dymnos' accomplices were tried first. They had already confessed and accused each other. (Wolves howl every night in Baktria, so I can't be sure of the sounds I heard.) After each trial the Macedonians shouted, and the man was led away.

Last appeared Philotas, whom I knew by his height, and the King, whom I knew by everything. They seemed to stand a long time there; one could tell by their gestures which was speaking. Then witnesses testified, above a dozen. Then the King spoke again; the Macedonians shouted, louder than all the other times. Then it was over.

I was told the evidence later. Except for the brothers', it had all been about Philotas' pride and insolence, and his speaking against the King. He would call him The Boy, and credit all his victories to Parmenion and himself; used to say he'd been vain from a child, and would rather be King of fawning barbarians than a decent Macedonian. Now he had swallowed whole the politic flatteries of Egyptian priests, and would be content with no less than deity; God help the people ruled by a man who thought himself more than mortal.

The executions would be next day; stoning for the lesser men; for Philotas, a squad with javelins. In Persia, they would have bricked up such men in a cold furnace, and stoked it slowly. And the King would have asked no man's leave.

Had Philotas, when he hid the plot, just seized the chance to profit by others' risk; or was he himself behind it? This was still unproved.

The King being shut up in council, for pastime I went back to the tower-top. Already the stakes were being sunk for the executions. On the roads and passes, I could see the guard-posts. Something moved on the western road; three men in Arab dress, on racing dromedaries. They caught my eye by the beauty of their action, after the great shaggy Baktrian camels. No creature that carries man is swifter or more enduring. They went up with their smooth stride towards the pass, and I looked to see them turned back. But after a moment's pause at the guard-post, they were let through.

I went down, lest the King should need me. Soon after, his council left. As they turned to the stairs, Hephaistion was last. The King beckoned him back. He went in, and bolted the door.

At other times, I should have found some dark place to grieve in. But it was nothing like that, as their faces told me. So I left my slippers in my cell, and crept up barefoot. The door-bolt was a great wooden thing; Hephaistion had been some time coaxing it. While he was drawing it back, I could be well away. You cannot learn too much of the one you love.

Hephaistion was saying, "I always thought he carried tales to your father. I told you so."

"I know you did." I heard again the voice of the distant boy. "But you never liked him. Well, you were right."

"Yes, I was. He hung round you from ambition, he always envied you. You should have listened in Egypt. This time, we have to know."

The King said, "Yes. We must know now."

"And don't take it to heart after. He's not worth it, never was."

"No. I shan't do that."

"He's been living soft, Alexander. It won't take long."

His voice came close to the door, and I made ready to run; but the King said, "Wait." So I crept back again.

"If he denies his father knew, don't push him to extremity."

"Why not?" Hephaistion asked. He sounded impatient.

"Because it makes no difference."

"You mean," said Hephaistion slowly, "that you'll—?"

"It is done," said the King. "Nothing else was possible."

There was a pause. Their eyes spoke, I suppose. Hephaistion said, "Well, it's the law. A traitor's near kin. It's only the manner of it."

"It's the only way."

"Yes. But you'll feel better, if you know he's guilty."

"Could I know from that? I won't lean on a lie, Hephaistion. It was necessary, and I know it. That is enough."

"Very well. Let's have it over." Hephaistion moved to the door again. I was in my cell long before he got it open.

After long enough, I asked the King if he needed anything. He was still standing where he must have been before. "No," he said. "I have something to see to," and went off by himself down the winding torchlit stair.

I waited, listening. At Susa, while still a slave, I had gone like other boys to the place of punishment. I had seen a man impaled, and flayings, and other things. Three times I had gone, drawn as boys are against their will to horrors. There were crowds that went every time; but I had had enough. I had now no wish to watch Hephaistion's work. It could be nothing much, to what I had seen already.

In time I heard the scream of a powerful voice. I felt no pity. What he had done to my lord, nothing undoes; the first betrayal by a friend. I, too, could remember losing childhood in a moment of time.

The scream sounded again, less like a man, more like a beast. Let him suffer, I thought. My lord has not only suffered a broken faith. He has taken a burden he will never again be free of.

I had understood his secret words to Hephaistion. Parmenion ruled like a king, in the lands behind us. Among his own troops, he could never be arrested, never be put on trial. Guilty or innocent, he would have his blood-feud the moment he got the news. I pictured our army and all its followers, in the freezing Baktrian winter, supplies cut off, no reinforcements; the conquered satraps, released by Parmenion's troops, tak-

ing us in rear; around us, Bessos and his Baktrians closing in.

I knew the errand of the dromedaries, swiftest of all
beasts that carry man: to outrun the news, carrying
death.

Such burdens fall only upon kings. He bore it all his
life, and, as he foresaw, he bears it dead. Since I am
one of many thousands who, because he took it on
him, are still alive, it may be said I plead my own
cause; but to the end of my days, I shall never see what
else he could have done.

The screams did not last long. A man in Philotas'
case has not much to lose by talking quickly.

The King came to bed late. He was stone-cold sober,
as if at war. He scarcely spoke to me, except to thank
me now and again, lest I should suppose him angry.

I lay in my little cell, wide awake, as I knew that he
would be. The night wore on; the guard clanked and
muttered below; the wolves of Baktria howled. Never
be importunate, never, never, never. I dressed and
gave on his door the tap he knew, and did not even
wait for leave to enter.

He was lying half turned away; Peritas, who always
slept unstirring at his bedfoot, was standing by him,
pawing the blanket as if concerned. Alexander was
rubbing his ears.

I came and knelt on the other side, and said, "My
lord, may I say good night to you? Just good night?"

"Bed, Peritas," he said. The dog went back to its
blanket. He felt my face and hands. "You're cold. Get
in."

I dropped off my things and came in beside him. He
warmed my hands on his breast, as he had rubbed
Peritas' ears, in silence. I reached up and stroked his
hair back from his forehead. "My father was betrayed
by a false friend," I said. "He told me so before they
killed him. It is terrible from a friend."

"When we get back," he said, "you can tell me who
it was."

The dog, after turning round two or three times, got

up to look, then went back to bed, as if satisfied he
was now being well cared for.

I said, "It is death to mock the gods. At Susa, I had
a slave from Egypt; not a common man, he had served
a temple. He said no oracle is as pure as the one at
Siwah."

He took a deep breath, and lay looking upward at
the rafters, where the shadows of cobwebs moved with
the flickering lamp. After a while, I put an arm across
him, and he laid his hand on it to keep it there. He was
silent a long time, holding my arm around him. Then
he said, "I have done a thing today that you don't
know of, which I shall be blamed for by men to come.
But it was necessary."

"Whatever had to be done," I answered him, "you
are the King."

"It was necessary. There was no other way."

I said, "We lay our lives on the King, and he bears
them all. He could never do it, without the hand of the
god."

He sighed, and drew my head upon his shoulder.

"You are my King," I said softly. "All you do is well
done to me. If ever I am false, if ever my faith forsakes
you, may I never enter Paradise, may the River of
Ordeal scald me all away. You are the King, the son
of the god."

We lay quiet, just as we were, and at last he slept. I
closed my eyes in contentment. Some Power must have
directed me; I had come when I was truly needed.

15

ALONG WITH Philotas, there died by the javelins Alexandros of Lynkestis, next heir, by side descent, to the throne of Macedon. His brothers had conspired in King Philip's murder; nothing being proved against the eldest, Alexander had taken him with the army. Now it seemed that Dymnos and the rest had meant to make him King; a decent Macedonian, who would keep barbarians in the place the Greek gods meant for them.

He had been warned of his trial, and prepared a speech of defense; but, before the Assembly, could only utter a senseless stammer. He had looked, they said, like a croaking frog; and they condemned him out of contempt, saying they were well shot of such a king. One or two of the accused made good their case and were set free. We were on the march again, by the time the news came in of Parmenion's death.

The men took it quietly. They had themselves condemned Philotas; they were ready to suppose there was evidence against his father. It was the veteran officers,

the old school of King Philip's training, who remembered Parmenion had won him a victory the day
Alexander was born; it was these who brooded. Philip,
it seemed, had been a proper Macedonian. Having freed
the Greek cities of Asia, he would have been content
to go home, and be master of Greece, which was what
he had always wanted.

Our moving city dragged on over barren moors
scorched brown with summer, now chilled with
autumn winds that sang through the broken crags. It
was harsh country; among the camp-followers the sickly
died; someone from their home place would scratch
them a grave in the hard ground. Nobody starved; the
wagon trains came from the west, and droves of cattle
lean with traveling. We labored along, mostly without
Alexander; he was scouring the wastes for Bessos, who
was reported moving east.

After days or a half-month, they would come back,
thin men upon thin horses, having outrun their
supplies. Or now and again some stubborn hill-fort
would hold out, and he would make a siege-train;
catapults taken apart to load on mules, wood for
ladders if the land was treeless; if he could bring one up,
a jolting siege-tower, drawn by ten yoke of oxen;
litters for the wounded, if it was too rough for wagons.
He would ride up and down the line, seeing everything
for himself. It was almost beyond belief, out of so many
thousand men, how many he knew. Often they
laughed; the soldier with the King, or the King with
the soldier.

The soldiers knew their part in him well enough.
Most had not even seen him in Persian dress; they
knew him in hard-worn Greek clothes, and armor of old
leather with the bits of iron plating working through at
the edges. They wanted no properer Macedonian than
their young unbeaten general, who sweated or froze or
starved with them, never sitting down till he had seen
them fed and their wounded cared for; never sleeping
drier than they; snatching victory out of peril. What
did they care if he appointed Persian satraps, when
some Macedonian might have ruled and fleeced the

province? They looked for their share of loot, and he shared it fairly. If he slept with Darius' boy when he had the time, what of it? He had a right to his share too. But they began to think about home.

They had had the cream of the spoils, the wealth of the great cities. They had swum in gold. Once, I was told, a transport mule in the treasure-train had foundered; the trooper who led it, careful of the King's goods, had shouldered the heavy pack, staggering under it. Along came Alexander, and said, "Bear up a little longer. Just get it to your tent. It's yours." So they had lived. They had had their pickings from the Persians, and wanted no more part of us.

Not so with Alexander. His hunger grew by feeding. He loved victory; Bessos was still unconquered. He loved magnificence; our palaces, our manners, had shown him what that could be. As a boy he'd been taught to despise us; he had found beauty and valor among our lords, bred in for generations; also, he had found me. He loved kingcraft; here was a whole empire, weak with misrule, whose bridle had scarcely felt his hand. Above all, he had his Longing. That moment of eager joy I had felt at the Kaspian Gates with the pass ahead, with him reached far into the distance, craving for wonders rumored in travelers' tales. Great anguish lies in wait for those who long too greatly.

Still he kept his soldiers faithful. Like Kyros, he cast his spell. He told them too that to retreat without settling Bessos would invite contempt, and a rising of all the tribes; they would lose their victories and their glory. They still cared for that. They had proved themselves masters of the barbarians, and valued it.

From them he would come back to me. As for sex, he was glad of it, having been a long time without; but he could have gone longer, there were things he needed more. He liked to return to his other kingdom, and find love there; to know there is one beauty of the sun, another of the moon. He liked, I found, to be sent to sleep with the long tales of the bazaar, about princes seeking the phoenix's egg, riding to towers of adamant ringed with flame, or coming in disguise to enchantress queens. He liked to hear about the court at Susa. At the rites of the getting-up, the bedtime and the bath, he could not keep from laughing; but to the etiquette of audience he listened carefully.

He trusted me. Without trust he could not live. He trusted Hephaistion, too; not all to my misfortune, as now it proved.

Philotas' power had proved too great for one man. The King now divided it between two commanders: Black Kleitos, a veteran officer he had known since childhood, and Hephaistion.

If trust were everything, Hephaistion would have had it all. But the army had its politics; already the parties were dividing. Hephaistion was known as the King's right hand in everything new he was doing. He had learned our forms of courtesy; was as tall and handsome as the Iranian lords, who admired and liked him; he was Persianized, said the men of the old school. Stocky bearded Kleitos, getting the same rank, was a surety they were not left out in the cold.

What all this meant to me, was that often Hephaistion would go out on his own campaigns.

He had proved himself well in war. He was a lord's son of Macedon, and required honor, even if it took him from Alexander's side. I wished him all of it he could go and find, I who required one thing alone.

About harvest-time, we came to the Valley of the Benefactors. To find this place delighted Alexander. I had told him the story, left out like so much else from his book on Kyros, of how these people had brought his army food when they were starving in the wasteland; how he found them so virtuous, he freed them from tribute and let them rule themselves. It was he who named them. Their breed endured; slow, shy, quiet, broad-faced people, friendly even to soldiers, since none had troubled them since Kyros' day. Their valley was wide and fertile, sheltered from the lancing northern winds. Alexander rested his men there, bought their produce at the best rate they'd ever had, and promised a hanging out of hand to whoever harmed them.

He himself, who could never be idle anywhere, used to ride out hunting. Often he let me come along. Xenophon, he told me, said hunting was the image of war. It was for Alexander. Dangerous rocky ground, long runs, a fierce quarry, lion or boar for choice were what he looked for. I remembered Darius in the royal park, shooting at driven game. After Alexander's hunts, I felt nearly dead. But I'd have died sooner than own it; before long I hardened, and came back just hungry for my supper.

While we were camped there, a Persian lord gave a great birthday feast, and asked the King to honor it. He came to bed hardly drunk at all. Persians drink deep on their birthdays; but they hold it better than Macedonians. He was always careful among them, and watched his friends as well.

As I was settling him into bed, he said suddenly, "Bagoas, I've never asked you, in all this time. When is *your* birthday?"

He could not make out why I was crying. I knelt by the bed with my head in my arms, and he patted me as if I had been Peritas. When at last I got it out, he leaned over me, and I heard him swallow a sob. It was absurd; I ought to have been ashamed.

He would not await the day, since, he said, I had missed so many, but next morning gave me a beautiful Arab horse and a Thracian groom; and two days later, when the jeweler had finished it, a ring with his portrait carved on chalcedony. I shall be buried with it. I have put that in my will; along with a curse, to keep the embalmers from stealing it.

Not only were the Benefactors a kindly people; they had worked out just laws among themselves. He greatly took to them. Before he went, he offered to double their lands; but they asked just for the tail-end of their valley, the one bit they did not own; it would round them off, which was all they wanted. He sacrificed to Apollo in their honor.

Bessos was lingering in the north, with no sign of raising a powerful army. While his generals and satraps were subduing the country round about, Alexander moved eastward, towards the outer skirts of Great Kaukasos; taking his time, making his mark; here and there founding a city.

I remember, the first I saw him make was upon this march; one of his Alexandrias. The site was a rocky hill, easy to defend; on a good trading route, as the Phoenician merchants told him; with a clean year-round spring for the public fountain, and good land next it. It commanded a pass for caravans, which had harbored robbers. Every day he was scrambling over it, with his architect Aristoboulos; marking out the places for the garrison fort, the market, the gates and their defenses, making sure the streets were well laid out, with channels to drain off the muck. He thought nothing like that beneath him. He had slaves to quarry and hew the stone, and free craftsmen to do the building. It amazed me, how quickly it all went up.

Then he had to people it. He would put in veteran soldiers, not all of them Macedonians; there were Greeks, and free Thracians, mostly with women and children they'd gathered on campaign; they were glad to be given a farm, though some grew homesick later. Some of the craftsmen settled there. They might not be very good, or they would have followed the lords and generals; but here they would not have rivals, and they brought something into the wilds, of Susa or of Greece. For all these people Alexander left laws, never too foreign to their ways or the gods they followed. He had a feeling for what they would understand, and see the justice of.

He put his whole soul into this city, all day till suppertime. He did not get drunk—there was good water up there, so nobody sat down thirsty—but after the day's work, he liked to sit talking with the cup before him. Founding a city always stirred his mind. He knew it would make his name live among men to come; it made him think of his deeds. At these times he liked to go back over them, some said too much. Well, he did them. Does anyone deny it?

He would talk to me sometimes, after, the wine still in him, his spirit still burning it up. I asked him once if he had known, before he crossed to Asia, he would be Great King. He said, "Not at first. It was my father's war; I wanted to win it faster than he'd have done. I was appointed general of the Greeks, to free the Greek Asian cities. When I'd done it, I disbanded their troops; and after that it was my own." He paused; then, seeing that I understood, said, "Yes, it was after Issos. When he ran away, leaving me his chariot and his royal mantle and all his arms; his friends' bodies who had died for him; his wife—even his mother!— then I said to myself, If that's the Great King, I think I could do better."

I answered, "Kyros himself did less."

I know the envious Greeks have written that I flattered him. They lie! Nothing was too good for him, or half good enough. I felt the impatience of his greatness, reined and curbed by the dullness of lesser men. They say I took his gifts. Of course I did. The best of them was to see his delight in giving. I took them in love; not, like some who claimed to be his friends, in covetousness soured with envy. If he had been a hunted man with a king's price on his head, I would have gone barefoot with him through Asia, starved with him, lain down in the market stews to buy him bread. All that is as true as the face of God. So had I no right to make him happy in his victories? There was never a word that did not come from my heart.

When the city was founded, he sacrificed, and dedicated it to Herakles and Apollo. I did a dance for Apollo, who, Alexander thought, must be the same as Mithra. I hope both gods were satisfied; I danced only for him.

I was someone now at court. I had my two horses, my baggage mules, my tent, and some pretty things in it. As for power, I wanted that over one heart alone. Sometimes I remembered Susa, and all those who had tried to buy my interest with the King. Only unwarned newcomers tried it now. The Persians said, "Bagoas the eunuch is Alexander's dog. He will feed from no other hand; let him be." Macedonians said, "Watch out for the Persian boy; he tells Alexander everything."

Sometimes, when I waited on him in his bedchamber, he would say I ought not to do servants' work; but that was just his courtesy. He knew I lived for it. He would have been sorry, too, to do without me.

We marched eastward towards the heights, over high passes, with only the tracks the herdsmen made, following the poor grass with the seasons. In the rock-clefts grew little bright dry flowers like jewelers' work. Great skies spread to dark horizons. I lived in the hour, I was young, the world unrolled for me; as it did too for Alexander, riding always ahead, to see the next turn of the road.

Of an evening he asked me to teach him Persian. (I had taught him some, but not of a kind which would do at all for an audience.) The sounds are hard for westerners; I never pretended he spoke it well. If he was cross from disappointment, it was over in a moment. He knew I saved him from making a fool of himself in public, which his pride could not endure.

"See what mistakes I still make in my Greek, Iskander." I had put in a slip or two, to cheer him up.

"How are the lessons? Has he tried you with reading yet?"

"He only has two books, and they're both too hard for me. He asked Kallisthenes to lend us one; but he said the sacred treasures of Greek thought were not to be smudged by barbarian fingers."

"He said that to your face?"

I had not reckoned on his being quite so angry. This Kallisthenes was so grand he must not be called a clerk, but a philosopher; and he was writing Alexander's chronicle. I thought my lord deserved someone who would better understand him; but one must go carefully with great men.

He said, "I am tiring of this fellow. He's too full of himself by far. I only took him on to please Aristotle, who's his uncle. But he has all the old man's set notions, whose errors I had to find out for myself, and none of his wisdom for which I honor him. He taught me what the soul should reach after. He taught me the skill of healing, which I've saved some lives with; and how to

look at the natural world, which has enriched my life.
I still send him specimens, wild beasts' skins, plants,
anything that will travel . . . What's this blue flower?"
He took it from behind my ear. "I never saw that before." It was nearly dead, but he pressed it carefully.

"Kallisthenes has none of that," he said. "Does he
often insult you?"

"Oh, no, Sikander—"

"Al-ex-ander."

"Al'skander, lord of my heart. No, mostly he
doesn't see me."

"Never mind if he thinks himself too good for you. I
see signs that it will be my turn next."

"Oh, no, my lord. He says it's he who will make
your fame." I had heard that myself, and thought he
had better know.

His eyes turned pale. It was like watching a storm
from shelter. "Will he so? I have left a few marks about
the world, to be remembered by." He started pacing the
tent; if he'd had a tail he would have lashed it. "He
wrote of me first with such fulsomeness that the truth
stank like a lie. I was a boy, I didn't see the harm it did
me. I rounded Cape Climax with god-sent luck and
good guessing, but he had the waves bow before me.
And heavenly ichor flowing in my veins! Men enough
have seen the color of my blood, and so I told him. And
none of it from his heart."

The sun was setting into a great horizon, the moor-
lands darkening in waves, the watch-fires budding
flame. He stood to look, putting away his anger, till the
slave kindled the lamps. "So you've never read the
Iliad?"

"What is that, Iskander?"

"Wait." He went into his sleeping-place, and came
back with something gleaming in his hands. "If
Kallisthenes is above bringing you Homer, I am not."

He put on the table what he held; a casket of pure
white silver, gold lions on its sides, the lid inlaid with
malachite and lapis, carved into leaves and birds.
There could not be two in the world. I gazed in silence.

He looked at my face. "You have seen this before."

"Yes, my lord." It had stood by Darius' bed, under the golden vine.

"I might have thought. Does it hurt you? I'll put it away."

"Truly no, my lord."

He put it down again. "Tell me, what did he keep in it?"

"Sweets, my lord." Sometimes, when he was pleased with me, he used to put one in my mouth.

"See what I use it for." He lifted the lid; I caught the scent of cloves and cinnamon. It choked me with the past; for a moment I closed my eyes.

He brought out a book, even more worn and mended than the Kyros one. "I've had this since I was thirteen. It's old Greek, you know, but I'll make it a little easier. Too much would spoil the sound."

He read a few lines, and asked if I had understood.

"He says he is going to sing about the anger of Achilles, which brought terrible trouble to the Greeks. Men died in great number and the dogs ate them. And the kites, also. But he says it fulfilled the will of Zeus. And it began when Achilles quarreled with—with some lord who was powerful."

"That's very good. It's a crying shame you've had no books yet. I'll see to that." He put the book away, and said, "Shall I tell you the story?"

I came and sat by his knees and laid my arm across them. If it kept me here, I did not care what kind of tale he told me. Or so I thought.

He told just the tale of Achilles; leaving out what I would not understand. So, after he had quarreled with his Great King and refused allegiance, we came quite soon to Patroklos, who had been his friend from boyhood; who took his part and comforted his exile, and died of taking his place in battle; and how Achilles avenged him, though it had been foretold his own death must follow. And after the duel, while he slept in weariness, Patroklos' ghost came to him in his dream, to require his funeral rites and recall their love.

He did not tell it with art, like the taletellers in the market, but as if he had been there and remembered everything. At last I knew where my rival stood, grafted into his spirit, deeper than any memories of the flesh. There could be only one Patroklos. What was I, to that, but the flower one sticks behind one's ear and throws away dead at sunset? In silence I wept, and scarcely knew that my eyes were shedding tears, as well as my heart.

He lifted my face, and, smiling, wiped my eyes with his hand. "Never mind. I cried too, the first time I read it. I remember it well."

I said, "I am sorry that they died."

"They too. They loved their lives. But they died unfearing. It was living without fear, that made their lives worth loving. Or so I think."

He rose and picked up the casket. "Look, you have been nearer it than you knew." He moved the pillow of his bed, and opened the bed-box. A dagger was there too, honed like a razor. Every second king of Macedon had been murdered, and sometimes two kings running.

Long after this, I caught my name as I approached his tent, and heard him say, "I tell you, when he heard the story of Achilles, his eyes were full of tears. And that fool Kallisthenes talks of Persians as if they were Scythian savages. The boy has more poetry in one finger than that pedant has in his head."

At autumn's end, we reached the southern spurs of Parapamisos. They were already shawled with snow. Far to the east, they join Great Kaukasos, the wall of India, which goes on higher and higher, further than anyone knows.

On a spur of their foothills, sheltered from the north wind, he made the year's third Alexandria. By the time of the first snowfall, it was ready for us to winter in. After some of the king-houses, like ogres' lairs in legends, it was good to smell clean new wood and wallpaint. The governor's house had a porch with columns, in the Greek style; and a plinth in front, for a statue of Alexander.

It was the first he'd had done since I had been with him; but he, of course, was as used to taking his clothes off for this as for his bath. The sculptor made drawings from all around him, seven or eight studies, while he gazed into the distance making himself look beautiful. Then he was measured all over with the calipers. Then he could go off hunting, and need not come back till the face was being finished. It was very fine, both calm and eager; true to his soul, though of course it left out the sword-cut.

One evening he said to me, "The new thing has begun. Today I sent orders back to the cities, to make me a new army. This one I'm growing from seed. I'm having thirty thousand Persian boys taught Greek, and trained to use Macedonian weapons. Does that please you?"

"Oh, yes, Al'skander. It would please Kyros too. When will they be ready?"

"Not for five years. They must start young before their minds get fixed. By then, I should hope, the Macedonians will be ready as well."

I said I was sure of it. I was still of an age when five years seem half a lifetime.

The air grew soft in the foothills, delicate flowers pierced the melting snow. Alexander decided he could cross straight over the mountains after Bessos.

I don't suppose even the local shepherds warned him. They only went up with the summer snow-line. He guessed the high passes would be hard, and went ahead with the soldiers; but I doubt he knew what they were in for. It was terrible even for us, who had their beaten way to follow, with more supplies. I, who love mountains, felt that these hated men. My breath labored, my feet and my fingers burned as I beat the blood back into them. People huddled at night for warmth, and I had many offers, all with fair promises to treat me like a brother; meaning that when it was too late I would not dare to tell. I slept with Peritas, whom Alexander had left in my care; he was a big dog, and there was a good deal of warmth in him.

Our hardships were nothing to the army's. With no fuel on the barren rock to cook their meat, they had to thaw it on their bodies, or were lucky to have it warm from some horse that had fallen dead. Their bread ran out, and they fed on the herbs the cattle eat. Many would have slept into the snow-death, but for Alexander struggling on foot along the column, finding them where they lay, dragging them to their feet, and putting his own life into them.

We overtook them at the border fort of Drapsaka, on the other side. There was food to be had; below, Bessos had wasted the land to starve us out.

I found him in a lodging of old roughhewn stone. His face was all burned with cold, and it seemed that only his sinews held his frame together. I was still not used to a king who starved with his men. "That's nothing," he said. "That soon comes back. But I can't yet believe I'll ever be warm again."

He smiled at me, and I said, "You will tonight."

I did not have the chance to warm him long. Once his men were rested and fed, before a full month was up he was off down into Baktria.

I was now of fighting age. Eunuchs before, among them my wicked namesake, had borne arms. I kept thinking how Hephaistion had been with him on the mountains; keeping him warm, maybe. So the night before he went, I asked him to take me with him; saying my father had been a warrior, and if I could not fight at his side, I would be ashamed to live.

He answered gently, "Dear Bagoas, I know you'd fight at my side. And you would die there, and quickly too. If your father had lived to train you, you would have made a soldier up to my best. But it takes time; and the gods willed otherwise. I need you now where you are." He was proud, but not for himself alone; he had feeling for the pride in others.

Just then Peritas, who had been terribly spoiled from sleeping in my blankets, tried to creep by stealth on the bed, though he weighed it down and took up all the room. So it passed in laughter; but I was left behind again, for Alexander went ahead with the troops, expecting Bessos.

He was not there; nothing was there but snow, still thick on those high uplands. He had not found much to ravage; in winter the people there bury everything, their vines, their fruit trees, even themselves, for they live in sunk beehive huts which the snows cover all over; they hole up with all their stores, and come out in spring. Soldiers clemmed with hunger would see a wisp of smoke rise through the snow, and dig down to the food. They said the stench was dreadful, and everything tasted of it; but they did not care.

With the spring, we followers caught up; the court and the royal city took form and traveled onward. Then news came that Bessos had crossed the Oxos, east. He was on the run, with a poor following. Nabarzanes had been the first, but not the last, to know he had looked for a king in vain.

Alexander marched slowly through Baktria. No one resisted him; so wherever he went, he had to take surrenders, and get his new lands administered. For Bessos, once again there was no hurry.

The next we heard of him, was from one of his own lords, a man well on in years, who came on a weary horse, his clothes and his beard full of dust, to give himself up to Alexander. This, he explained through me (I was interpreting, for the sake of secrecy), was what he had urged Bessos himself to do, when he held a war council. Gobares, who now addressed us, had cited Nabarzanes as an example, which was surely rather simple of him. Bessos had taken drink, and at the mere sound of the name made for Gobares with drawn sword. He had scrambled off, faintly pursued since he was well respected; and here he was, ready in return for pardon to tell us all he knew.

Bessos' Baktrian levies had now deserted him. He had never led them, only fallen back before Alexander. They had gone home to their tribal villages; their surrenders could be trusted. All Bessos had left were those who had escorted Darius to his death; a remnant who shared his flight not from love, but fear.

He was making for Sogdiana, in which his last hopes lay. The Sogdians, Gobares said, do not like strangers, and would be loath ("At first," he said polite-

ly) to accept a foreign king. So Bessos would cross the
Oxos, and burn his boats behind him.

"We will cross that river when we come to it,"
Alexander said.

Meantime, he had to choose a satrap for Baktria. I
awaited this with sadness; the second Persian satrap of
Areia had rebelled, and he had had to send them a
Macedonian. Nonetheless, he gave Baktria to a Persian.
It was Artabazos. He had lately told Alexander he was
getting too old to march about any longer; the moun-
tain-crossing had left him rather tired. I have heard he
ruled his province with prudence, vigor and justice; retired from office at ninety-eight; and died at a hundred
and two, from riding a horse that was too fresh for him.

So now it was time to go north and cross the Oxos.
We'd been near it in the mountains; it takes its rise
there; but for leagues it dashes through rocky gorges,
where only a bird could go. The hills open out on the
threshold of the desert; after that, it slows and widens
on into the furthest wilderness, where at last, they say,
it sinks into the sand. We were to cross at the first
ferry, where the road goes on to Marakanda.

We went down pleasant warm slopes with vines and
fruit trees. The holy Zoroaster, who taught us to worship God through fire, was born in those parts.
Alexander heard this with reverence. He was sure the
Wise God was the same as Zeus; and had seen him in
fire, he said, since childhood.

We had enough of fire before long. When we came
down into the Oxos valley, the desert wind from the
north was blowing. It comes in midsummer, and living
things all dread it; it's as if the air had been passed
through a furnace, and blown at you with bellows. We
had to wrap our heads in cloth, to save them from the
burning, pelting sand; four days of it, before we
reached the river.

It's a great sight when you get to it; it was at least
for me, and all who had not seen the Nile. The desert
deer on the far side looked small as mice. The engineers stared at it in dismay. They had brought wagons

full of timber with them; but what with its great width, its depth and its shifting sands, they could sink no piles. To bridge it was impossible.

Meantime the ferrymen met us with lifted hands, begging for bread. They had owned flat boats, with yoke-poles for a pair of horses, which were trained to swim them across. Bessos had burned the boats on the far side, gone off with the horses, and paid nothing. Alexander offered gold for anything they had left.

At this the poorest brought out their hidden wealth; rafts of hide blown up with air, to float with the current. That was all there was; and that, Alexander said, was what we would cross on, making the rest ourselves.

There were hides in plenty; the tents were made of them. The tentmakers studied the native craft, and oversaw the work. The insides were stuffed with straw and dry rushes, to keep them buoyant longer.

I've seldom been so scared as when the moment came to push off. My two servants shared the raft with me; we swam the horses and the mules. When the current tugged, the beasts began to flounder, the Thracian moaned out prayers to some Thracian god, and I saw further on a bigger raft overturning, I thought I was bound for another River. But this was the first time I had shared Alexander's danger, I who had talked of fighting at his side; and I could see my body-servant, a Persian from Hyrkania, watching me, in search of encouragement, or maybe to see how a eunuch would behave. I will see you dead, I said to myself, before you shall make a tale of me. So I said people crossed like this every day; and showed them that the men from the capsized raft were still holding on to it. The horses got the feel of the river and pulled us on; and we reached the shore hardly even wet.

Even the women and children crossed like this. They had to; it was leagues through the desert to the nearest ford. I saw one raft with a woman on it hiding her eyes, and five children screaming with pleasure.

All in all it took five days. The rafts had to be dried and made into tents again. Alexander gave timber to the ferrymen, to make good their boats.

Horses had died in the march through the burning wind. I thought I would lose Lion; his chestnut coat was staring and his head was down. Oryx, the one I'd had from Alexander, was a fine strong beast and bore up better; but Lion was dear to me. He just lived through it; so did old Oxhead, nursed all the way, often with the King's own hands. He was twenty-seven now, but built to last.

Soon we could take it easier. The last two Baktrian lords to follow Bessos sent word that Alexander could have him with their leave. The village where he was lodging would give him up.

We were now in Sogdiana. This was the first-fruit of it. They have no laws worth speaking of, but the law of blood-feud; even guest-friendship does not count for much there. If you are a little luckier than Bessos was, you may be safe under their roof; further along the road, if you have anything worth taking, they will ambush you and cut your throat. Their chief sports are robbery and tribal wars.

Alexander disdained to pick up Bessos himself. He sent Ptolemy, with a good-sized force since he had to deal with traitors. He did not need it; the Baktrian lords had made off; the mud-walled fort let him in for a small reward. Bessos was found in a peasant hut, with only a couple of slaves.

If Darius' spirit looked on, he must have felt well avenged. The lords who gave Bessos up had learned from his own example; they wanted him out of the way, to keep Alexander quiet while they prepared for war.

Ptolemy had had his orders. When Alexander came up with the army, Bessos was standing by the road, stripped naked, his hands tied up to a wooden yoke. At Susa I had seen this done to a famous bandit before they put him to death. I had never told the King of it; he must have asked Oxathres what was proper.

Nabarzanes had been right; there was nothing of a king in Bessos. I'm told that when Alexander asked him why he had dragged his lord and kinsman to so base a death, he pleaded he had been only one of many about Darius, who had agreed on it to win Alexander's favor. He did not say why in that case he had assumed the Mitra. The Susa bandit had put on a better face. Alexander ordered him flogged, and kept in chains for his trial.

The traitor lords, who had hoped to keep Alexander quiet, should have known better. He marched straight on into Sogdiana. It was part of the empire, and he meant to keep it so.

The Sogdians live in a land of great dun hills and fearsome gorges. Along every pass there are forts full of armed robbers; the caravans have to hire small armies of guards, to get safely through. Sogdians are handsome; hawk-faced, with the carriage of princes. Nearly all Sogdiana is made of rock; but they build on it in mud, like swallows, because the men think craftsmanship beneath them. They can ride horses where you'd not think a goat could go; but they don't regard their oaths if it does not suit them. Alexander was quite taken with them, till he found this out.

All seemed to go well at first. The city of Marakanda surrendered; so did the line of forts down by the Jaxartes River. Beyond that are the grasslands, and the Scythians against whom the forts had all been built.

Alexander now summoned the chiefs to his camp, to meet him in council. He wanted to tell them he would rule them justly, and ask what their laws were now. The chiefs, who knew just what they would do if they were Alexander, never doubted he wanted them there to take their heads. So of a sudden the river-forts were stormed by yelling Sogdians, and their garrisons butchered; Marakanda was under siege; a forage party from our own camp was cut to pieces.

He dealt first with that. The raiders had a roost on a mountain crag. The signal-smoke went up from the tall cresset by his tent; the troops fell in; he set out for the place, and took it.

They brought him back on a litter, and laid him on his bed. The surgeon was waiting in the tent, and so was I. An arrow had smashed into his shin, and split the bone. He had made them tug out the barb in the field, and sat his horse till the fort was taken.

When we soaked the stuck bandages off, splinters of bone came with them. More chips were sticking through the skin; the doctor had to work them out.

He lay looking upward, still as his own statue; not even his mouth moved. Yet he had wept for the maimed slaves of Persepolis; for old Oxhead; for Achilles and Patroklos, dead a thousand years; for my forgotten birthdays.

The surgeon dressed the wound, told him to keep quiet, and left. I stood one side of the bed with the bowl of bloodstained water; on the other stood Hephaistion, waiting for me to go.

I turned, with my dirty bowl. Alexander looked round, and said—the first sound he'd made—"You were good with the bandages. Light-handed."

He kept quiet for about seven days; that is, he went by litter, instead of riding, downhill towards the Jaxartes river-forts. First he was carried by an infantry detail, till the cavalry complained of being denied the privilege. He then let them take turns. At night, when I changed the bandages, he confided to me that the cavalry, being unused to marching, were inclined to jolt.

I rode ahead with the army, this time; he was used to my doing the dressings. The doctor smelled at the wound each day; if the bone-marrow putrefies, it mostly kills a man. Bad as it looked, it scabbed over clean at last; but it left a dent on his shin, which he had for life.

Before long he rid himself of the litter by getting on a horse. By the time we reached the river grasslands, he had started to walk.

Doriskos had once said to me, "He's said to be over-trusting; but if you break your pledge, God help you." I was now to see the truth of it.

He took five forts in two days; at three of the assaults he was there himself. All had sworn him loyalty, and all had helped murder their garrisons. If

Sogdians thought that to honor his given word a man must be soft in the head, they were now shown reasons they would understand.

So now I saw what I'd not seen all through Baktria; the herd of wailing women and children, driven into camp like cattle, the spoils of war. All the men were dead.

It happens everywhere. Greeks do it to other Greeks. My own father must have done it, in Ochos' wars; though Ochos would never have given such people a first chance. However, this was the first time for me.

Alexander did not mean to drag along this horde of women; he was planning a new city here, and they would give the settlers wives. But meantime, soldiers short of a bedmate-slave were getting their pick. A woman would be led away; sometimes young children with wet dirty faces would stumble after, sobbing or screaming, to be cared for when her new master gave her time. Some of the young girls could scarcely walk; their blood-stained skirts showed why. I thought of my three sisters, whom I'd long managed to forget.

This was the slag of the fire, when the bright flame had passed. He knew what he was born to do; the god had told him. All those who helped, he would receive like kindred. If he was checked, he did whatever was necessary; then went on his way, his eyes on the fire he followed.

The sixth city was Kyropolis, the strongest; not built by the river, of mud-brick, but on a hill-flank, of stone. It had been founded by Kyros, no less; so Alexander had sent the siege-train on with Krateros, and ordered the assault saved up for him. He pitched his tent quite near the siege-lines, to save a walk, so I saw some of the battle. A great splinter of bone had just worked up through the scab on his shin. He made me tug it out, saying the doctor talked too much, and I was neater-handed. The blood was clean. "I've good-healing flesh," he said.

The engines were set up; two siege-towers, clad with hide; a row of catapults, like huge bows laid on their sides, shooting bolts of bronze; and the battering-rams under their housings. In honor of Kyros, he put on his best armor; his silver-burnished helmet with white wings, and his famous belt from Rhodes. Because of the heat, he refused his jeweled gorget. I heard the men cheering, as he rode up to the lines. The assault started soon after.

I felt the rams' thumping through the ground. Great clouds of dust flew up, but no breach appeared. For some time I saw the silver helmet, till it passed round a turn of the wall. Not so long after, yells and shouts rose up to heaven. The great gates of the fort were open; our men poured in. The walls were covered with soldiers fighting hand to hand; I could not think why, if the Sogdians had opened the gates. They had not; Alexander had done it.

The fort had its water from a river led under the walls. It was low in summer; its channel would let in a stooping man. He led his party in himself, wounded leg and all. The Sogdians, concerned about the rams, had not watched the gates well. He fought his way through, and pulled back the bolts.

Next day he came back to camp. A knot of officers was with him, asking how he felt. He shook his head fretfully, beckoned me up, and whispered, "Bring me a tablet and stylos."

That came of leaving off his gorget. In the street-fighting, a stone had hit his throat and bruised his voice-box. Only a little harder, it would have broken the bone and choked him. But he had stayed there in command, whispering his orders, till the citadel surrendered.

He could bear pain like no one I ever saw; but not being able to talk drove him nearly mad. He would not rest quiet alone with me, who at a finger-sign would have known just what he wanted; when his voice improved he strained it and it went again. He could not endure to hear the talk at supper and stay mute; he ate in his tent, with a clerk to read to him from one of the books he sent to Greece for. They had started building his new city, so he was soon riding out there, finding of course a hundred things to say. Even so, his voice was strengthening. He had a wonderful body for healing, in spite of all he did to it.

A new sight now appeared across the river; the house-wagons of Scythians, their horse-herds and black felt tents. They had heard of the Sogdian rising, and swept down like ravens to share the spoil. When they saw us, they withdrew and we thought them gone. Next day they were back; the men alone. They rode their small hairy mounts in whirling circles, waving their tufted spears and yelling. They tried to shoot across, but their arrows would not carry. Alexander, curious to know what they were saying with so much noise, sent for Pharneuches, the chief interpreter. The gist, it seemed, was, if Alexander wanted to know the difference between Baktrians and Scythians, let him cross the river.

We had this several days running, louder each time, and with gestures that needed no interpreter. Alexander was getting angry.

He had the generals in his tent, huddled around him so that he need not raise his voice. A whisper is catching; they all sounded like conspirators. I heard nothing till he said aloud, "Of course I'm fit! I can do anything but shout." "Stop trying, then," said Hephaistion, "or you'll be dumb as a fish again." As they argued their voices rose. Alexander said that if the Scythians got off now without a lesson, they would be sacking his new city the moment we had marched on. Since he meant to give the lesson himself, the others were much against it.

He supped in his tent, as sulky as Achilles. Hephaistion sat with him awhile, but left because he would keep talking. So I went back again; shook my head at all but sign language, and in due course put him to bed. When he caught my hand to keep me, I must own it was not without my contrivance. The bow had been strung too long. We did very well without words; and, after, I told him old tales till he went to sleep.

I knew, however, he would not change his mind about the Scythians. He thought that if he did not go himself, they would suppose he was scared.

The Jaxartes is much smaller than the Oxos. He had the rafts started next day, and sent for the seer Aristander, who always took the omens for him. Aristander came back to say the entrails of the sacrifice were unlucky. (We Persians have cleanlier ways of consulting heaven.) I heard it said the generals had been at him; but I would not have cared for going to that old blue-eyed Magus, and asking him to bend a prophecy. Besides, he was right.

Next day more Scythians than ever came. They were now an army. Alexander had the sacrifice done again; got another No; and asked if the danger was to his men, or him. To him, Aristander said; which to my mind proves his honesty. Of course Alexander prepared at once to cross.

It was with anguish of heart that I watched him being armed. Before two squires, I could not shame him with unseemly grief. I returned his parting smile; smiles are well-omened.

The Scythians were waiting to cut up the troops as they struggled ashore. They had reckoned without the catapults. Their bolts did not fall short like Scythian arrows. After one rider was shot clean through his shield and armor, they kept their distance. Alexander sent the archers and slingers on ahead, to hold them while the phalanx and the cavalry got over. Not that he waited for that himself; he was on the first raft to cross.

From across the river, the battle looked neat as a dance: the Scythians wheeling around the Macedonian square; then the smashing charge of the cavalry, left and right, closing till they ran off inland. In a great cloud of dust (it was a very hot day) they went streaming over the plain, Alexander's horse after them. Then there was no more to be seen, but the rafts paddling over to bring in our dead and wounded, not many; and the kites screaming over Scythian corpses.

For three days we waited their returning dust. Then they came. Messengers paddled ahead. Once more the doctor was waiting, and so was I.

When the squires set down the litter, I took one look and thought, He is dead, he is dead. A great wail

rose up in me, and I had almost uttered it, when I saw
his eyelids move.

He was pale as a corpse; his fair skin had no color
when the bright blood had left it. His eyes were sunk
as if into a skull. He stank, he who liked to be as clean
as a bride's linen. I saw that though too weak to speak
he had his senses, and that it shamed him. I took a step
to his side.

"It's a flux, sir," said a squire to the doctor. "I was to
tell you, he drank bad water. It was very hot, and he
drank from a standing pool. He's been purging blood.
He's very weak."

"I can see that for myself," the doctor said.
Alexander's lids fluttered. They were speaking across
him as if he were half gone; which he was, but it made
him angry. No one noticed but I.

The doctor gave him the draught he had prepared
when the message reached him, and said to the
squires, "He must be put to bed." They approached
the litter. His eyes opened, and turned to me. I guessed
what it was. He was lying in his dirt, he had been too
weak to help himself. He did not want them uncover-
ing him; it hurt his pride.

I said to the doctor, "The King wants me to see to
him. I can do everything." Faint as a breath he said,
"Yes." So they left him to me.

I sent the slaves for bowls and hot water and piles
of linen. I got rid of the bloodstained muck, and
washed him clean while he still lay on the litter, and
had the mess carried away. His backside was raw; he
had pressed on after the enemy long after he got sick,
getting off his horse to purge, and back again, till he
fainted. I rubbed him with oil, and lifted him into
the clean bed—he'd lost so much weight, it was easy
—and put a pad of clean linen under him, though he
had emptied himself by now. As I laid my hand on
his brow, feeling the fever, he whispered, "Ah, that's
good."

Soon after, Hephaistion, having got his men across
the river, came in to see him. I went, of course. It was
like tearing my own flesh. I said to myself, If he dies,

with that man and not with me, then truly I will kill him. Let him stay now, I will not grudge my lord his wish in his last hour. Yet he was glad of me.

However, he slept on right through the night on the doctor's opiate; wanted to get up next day, and did so the day after. Two days from that, he received an embassy from the Scythians.

Their King sent to say he was sorry Alexander had been vexed. The men who'd vexed him were lawless robbers, in whom the King had no part at all. Alexander sent back a civil answer. The Scythians, it seemed, had had their lesson, even though an unfinished one.

One evening, as I combed his hair, trying to ease out the tangles without hurting, I said, "You were nearly dead. Did you know it?"

"Oh, yes. I thought the god had more left for me to do; but one must be ready." He touched my hand; his thanks had been wordless, but none the worse for that. "One must live as if it would be forever, and as if one might die each moment. Always both at once."

I answered, "That is the life of the gods, who only seem to die, like the sun at his setting. But do not ride too fast across the sky, and leave us all in darkness."

"One thing," he said, "I've taken to heart from this. The water in the plains is poison. Do as I mean to do, and stick to wine."

16

SPITAMENES, ONE of Bessos' two traitor lords, was besieging Marakanda. When the first force Alexander sent had been cut up, he went himself. At the news of his approach, Spitamenes decamped, and escaped into the northern deserts. By the time the country was in order, winter was coming on. Alexander, to keep an eye upon the Scythians, wintered at Zariaspa-upon-Oxos.

It's a fair-sized town, north of the ferry; the river flows very wide there. They have channeled its waters round about, and made green things grow; beyond is the desert. In summer it must be a furnace. They've more cockroaches there than anywhere else I've known; most houses keep tame snakes to eat them.

Alexander had the governor's house, of real fired brick; a grandeur where mud-brick was the rule. He had good hangings and fine furniture to make it kingly. It pleased me to see him grow less careless of his state. He'd had a beautiful new robe made, purple bordered with white, the Great King's colors, for state occasions. For the first time, here, he put on the Mitra.

I took it on myself to say all Persians would expect it when he tried Bessos. To try pretenders, a king must look like a king.

"You are right," he said. "It's a Persian matter, and must be done the Persian way. I am taking advice upon the precedents." He was pacing about the room, and frowning to himself. "It will mean a Persian sentence. The nose and ears, beforehand. Oxathres will be content with nothing less."

"Of course, my lord. He is Darius' brother." I did not say, "Why else should he accept a foreign king?" He could see that for himself.

"It is not our custom," he said, still pacing. "But I shall do it."

He never said anything uncertain. Yet I feared he might change his mind, which would do him great harm among the Persians. My father had suffered only for keeping faith; why should this traitor escape? Besides, I owed another debt.

"Did I ever tell you, Al'skander, what Darius said before they dragged him away? 'I no longer have power to punish traitors, but I know who will.' Bessos thought he was speaking of our gods; but he said it was you he meant."

He paused in his stride. "Darius said that of me?"

"I myself heard it." I thought of the horse and the silver mirror and the necklaces. Even I had my obligations.

He paced a while longer; then said, "Yes, it must be by your custom."

I said to myself, Be at peace, poor King, whatever the River of Ordeal has left of you to attain Paradise. Forgive me that I love your enemy. I have made what amends I can.

From the street I saw Bessos led to his trial. He had shrunk, since that night I had recalled; his face was heavy as clay. He knew his fate. When first they took him, he had seen Oxathres riding by Alexander.

If he had surrendered along with Nabarzanes, he would have been spared. Oxathres came in later, and would never have got Alexander to break his given word. He kept it to Nabarzanes, whatever Oxathres wished. I often wondered why Bessos ever put on the Mitra. For love of his people? If he had led them well, they would not have forsaken him. I suppose Nabarzanes first tempted him to kingship; but he had not Nabarzanes' suppleness. He could not wield it, yet could not let it go.

He was tried in Greek and Persian. The council agreed. He would lose his nose and ear-tips; then be sent to Ekbatana, where he had betrayed his lord; and be crucified, before an assembly of Medes and Persians. It was all in order, and according to custom.

I did not join the crowd that saw him go. His wounds would be fresh; I was afraid he'd look like my father.

In due time, word came from Ekbatana that he was dead. He had been nearly three days dying. Oxathres had ridden all the way there, to watch. When the body was taken down, he had it cut up small, and strewn on the mountain for the wolves.

The court stayed at Zariaspa most of that winter.

From all over the empire, people made the journey, and Alexander entertained them with splendor, as he had learned to do. One evening before supper, he had put on his Persian robe, and I was draping the folds for him.

"Bagoas," he said, "before now I've heard from you what the Persian lords daren't tell me. How much do they feel it, that they make the prostration, and the Macedonians not?"

I'd known he would ask me in the end.

"My lord, they do feel it. That I know."

"How?" He turned round to look at me. "Is it spoken of?"

"Not before me, Al-ex-ander." I still had to go slowly, to get it right. "No one would do that. But you in your courtesy keep your eyes on the man you are greeting, while I can look where I choose."

"You mean they look angry, to see a Persian do it?"

This was less easy than I'd hoped. "Not quite that, Al'skander. We're brought up to do it before the King."

"You have said enough. It's when a Macedonian doesn't?"

I settled the pleats of his sash, and did not answer.

He moved restlessly, before I had it right. "I know. Why put you to the pain of telling me? But from you I always get the truth."

Well, sometimes he got what I knew would make him happy. But one thing he never got from me, was a lie that could do him harm.

That night at supper he kept his eyes well open. I think he saw a good deal, while they were fresh. This did not last all through supper, at Zariaspa.

He had said truly, that Oxos water is poison to those not bred to it. I suppose that among the natives, those whom it kills die young, before they have time to beget offspring.

No vines grow there; the wine comes in from Baktria. Baktrian wine is strong; but they reckon three parts of it to one of water, to kill the Oxos flux.

It was winter, and almost cool; no Persian host would have dreamed of offering wine before the sweets. But the Macedonians drank from the start, as always. Persian guests would sip for manners; the Macedonians drank deep as ever.

To be drunk now and then, what harm does it do a man? But give him strong wine night after night, and it takes a hold. If only my lord had wintered in the hills by a pure spring, he would have been spared much grief.

Not that he was really drunk every night. It would depend on how long he sat at table. He did not toss it down like the others, not at first. He would sit with the cup before him, and talk, and drink, and talk again. Cup for cup, he drank no more than before. But Baktrian wine should be mixed with two-thirds of water. Each cup he drank was twice the strength he was used to.

Sometimes after a late night he would sleep as late as noon; but for serious business he was always up, brisk and ready. He remembered even my birthday. At supper he called for a toast to me; commended my faithful service; gave me the gold cup he had drunk from, and then a kiss. The veteran Macedonians looked much scandalized; whether because I was a Persian, or a eunuch, or because he was not ashamed of me, I can't say. I suppose all three.

He did not forget the prostration. It was on his mind. "It will have to be changed," he said to me. "And not with the Persians, it's far too old. If Kyros began it as they say, he must have had a good reason."

"I think, Al'skander, to reconcile the peoples. It was the Median custom, before."

"You see! Fealty from both, but neither people to lord it over the other. I tell you, Bagoas, when I see some Persian whose title goes back before Kyros' time, and who has it written all over him, bowing to the ground; and a Macedonian my father made out of nothing, whose own father wore sheepskins, looking down as if at a dog, I could knock his head off his shoulders."

"Don't do that, Al'skander," I said, only half laughing.

The hall downstairs was quite big, but the upstairs rooms were cramped; he turned about like a leopard in a cage. "In Macedon, the lords have learned so lately to obey the King at all, they think that's doing a favor. At home, in my father's day, he would put on fine manners for foreign guests; but when I was a boy, supper was like a feast of peasants . . . I know how your people feel. I draw my blood from Achilles and from Hektor, and before that from Herakles; we won't speak of anything else." He was on his way to bed; not very late, but still the wine had exalted him. I was afraid his bath would get cold.

"It's simple with the soldiers. They may think I have my fancies when off the field; but on it, we know each other. No, it's the men of rank, those I must entertain with Persians . . . You see, Bagoas, at home they think prostration is for gods."

There was something in his voice, which told me he was not just instructing me. I knew him. I felt the current of his mind. Why not? I thought. Even the soldiers feel it, though they don't know what they feel.

"Al-ex-ander," I said, letting him know I was weighing every word, "everyone knows that the oracle at Siwah cannot lie."

He looked at me with his deep grey eyes, saying nothing. Then he pulled his sash undone. I disrobed him. He gave me another look. I saw, as he meant, the catapult wound on his shoulder; the sword-slash across his thigh; the purple dent on his shin. Truly, those wounds had run blood, not ichor. He was remembering, too, the time he had drunk bad water.

His eyes rested on mine, half smiling; yet with something in them that neither I, nor anyone would reach. Perhaps the oracle had, at Siwah.

I touched his shoulder, and kissed the catapult wound. "The god is present," I said. "The mortal flesh is his servant and his sacrifice. Remember us who love you, and do not let the god take it all away."

He smiled and held out his arms. That night the mortal flesh received its due. Though gentle, it was as if he mocked himself. And yet the other presence stood waiting, ready to claim him back again.

Next day he was shut up with Hephaistion a long time alone, and the old sickness bit my heart. Then there was much coming and going among the King's best friends; then messengers went out, summoning guests to a great supper of fifty couches.

On the day, he said to me. "Bagoas, you know what I've had in mind? Tonight we shall try for it. Put on your best clothes and look after my Persian guests. They know what to expect, Hephaistion has been seeing them. Just make them feel valued; you with your court manners can do that best."

So, I thought, after all he needs me too. I put on my best suit, which by now was a very good one, crusted

with gold embroidery on a dark-blue ground; and
came to dress Alexander. He wore his grand Persian
robe, but a low coronet, not the Mitra. He was
dressed for Macedonians too.

If only, I thought, they would keep the wine till
dessert-time. This will be delicate business.

The hall was splendidly garnished for the feast. I
greeted the Persian lords, in the proper way, and led
each to his supper couch, with compliments where they
would be acceptable, on someone's famous ancestor,
breed of horses, and so on; then I went to attend on
Alexander. The meal went smoothly, in spite of all
the wine; the dishes were carried out. Everyone made
ready to toast the King. Someone got up; as people
thought, to propose it.

This one was certainly sober. He was Anaxarchos, a
tame philosopher who followed the court about; the
kind Greeks call a sophist. As for wisdom, he and
Kallisthenes had not half enough between them to make
one good philosopher. When Anaxarchos rose, Kallisthenes looked as angry as an old wife with a young
concubine, at not having been asked to speak first.

Certainly, he'd not have done it so well. Anaxarchos
had a well-trained voice, and must have conned his
speech by heart with every grace-note. He led off
about some Greek gods who'd started life as mortals,
and been deified for their glorious deeds. Herakles was
one, the other Dionysos. Not a bad choice; though I
doubt he had what I had in mind, which was that
Alexander had some of both in him: the urge to great
labors beyond reach of all other men; and the beauty,
the dreams, the ecstasy . . . did I think, then, the madness also? I expect not; I can't remember.

These divine beings, said Anaxarchos, while on
earth, had shared the trials and sorrows of the human
lot. If only men had seen their godhead earlier!

Then he rehearsed the deeds of Alexander. The
plain truth, though known already, struck home even
to me. Anaxarchos said that when it pleased the gods
—let them keep the day long from us!—to call the
King to themselves, no one would doubt that divine

honors would at once be paid him. Why not offer them
now, to comfort him through his labors; why wait till
he was dead? We should all take pride in being the
first to give them, and to symbolize it with the ritual
of prostration.

All through the speech, I had been watching faces.
Not the Persians'; they had been prepared, and were all
grave attention. The King's friends, in the secret too,
were doubly busy, applauding and watching others; all
but Hephaistion, who for most of the time was watching Alexander, as grave as the Persians, and more at-
tentive still.

I moved from behind his couch, to where I too
could see him. I perceived that Anaxarchos' words,
planned for use, had become a pleasure. Though nowhere near drunk, he had of course been drinking; the
shine had come into his eyes. He fixed them on the
distance, as he did for the sculptors' drawings. It would
be beneath him, to look about and see how people
took it.

Most of the Macedonians took it, at first, as a long-
winded way of proposing the toast to the King. Cheerful with wine, even the veterans applauded. They were
too slow to see where it was leading till the very end,
when they looked as if hit suddenly on the head.
Luckily I'd been trained against ill-timed laughter.

Others had seen it coming. The time-servers, each
eager to be first in the race to please, could hardly wait
for the speech to finish. Most of the younger men
looked startled at first; but, for them, King Philip's day
was when they were boys made to do as their fathers
told them. Now was the time. Since Alexander led
them, there had always been something new. He
might be going rather far, but they would go along
with him.

The older men were dead set against it. Oh, yes! I
thought. You are angry that he wants a god's saluta-
tion. If you guessed he was trying to level you with us,
how much angrier you'd be! Sulk, then; you're too few
to matter.

Anaxarchos sat down. King's friends and Persians

applauded; no one else. A kind of stir began. The Persians with gestures of respect stood by their couches, preparing to come forward. The King's friends got up too, saying, "Come, let's begin." The sycophants, twitching with eagerness, waited upon precedent. Slowly, the other Macedonians began to rise.

Suddenly Kallisthenes stood up, and in his harsh voice said loudly, "Anaxarchos!" All movement ceased in the hall.

I'd been watching him. I knew the King had been cooler to him, since what I'd said. Resenting Anaxarchos' speech, he had hung on every word, and caught the drift quite early. I had guessed he would be up to something.

If both these were philosophers, they were pretty different. Anaxarchos' robe had embroidered borders; his silvery beard was combed like silk. Kallisthenes', which was black, was thin and straggly; his plainness of dress, since Alexander paid him well, was boorish for a state dinner. He stood well forward, to give us all a view of him. Alexander, who when his friends hailed him had returned from his distance to give them a welcoming smile, now turned, and fixed his eyes on him.

"Anaxarchos," he led off, as if they were debating in some public street instead of in the Presence, "I think Alexander not unworthy of any honor proper to mortal man. But bounds have been set between honors human and divine." Of these latter, he gave a catalogue which I thought would go on forever. But such honors, he said, when offered to a man, insult the gods, as royal honors offered a common man would insult the King. At this I heard, all about the hall, low murmurs of assent. Like the storyteller who has caught his audience, Kallisthenes started to bloom. He reminded Anaxarchos he was advising a leader of the Greeks, not some Kambyses or Xerxes. The contempt with which he named these Persian kings was much to the Macedonians' taste. I saw the Persians exchanging looks. Hiding my shame and anger, I went among those of the highest rank, and made a business of handing sweets. Since I started going to theaters, I've seen how an actor can spoil another's big scene. In my youth and ignorance, I had some such notion myself.

Not put out at all by me—what does a barbarian eunuch matter, serving a barbarian lord?—Kallisthenes went on to say that Kyros, who had founded the prostration, had been humbled by the Scythians who were poor but free. I would only have said myself that he failed to catch them; but more to the purpose, it was aimed at Alexander. Everyone must have known how he honored Kyros; certainly Kallisthenes did, who had once had his trust. He gave it a clever turn by adding that Darius, who had received prostration, had been routed by Alexander who had done without. This licensed the Macedonians to applaud.

They did; and it was clear they were not applauding the hollow compliment. He had brought over all the doubtful ones, who would have complied if let alone. And what he'd caught them with was not respect for the gods, but contempt for Persians. When he named Darius, I didn't miss the spiteful glance that he aimed at me.

One must be just to the dead, who cannot answer. Maybe one should credit him with courage; maybe just with a blind complacency. The applause of the Macedonians was a brief delight; Alexander's anger would last.

Not that he made a show of it. After this slap in the face, he was concerned to keep his dignity. In his clear skin the flush showed like a flag; but his face was calm. He beckoned up Chares, spoke to him quietly, and sent him on a round of the Macedonian couches, to tell the guests that if the prostration was against their minds, they need think no more of it.

The Persians had not followed Kallisthenes' speech, since the interpreter had not thought fit to translate it. His voice when he named the kings must have told its tale. They saw Chares going round, and those who had risen settling back on their couches. There was a silence. The Persian lords looked at each other. Then, without a word exchanged among them, the lord of highest rank came forward, crossing the hall with the carriage such people have learned in childhood. He saluted the King, and went down in the prostration.

In order of precedence, all the others followed.

It was beautiful. No man of breeding could fail to see it was an act of pride. If these uncouth westerners thought themselves above the ancient courtesies, it was beneath a gentleman's notice. Most of all, though, it was done for Alexander, who had tried to offer them honor. As the foremost faced him, before making his bow, I saw their eyes meet in perfect understanding.

To each, as he made reverence, the King bent graciously; the Macedonians muttered on their couches; till near the end of the line came an oldish man, rather stout, and stiff in the knees, and got down as best he could. Everyone knows that one should not stick out one's backside; all the others had sunk with grace; but any fool could see the poor man's infirmities. I heard a snigger somewhere among the Macedonians; then one, a Companion called Leonnatos, gave a loud guffaw. The Persian, just then struggling to rise with a little dignity, was so shocked that he stumbled. I was behind him waiting my turn; I stepped forward, and helped him to his feet.

Concerned with this, I did not see Alexander till he was halfway there. His robe swinging about him, he came down the room as if his feet did not touch the ground, light as the lion running up for its spring. I don't think Leonnatos saw him coming at all. Without a word, eyes fixed in a wide pale stare, he grasped Leonnatos' hair with one hand, his girdle with the other, and heaved him off his couch onto the floor.

They say that in battle Alexander seldom fought in anger; that mostly he was light of heart, and often smiling. Yet now I thought, How many men's last sight has that face been? Leonnatos, floundering upon the floor as angry as a bear, took one look and paled. Even I felt a little cold breath chill my neck. I looked at his sash, to see if he had a weapon.

But he just stood quietly, hands on hips, no more than a little short of breath, and said, "Well, Leonnatos, now you're down there too. And if you think you look graceful, I wish you could see yourself." Then he walked back to his supper couch, and spoke coolly to those about him.

A boor has been punished, I thought. No one was hurt. It was foolish to be afraid.

The party broke up early. Alexander came to bed sober. The rage of the lion had gone; he was restless, pacing the room, spoke of the insult to my people, and then burst out, "Why has Kallisthenes turned against me? How did I ever harm him? He's had gifts, consequence, anything he asked for. If he is a friend, give me an honest enemy. Some of those have done me good; he came to do me harm. He hates me, I saw it. Why?"

I thought, Perhaps he really believes divine honors should be kept for gods. But I remembered the Greeks had given them to men before. Besides, there had been something else. When you are used to courts, you get the feel of it. He was a Greek; I could not tell who might be behind him. I just said, therefore, that it seemed he wanted to form himself a faction.

"Yes; but why, that's the thing." With some trouble, I got him to disrobe and take his bath. I had no comfort to offer which suited his mood just then, and I feared he would not sleep.

It was not only his being robbed of his rights, which he'd known for his due while they were being proclaimed. They had failed in love to him. He felt it too deeply to speak of it. Wounded in the moment of exaltation, he was bleeding still. Yet he had contained his anger; it was the insult to the Persian, had loosed it off. He had ended in thought for us, as he had begun.

I had put him to bed, and was seeking some word of comfort, when a voice at the door said, "Alexander?" His face lightened as he said "Come in." It was Hephaistion. I knew he'd have come in without knocking, but for knowing I would be there.

I left them together. On the day of the oracle, I

thought, he was there waiting, he was told it all. Now he is here to do what I cannot. And once more I wished him dead.

As I tossed on my pillow, I said to myself at last, Do I grudge my lord the herb that will heal him, because another gathers it? No, let him be healed. Then I cried my eyes out, and fell asleep.

At the winter's end, Alexander moved his court to Marakanda. We were free of the poisonous Oxos and the hot plains. Now, I thought, all will be well.

It was like a paradise, after Zariaspa; a green river valley in mountain foothills; tall white peaks above; the water like liquid ice, and clean as crystal. Already in the many gardens almond trees were budding, and small delicate lilies sprang from the melting snows.

Though in Sogdiana, it is not wild like the backlands; it is a crossroads for caravans; you meet people from everywhere. The bazaars sell horse-collars set with turquoise, and daggers with wrought-gold sheaths. One can buy Chin silk there. I got enough for a coat, sky-colored, embroidered with flowers and flying serpents. The dealer said it had been a year upon the road. Alexander said Chin must be in India, there was nothing further than that but the Encircling Ocean. His eyes glowed, as always when he spoke of distant marvels.

The citadel perches westward above the city; a good-sized fort, with a real Palace in it. Here Alexander did a great deal of business, which had not reached him in the north. He entertained many Persians of high rank; and, as I saw, felt no better about the prostration.

Leonnatos had been forgiven. He was a man, Alexander said to me, who was a good fellow in the main, and would have had more sense when sober. I answered that things would be better here, where we had mountain water.

I spoke only in hope for him. He had drunk strong wine too long beside the Oxos; he had the taste for it. Here he tempered it more, maybe half and half; but that's not enough for Baktrian wine.

If the talk was good, he would talk more than he drank, and even if he sat up late, all would be well. But at other times, he just set out to drink. All Macedonians do it; by the Oxos, they'd come to do it more than before.

Never in his life was he drunk upon campaign. His victories had been too brilliant; his enemies left him time for it. He never did it when he had to be up early, even if it was only to hunt. Sometimes he'd be two or three days at that, camping in the hills; it cleared his blood, and he'd come back fresh as a boy.

He was getting into our ways. At first, I think, to show us we were not slighted; but then he took to them. Why not? He was far above the land he came from, as I'd seen from the very first. He was civilized in his soul; we showed him the outward forms of it. Often now, at audiences, he wore the Mitra. It suited him, being shaped so like a helmet. He had taken into his Household several Palace chamberlains, who hired Persian cooks; Persian guests now got real Persian banquets, and though he always ate sparingly, he did not dislike the food. Feeling him move into harmony with our ways, many who had served him first from fear now did it willingly. His rule was both strong and just; it was a good while since Persia had had both together.

The Macedonians, though, were feeling wronged. They were the victors, and they thought it their due to have it shown. Alexander knew it. He was not a man to give up easily. He tried once more to bring them round to the prostration. This time, he started at the top.

No big feast this time, no Persian guests. Friends he could trust, and Macedonians of importance, who he hoped could be persuaded. He told me the plan, which I thought would persuade anyone. He had the gift of grace.

I was not to be there. He did not tell me why; he knew well enough he need not. Still, resolved to witness it, I slipped into the service anteroom, and posted myself where I could see in through the door. Chares said nothing. Within reason, I could do pretty much what I chose.

All the King's close friends were there; Hephaistion, Ptolemy, Perdikkas, Peukestas; Leonnatos too, grateful for forgiveness and ready to make amends. As for the others, they knew what was to happen. When Alexander had told me one was Kallisthenes, I looked my doubts; but he said Hephaistion had talked to him and he'd agreed. "And if he breaks his word, I don't intend to notice it. This won't be like last time. It will do him no good with the others."

It was quite a small party, fewer than twenty couches. I saw Alexander kept down the drinking. As long as he lived, there was no pleasure he was a slave to, when he put his will to it. He talked, and drank, and talked.

No one could talk like him, when he chose and had someone to talk to; with a Greek, plays and sculpture and poetry and painting, or the planning of cities; a Persian he would get to talk of his forebears, his horses, the customs of his province, or of our gods. Some of his Macedonian friends had gone to school with him, under Aristotle of whom he still thought so much. With most of the others, who had never read a book and could just about scrawl on wax, it had to be their concerns, their kills at the hunt, their love affairs, or war; which, if the wine had gone briskly round, would soon lead to Alexander's victories. I suppose it's true that he sometimes talked too much of them. But any artist likes to relive the best of his art.

Tonight, with well-tempered wine, it all went smoothly. He had the right word for everyone. I heard him ask Kallisthenes if he'd lately heard from Aristotle, which for some reason he answered awkwardly, though he covered it just after. Alexander told the others that as well as his own rarities, he'd ordered the satraps of all the provinces to send anything strange their huntsmen found to the philosopher; and had given him a vast sum, eight hundred talents, to house his collection. "Someday," he said, "I must go and look at it."

The tables were cleared; no Persian sweets that night. There was an air of expectation. Chares himself, whose office was far above serving anything, bore in a beautiful gold loving-cup. It was Persian work, I daresay from Persepolis. This he put in Alexander's hand.

Alexander drank; then held it towards Hephaistion, whose couch was on his right. Hephaistion drank, handed the cup to Chares, rose from his place; and, standing before Alexander, performed the prostration. He did it perfectly. He must have practiced for days.

I drew well back out of sight. This I was not meant to witness, and I knew it was fair enough. I had been bowing to the ground most of my life; so had my forebears back to Kyros' day. It was just a ceremony, we did not feel it humbled us. For a Macedonian with his pride, it was something else. He had a right, this first time at least, not to have Persians there; and especially not me.

He got to his feet as gracefully as he'd gone down (I'd seen nothing better at Susa) and stepped towards Alexander, who took him by the shoulders and kissed him. Their eyes met smiling. Hephaistion got back on his couch; Chares took the cup to Ptolemy. So it went on; each saluted the King, and was then embraced by the friend. This time, I thought, not even Kallisthenes can be sour.

His turn came near the end. As if by chance, Hephaistion spoke just then to Alexander, who turned his head to answer. Neither watched Kallisthenes.

I watched him. I wanted to decide how much respect he deserved. I soon knew. He did not refuse; he drank from the cup, then walked straight up to Alexander, who he thought had noticed nothing, and presented himself to be kissed. I could picture him later, boasting of having been the only one not to bow. One could scarcely believe a grown man could be such a fool.

Hephaistion's eyes signaled to Alexander. He said

nothing. Kallisthenes had had the chance to keep his word. Having broken it, he would be despised by the most powerful men at court; also resented, for setting himself above them.

It was well reasoned; except that they resented him too much. As Alexander turned to him, one called out, "Don't kiss him, Alexander! He never bowed."

The King, having been told, now had to know. He raised his brows at Kallisthenes and turned his face away.

Enough, one would suppose. But Kallisthenes could never let either well or ill alone. He shrugged, and walked off saying, "Oh, well! So I go short of a kiss."

I suppose if you can keep cool in the front line of battle, to do it with a Kallisthenes is nothing much. Alexander just beckoned Chares, who overtook Kallisthenes as he reached his couch. Looking—if you can believe it—quite surprised at his dismissal, he got up again and went out. I greatly approved the King's not deigning to address the man himself. Yes, I thought, he is learning.

The last few bowed, as if nothing had happened; the party went on like any friendly meeting. But it was spoiled. Kallisthenes had cut an ignoble figure; but he would make his own story out of it, and encourage others. I thought it over.

The King came to bed early. I listened to all he told me (remember, I'd not been there), then I said, "I would do much more for a kiss than that. I will kill this man for you. It is time. Just give me the word."

"Would you do that?" He sounded wondering, more than eager.

"Of course I would. Each time you go to war, your friends are killing your enemies. I've never killed anyone for your sake. Let me do it now."

He said, "Thank you, Bagoas. But it's not the same."

"No one will know. The caravans bring subtle drugs from as far as India. I will disguise myself, when I buy. I know what to do."

He took my face in his hand, and said, "Have you done this for Darius?"

I did not reply, No, this is just the plan I made for killing your lover. "No, Al'skander, I have only killed one man, and that was in a fight, to keep his hands off me. But I will do this for you; and I promise you, I won't botch it."

He let my face go, quite gently. "When I said it was not the same as war, I meant not for me."

I should have known. He never killed by stealth in all his life. He had made no secret of Parmenion's death, once it was done. There must have been a score of men who could have rid him of Kallisthenes and made it look like nature; but what he would not own to, he would not do. And yet, if he had let me serve him as I wished, it would have saved much trouble, and some lives.

After this, he said no more about the prostration. With the Macedonians, he just went back to the old drinking-parties. Yet there was a change. Those who had agreed to bow, from love, or loyalty, or understanding of his reasons, or simple flattery, resented those who'd refused as putting contempt upon them, and slighting the King. Men had now shown where they stood; where there had been uncertain talk, there was bitterness and faction.

Yet when we Persians bowed down, they thought nothing of it. Oh, no; we were just displaying our abject natures. It was only blasphemy when done by Macedonians.

There had been bad blood already between the parties. The force that had first failed to relieve Marakanda had been cut up with some disgrace. They had dislodged the besiegers; but had then gone on to attack a large force of Scythians, and were cornered in a river gorge. Pharneuches the interpreter had been attached to them as envoy; the Macedonian officers, of horse and foot, tried to get him to assume command. No one will know the whole truth; the few survivors put the blame here or there; but it seems the cavalry commander made off with his men across the river, leaving the foot in the lurch; they scrambled after as best they could; all were stranded on a river island, sitting targets for Scythian arrows; and not many swam away to tell the tale. Marakanda had been besieged again; Alexander himself relieved it, rode on to find what was left of the wretched corpses, and gave them burial.

He was furious at having good men butchered by such bungling, and said he could spare Pharneuches less than such commanders. His own friends said these were men who'd not thought Persians good enough to eat with; only to shoulder their commands when things looked bad. There was rancor about it; it made them more quarrelsome in their drink. Each night I was uneasy lest some brawl should start in the King's presence. That was the worst I feared. God spared me from foreknowledge.

It was about this time that Kleitos the Black (so called from his bushy beard) called at the Palace, asking for the King.

It was he who shared with Hephaistion command of the Companions. If you wanted a type of the old school, you found it here. Alexander always humored him, because he had known him from the cradle; he was the younger brother of the royal nurse, a Macedonian lady of good blood. He would be about a dozen years the King's elder. He had fought under King Philip; he liked the old ways, free-spoken among one's peers, despising foreigners. I suppose he could remember Alexander at a year old, tumbling about and puddling on the floor. It takes a small mind to remember such things against a great one; but I don't think, even by trying, Kleitos could have made his mind much larger. He was a very good soldier, and brave in battle. Every time he saw Persians, you could see him wishing he had killed more than he had.

It was a pity, therefore, that when he came for audience, Oxathres was the bodyguard on duty.

I was passing at the time; and hearing him addressed as if he were a servant, paused to look. Though he disdained to notice the rudeness, he did not mean to leave his post and run on errands; he beckoned me up, and said in Persian, "Bagoas, tell the King that Kleitos the Commander asks to see him."

I replied in the same tongue, and made him a little bow; it seemed proper not to forget what our stations had been at Susa. As I turned to go, I saw Kleitos' face. Two barbarians between him and the King, and one a eunuch! Till then it had all felt natural; now I saw what he thought of being announced by a Persian whore.

The King saw him quite soon. His business was nothing out of the way; I overheard it. It was only when he came out, and saw Oxathres at his post, that his brow grew black again.

Soon after this, the King gave a big supper, mostly for Macedonians; a few Greeks were there, envoys from western Asia; and some Persians of importance in the province, whose offices he had confirmed.

His Household had grown to match his state; it was fit to look after guests of any rank. I could have gone shopping in the bazaar, or watched some dancing, or lit my lamp and read my Greek book, which had become a pleasure. Yet I went to the supper hall. No strange chance took me there. I was just anxious, and hung about. Such warnings may come from God; or from feeling the weather, as shepherds can. If God had sent me, he would have found me some good to do.

It was strange from the very outset. Alexander had done sacrifice that day to the Dioskouroi, the twin heroes of the Greeks. Kleitos had planned a sacrifice of his own; to Dionysos, for this was the god's day in Macedon, and he was always one for the old customs. He had poured libations on his two sheep, ready to slit their throats, when he heard the horn blow for supper; so he left everything, and went. But the silly sheep, taking their butcher for their shepherd, trotted along behind him, and followed him through the door. Everyone shouted with laughter; till it came out that these were beasts of sacrifice, dedicated already. The King was disturbed for Kleitos at this omen, and sent to the priests to sacrifice for his safety. Kleitos thanked him for the kind thought; and the wine came in.

I could see at once this was a night when Alexander

felt like drinking. He set the pace; the wine-pourers
went round so fast, everyone was tipsy by the time the
meat was finished; when, at a decent Persian feast, the
wine would first have come in. I am angry to this day,
when ignorant Greeks say we taught the King deep
drinking. Would to God he had learned from us.

There was a dessert that day; beautiful apples from
Hyrkania. They had traveled well; Alexander had
made me take one before supper, in case there should
be none left. He was never too busy to think of things
like that.

It seems the nature of man to turn God's good gifts
to evil. At all events, it was over these apples that the
talk began to go wrong.

The fruits of all earth's four quarters, said Alexander's friends, now reached him from his own lands. The
Dioskouroi had been deified for conquests far less than
his.

Now I know, from my later reading, that this is
true. The furthest the Twins ever got from their Spar-
tan home, was up to the Euxine in Jason's ship; about
as far as from Macedon to western Asia, and just the
coast at that. Their other wars had been these little
Greek ones, cattle-raids, or getting their sister back from
some king of Athens; all quite near home. Good
fighters, no doubt; but I never heard they could fight
hand to hand while leading men in battle. One of them
was just a boxer. So Alexander did not deny he had
excelled them. Why should he? Yet I felt the breath of
trouble.

Sure enough, the old school started to raise the cry
of blasphemy. At this, the King's friends shouted out
(by now everyone was shouting) that the Twins had
been born as mortal as Alexander; and it was only spite
and envy, putting on a false face of reverence, which
had denied him the same honors, better earned.

As if touched by the ferment in the hall, I had
helped myself well to wine out in the anteroom, and
was in a haze; as one is in dreams where disasters
loom, but one knows one can do nothing. Sober,
though, I would have known the same.

"Alexander this, Alexander that, all Alexander!" Kleitos' thick raucous voice topped all the rest. It brought me from the anteroom to the entry. He was standing up in his place. "Did he conquer Asia by himself? Did *we* do nothing?"

Hephaistion yelled back (he was as drunk as all the rest), "He led us! You didn't get as far in Philip's day."

This was just the thing to double Kleitos' anger. "Philip!" he cried. "Philip started with nothing! How did he find us? Tribes feuding, rival kings, enemies all round. He was struck down before he was fifty, and where was he then? Master of Greece; master of Thrace to the Hellespont; all ready to march to Asia. But for your father," he shouted straight at Alexander, "where would you be today? Without the army he left you ready? You'd be still beating off the Illyrians."

I was shocked to the soul that such insolence was being heard by Persians. Whatever was done to the man later, he must be got out at once. I looked for the King to order it.

"What!" he shouted back. "In seven years? Are you off your head?"

Never had I known him so to forget himself. It was like some trooper in a tavern. And the drunk fools of Macedonians did nothing but shout along with him.

"—still fighting the Illyrians!" bawled Kleitos over again.

Alexander, who was used to being heard above a battle when he raised his voice, lifted it now. "My father was fighting the Illyrians half his life. And they never kept quiet till I was old enough to do it for him. I was sixteen. I drove them leagues beyond their borders, and there they've stayed. And where were you? Lying up with him in Thrace, after the Triballians had thrashed you."

I had long heard that Queen Olympias had been a turbulent jealous woman, who taught him to hate his father. This, I thought, is what comes of their having no one trained to manage their harems properly. I could have sunk with shame.

A roar of dispute broke out. The disaster by the river was fought over once again. During the hubbub Alexander came to himself a little. He called for silence, in a voice that at once procured it; I could see him fighting for calm. Presently he said to the Greek guests sitting near, "You must feel like demigods among wild beasts, in all this uproar."

Kleitos had heard. Purple with drink and fury, he yelled, "Beasts now are we? And fools and bunglers. It'll be cowards next. That's what it will be! It's we, the men your father made us, *we* put you where you are. And now his blood's not good enough for you, you son of Ammon."

Alexander was dead silent a moment; then he said, not loudly but in a voice so deadly it cut through everything, *"Get out."*

"Yes, I'll go," Kleitos said. "Why not?" Suddenly his arm shot out and pointed straight at me. "Yes, when we have to beg barbarians like that creature there for leave to see you, better stay away. It's the dead, it's Parmenion and his sons, it's the dead are lucky."

Without a word, Alexander reached to his dish of apples, drew back his arm, and hurled one at Kleitos' head. It hit dead on; I heard the clunk on his skull.

Hephaistion had jumped to his feet, and was standing by Alexander. I heard him say to Ptolemy, "Get him outside. For the gods' love, get him *out.*"

Ptolemy went over to Kleitos, who was still rubbing his head, took his arm and eased him towards the outer doors. Kleitos turned and waved the other arm. "And this right hand," he said, "saved you at Granikos, when you'd turned your back on Spithridates' spear."

Alexander, who had on his half-Persian robe, grabbed at his sash, as if he hoped to find a sword there. Perhaps in Macedon they'd even worn them at supper. "Turned my back?" he shouted. *"Liar!* Wait for me, don't run away."

Now he had good cause for anger. Though Spithridates' kin had always claimed, at Susa, that he'd fought hand to hand with Alexander, they had done him too much honor; he had tried to take him from behind when he was fighting someone else. Kleitos, coming up in turn behind Spithridates, had cut through his lifted arm. Any soldier in reach, I suppose, would have done the same; and Kleitos boasted of it so often that everyone was sick of it. To say Alexander had turned his back was truly infamous. He was already on his feet, when Hephaistion and Perdikkas gripped him round the middle. He struggled and cursed them, trying to break their hold, while Ptolemy shoved Kleitos towards the doors, still uttering some defiance swamped by the noise. Hephaistion said, "We're all drunk. You'd be sorry after."

Alexander, wrenching at their arms with both hands, said between his teeth, "This is how Darius finished. Is it fetters next?"

He is possessed, I thought; it is more than the wine; he must be saved. I ran up to the struggling knot of men. "Al'skander, it wasn't like this with Darius. These are your friends, they don't wish you harm." He half turned and said "What?" Hephaistion said, "Go away now, Bagoas"; speaking impatiently, as if to a child who comes up for notice when everyone is busy.

Ptolemy had walked Kleitos down the hall to the doors, and pulled them open. He nearly got away and back into the hall, but Ptolemy kept his hold. They vanished and the doors closed after them. Hephaistion said, "He's gone. It's over. Don't make a show of yourself, come and sit down." They let him go.

He threw back his head, and gave a great shout in Macedonian. A score of soldiers came running in from outside. He had called the guard.

"Trumpeter!" he said. The man stepped forward. It was his duty always to be in reach of the King. "Sound the general alarm!"

The man lifted his trumpet, slowly, putting off the moment to blow. It would have turned the whole army out. From his post he must have heard nearly everything. Hephaistion, standing behind the King, signed to him "No."

"Sound the alarm," said Alexander. "Are you deaf? *Sound the alarm.*"

Again the man raised the trumpet. He saw the eyes of five or six generals fixed on him, saying no. He lowered it. Alexander hit him in the face.

Hephaistion said, "Alexander."

For a moment he paused, as if coming to himself. He said to the gaping guards, "Go to your posts." The trumpeter, after one anxious glance, went too.

Early in the uproar, the Persians had excused themselves to the chamberlains, and slipped away. The ever-curious Greeks had stayed much longer, then scrambled off without ceremony when the guard was called. It was now all Macedonians; their own quarrel forgotten, gaping like rustics beside whose village brawl a thunderbolt has fallen.

I thought, They should have let me near him. When I named Darius, he heard. Never mind what they do, I am going back to him.

But he was free now, striding down the hall, calling for Kleitos as if he were still in hearing. "All this faction in the camp, it's all your doing!"

He passed by me unseeing; and I let him pass. How could I take hold of him before all these people? There had been enough unseemliness. That he should have wished to chastise this insolent boor with his own hands, instead of sending for the executioners! What king could think of such a thing, except one reared in Macedon? It was bad enough, without his Persian boy dragging at his arm in sight of everyone. I expect it made no difference, I daresay he would have shaken me off unheard. Yet even now, I wake in the night and think of it.

Just then, Ptolemy slipped in quietly through the service door, and said to the others, "I walked him right outside the citadel. He'll cool off there."

The King was still calling "Kleitos!" but I felt better. He's just fighting drunk, I thought. It will soon go off. I'll get him into a good hot bath, and let him talk. Then he'll sleep till noon, and wake up himself again.

"Kleitos, where are you?" As he reached the outer doors, they burst wide open. There stood Kleitos, red-faced and panting. He must have started back as soon as Ptolemy left him.

"Here's Kleitos!" he shouted. "Here I am!"

He had come back for the last word. He had thought of it too late, and would not forgo it. It was his fate to be given his wish.

From the doors behind him, a guard came in doubtfully, like a muddy dog. He'd had no orders to keep out the Commander; but he did not like it. He stood spear in hand, looking dutiful and ready. Alexander, checked in his stride, stared unbelievingly.

"Listen, Alexander. *Alas, ill rule in Hellas . . .*"

Even Macedonians know their Euripides. I daresay everyone there but I could have completed these famous lines. The gist of them is that the soldiers do it all, the general gets it all. I don't know if he meant to go on.

A flash of white went to the door, and turned again. There was a bellow like a slaughtered bull's. Kleitos clutched with both hands at the spear stuck in his breast; fell and writhed grunting; jerked in the death-spasm. His mouth and eyes fixed, wide open.

It had been so quick, for a moment I thought the guard had done it. The spear was his.

It was the silence, all down the hall, that told me.

Alexander stood over the body, staring down. Presently he said, "Kleitos." The corpse glared back at him. He took the spear by the haft. When it would not come, I saw him begin the soldier's movement to brace his foot on the body; then flinch and pull again. It jerked out, a handspan deep in blood, splashing his clean white robe. Slowly he turned it round, the butt on the ground, the point towards him.

Ptolemy has always maintained that it meant nothing. I only know I cried, "No, my lord!" and got it away. I took him unready, as he had done the guard. Someone reached over and carried it out of sight. Alexander sank on his knees by the body, and felt over its breast; then covered his face with his bloody hands.

"Oh God," he said slowly, "God, God, God, God."

"Come away, Alexander," Hephaistion said. "You can't stay here."

Ptolemy and Perdikkas helped lift him to his feet. At first he resisted, still searching the corpse for life. Then he went with them, like a sleepwalker. His face looked dreadful, all striped with blood. The Macedonians, in little knots, stared as he passed. I hurried after him.

At the door of his room, the squire on guard started forward saying, "Is the King wounded?" Ptolemy said, "No. He doesn't need you." Once inside, he flung himself on the bed, face downward, just as he was in his bloodstained robe.

I saw Hephaistion looking about, and guessed what for. I wetted a sponge and gave it him. He pulled at Alexander's hands and washed them, then turned his head this way and that, and cleaned his face.

Alexander pushed at him and said, "What are you doing?"

"Getting the blood off you."

"You will never do that." He was sobered. He knew it all.

"Murder," he said. He spoke the word over and over, like a foreign one he was trying to learn. He sat up. His face was nowhere near clean. I would have sent for warm water, gone quietly about it, and done it properly. "Go, all of you," he said. "I want nothing. Leave me alone."

They exchanged looks and moved towards the door. I waited, to care for him when his first grief was spent.

Hephaistion said, "Come out, Bagoas, he wants no one here."

"I am no one," I answered. "Just let me put him to bed."

I took a step to him; but he said "Everyone go"; so then I went. If Hephaistion had kept his mouth shut, I'd just have sat quietly in a corner till he forgot about me. Then, later in the night, when the life runs low, he would not have been sorry to have me tend him. They had not laid a blanket on him, and the nights were cold.

They went off talking together. In my room I kept my clothes on, in case he called for me. I could well understand, having brought on himself so dreadful an indignity, he could bear no one near him now. My heart shed blood for him. We had taught him enough in Persia, for him to feel his shame. When Nabarzanes had asked Darius to step down for Bessos, and the King had drawn his scimitar, it had been almost a courtly scene, compared with this.

I pictured such a person as Kleitos insulting the King at Susa, if such a thing could be conceived. The King would just have motioned with a finger, and the proper people would have appeared. The man would have been taken off with a hand over his mouth; the feast would have proceeded decently; and next day, when the King had rested, he would have decreed the mode of death. It would all have been quiet and seemly. The King would have done no more than move his hand.

I thought, He knows he forgot his dignity, before Greeks and even Persians. He feels he has lost esteem. He needs comfort, and to be reminded of his greatness. In all this trouble, he should not be alone.

In the dead hour after midnight, I went along to his room. The squire on duty looked at me, unmoving. From outside, I could hear the high whining of Peritas, and knew he must be weeping. "Let me in," I said. "The King needs attendance."

"Not your kind. Nor any other. Those are my orders."

This youth, Hermolaos, had never left me in doubt of what he thought about eunuchs. He was glad to keep me out; he had no feeling for his master's grief. The sound tore at my heart; I could hear it now. "You have no right," I said. "You know I have the entry." He just held his spear across the doorway. Gladly I would have sunk a knife in him. I went back to bed, and did not close my eyes till morning.

When the night guard had changed, between dawn and sunrise, I went again. It was Metron now. I said, "The King will expect me. Nothing at all has been done for him since before supper." He was sensible, and let me in.

He lay face upward, staring at the ceiling beams. The

blood on his robe had turned dark brown. He had done nothing for himself, not even pulled on the blanket. His eyes looked fixed like a dead man's.

"Al'skander," I said. Dully his eyes moved, empty of welcome or displeasure. "Al'skander, it's almost morning. You have grieved too long."

I laid my hand on his brow. He let it lie just long enough not to slight me, and turned his head away. "Bagoas. Will you take care of Peritas? He can't stay shut up here."

"Yes, after I've seen to you. When you've taken these things off, and had a bath, you may still get a little sleep."

"Let him run by your horse," he said. "It's good for him."

The dog had jumped up, and was padding from one to the other of us, full of trouble. He sat down when I told him, but his head still turned about.

I said, "The hot water's coming. Let us get these dirty clothes off." I hoped this would work with him. He hated not to be clean.

"I have told you, I want nothing. Just take the dog and go."

"Oh, my lord!" I cried. "How can you punish yourself for such a fellow? Though the work was beneath you, it was still a good work done."

"You don't know what I have done," he said. "How should you? Don't trouble me now, Bagoas. I want nothing. His leash is in the window."

For a moment he growled at me; but Alexander spoke to him, and he went meekly. There were three jars of hot water standing by the door, and a slave was toiling up the stairs with another. I could only send them back.

Metron moved from the door, and said softly, "Won't he have anything done?"

"No. Only the dog looked after."

"He's taking it hard. It's because he killed a friend."

"A *friend?*" I must have stared like an idiot. "Do you know what Kleitos said to him?"

"Well, but he *was* a friend, since they were boys.

He'd a name for being rough-spoken . . . You'd not understand, not having lived in Macedon. But haven't you found that friends' quarrels are the bitterest?"

"Are they?" I said, having no knowledge of it; and led the dog away.

After I'd given him his run, I hung about the door all day. I saw food brought in at noon, and sent out untasted. Later on, Hephaistion came. I could not hear what he said, because of the guard at the door; but I heard Alexander cry out, "She loved me like a mother, and I give her this." He must have meant his nurse, Kleitos' sister. Hephaistion left soon after. There was nowhere to withdraw to; but when he saw me he said nothing.

The King sent out, untouched, a good hot supper. Next morning, early, I brought an egg posset to put some strength in him. But a different guard was there, and turned me off. He lay fasting all that day.

After that, people of importance started coming, begging him to take some care of himself. Even the philosophers came, to preach at him. To me, it was beyond belief they should send Kallisthenes. I thought quickly and walked in after him. If *he* could enter, so could I. I wanted to see about the drinking-water; I remembered the pitcher had not had much in it.

It was just as it had been, quarter full. In two days, and with the thirst a man has after wine, he had not even drunk.

I sat down in a corner, too distressed to listen to Kallisthenes. I think he tried, in his way, to be of use, saying the virtue of repentance was next best to leaving the deed undone. To my mind, his mere presence, setting himself up, was an affront; but Alexander listened quietly, and at the end said without anger that he wanted nothing, but to be alone. I remained, as I'd hoped, unnoticed.

But then in came Anaxarchos, and asked why Alexander lay grieving there, when he was master of the world and had the right to do as he chose. Him too the King heard with patience, though in his state even the grasshopper must have been a burden. Then, just as the stupid man was going, he felt moved to add, "Come, let Bagoas here bring you food and make you fit to be seen." So I was noticed, and sent out with the sophist, my trouble all gone for nothing.

The third day came; nothing was changed. The news was all over the camp. The men were not strolling the town, but milling in their quarters, or sitting about before the palace; they kept sending to ask after the King. You could not be long with Macedonians, without guessing they killed each other in drinking-brawls pretty often; it had taken them some time to be anxious for him. But they knew that what he willed, he did; and they began to fear that he willed to die.

I had lain fearing it half the night.

I was glad to see Philippos the doctor go in. Though it was before my time, I knew the story of how the King, when very sick, had trusted him enough to take his draught, though Parmenion had just written that Darius had bribed the man to poison him. He'd handed him the letter to read, and meantime swallowed the medicine. But he came out, now, shaking his head.

I *must* get in, I thought; and I brought two gold staters, to bribe the guard. If he'd asked for a jar of my blood, I would have given that.

As I went to speak to him, the door opened, and Hephaistion came out. I stood aside. "Bagoas," he said, "I want a word with you."

He led me down into the open courtyard, away from eavesdroppers; then he said, "I don't want you to see the King today."

Because of his great power, I tried to hide my anger. What if he sent me from my lord? I said, "Is that not for the King to order?"

"True." I saw, surprised, that he too was holding back; what had he to fear from me? "If he asks for you, no one will keep you out. But stay away till he does."

It shocked me. I had thought better of him. I answered, "He is killing himself like this. If he is saved, do you care who saves him? I do not care."

"No," he said slowly, looking down from his tall height. "No, I daresay." He still spoke as if to a tiresome child, but one he had half forgiven. "I doubt he will kill himself. He will remember his destiny. He has great endurance, as you'd know if you'd soldiered with him. He can stand a great deal of punishment."

"Not without water," I said.

"What?" he said sharply. "He has water there, I saw it."

"It is just as it was when you fetched me out the first night." I added, "I concern myself with these things, when I am allowed."

Still he held back. "Yes, he must take water. I will try to make him."

"But not I?" I regretted, now, not having poisoned him at Zadrakarta.

"No. Because you will go in there and tell him the Great King can do anything."

What I had meant to say was different, and no business of his. I answered, "So he can. The King is the law."

"Yes," he said. "I knew you would tell him that."

"Why not? Who will give him respect, if traitors can spit in his face? At Susa, a man like Kleitos would have prayed for the death he got."

"I don't doubt it," he said. I thought of Philotas' screams, but did not remind him. I only said, "Of course, if the King had been himself, he would not have soiled his hands with it. He knows that now."

He took a deep breath, as if restraining himself from clouting my head. "Bagoas," he said slowly, "I know the Great King can do anything. Alexander knows it too. But he also knows he is King of the Macedonians, who can't do everything. He cannot kill a Macedonian, with his own hand or anyone else's, unless Assembly has voted. This he forgot."

I remembered him, then, saying, "You don't know what I have done."

"It is not our custom," I said, "to bring in the wine so early. Think how he was insulted and defied."

"I know all about that. I knew his father . . . But that's no matter. He broke the first law of Macedon. And he was not master of himself. That's what he can't forget."

"But," I cried, "he must forgive himself. He must, or he will die."

"Of course he must. Do you know what the Macedonians are doing now? They are calling an Assembly, to try Kleitos for treason. They'll convict him, and then his death will be legal. It was the men who wanted it. They are doing it to make Alexander forgive himself."

"But," I said staring, "don't you want that too?"

"Yes," He spoke as if I might not understand Greek. "Yes, but I am concerned with the terms on which he does it."

I replied, "I am concerned only for him."

Suddenly he shouted at me, as if at some awkward soldier. "You fool of a boy! Will you listen to sense?" It winded me like a blow, after his quiet.

"Have you noticed," he said, standing over me with his fists upon his belt, "that Alexander likes his men to love him? Yes or no? Well, his men are Macedonians. If you don't know what that means by now, you must be deaf and blind. In Macedon, any freeman can speak man to man with his chief; chief or freeman can speak to the King. And I tell you this; they can much better understand what Alexander did to Kleitos in the heat of anger, which might have happened to any one of them, than they'd understand an execution in cold blood next day. That would have threatened all their freemen's rights, and they'd have loved him less. If *you* love him, never tell him he is above the law."

His earnestness transformed him. I said, "Anaxarchos told him that."

"Oh, Anaxarchos!" He shrugged. "But he might listen to you."

He had owned it. It could not have been easy. I owed him some return.

"I understand you. I see that you must know best.

I won't say those things to him; I promise. May I see him now?"

"Not now. It's not that I doubt your word; but at present, he's better among Macedonians."

He went away. He had taken my promise, and given nothing back. I had never craved for power, as some eunuchs do; only for love. Now I understood what power is good for. He had it. If I had had it, someone would have let me in.

All that long day, I kept going to ask the guard if the King had eaten or drunk. The answer always was that he'd said he wanted nothing.

The soldiers had tried Kleitos, and pronounced him a traitor, justly put to death. Surely he would take heart from this proof of love? But not even this had moved him. Could it really be true he felt that he'd killed a friend? I remembered the bad omen of the sheep, and his sacrifice for Kleitos' safety. He had asked him to come and share the good apples, too.

The sun rose to its zenith; the sun declined. How many suns more?

I kept to my room till the night was late, lest Hephaistion should see me. When all was quiet, I took a pitcher of fresh spring water, and a clean cup. All would depend on who was the night-guard squire before the door. God was kind to me. It was Ismenios. He had always treated me well; and he loved the King.

"Yes, go in," he said. "I don't care if he curses me after. I went in myself, when I came on guard. But he was asleep; I didn't dare wake him."

My heart nearly ceased its motion. "Asleep? Did you hear him breathing?"

"Oh, yes. But he looks half dead. Go in and try."

The door made no noise. It was dark; he had put out the night-lamp. After the torch outside, at first I could only discern the glimmering windows. But there was a moon, and soon I saw him clearly. He was still asleep. Someone had put a blanket on him, but it was tossed half off. He was still in his bloodstained robe. His hair was matted, his skin drawn. Fair though it was, his beard had begun to show. A filled pitcher stood untouched by him. His lips were cracked and dry; in his sleep he was trying to wet them with his tongue.

I filled my cup. Sitting by him, I dipped two fingers, and trickled the water on his mouth. He licked at it like a dog, still sleeping. I went on till I saw him start to wake; then I took his head on my arm, and tilted the cup gently. He drank, and gave a great sigh, and drank again. I refilled it, and he drank that too.

I stroked his hair and brow, and he did not draw away. I did not beg him to come back to us; he'd had enough of that. I said, "Don't shut me out any longer. It is breaking my heart."

"Poor Bagoas." He laid a cold hand on mine. "You can come in tomorrow."

I kissed his hand. He had broken his fast before he knew it; he would end it now. Yes, now, I thought; not with officious fools around him, urging him on like a fractious child.

I slipped out of the door, and whispered to Ismenios, "Send someone to wake a cook. Egg posset, with honey and wine, and soft cheese crumbled in. Hurry up, before he changes his mind." His face lit up, and he gave me a great clap on the shoulder; which was more than Hermolaos would have done.

I went back to the bed. I didn't want him falling asleep before the posset came, then waking to say he would have nothing. But his eyes were open. He knew what I'd been about, and understood. He waited quietly, and I talked of little things, such as Peritas' doings, till Ismenios scratched at the door. The posset smelled good. I made no speeches, just lifted his head again. Soon he took the bowl from me, and finished it.

"Sleep now," I said. "But you must send for me in the morning, or they won't let me in. I shouldn't be here now."

"Enough people have been let in," he said, "whom I didn't want. You I do." He kissed me, and turned on his side. When I showed Ismenios the empty bowl, he was so pleased that he kissed me, too.

So next day I bathed and shaved and combed him, and he looked almost himself again, though very worn.

He kept his rooms; it would take more courage to show himself again, than to lead the charge at Gaugamela; so he would do it soon. The soldiers, hearing he'd taken food, were giving themselves the credit, because they had condemned Kleitos. This was best; they were welcome to it, for me.

Later, the priest of Dionysos came for audience. He had taken omens, and the god had spoken. It was his anger had caused it all. On his Macedonian feast-day, Kleitos had left his sacrifice unfinished (had not his unoffered victims followed him in reproach?) and Alexander had worshipped the Heavenly Twins, instead. For this, the deity's sacred frenzy had been sent on both; and after that, neither was answerable for what he did.

I could see this gave Alexander comfort. I don't know why he had chosen the Twins that day. But I remembered the talk at supper, about his exploits surpassing theirs (which was true) and his deserving the same divine honors; and I guessed he had tried once more to have his people share the prostration with the Persians. Who could have guessed it would end so cruelly? But Dionysos is a cruel god. I had found a dreadful play about him, in one of the books Alexander had had sent from Greece.

He gave orders for a great propitiation sacrifice. Then he spent the day with his closest friends, and looked a little better. He retired early; it was suffering more than fasting that had worn him out. When he was settled, I put out the great lamp and set the night-lamp by him. He took my hand, saying, "Before I woke last night, I dreamed of a good spirit."

I thought of my life, and smiled. "The god sent that, to tell you his wrath was over. He released you then; that was why you drank."

"I dreamed of a good presence; and it was true."

His hand felt warm. I remembered it before, stone cold. I said softly, "The god's madness was truly there; I myself felt it. Do you know, my lord, I only went to have a look at the feast, and even so it seized me? I snatched at the wine as if compelled; and all that came after, I seemed to dream in madness. It was a visitation. I felt it everywhere."

"Yes," he said slowly. "Yes, it was strange. I was driven out of myself. Kleitos, too. Look how he came back. The god led him, as he led Pentheus to his fate, and caused his own mother to perform it." He knew I had read the play.

"No one can help himself when a god possesses him. Sleep in peace, my lord. He has forgiven you; he was only angry because you're dear to him. A slight from you hurt him more than from anyone else."

I sat down by the wall, in case he should be wakeful and want to talk; but he slept soon, and lay quiet. I went away well content. What can compare with giving comfort to the one you love?

I had kept my promise to Hephaistion, too.

17

MOST OF that year, and the next, we were in Baktria and Sogdiana. It was a long, hard war. You never know where you are with Sogdians. They are mostly at blood-feud with the tribe in the next hill-fort, over the rights to water, or women carried off while gathering wood. They would swear loyalty to Alexander till he had reduced these people; then, if he took their surrender and did not cut all their throats, would turn on him themselves. Spitamenes, their best general, was killed by Sogdian enemies; they sent Alexander his head, for a reward, but were no more to be trusted after. Our men never left a dying man on the field, however hard pressed they were, to be found by Sogdians. He would thank them for the death-stroke.

Alexander would be gone for weeks on these local wars. I missed him, and was forever anxious; but had my consolation. On campaign he was always sober. He had good mountain water. Soon he had sweated and rinsed the strong wine out of his blood, and was much as he used to be; enjoying sometimes a long night of spun-out talk and drinking, a long sleep after; moderate in between. The dreadful lesson of Marakanda lasted him all his days. He was never again seen disordered in his wine, let alone violent. Even his slanderers don't deny it.

A lesser man might have held it against me, that I'd seen him in despair and shame. But he only remembered I had brought him comfort.

Once he had to recross the Oxos; it was easy this time, everything ready and better weather. I might hardly remember it, except that a miracle happened there. They had pitched the King's tent, and I was seeing his things set out, when I heard the squires exclaiming. Right by the tent, which was not far from the river, was a dark welling spring. They had skimmed the scum off, in case it might serve for horses; and found that it was oil!

Alexander was fetched to see the wonder. We all rubbed it upon our arms, and it spread smoothly. He sent for Aristander the seer, to read the omen. He sacrified, and announced that as oil anoints the wrestler before the games, the portent stood for labors, but its generous flow for victory and wealth.

We tried some in the King's lamp at night. It burned quite well, but made a foul smoke; the lamp had to be taken outside. He wanted to taste it, but I said it might be as bad as Oxos water, which changed his mind. Leonnatos was for throwing a lighted torch into the pool, to see what happened; but Alexander thought it would be impious, towards a gift of the gods.

He had the labors it foretold. He was forever off in the mountains, often with small forces, for he had to divide his troops; he was resolved to bring Sogdiana under law. He learned wonderful skill and cunning in taking hill-forts. Many tales came back, of his endurance in cold or heat (you get extremes of both in Sogdiana); of a frightful storm, thunder and lightning-bolts followed by hailstones, and bitter cold, when men were perishing of despair and terror, freezing in their tracks, till, seeking the stragglers out in the maze of a black forest, he shook them alive and got them making fires. He was at last sitting down to get warm himself, when a soldier came staggering up, half dead on his feet, hardly knowing where he was. Alexander took off with his own hands the icy armor whose straps made his fingers bleed, and sat the man in his own chair by the fire.

(King Ptolemy, who was there, is putting such things in his book, to be known by men to come. Sometimes about other matters he sends for me, and I tell him whatever I think my lord would like to be remembered for. Seeing I followed his golden bier all the way here to Egypt, King Ptolemy in kindness found room for me in his Household. He speaks louder than he knows, now he's a little hard of hearing [he is my elder by twenty years], and sometimes I hear him say, quietly as he supposes, to a foreign guest, "Look there. Don't you see there has been great beauty? That is Bagoas, who was Alexander's boy.")

In camp I read Herodotos with Philostratos. He begged my pardon for the choice of book; he had not many; but as I told him, it was no news to me that Xerxes had been beaten in Greece; my great-great-grandfather had served with him.

Philostratos and I had grown fond of one another; only as teacher and pupil, though I saw Kallisthenes sniffing. When the King was at war, and the chronicle was up to date, he had not much to do till the King got back with his squires, whom Kallisthenes had the teaching of. They being of noble birth, and likely to command men later, Alexander did not want them ignorant. He had never taken this work from the philosopher, even after they were estranged. I thought it overgenerous, myself; but then, he had Aristotle to consider.

Just now Kallisthenes was going over his library; we could see through his open tent-flap the racks of scrolls. Philostratos went in, and had another try at borrowing one, so that I could read Greek verse; he had only taught me what he knew by heart. I heard him get a dry No, and tell Kallisthenes he'd be lucky if

one of his pupils showed half my promise. Kallisthenes
said *his* pupils showed promise in the noble art of
philosophy, not mere book-reading. Philostratos said,
"Can they read?" and walked out. They did not speak
for a month.

Next time Alexander came back, I asked him to give
Philostratos a present. He loved being asked for things.
I don't think my story about Kallisthenes did the
present any harm either. "But what for yourself?" he
said. "Don't you think I love you enough?"

"I had presents at Susa without love," I said. "You
give me all I need. And my best suit is still as good
as new; or nearly."

He laughed and said, "Buy another. I like to see you
come out in something new; like a pheasant in spring
feathers." He added gravely, "My love you will always
have. That is a sacred bond to me."

Soon he was off again. I had my new suit made in
deep red, embroidered with gold-spangled flowers. The
buttons were jeweled roses. I put it away to wear when
he came back.

I should soon be twenty. Alone in my tent, I often
looked in the mirror. For people like me, it is a dangerous age.

Though my looks had changed, it seemed I had
beauty still. I was slim as ever; my face had not
coarsened but fined. There is no salve like love.

It did not matter that I was a boy no longer. I had
hardly been that when he saw me first. He was not a
boy-lover; it was the comely young men around him
that pleased his eye. One of them, a squire called
Philippos, had lately died for it. I could see Alexander
was fond of him; maybe there had been some night
upon campaign—I can think of it gently now. At all
events, the youth felt a burning loyalty, which he
longed to prove. They made a long pursuit after the
Sogdians, in summer heat; his horse gave out, one of
many; so he ran on foot by the King's horse, fully
armed, and refused a mount he was offered, to show
what he was made of. At the end of the chase, they
found and fought the enemy. He stood by the King in

the van; then, when it was over, suddenly the life went out in him, like the flame of an emptied lamp. He lasted just long enough to die in Alexander's arms. Even I could not grudge him that.

Yes, I thought at the mirror, he will always love me. He never takes love without return. But when desire begins to fail, it will be a day of grief. Holy Eros! (for I knew the god well by this time) let it not be yet.

As the country was subdued, he was founding cities. Hephaistion founded some of them. He had learned Alexander's eye for a good site, and though rough-tongued among Macedonians, had good manners and good sense with foreigners. Gladly I gave him credit for all his virtues, once he was out of sight.

What use to scourge oneself with jealousy of the past? He'd not had ten years of it before me, my first guess; he had had fifteen. They had been together since I was a baby learning to walk. The future no man knows; the past has been, now and forever.

We wintered in a rocky sheltered place called Nautika, with a waterfall and a cave. Alexander was up in the citadel tower again; reaching his bedchamber through a trapdoor in the floor. I was scared to death he would stumble on the ladder, some night after supper, though he'd never been known to fall however drunk he was. The room had a big hearth under a hole in the roof; snow would come through it and hiss upon the fire. He and Hephaistion would sit by it talking, with Peritas stretched out like a great rug. But the nights were mine. Sometimes he'd say, "You can't go out there, it's freezing," and take me in just to keep me warm. He was always a giver.

In the room below, heated by fire-baskets and full of drafts, he would do business most of the day. At one end was his chair of state and place of audience; at the other, behind a curtain, his working-table, full of tablets and records, and letters from half the world. The more lands he conquered, the more work he had.

There were the soldiers to look after, and keep in shape through the idle time till the passes opened. He held games, for which everyone had to be ready on the first fine day. Once we even had a play, with a proper stage and good actors out from Greece. Actors would go through water, fire and ice, to go home and say they had played before Alexander. Philostratos sat by me, and explained in whispers the finer points. Kallisthenes, sitting among some of the squires he favored, sniffed at us, and said something that made Hermolaos smirk.

Spring broke at last; huge snowslides thundered down the mountains; streams turned to brown cataracts, hurling along the wreckage caught in their rush. The best passes opened. Sogdian robbers came out from their dens, awaiting the first caravans, but met with troops instead.

The land seemed quiet under Alexander's garrisons; till news came in that a powerful chief, who the year before had submitted and pledged fealty, was up in arms raising his tribesmen. An old story, except that he owned the Sogdian Rock.

It had the name of the strongest place in Asia; a huge sheer crag, its upper part full of caves. Generations of chiefs had burrowed there; it would hold a small army, with stores for years. They had tanks to catch the snow and rain, and store it against summer. It was reported snow still lay thick there; but the chief had already sent up his warriors, wealth and women, while he himself went rousing the countryside.

Alexander sent to him, offering a parley to his envoys. It was now known that envoys' heads returned from Alexander still on their shoulders; so two swaggering tribesmen came. When he offered free pardon for free surrender, the envoys laughed, and said he could go or stay; he would take the Sogdian Rock on the day his men grew wings.

Calmly he ordered them to be fed, and they took their heads safely home. A Sogdian chief, getting that message, would have left their heads till the last, when they'd have been glad to part with them. Alexander merely decided to have the Rock, if it took a year.

The whole camp marched there. One could see it for miles. Closer up, it really seemed a task for eagles.

There was no easy side; it was precipice all round, plunging down to ragged rocks. One could just trace the goat-track the people had gone up by, because it had caught the snow; every yard was commanded by the mouths of the caves above.

The army made camp just out of bowshot. Behind them, the swarm of followers, sutlers and grooms and slaves, merchants and clerks and horse-traders, singers and painters and sculptors, carpenters and tanners, dancers and ironsmiths, jewelers and whores and bawds, spread about the Rock.

People have written of this enterprise, as if the King had been a boy taking up a dare. Of course that was always in him; he would have kept it into old age. But the Rock commanded leagues of country; he could not leave it unconquered in his rear. Also the Sogdians, who understand little except strength, would have despised his power, and cut his cities to bits as soon as he had moved on.

The chief, Oxyartes, did not live in this eyrie in peacetime. His house and his tribal village were at the foot of the trackway. Alexander would not let the soldiers burn them, lest it be read as a sign that he meant to give no quarter. In the cave-mouth, little figures, as small as if carved on rings, stood looking down. On the steeps below, where in summer one would not have seen foothold for a rock-rabbit, winter had picked out in white the tiny ledges, or the cracks that gashed the cliffs. It was full moon. Even at night, one saw the gleam of the snow. Alexander rode all round it, looking.

Next morning, he called for a muster of mountaineers. A small crowd reported; mostly hillmen born, who had climbed for him in other sieges. From all who came forward he picked three hundred. To the first man on the summit, he would give twelve talents, riches for life; to the next eleven, and so on for the first twelve. They were to go up that night, by the steepest side, which could not be seen from the caves. Each would carry a wallet of iron tent-pegs, a mallet to drive them in, and a strong light rope, to hitch himself to one peg while he fixed the next.

It was a cold clear night. I had everything ready, but he would not come to bed. This was the first really dangerous action he had not led himself. There could be no leader; each took his own way to the top. He had not the skill. But he could scarcely bear it, not to be risking his neck with them. When they had climbed too high to be seen in the dim light, he came in, but still paced about. "I saw three fall," he said. "We shall never find them for burial. They lodged up there in the snow." He lay down in his clothes, with orders to be called at the first light.

He woke uncalled, while it was still too dark to see much. Some of the officers were waiting for him. The top of the Rock was a dark loom in the faint sky. As its edges sharpened, Alexander stared up devouringly. His eyes were good; but Leonnatos could see far things like a hawk, though when he wanted to read, he had to hold the writing out the length of his arm. He pointed up, and cried, "They're there! They're signaling!"

The rising light showed them clustered on the blunt summit, as thick as cormorants. They had unrolled the long strips of linen they had carried bound around them; the signals streamed in the breeze.

Alexander stepped out, lifted his shield and flashed it at them. The trumpet squealed under the crags; the big voice of the herald bawled to the defenders to look above them; Alexander had found winged men.

The chief's son, who was in command, at once asked terms of surrender. He could not see how many were up there, or what arms they had, which were none; their pegs and mallets had been enough to carry. Thirty had died, one man in ten. Their graves were the maws of kites; but Alexander gave them a rite of honor, with an empty bier, after the custom of the Greeks.

It took two days, for all the people to come down from the Rock with their goods and gear. I wondered how the women could manage the giddy path, in the wide skirts of Sogdiana; but I suppose they had done it often, in the endless tribal wars.

The chief's son, who never learned that the King's

eagles had had no claws, came and pledged himself, promising to send a message to his father. To seal their compact, he begged the honor of entertaining the King to a royal feast.

It was agreed, for two days later. I was only afraid they meant to knife him as he sat at meat. It would be nothing much, for Sogdians.

I dressed him for it, in the Mitra and his grandest robe. He was in good spirits. Though he grieved for his mountaineers, this stronghold might have cost many hundred lives. The enemy had shed no blood at all, and were grateful enough to promise anything.

"Take care, Al'skander," I said as I combed his hair. "He may offer you his daughter, like that Scythian king."

He laughed. His friends had been very pleasant about the matter, picturing the bride being cut out of the clothes she'd been sewn up in some winters back, having the rancid mares'-milk fat scraped from her hair, her vermin picked off, and so on, to make her lovely for the marriage bed.

"If that young man has a daughter, she's under five. You must come to the feast, it should be worth seeing. Put on that new suit of yours."

The chief's son, Histanes, had certainly spared no pains. A lane of torches led from the camp to his hall. Music came out, quite good for Sogdiana. (I had once heard Alexander compare Persian singing to the yowl of mating cats; but he hadn't known I was listening.) The King was embraced by his host upon the threshold. It was a big hall. Oxyartes must be rich as well as powerful. Hangings of scarlet, stitched with ramping lions and leopards, smoldered in the light of torches enough to warm the air. The high table was set with gold and silver; gums I had not smelled since I left Susa burned in the fretted censers. If some of the Macedonians thought the place would have been worth sacking, they had to keep it to themselves.

The food was good and spicy; the caravans from India pass that way. Alexander and the host had an interpreter standing by them; the other Macedonian guests got along as best they could, letting their dishes be heaped up twice for good manners. Alexander, light eater as he was, performed this duty. He is wishing, I thought, they'd bring on the wine instead.

The sweets came in, and the wine. Histanes and Alexander pledged each other, exchanging compliments; then the interpreter stood forth and addressed us all in Greek. To honor the King, the ladies of the household would appear and dance. This was something indeed, in Sogdiana, where to look at their women is a matter for long knives.

I was at the foot of the table, near the royal squires. Ismenios had moved over to sit by me. His friendliness had increased; if he wished, as I thought, for more, he kept it to himself from loyalty to Alexander. I was his debtor for much kindness, and for smoothing my way with the others when he could.

The Sogdian youth on my other side now addressed me in their uncouth Persian, which I could barely understand. With both hands he drew female curves in the air, smiling and rolling his eyes. I said to Ismenios, "It seems there's beauty in store."

"They'll perform up at the top," he said, "for the King and generals. Only their backs for us. We must make do with one another."

The musicians struck up a stately measure; the women entered, stepping to the beat, not dancing yet. Their heavy clothes were crusted with embroidery; gold chains, hung with gold pendants, circled their brows; massive rings on their arms and ankles clashed as they moved, or tinkled with little bells. We had hardly glimpsed them before they turned away from us to bow, with arms crossed on their breasts, before the King.

Histanes pointed, no doubt at the chief's close kin, for some of them bowed again. Alexander inclined his head with a glance for each. I thought he paused, once, before his eye moved on. Ismenios said, "Yes, one of them must be beautiful, to make the King look twice."

The music quickened; they began to dance.

In Persia, only such women dance as are trained in

it to rouse men. This dance was decent and seemly; they hardly showed more than their hennaed feet, as they twirled their heavy skirts and clashed their anklets. Their bending had grace, without invitation; their swaying arms were like rippling barley. But you would be foolish, to call this modest dancing. These ladies were above modesty. Its place was taken by pride.

Ismenios said, "All very proper. One's own sister could do all that. Maybe we'll have real dancing later. Now *you* could have showed them something."

I hardly heard him. The women wheeled in slow circles, or joined in a winding chain. Alexander's eyes, as they turned with the wheel or followed the chain along, were always fixed on one link.

He liked all things good of their kind. I had heard him praise a fine woman, often enough. Yet my belly shrank on itself, and my hands grew cold.

He spoke to the interpreter, who pointed questioning. Alexander nodded; he was asking who that one was. Histanes replied, with some increase of dignity. She must be someone of rank, no doubt his sister.

The music grew louder; the line of women turned, and came down the hall. All of us guests must have our share of honor.

I knew at once which she was. Yes, a sister; I saw the likeness; he was a handsome man. She was about sixteen, full womanhood in Sogdiana. Pure ivory, faintly tinted, and not by art; soft hair, blue-black, small fronds brushing her cheeks; a clear forehead under the gold pendants; brows with a perfect arch, over large brilliant eyes. She had the kind of beauty that is famed for leagues around, and made no pretense of not knowing it. Her one defect was that her fingers were not quite long enough, and the ends too pointed. I had learned to look for such things in Darius' harem.

Alexander's eyes were following her still, waiting for her to turn his way again. She passed by me, sitting there in the new suit he had liked so much; and he never saw me.

The Sogdian youth pulled at my sleeve, and said, "Roxane."

They danced back to the high table and made sweeping bows. Once more the interpreter hovered. As they turned to go, Histanes beckoned his sister. She came up; Alexander rose to his feet, and took her hands. He spoke and she replied. Her profile, now turned my way, was carved without flaw. When she went out, he stood till she had gone.

Ismenios said, "Well, one knows one's in Sogdiana. No Persian girl would have done that, would she?"

I answered, "No."

"Still, Alexander asked to speak to her. I thought so, didn't you?"

"Yes. I thought so."

"And sober as a judge. I expect he was just honoring the host. It's true, she's beautiful. Of course she's darker; but she has somehow a look of you."

"You flatter me." He had always been kind. He sat there smiling over his wine with his clear blue eyes, his flaxen hair a little damp from the heat, turning the knife in my heart.

Up at the high table, Histanes and the King were busy with the interpreter. Alexander had barely touched his wine. The room grew hot; I loosed the neck of my coat, with its ruby-clustered buttons. The last hand to open it had been his.

I had found him Hephaistion's boy, and with me he had wished for manhood. It had been my pride. So now I had given him to a woman. I sat in the hot torchlight, tasting death, and being pleasant to those around me, as I had been taught when I was twelve years old.

18

I<small>N HIS</small> tent I awaited his return, listening to my demons.

I answered them: So he has chosen a concubine. Darius had more than three hundred. How am I wronged? Any other king would have been married before he met me; from the first I would have shared him, with who knows how many, awaiting the night of favor.

Oh yes, they answered. But those were the days when you had a master. You have had a lover since then. Get ready, Bagoas, you have felt nothing yet. Wait till he comes to bed. Perhaps he will have her with him.

Perhaps so, I told the demons. But he is my lord whom I was born to follow. He never turns away love; nor can I take it back though it scalds my soul like the Fiery River. Thus it is. So go, and laugh somewhere else.

The feast had been over a long time. Was he still bargaining with her kin? At last I heard him; but he

had with him most of his chief generals, the last thing
I'd expected. Late as it was, they all came in, and
talked in the outer chamber. It was well I listened; I
had time to get over the shock of what I heard. At
first I could not believe it.

Hephaistion stayed on last. They talked too quietly
for me to overhear. Then he went too, and Alexander
came in.

"You shouldn't have waited up. I ought to have sent
you word."

I said it was nothing, and that his bath-water was
on the way. He paced about; and no wonder. I knew
he would speak before long; he could not keep it in.

"Bagoas."

"Yes, Alexander."

"Did you see Oxyartes' daughter, Roxane? She was
presented, after the dance."

"Yes, Alexander. We were all speaking of her beauty."

"I shall marry her."

Yes, it was well I was prepared. One more astounded
silence would have been too much for his temper, I
daresay.

"May you be happy, my lord. She is truly a pearl
of light." A Sogdian! A mere chief's daughter! Useless
to hope he had not yet asked for her, and would wake
in his right mind tomorrow. I could see it was too late.

He was pleased with my words. I'd had time to get
them ready. "They're all against me," he said. "Hephaistion will stand by me; but he's against it too."

"My lord, they only think no one at all is worthy
of you."

He laughed. "Oh, no! Some Macedonian girl I never
set eyes on, carted out to me hit or miss; *she'd* have
been worthy . . . Roxane. What does it mean in Persian?"

I answered, "Little Star." He was pleased with that.

The bath-water came, and I had a chance to undress
him. When the slaves had gone, he said, "I've known
a long time I ought to marry in Asia. It is necessary.
The peoples *must* be reconciled. It can only begin with

me. This is the one way left. This, they'll have to accept."

I said, "Yes, Alexander," thinking, Suppose they won't?

"But since I knew this, I've not seen a woman I could put up with, until tonight. Have you ever seen her equal?"

"Never, my lord, even among Darius' ladies." I think this was really true, but for her hands. "Of course, I never saw the Queen. That would not have been permitted." I said this to make sure he never brought me into her presence.

"I only saw her once; and again when she was dead. Yes, she was beautiful; like a lily on a tomb. Her daughters were children then. They are older now, but . . . Well, they are his too. I will not breed a son from the stock of cowards. This girl has spirit."

"Without doubt, Alexander. One can see it in her eyes." *That* was true enough. What sort, was another thing.

He was too restless to sleep, but paced about in his bath-robe, running on about the wedding, how he was sending word to Oxyartes her father, and so on. Strange to say, I found comfort in it. He would never have made me listen to all this if he meant to turn me away; it was not in him. I could see such a thought had never entered his head.

Of course, he knew it was the girl he desired at present; but it was not from carelessness he did not know my pain. Affection ran deeper in him than passion, always. He had given it to Philotas, whose treachery had cut him like a lover's. He had given it me, and still felt true to it. Suddenly I wondered if Hephaistion had felt as I did.

At last I got him to bed. It was not far short of morning. "Bless you, in the name of both our gods. You are the only one who has understood." He drew down my head and kissed me. The held-back tears flooded my eyes; but I got out before he knew it.

Oxyartes came in a few days later, to make peace. Of course Alexander did not give him back the Rock,

which he meant to garrison; but the chief had made a
pretty good bargain, if his grandson was to be Great
King. When he got the news that Alexander meant to
marry the girl, whom any other victor on earth would
have taken as prize of war, I expect he could not believe his ears.

The wedding feast, now preparing, looked like making the last one seem a mere family supper. The kindred had been summoned, they were decking the bridal
room. All I wished to know was what Alexander meant
to do with her when he moved on. Sogdian women are
not like ours. What if she expected to live with him
in his tent, doing everything for him, only going inside
when men appeared; seeing no reason for my presence
but as her servant? If he lets that happen, I thought, it
will be a good time to die.

Then appeared a fine new tent, and a splendid wagon, roofed and curtained with embroidered leather. My
heart revived.

He called me to him and laid a hand on my shoulder.
"Will you do me a kindness?" "How can you ask?"
"Come to Roxane's tent, and tell me what is wanting. I
don't know much of these things. I have taken advice;
but these people never lived at court."

I smiled back at him and he led me in. I could
have told him this Sogdian girl had never guessed such
splendors existed, and would not know the use of half
the toilet things. But I went gravely round, spoke well
of orange-flower water if it could be obtained, and
said nothing else was lacking. The bed was very grand,
in the heavy style of the province. There came back to
me the scent of cedar-wood, and the salt breeze of
Zadrakarta.

As the day approached, it was clear the Sogdians
were happy, but no one else was. Macedonians of rank
took it very ill. If he had traded the girl for her
brother's life, and had her dragged to his tent, it would
have been a trifle; a scream or two would have been
worth some bawdy jokes. But marriage, that affronted
their victors' status. If he'd first taken a Macedonian
Queen, and added this girl as a minor wife (his father,

so they said, had had many such), they would not
have grumbled. As it was, many had a daughter at
home, whom they thought should have been preferred.
They were only kept quiet by his not conferring the
rank of Queen on her. I was pleased to see he was not
so far gone as that.

As for the men, all soldiers like oddities in a leader
they admire; they like him to be a legend. They were
used to the Persian dancing-boy; if he'd had no one
for his bed, they'd have wondered what was wrong
with him. But this was another thing. They had fought
to subdue Sogdiana, because he said it was necessary;
now it was rumored he thought of India. They started
wondering if he meant to go home at all. He had
spread his wings; the whole earth was his home. But
they thought of their villages, the hills where they'd
herded goats in boyhood, and Macedonian children
by Macedonian wives.

Whatever we all thought, the day arrived, true to its
time as death. While I dressed him for the feast, he
smiled to himself, as if now it was come he hardly
believed it could be happening. A crowd of his friends
came in, to wish him joy in the usual way. It pleased
them when he did not put on the Mitra—he was taking
a wife, not a Queen—and the jokes grew lively. Nobody noticed me; except that once Hephaistion glanced
my way when he thought I did not see; in curiosity, or
triumph, or pity, there was not time to guess.

The feast began; a blaze of light and heat and gold
and color, reeking with roast meats; the great barbaric
heaps of the bride-goods on their stands; bridegroom
and bride enthroned. It was a fine still night; all the
flames burned upright. There was deafening music, everyone shouting over it. The bride looked about with
her glowing eyes, as if no one had ever taught her
to cast them down; till Alexander spoke to her through
the interpreter, when she turned them upon him.

They brought in the ritual loaf, for him to divide
with his sword. He broke off a piece from her half,
gave it her to eat, and tasted his own. They were now
man and wife. We all rose to our feet to cheer them.

My throat closed; I could not utter a sound. The torches stifled me and burned my eyes. Yet I kept my place, ashamed to be seen going. If I stayed much longer, they would be bedding the bride.

In the shoving crowd, a hand slid under my arm. Without turning, I knew it was Ismenios.

"She is beautiful," I said. "Are you envying the bridegroom?"

"No," he said in my ear. "But I did before."

I leaned a little nearer. It seemed to happen of itself, like blinking against dust. He eased me out from the press. We found coat and cloak in the heap outside, and went out under the cold Sogdian stars.

It was nearly as bright outside as in; great cressets flaring everywhere, and a horde of tribesmen gorging on whole carcasses, spitted over the fires; singing, roaring, bragging, setting their dogs to fight each other, dancing in rings. However, they were all where the food and drink was; we soon got free of them.

No snow had fallen since before the siege; the ground had dried. We found a round hidden place among the boulders, and he spread his cloak. The grass had been well pressed down; I expect the whole village went there. I did not say so to Ismenios, who thought it a paradise created for us alone.

It surprised him, how quickly I divined his wishes. I don't know why; they were nothing out of the way. I'd have thought myself lucky, any afternoon in Susa, to get such an easy client. He was eager to please, and I to be pleased by almost anything. Oromedon would have warned me what to expect: I had almost forgotten those early days. "It comes of anger, and the soul's resistance." When I caught my breath, Ismenios thought it was from rapture, and was happy. He had been a good friend, when other squires were plaguing me. I had learned young how to give thanks to those who did not ill-use me.

I don't know how long we were there; it felt like half the night. He had wanted me for a year, and seemed a stranger to fatigue. At last, after we had lain awhile under my coat, we agreed the night grew too cold to stay.

A late waning moon was up. Ismenios gazed at it floating beside the Rock; I leaned upon his shoulder. Making sure he got all he wanted had given me something to think about, which was worth as much to me as any of it to him. I said, "We have dreamed, dear friend. Another time, we might awaken. Let it be a dream forgotten at morning." That seemed a better way of saying it than, "Never remind me of this, for fear I should stick a knife in you."

He put an arm round my waist. A handsome youth; it had not always been my lot to pick and choose. Speaking quite sensibly—indeed he had never been stupid—he said, "I promise. Never a word, not even if we're alone. I'm lucky having it to remember. Of course, he'll want you back. Anyone would."

Up the Rock, a great fire leaped in the cave-mouth. Even on his wedding night, Alexander was not so besotted as to leave the place ungarrisoned; but had sent them plenty of good cheer to keep the feast.

In the hall there was lazy broken singing, from those guests who always linger till morning, to see the bride-sheet displayed. For the first time, I started wondering how he'd fared. He must be very much out of practice, if indeed he'd ever been in it, and a virgin of sixteen would not be much help. For a moment my demons, returning, made me wish him to fail, and seek me for consolation. Then I thought what it would do to him, who had never known defeat; so I caught back my evil wish and killed it. When Ismenios had left me with speaking eyes, and gone to bed, I stayed, lost in the crowd, till daylight came with music, and some wellborn old crone appeared to flap the sheet at us. It bore the red badge of victory. Alexander was still unconquered.

Next day, there was so much ceremony that I scarcely saw him, except when he came to his tent to change his clothes. He seemed pleased with himself (from bliss or from achievement who could say?) and looked brisk

and fresh. Ismenios was on duty with blue lines under
his eyes, and a soft secret smile he took care not to
turn on me.

The bride was being visited by a hundred women;
you could hear the chatter in the bride-room from out
of doors. Not having traveled deaf in Darius' harem
wagons, I knew the questions, and wondered how she
replied.

I never went near the door, but would send a servant to leave his morning clothes with the eunuch
there, or take away his supper robe. One must start
as one means to go on.

When he came for his bath at evening, I felt as I
sluiced him down that I washed her off him; to such
follies will jealousy bring the heart. Suddenly he said,
"I shall have to have her taught Greek."

"Yes, Alexander." How had he managed without
speech? I had cured his old sadness—perhaps for good,
perhaps not—by coaxing, gossiping, confiding, telling
secrets or old tales. He loved a spell of this, before
he was ready again. Sometimes he would just fall
asleep to the sound of my voice; it was all one to me,
so long as he kept me by him. Now there was this
girl, without a word to say to him, just lying waiting
for more.

"Your teacher, Philostratos, do you think he'd do?"

"None better," I said, delighted to enrich him after
all his kindness. "And he has picked up a little Persian,
from teaching me."

"She doesn't understand mine." Sogdian is to pure
Persian as Macedonian is to Greek. He went on quickly, "Yes, he seems just the man."

"Not Kallisthenes?" I said, recalling an old joke;
but he said unsmiling, "When iron floats. He is taking
more on himself than will do him good."

I should have thought. Anyone could guess what
Kallisthenes would say of barbarian weddings, and
half-Sogdian heirs being bred to rule over Greeks.

"He must have written by now to Aristotle. Well, I
have written too. The old man must try to understand
what I am doing."

"Yes, Alexander." There was a purple bruise on his neck. She must have bitten him. How did that go, I wondered; it was not in his style at all.

However it went, a week had not gone by before, hearing of a tribe that had refused submission, he was off upon campaign. Since the rebels lived no great way off, he said it was not worth while to move the court, nor tire the Lady Roxane with rough travel over snowy passes; he would soon be back.

At this news, I sat down to think.

If I just packed and assumed that I was going, he would quite likely take me along. I would be there, she not; what could be better? Well, perhaps one thing. What if we see who is missed the most? A big stake, upon one throw of the dice. All the same, I'll throw.

So I assumed I was to be left, as often before, and he marched away. As his long train vanished over the passes, I would have taken back my stake again. But it was down.

If I'd gone, he would not have had much time for me. The rebels lived in a rock-fort, with a great ravine before it, supposed to make it impregnable. Alexander spent about three parts of a month, in terrible weather, getting the ravine filled up, till he could bridge the gorge. Since no one inside had ever thought of such a thing being possible, they were much put out when arrows began to hit them, while their own, aimed at the working-parties, fell on thick bullhide screens. They sent down a herald, asking for Oxyartes to act as envoy.

Alexander sent for him, I think he was some kin to the chief. He went up, reported his daughter's marriage, declared Alexander both invincible and merciful. The chief surrendered, invited Alexander into his stronghold, provisioned the army from his stores laid up for the siege; was confirmed in his rank and given his fortress back. Thus the war ended.

Meantime, still at my Greek with Philostratos, I could not keep from asking him how he got on in the harem. He said he had to teach in the presence of two old women, the girl's three sisters, and a eunuch armed to the teeth. "You don't know when you're well off," I said. "Oxyartes wanted to have you cut, before you were let inside." I laughed aloud at his courteous efforts to control his face. "Don't worry, Alexander was very firm. And how are the lessons going?"

He said the lady was eager to learn, even to impatience. On this he looked uneasy, and quickly opened our book.

Soon after, the chief eunuch of Oxyartes' harem came seeking me. His condescension surprised me; though unpolished, he was very pompous; but his errand surprised me more. It was a summons to see the Lady Roxane.

So, then, she knew. Never mind whether through spiteful tattle, or from sending out spies herself; she knew.

Of course I was not going near her, now more than ever. I said I was in despair that I could not rejoice my eyes with her gracious presence; but I dared not attend the harem without the King's command. He nodded gravely. It is not usual, anywhere, to bring people of my looks into a harem, even when cut; Darius had never sent me once without him. I could see the eunuch uneasy with his errand. Perhaps, I asked, he could tell me why his lady had wished to see me?

"As I understand," he said, looking me up and down, "she wished to ask why, since you are a dancer, you would not dance at her wedding, to bring good fortune to her and to your master."

"Dance at her wedding?" I must have stared like a fool. "It is the custom of our country," he said, "for a eunuch to do so in woman's dress."

"You may tell your lady that I did not refuse to dance; the King did not command me. It is not a custom of his people." Someone must have performed after I left the hall. So he had crossed her will on his wedding eve, rather than give me pain. Had she known then, already?

He came back soon after.

His forerunners came at noon, he himself at sunset. No doubt he excused himself to Oxyartes on account of his late return; he dined in camp, with a few friends, and the officers he'd had with him.

They did not sit long over the wine. They fought the campaign over, debating how long it would have taken if the garrison had held out; then he said he was going to bed. Nobody asked him where.

He came inside. I had everything ready as he liked it. He greeted me with a kiss, and it was a little more than a greeting; but I did not presume on that. What if he goes over there, I thought, as soon as he has bathed? I will not invite the cruelties of hope.

I bathed him; I rubbed him dry. Would he ask for fresh clothes? No. I turned back the bed for him.

Going about the sleeping-place, folding his things, kindling the night-lamp and putting out the great one, I felt his eyes. At last I ceased to rebuke my heart for singing. All the same, he would have to ask.

I stood the night-lamp by the bed, and said, "Is there anything else, my lord?" He answered, "You know well."

As his arm received me, he gave a little sigh; just as when he came back from a fight and a long ride, dusty and bruised, and found his bath just right for him. A hundred verses of tenderest love, sung to the lute, could not have given me half the joy.

Next day, he set about the great pile of business that had come in while he was gone; envoys from cities of western Asia, men who'd ridden for leagues with grievances against satraps; letters from Greece, from Macedon, from his new cities. He was at it all day and on into the night. I don't know if he got in a courtesy call at the harem. At night he just dropped into bed and slept.

The day after, I heard that someone was asking for me at my tent. Here a young boy, whom I'd never seen, put in my hands an inlaid silver dish. Lifting the lid, he showed it was full of sweetmeats; with a slip of parchment in a fine Greek script. It read, A GIFT FROM ALEXANDER.

I gazed in surprise. When I looked again for the boy, he'd gone.

I took the dish inside. Though I knew all his things, it was new to me. It was costly, but unrefined in style; it would have been thrown out of doors at Susa. It looked to me like Sogdian work.

The note was odd. He used no ceremony with me. Anything like this, he'd just send by a servant, whom I would know, with a message by mouth that he hoped I would enjoy it. The writing was delicate, nothing like his impatient hand. Recognition came to me. I thought that I understood.

I went out, and threw a sweet to the wretchedest of the pi-dogs that hung about the camp. He followed me, in the hope of more. In my tent I gave him half the dishful. I had no need to tie him; the poor mangy creature sat down on my carpet, believing that at last he'd found a master to care for him. When he jerked about, and died with yellow foam upon his jaws, I felt like a host who has murdered a trusting guest.

I stared at the corpse, and thought of what I had planned once at Zadrakarta. Who was I to be angry? But at least I had not done it.

He will have to know, I thought; and not only because I want to go on living. Who can tell what next? By now, I doubt if the shock will kill him.

I went to his tent as his day's business was done, showed him the dish and told my story. He listened in silence, only his eyes looking deeper-set. "This came in the dish, Alexander," I said, and handed him the writing.

He took it between finger and thumb, as if it were poisoned too. "Who wrote this? This is a scholar's hand."

"My lord, it was Philostratos." He stared at me. I said, "I showed it him and he owned it freely. He could not understand how I came to have it. He wrote out a dozen, he said, for the Lady Roxane, to put in her chest with your wedding gifts to her. What must have happened," I said, looking down, "is that someone stole it." I added, "I told him nothing, my lord; I thought it best."

He nodded, frowning. "Yes, say nothing more to him. I shall not have him questioned." He covered the dish and put it in a coffer. "Eat only from the common table till I give you word. Drink nothing that has stood in your tent unwatched. Tell no one. I shall see to this myself."

It was remarked that the King found leisure that afternoon to visit the harem. He was gone some time, which all thought proper in a bridegroom. At bedtime he said, "You can feel safe now; I've dealt with it."

I thought that would be all; but presently he said, "We are bound in love; you have a right to know. Come and sit here." I sat by him on the bed. He was tired, it would be a night for sleep. "I took the sweets to her, and I could see she knew them. I offered her one, smiling at first. When she refused, I looked angry, and made as if to force her. She did not plead, she flung them down and trampled them. She has spirit, at least." He spoke not without approval.

"But the time had come to tell her what she must not do. And here I met a difficulty. I could not bring in an interpreter to hear of such a business. The only one I could have trusted would have been yourself, and that would have been too much. She is, after all, my wife."

I agreed that this was so. There was a lengthening silence. At last I dared to say, "So, my lord, how did you manage?"

"I beat her. It was necessary. Nothing else was possible."

Deprived of speech, I looked about the room. What had he used? He did not own a whip. Neither Oxhead nor Peritas had known the touch of one. But there it was on the table, with ten years' wear on it, borrowed, as I guessed, from a huntsman. She must have been awed by the use that it had seen.

Since there was nothing at all that could be said, I held my peace.

"She thought the more of me. I hadn't considered that."

So that was why he'd been so long gone! I pulled my face straight in time. "My lord, the Sogdian ladies have a great regard for strength."

He eyed me sideways, considering whether he could permit himself to share the joke, and deciding it would be improper. I rose gravely and smoothed the bed-clothes. "Sleep well, Al'skander. You have labored and earned your rest."

Later I thought about it. He was warm, not hot; gentle, in giving and taking; his pace was slow, he liked the pauses of tenderness. I'm sure he had never asked himself whether we suited so well because I was what I was. I could imagine the care he would take with a young maiden. So now he knew that she'd simply thought him soft.

Soon after this, the camp was struck. The bride bade her kin farewell, and was received into her wagon train. We were bound west for Baktria, to put the province in order. Some of its satraps and governors had failed their trust; and all must be left secure, before the march to India.

19

H E VISITED his new
cities, heard causes, removed a governor here and
there who was extortionate, corrupt or weak. Except
for a few short forays, against robber bands that were
preying on the trade roads, the court went with him.
Now, besides the usual horde, there was the long wagon
train of Roxane, with her ladies and maids and eunuchs.

At first, he used to visit her pretty often, mostly in
the afternoon. It soon appeared that he did not like
sleeping the night there. He liked to have his own
things around him, among them me; to retire late if he
wished, and sleep on undisturbed next morning. In the
afternoon, he could exchange civilities in such Greek
as the lady had, perform his husband's duty, and go
away.

She was not with child. Such things are not long a
secret. Those who had known him from a boy in
Macedon, said he had never yet had offspring; but then,
they added, he had never cared for women, so that
meant little.

No doubt her kin awaited the news with eagerness; but I saw none elsewhere. The Macedonians had
not grown to love the Sogdians, having found them
brave, but cruel, and not averse to treachery. True,
the King was now kin to half the noble Sogdians, and
the province was at peace. But the soldiers, who wanted
no Sogdian heir to rule their sons, were hoping she
would be barren.

Still they followed him. He drew them as a comet
draws its tail, by his light and fire. Besides, he was
head of their family. They could come to him as if
to their tribal chief at home. Half his business was
about their affairs. All who had campaigned with him,
Macedonian, hired Greek, wild painted Thracian,
knew some tale like that about the frozen soldier he'd
set in his own chair by the fire. And he was unde-
feated. That above all.

As for me, my grief was healing. True, when he'd
been with her he had nothing for me but his love; but
I could live well on that, and I guessed my fasts would
shorten. She tired him out. I could tell, though he
never said so. He did two men's work, a king's and a
general's; often enough a fighting soldier's as well. I
had always been content with whatever the day's
toil left him; he could come to me for a little drowsy
pleasure, given with love, followed by rest; and I would
slip away to let him sleep at ease. I don't think in the
harem tent it was quite so simple. Perhaps the beating
had raised false hopes.

Little by little, at any rate, his visits grew less fre-
quent; or he was out again in barely the time it needed
to ask after her health.

Philostratos had a box of new books, just come from
Ephesos. He had been too poor to order from a good
copying-house, and pay the costly cartage, till I'd asked
Alexander to make him that first present. He unpacked
them like an eager child; now, he said, we could
read Greek verse.

It was strange after the Persian; sparer in language,
stricter in form; but in time yielding up its treasures.
When I first read the entrance of Hippolytos, offering

his mountain flowers to the pure goddess he alone can see, my eyes ran over. Philostratos, somewhat awkwardly, patted my hand, supposing I wept for my former life—who knows, perhaps even for my present one.

Not all my thoughts were on Euripides. In the next tent—the camp slaves always pitched them the same way—Kallisthenes taught the squires. I heard things as I passed; even where I sat, if he forgot to keep his voice down.

Ismenios, though he had kept his word with honor, would talk to me when he could. One day I asked him what he thought of the lessons. He laughed. "I've not been for a three-month. I got sick and tired of them."

"Truly? When I missed you, I thought you must be on duty. Do you mean he's never told on you? You could be punished, surely?"

"Oh, yes. I suppose he's glad to be rid of me; he thinks I'm too stupid for philosophy. It's all we get now; meaning his opinions, of which I've had enough. When first we joined, we used to learn something useful."

Too stupid, or too loyal? Yes, maybe his absence was welcome. He was simple, compared with me who had served at Susa. Hearing what he disliked, he went away, when I would have stayed to listen.

My Greek was so fluent now, that Alexander was telling me not quite to lose my Persian accent, which he had grown fond of. But if Kallisthenes passed, I was always mute. It pleased him that a young barbarian could not master the tongue of Zeus' chosen race. I don't suppose it entered his head that Alexander ever *talked* to me.

I was indeed scarcely worth attention. The Persian boy was an old story; nothing in outrage, compared with the Sogdian wife.

Since the wedding, Kallisthenes had flaunted his austerity. He had been absent from the feast, pleading sickness, though he was about next day. Alexander, still willing to patch things up, even asked him to supper later, but got the same excuse. Few people were asking him anywhere; he was dour company and killed the mirth. Had I known it then, he was acting the new Athenian philosopher (old Sokrates, they say, was a good man at a party); and if I'd known more of Greece, perhaps I'd have guessed why. Even in my ignorance, I thought he called for watching, and would dawdle as I passed his class. For certain matters, he used a different voice.

Spring had broken. White flowers scented like jasmine opened on wayside thorns; lilies grew by the streams. Icy winds still whistled down the gorges. I remember a night when Alexander and I lay wound together; he disapproved of extra blankets, which he thought were softening, but did not object to me.

"Al'skander," I said, "who were Harmodios and Aristogeiton?"

"Lovers," he said sleepily. "Famous Athenian lovers. You must have seen their statues on the terrace at Susa. Xerxes took them from Athens."

"The ones with the daggers? The man and boy?"

"Yes. It's in Thukydides . . . What's the matter?"

"What were the daggers for?"

"Killing the tyrant Hippias. Though they never did it. They only got his brother, which made him more tyrannical." He roused himself to tell the story. "But they died with honor. The Athenians set great store by them. I'll send them back sometime. Very old statues. Stiff. The beautiful Harmodios, he's not fit to do up your shoes."

He would be asleep in a few more moments. "Al'-skander. I heard Kallisthenes telling the squires they killed the tyrant, and it was a noble work."

"Did he? Thukydides says it's a common error in Athens. There's an old song, I've heard it, about how they freed the city."

I did not say, "He spoke in a different voice." I had seen conspiracy at Ekbatana; I had felt it first with my skin; I thought that I felt it now. But though I spoke the language, I had not yet learned its little mysteries, the changes of note, the pauses, where secrets show.

"Well, don't kill him." He ran his hand over me laughing. "Aristotle would never forgive me." A draft came down the bed; we closed in a tighter knot. He had done three men's work that day, and was soon asleep.

A half-month later, while I combed his hair before supper, I told him that Kallisthenes had singled out Hermolaos and was forever in his company out of lesson-time. He replied that it was a pity, but love is blind.

"It's not love. Sostratos is his lover. I've watched him, he doesn't mind. Sometimes he's there too."

"So? I've been wondering what has gone wrong with their manners. That must be Kallisthenes. He never did know the difference between civility and servility. How tedious the man is. But he's a southern Greek, you must remember. Six generations they've prided themselves on never owning a master; it's destroyed half their greatest men. Xerxes got down as far as Attica, only because they wouldn't follow one leader. That's why my father too could have sacked Athens if he'd wanted, and so could I. But between Xerxes and us, three generations, till envy wrecked them again, they were truly great, and Athens was the heart of it. I've only been there once. But one feels it still."

"Al'skander, do you never comb it through when you're away? Underneath it's all in knots. If Kallisthenes hates a master, why did he come?"

"Because my father refounded Aristotle's home town as a fee for tutoring me. It was burned out in the Thracian wars when I was a boy; so was Olynthos, where Kallisthenes comes from. He thinks he's worth as much, though he's never said so. But why Aristotle sent him, was to keep me Greek. That's the real reason."

His hair was done, but I played with it to keep him talking.

"Ochos killed his best friend by torture, a man he'd studied with. He got the news in Macedon. 'Never forget,' he said to me, 'to treat Greeks as men, and barbarians as cattle created for men's use.' " He laid my hand to his cheek.

"A great mind; but it's never followed me here. I

write to him; I tell him each time I found a city, because he taught me civics and law. But I disappoint him. He can't see why, with a shake-up of Baktrians and Thracians and paid-off Macedonians and a few landless Greeks, I have to leave them a garrison and a code, not a constitution. The Greek cities of Asia, there I could make democracies; they understand it. But one must have justice, before all . . . I still send him gifts. I never forget my debt to him. I even put up with Kallisthenes, though he'll never know what it costs me."

I said, "I hope, my lord, he will never cost you more. It is time you had your hair cut." He never had it curled, and left it to hang in careless locks like a lion's mane; but he had it cut with care, to keep its shape. In early days, I stole a piece from the barber's cloth. I have it now, in a little golden box. It is still as bright as the gold.

I said no more. If I made myself tiresome, he would listen less. His patience was shorter, on the days when he'd been to the harem.

With the spring, we moved our camp higher up the hills, to a slope by a tumbling river, clothed in a forest of ancient cedars. Even at noon the sun was sifted and mild. Anemones grew there. The stones in the clear brown stream were like polished bronze. The scent of the cedars bettered Arabian spices; their sheddings gave to the tread like harem carpets. It was a place for happiness.

Though the forest was a paradise to ride in, I still found time for my Greek, and for watching Kallisthenes, and his favorite pupils.

He never, of course, had all the squires at once. Some were on duty, the night guard would be sleeping. They were assigned to their watches, though Alexander was not strict if they asked to change. Hermolaos and Sostratos had been let serve together. It was their watch that Kallisthenes took trouble with.

I've thought of him often, since I lived in Egpyt and read more books. He saw himself as a Greek philosopher; he knew, as I do now, that old Sokrates would never have made prostration; nor would Plato. But Alexander would no more have asked it of *them*, than he would of Aristotle if he'd made the journey. My lord recognized greatness of heart and honored it, as later he showed in India. He did not honor Kallisthenes, who had first flattered, then insulted him. Why should he? There are always men who take their own measure against greatness, and hate it not for what it is, but for what they are. They can envy even the dead.

So much Alexander saw. He did not understand, since it was not in him, the power such men have to rouse in others the sleeping envy they once had a decent shame of; to turn respect for excellence into hate. Nor did Kallisthenes understand it in himself. Vanity begets it, vanity covers it up.

Did he see he was unlike his followers, almost their opposite? He looked back to a greater Greece long dead. To these Macedonian youths, Greece was just a name; he was something new, a fashion in defiance.

Certainly both Hermolaos and Sostratos showed it, and they were making their mark on others. Alexander was taking notice. The squires' privilege was that they served directly under the King; no one else could punish them. Sostratos was reprimanded and put on extra guard; Hermolaos was cautioned.

They were at the end of their term of service; as soon as a new batch arrived from Macedon, they would be relieved. They were not boys being watched for awkwardness, but men, for insubordination; this they knew. An uneasy time. Alexander, when he gave me one of his many presents, said, "But for you, I'd be putting up with those louts in here."

So things stood, when he went up the mountain hunting.

I loved the hunt, though I never killed much; the rough ride, the keen upland air, the tall hounds finding and baying; the waiting tiptoe at the covert, to see what would come out. From tusk-roughened bark and droppings, we knew this time; it would be boar.

One side of the range was bare, the other full of

wooded folds and hollows. In a shade sweet with
crushed flowers, the hounds bayed the thick covert,
rank for them with boar-scent. Alexander gave his
horse to a squire; all the men dismounted. I too,
though I was terribly scared of boar. They can knock
you over, and tusk you open as you fall; if I got one
on my spear I could never hold it. Well, I thought, if
I die, he will remember me forever beautiful. And not
a coward.

The men stood straddled firmly, spears leveled, knees
bent a little to take the shock if the boar should break
their way. The hounds were slipped into the covert.
The squires stood near the King, a custom brought
from Macedon.

Something black shot out; there were furious grunting squeals. Perdikkas had killed. He was briefly
cheered; the hounds were still working within. The
noise came the King's way; he smiled with eagerness,
like a boy. Finding my own teeth clenched together,
I made myself smile too.

A tusked snout pushed forth; a great boar stood
at bay, a little sideways from Alexander, staring at the
invaders of its home, choosing an enemy. Alexander,
moving springily, stepped forward lest it should charge
a squire. But at the moment the boar broke out, Hermolaos ran forward, and took it on his spear.

It was unheard-of insolence. Alexander would have
yielded the game to any friend who had right of place
when it broke; but the squires were only there to attend him, as they were in battle.

The boar had been badly struck, and fought fiercely.
Alexander, himself not moving, signed to the other
squires to help. When the bloody, untidy work was
done, he beckoned Hermolaos. He came defiant, to
meet eyes he'd seen in displeasure, but never before
in anger. He paled. It was not a sight to forget.

"Go back to camp. Return your horse to the lines.
Go to your quarters. Stay there till you are sent for."

There was a hush among the rest. "Return your
horse" meant he was to be dismounted; a squire's
greatest disgrace, save one.

He moved to another wood, and the hunt continued. I think we ran down a stag. Then we went back. Alexander never liked putting off.

That afternoon he had all the squires paraded; a good many, when one saw all the watches together. He told them he knew who was giving good service, and they had nothing to fear. Some had grown slack and impudent; they had been warned already, in vain. He gave out the offense of Hermolaos, who had been brought under guard, and asked him what he had to say.

I've been told that in Macedon, no youth comes of age till he has taken a boar alone. (It was a man as well, in King Philip's day.) I don't know if Hermolaos had this in mind; certainly Alexander imposed no such condition. At all events, Hermolaos said, "I remembered I am a man."

I too remembered something; Kallisthenes exhorting his class to remember they were men, and using his different voice. I don't know if Alexander guessed whence the words had come. He just said, "Very good. Then you are fit to take a man's punishment. Twenty lashes, tomorrow at sunrise. The corps will attend to witness it. Dismiss."

I thought, If Sostratos is anything of a lover, it will be worst for him. Well, he should not have encouraged his friend in insolence; he is the elder.

All the same, having myself seen wounds and pain in the body that I loved, I could not help but pity him.

It was the first time a squire had been flogged in Alexander's reign. He bore it quite well. The lash did not lay him open to the bone, as I'd seen it done at Susa; but it cut him, and I daresay he didn't know it could be worse. It would scar him, a disgrace whenever he stripped for exercise. A Persian could have kept it hidden.

I saw Kallisthenes put his hand on Sostratos' shoulder. A kindly gesture; but Sostratos, with eyes only for his beloved, could not see the face behind him. There was pleasure in it. Not a relishing of the pain, but the look of one who sees events fall out as he would wish.

Well, I thought, if he hopes this will turn the soldiers against the King, he's a fool; they understand discipline. I did not think it worth mentioning to Alexander; especially as things seemed to get better afterwards. The lessons I overheard were nothing out of the way; the different voice had gone. Perhaps he repented having harmed his pupil. Hermolaos, when after his cuts had scabbed he returned to duty, had become very correct; Sostratos also.

It was about this time, that the Syrian soothsayer began to hang about the King.

She had followed the camp for months, a little brown thing, young-old, in tattered clothes stitched with gold thread, and tawdry beads. She had a familiar spirit, and would wander about till he pointed out a man to her. Then she would tell him she'd luck to give him, for a loaf or a silver bit. They laughed at first, till they saw that those who gave, got the luck she promised. She would not divine for everyone; her Master must show the man. She came to be thought well-omened, and never starved. But once, some drunk bullies baited her; she was frightened at first, then looked at the leader suddenly, as if she'd only just seen him, and said, "You will die about noon, the third day of this moon's waning." He fell in a skirmish, on the day. After that she was left in peace.

Once or twice she had offered Alexander luck for nothing. He'd laughed, made her a gift, and not stopped to listen. You were pretty safe in prophesying him victory; but later, when he'd stayed for a word or two, he found small things she foretold fell pat, and would hear her out. With his gold, she bought herself a new gaudy dress; but as she slept in it, it soon looked much like the old one.

Of a morning, I used to enter the King's tent by the back way, that went straight into the sleeping-place. (It had been made for Darius, to bring in his women quietly.) One day I found her there, squatting cross-legged outside. The squires had not turned her off, because Alexander had told them not to. "Why, mother,"

I said, "have you been here all night? You look like it."

She roused herself, and shook the coins in her ears, two that Alexander had given her. "Yes, little son." (I was a full head taller.) "Master sent me. But now he says it's not yet."

"Never mind, mother. When the luck-day comes, you know the King will listen. Go along and sleep."

About a month after the boar-hunt, Perdikkas gave a party for Alexander.

It was a big one; all his best friends; also their mistresses, if they were suitable; meaning as a rule Greek hetairas of good standing. There were of course no Persians. A Persian gentleman would rather die than show in public the very least of his concubines; even Macedonians who had ladies taken in conquered cities, did not put them to this disgrace. Alexander would not have allowed it.

Through the open tent-flap I saw Ptolemy's Thais, crowned with roses, sitting on his supper couch near Alexander. She was an old friend, almost of his boyhood, having been Ptolemy's mistress before he crossed to Asia; being then quite young, she was in full beauty still. Ptolemy kept her almost like a wife, though not so strictly, which, after her fame in Corinth, she would not have endured. Alexander had always got on well with her. She was the girl who'd called to him, at Persepolis, to burn the Palace.

He was dressed all Greek tonight, in a blue robe trimmed with gold, and a wreath of gold leaves, into which I had stuck fresh flowers for him. I thought, He has never been ashamed of me. I might be sharing his couch, if it weren't that he knows it would grieve Hephaistion. Already it was growing easier to forget Roxane. Hephaistion I never forgot.

Alexander had told me not to wait up. Yet in his tent I dragged out my little tasks. I felt an odd guilt at the thought of leaving, though, as I'd first watched the feast, it was already late.

Round the tent the night guard was on duty, the usual watch of six; Hermolaos, Sostratos, Antikles, Epimenes, and a couple more. Antikles had changed over from another watch just lately. I stood in the back entry, smelling the night, hearing the hum of the camp, a dog baying—not Peritas, whom I'd left fast asleep inside—and the laughter from the feast. Light from the open tent slanted between the cedars.

The women were leaving. They squealed and giggled as the soft cedar-mast tripped their tipsy feet. Their torchbearers led them off among the trees. In the tent, someone plucked a lyre, and they started singing.

Held by the beauty of the night, the flitting lights and the music, I lingered, I don't know how long. Suddenly Hermolaos was by me. I'd not heard him, on the soft ground. "Are you waiting up, Bagoas? The King said he'd be very late." In the past, he'd have put a sneer in it; now he spoke very pleasantly. I thought again how his manners had improved.

I was saying I was off to bed, when I saw a torch approaching. I must have dreamed a good while. It was lighting Alexander. Perdikkas and Ptolemy and Hephaistion were seeing him home. They looked steady enough on their feet, and were all laughing together.

Glad to have waited, I was about to go inside, when I saw in the jumping torchlight the Syrian woman. She came flitting along, like a night-owl, to Alexander; tugged at his robe, and reached up to straighten his chaplet. "What now, mother?" he said smiling. "I've had my luck for tonight."

"Oh, no, my King!" She grabbed him again with her little nut of a fist. "No, child of fire! My Master sees you, he sees your best luck to come. Go back to the feast, rejoice till sunup, your life's best luck is there for you. There's none for you here, my darling, none here at all."

"You see?" said Perdikkas. "Come back and bring luck to *us*."

Alexander looked at them laughing. "The gods give good advice. Who's for a dip in the river, before we start again?"

"Not you," Hephaistion said. "It's snow-water, like the Kydnos, and you know that nearly killed you. Let's go and sing."

They all went back, except Ptolemy and Leonnatos, who were on bodyguard duty next morning. Returning to the tent, I saw the squires had left their stations and were in a huddle, muttering. Slack discipline, I thought. Well, I'm for bed.

Yet still I did not go. After the soothsayer, the night now felt uncanny. I did not like her saying there was no luck for Alexander here. I went in. The squires still had their heads together; anyone could have entered, like me, unseen. I thought, They'll never make soldiers.

At the bed's foot, Peritas lay stretched out snoring. He was a dog who dreamed, jerking his paws, and with soft squeaks chasing his dream-quarry. But he was still, and never raised his head for me.

I will watch, I thought, for my lord's bad luck, since not even the dog is doing it. I rolled in my blanket, in a corner out of the way, in case the King's friends came in with him. The cedar-mast made the floor soft as a mattress. I closed my eyes.

I awoke to daylight. Alexander was there. The tent seemed full of people. They were the squires of the night guard; why? Their watch ended at dawn. He was speaking to them with great kindness, saying he understood what they'd done, and here was something to mark it. He gave each a gold piece and a smile, and sent them off.

He did not seem much the worse for his long night; the talk must have been good. He never flung down the wine as he used by the Oxos, or at Marakanda.

The last squire out was Sostratos. By chance he looked my way, and gave a violent start. No wonder, I thought, when none of you had your eyes open.

Alexander said, as he dropped his clothes off, that I ought to be in bed. I asked if the promised luck had come to him.

"Yes. But I had it here, after all. You saw who the night guards were; all the bad squad. They were relieved at dawn; but when I got back, they were all still at their stations, standing by. They meant it for a sign to me. I've never yet been hard on a man who asked for pardon. If I'd turned in early, they'd have had no chance to do it. I must give the Syrian something. By Herakles, though, I'm tired! Let no one near me all day."

I washed and changed, took a canter through the forest, and, the camp now growing busy, went back to make sure he was undisturbed. He slept like the dead; so, strangely, did Peritas still. I felt his nose, but it was cool.

There were voices in the outer tent, which I thought too loud. The bodyguards, Ptolemy and Leonnatos, had two men there making a great to-do. In one, to my surprise, I recognized young Epimenes of the night guard, sobbing, his face in his hands. The other said, "Forgive him, sirs, he's been in such great distress." At this I came forward, saying to Ptolemy that the King was sleeping, and had asked for quiet.

"I know that," said Ptolemy shortly. "But I shall have to wake him. He's lucky to be alive. Leonnatos, can I leave these two with you?"

Whatever was this? It was unheard of, to wake him against orders in his first dead sleep. But Ptolemy was no fool. I went in behind him, without excuse, taking myself for granted.

Alexander had turned on his back and was snoring softly; he had to be very deep to do that. Ptolemy stood over him and called his name. His eyelids creased, but he did not stir. Ptolemy shook him.

He returned as if from death. His eyes looked blind. With a great sigh he forced back sight into them, and said, "What is it?"

"Are you awake, Alexander? Listen. It's a matter of your life."

"Yes. I'm awake. Go on."

"There's a squire, Epimenes, was on guard last night. He says they'd all planned to kill you in your sleep. If you'd gone to bed, they'd have done it."

Alexander's brow creased deeply. Slowly he sat up naked, and rubbed his eyes. I came with a towel wrung in cold water; he took it and wiped his face. Presently he said, "Who's that weeping?"

"The boy. He says you were good to him this morning, and he was ashamed."

He had smiled at them. I remembered the first time he'd smiled at me.

"He told his lover," Ptolemy said, "because he didn't know what to do; they'd all taken some oath together. The lover's in the Companions; he soon made up his mind for him, and told his elder brother, to settle it."

"I see. Get me the man's name, I owe him something. And the rest of them? What were they going to do?"

"Wait. Wait till their turn came round again. They've been a full month, the boy says, working themselves into the same watch together. That's why they hung about this morning, after they were relieved. They couldn't make up their minds to having failed, after all their trouble."

"Yes," said Alexander slowly. "Yes, I see. Are there any other names?"

"One or two. I've taken them down. Do you want them from him or me?"

He paused, wiping the towel across his eyes. "No, arrest them all. I'll deal with it tomorrow. I can't come to a treason trial half asleep. But I'll see Epimenes." He stood up. I put a fresh chiton on him.

In the outer tent, the brothers fell on their knees, the elder with outstretched hands. Alexander said, "No, Eurylochos, don't ask your brother's life from me." The man went ashen. "No, you mistake me; I meant, don't deny me the pleasure of giving it you unasked." He had not meant to torment him; he was still barely awake. "I shall thank you later. You'll both be needed tomorrow, but set your minds at rest." He gave his right hand to each, along with a smile. I could see that from now on, either would die for him at a word.

When they'd gone, he said to Ptolemy, "Give out a free pardon for the next of kin, or they'll be running away all over Baktria. Why put them to that; we know where it all began. Arrest him. Keep him apart from the others."

"You mean Hermolaos?"

"I mean Kallisthenes. It's time. Will you do all that for me? Then I'll get back to bed."

He slept quite soon. He was used to living close to death.

At evening he woke, had a drink of water, ordered a night guard from the Companions, and slept again till sunrise. Then he sent for me.

"You warned me," he said. "Again and again you warned me. I thought . . ." He laid his hand on mine. He'd thought, of course, that I came from a corrupt court, and it was not my fault if I brought its suspicions with me. "I thought you were overanxious. You've heard Kallisthenes putting this in their minds?"

"I think so. Among Persians I'd have known. But I think so, yes."

"Tell it me all again. These people will be put to the question. I've no wish to drag it on. With something to go on, I can make it shorter."

I felt no such wish. My former pity had changed to sparks of fire. Whatever had to be done, I would gladly have done myself, if I'd had the skill. But I told all I remembered, starting with the Athenian lovers. "Yes," he said. "I read you a lesson and laughed at you. You asked me, What were the daggers for?"

"He was forever on about some tyrants in Greece. I don't remember their names. They lived in—in Si— Syracuse? And Tessaly."

"Thessaly. He was killed in bed. Go on."

"Then, after Hermolaos was beaten, it stopped. It was only the Good Life, or figuring with numbers. I thought he knew he'd been wrong. Now, I think he'd chosen his men, and wanted to keep it from the others. A few days back, when I was riding in the woods, he was there with all of them, and a couple more. I thought, then, he was teaching them about plants, as Aristotle did you."

"Why not, after I'd made light of you? Do you know who the others were?"

I did, and told him. I felt no reproach to him for heeding me so late. I loved him for finding it so hard to think the worst, even of a man he'd been at odds with. I did not remind him that I'd wanted to rid him of the fellow long ago. I remembered how he'd spoken gently to the waiting murderers, and made them gifts. It would leave a mark on him, as deep as the catapult bolt at Gaza.

The squires were taken out of the camp for questioning. Ptolemy, who I daresay was there, writes that they all confessed Kallisthenes had inspired them.

Later, Alexander found me in the tent giving milk to Peritas, who was sick from the drug they'd dosed him with, and would not eat. He said, "The other two names were those you gave me. I'm grateful to you for that." He caressed the dog, who had staggered to his feet to greet him. "I'm glad you were not needed there; you are too gentle for such work."

"Gentle?" I said. "They would have killed you sleeping, when not all together would have faced you waking, mother-naked with just your sword. No, my lord, you would not have found me gentle." He ran his hand through my hair, and did not believe me.

They went to their trial able to walk, which I suppose was proper. Not being Macedonian, I was only there to see them stoned. The stones came from the river-bed; clean, round and good to grip. But it would have outraged everyone, for a Persian to stone a Macedonian. There were willing hands enough. The vote for death had been passed by acclamation; even the fathers, if they were there, agreeing. By the old law of Macedon, they should all have died as well; not so much for being suspect, as to protect the King from blood-feud. Alexander was the first to grant free pardon.

When the condemned were brought, Alexander asked if any wished to speak. I understood, after Hermolaos accepted.

I will say he kept a good countenance, though his voice grew shrill. But as he spoke, every word came like an echo. It was the voice of a disciple—a steadfast one, that I concede to the dead—paying his master homage. To most of the Macedonians it was mere insolence; Alexander had to restrain them till the youth had done; but to those who'd heard the speeches on the prostration, it was proof. As they were led to the stakes, Sostratos passed me. It was he who had seen me in the tent that morning. He spat towards me. "Yes, and we'd have had you too, filthy painted barbarian whore."

It grieved me to stand still while others revenged my lord. Whenever I saw a strong man with a big stone, I prayed to Mithra, Avenger of Loyalty, "Send that for me." One such broke Hermolaos' head.

Kallisthenes I never saw again. Only Macedonians had right of trial before Assembly. Ptolemy thinks he was put to the question and then killed, but I doubt he was there, for I have heard a different story.

At the time, Alexander did not speak to me of it, so I did not ask. I felt things which went deep with him, and which he didn't think I would understand. But a long time after, when he was rather drunk and had forgotten he'd never told me, he said something from which I pieced it out. I think when they went over Kallisthenes' papers, they found letters from Aristotle. The philosopher had heard, it seemed, from his nephew how the King made barbarians his friends and officers; had required free Greeks to bow down to him along with this servile breed; had first taken to his bed a Persian eunuch, who'd even been in Darius' bed before; then stooped to marry a Sogdian savage, a mere dancer at a feast. And the philosopher had written (letters no doubt too precious to be destroyed) that such things would bring back the rule of tyranny and corrupt all good Greek ways. No means should be spared to make an end of it.

Old Sokrates and Plato had both been soldiers; Aristotle never. Maybe he'd had no thought that his words would beget more than other words. If so, he did not know men. Alexander, who did, and now knew more, had seen the effect; small wonder if he doubted the intention.

At all events, I heard long after of Kallisthenes alive in bonds, and that Alexander meant to try him in Greece before Aristotle, to show where his words had led, but that in India Kallisthenes died of sickness. One thing is sure, that in Athens, which Alexander had spared only to hate and slander him, Kallisthenes would have been a great man indeed if the King had died. To me he did not speak of it.

To Hephaistion he did. They sat long of an evening, talking quietly with Peritas at their feet. They had studied together with the philosopher as boys in Macedon and shared their thoughts. Hephaistion knew it all; not like a boy from Susa, whose only schooling had been in pleasing a king.

This I know; no more pressed flowers or strange beasts went from Alexander to the school at Athens. And this I understand; that as his power grew, he had often asked himself how his old teacher would advise him; but now it ended. Henceforward he would listen only to his own soul.

20

Iₙ ᴛʜᴇ end we did not start that year for India. In Sogdiana, they sent the King a whole new army to train, from provinces all over Asia. Though they'd been drilled by Macedonian officers, it's one thing to school a colt, another to get him knowing the master's hand.

For me it was strange indeed, to see the very peoples who'd made up Darius' army (often the same men) once more in a great host, but one so changed; no longer a formless mass of peasants with home-forged arms, waiting for chiefs in chariots to call them on, with the whip-men behind to urge them; but phalanxes and squadrons, forming or wheeling at a word.

Alexander inspected them in all his parade armor; he knew they would want to see a king. He flamed in the sun like the image of a god. When he threw them into maneuver, they went at it as if for a prize. There he was on a little hill, with his generals and some Persian officers, directing this vast host from his conquered nations, which had only to charge as one to sweep him from the earth. It could not happen, simply because he knew it could not. He was Alexander.

He returned to the Rock, taking his wife to see her kindred; all very properly done. One could tell they were grieved she was not with child; but he made them princely gifts, treated them courteously, and had taken no other wife. What could they say?

One was enough. He had far too much pride to bring the secrets of the marriage chamber, even to me. He knew that I understood. I have heard it said that some men choose wives in whom they see their mothers. From all I could learn of Queen Olympias, her son was one of them. But that he learned too late.

Of Olympias, I've heard she was fierce and beautiful, and brawled with her lord till the day he died, which it was whispered she'd had a hand in. She ate Alexander up with love, and made sure he and his father were never friends for long. All of us knew she had never learned the conduct of a lady; for her letters followed him all over Asia, intriguing in the affairs of Macedon, and quarreling with Antipatros, his regent there. Alexander had been heard to say, after reading one of them, that she charged high rent for the nine months' lodging she'd given him.

All of which goes to show, to my mind, that we Persians could teach the Greeks how to deal with women.

Maybe we'd taught Alexander. But also, gentle as he was with them, he had somewhere a deep core of iron, forged, I expect, when he freed himself from his mother. He had no brawls with Roxane. He never forgot he was Great King. She had her harem tent and her household; there she could rule. He would visit her now and again; if she was troublesome, he would leave, and be slower to return. I knew, as soon as he came back to me. There were certain signs, of relief from distaste elsewhere. I had been trained to understand such things.

The new squires had come out from Macedon. Even there, they'd learned of the traitors' fate. A scared huddle of boys, afraid to open their mouths, they were brought before the King. He was charming to them, and knew all their names in no time. In relief they fell over each other, trying to please him; spoke to me with respect, and gratefully took advice from me. They seemed very young. Since the last set came, I was four years older.

It was one of them who fetched me to Alexander, in the dark before dawn. He was sitting in his bath-robe on the side of his bed. Down the middle lay Peritas, taking up all the room. He had never been the same since the squires had drugged him.

Alexander said, "He tried to climb up, and I told him to get down. After a while he tried again, and something warned me."

"How old was he?"

"Eleven. He should have lived a few years more. He was quiet all yesterday. I had him in Illyria, from King Kotys' huntsman, when I'd fallen out with my father and gone away. He looked like a bear-cub. I had nothing much to do, and he was good company."

"You must have his likeness put on his tomb," I said, "so that he will be remembered by men to come."

"I'll do better for him than that. I'll name my next city after him."

It has a fine site, approved by the soldiers and the merchants, on a good pass to India. The tomb and the statue are by the gate as you go in. The city is called Perita.

When the passes froze, we wintered in eastern Baktria. Though urgent news came through, it was long before we learned how Kallisthenes was beginning already his long revenge, which he has not ceased from yet.

In Athens, the news of his arrest had been like kicking a wasp-nest. More than ten years had passed, since King Philip had beaten them in a battle not of his seeking, which their speechmaker Demosthenes had talked them into, bringing ruin to Thebes as well. (It was Alexander, at eighteen, who first broke their line.) After, Philip had shown Athens a mercy that astonished Greece. In spite of this, or (for who knows man's heart?) because of it, they had loathed him, and were suspect of privity to his murder; they loathed his son, who had never set foot there but once on a peaceful mission. While my lord lived, they kept quiet from fear; after, like jackals when the lion dies, they began to tear him.

It did even the great Aristotle no good, that he'd warned his pupil against Persians; he had to run for his life, as a friend of Macedon, and never dared return. A smaller man took his school; then the philosophers joined the chorus.

So now, for mercy and honor shown to my people, my lord is barbarous; a tyrant, because he punished his would-be murderers, the right of their meanest citizen; a mere vaunting soldier, though wherever he went he brought Greece with him, the Greece he honored, of which these liars are the unworthy heirs.

One good thing's come out of it; it determined King Ptolemy to write down the truth while he still has time. Now, he had rather work on his book than govern Egypt, which he mostly leaves to his son.

"Oh, my dear Bagoas!" my friends here say to me. "A man like you, who reads the best of the Greeks, how can you be content to die without seeing Athens? The voyage is nothing, in the good season. I can recommend you a ship; I will write out all the things you ought to see; I will give you letters to men of learning. What holds you back, when you've traveled so much further? Do go, before age overtakes you and journeys become a burden." So they say. But my lord in his house of gold here, my lord who is younger now than I—he understands why I shall never go to Athens.

Spring broke at last. It was time for India.

All winter the King had been seeing caravan masters, and Greeks from beyond Kaukasos, who had gone trading with the caravans and stayed on. Craving for Greek speech again, or just for gold, they came to tell him about the country beyond the mountains, the Land of Five Rivers.

These rivers flowed down from Kaukasos, the greatest being the Indus which received the rest. The Indians who lived between them were mostly at feud, and would welcome anyone who fought their enemies. Alexander said that it had been the same in Greece, which was how his father had conquered it.

From the man who had journeyed furthest, he learned one day that a half-month's march from the Indus was a river even greater. This stream, the Ganges, flowed not west but east, and ran into the Ocean.

I have seldom seen him so exalted. He was still full of it at bedtime, though he'd been talking of it all day. "The Encircling Ocean! We shall have crossed the world to its furthest end. We can sail north to the Euxine, or round south to Babylon. We shall stand at the end of the world."

"It will be remembered forever," I said, "by men to come."

I had been wearing my coat of the silk from Marakanda, with its flying serpents and flowers. Its blue gleam caught my eye (I had taken it off to bathe him); the buttons were of a pale green stone, heavy and cool to touch, carved with magic signs. According to the merchant, it had all been a year on the road. The liar, I thought; he was just putting up the price.

"What are you thinking of?" asked Alexander smiling. I was ashamed to have been so trivial, and said, "Of the altar you'll build, Al'skander, at the world's end, carved with your name."

"Ride with me tomorrow early. I must give Oxhead a canter, or he'll start grieving. His wind's still good. But I'm sorry he must cross the mountains." He still missed Peritas. Friends had offered him good dogs, but he would not have one. "You know," he said, "Oxhead is rising thirty."

I bent, as I washed him, and kissed his head. I had seen, where the lamplight caught the gold, two threads of grey.

When spring opened the passes, we marked our leaving with a holocaust. The new troops had brought only their own necessaries; but the old army was lumbered up with wagons and wagons of heavy loot—furniture, beds and bedding, hangings, carpets, clothing; meant,

I suppose, to be carted back to Macedon. They were no use meantime, unless to sell for a song by men in debt. The generals had whole trains of it. Alexander, though he always kept less than he gave, had some wagons of fine stuffs and carpets. He had everything carted out on a bit of heath, and the draft-beasts led away. Then he went up to his own wagons. A fire had been kindled near, with a pile of torches by it. Into each wagon, he threw a burning torch.

The officers, warned beforehand, followed suit. Even the men did not hang back too long. They had shed blood for all these goods, and carried them off in triumph; now they were tired of hauling them along. Besides, a love of fire is born in everyone; even a young child will try to grasp it; which proves that it is divine. As the splendid blaze went up, the men started flinging firebrands, at other men's things at first, then anywhere, laughing and shouting like boys, till the heat drove them back. But I watched the revel, I who had grown old without manhood when I was ten; I remembered the burning rafters of my father's house, and thought of the waste of war.

This time we crossed Parapamisos without much hardship; Alexander had learned from the time before. He stayed awhile in Alexandria, putting it to rights, the governor having proved a fool and rogue; meantime, he sent heralds over to Omphis, the nearest of the Indian kings, asking for his allegiance. His land had been subject to the empire since the first Darius' day.

Omphis came himself; the first Indian, except a few common soldiers, the troops had seen. He came with twenty-five elephants, on the first of which he sat like a glittering image in his painted howdah; a handsome man of good stature, darker than a Mede, but not so dark as an Ethiop. He wore ivory earrings; his mustache and beard were dyed bright green. We Persians like rich colors; the Indians prefer brilliant ones. Besides the gold sequins stitched to his clothing everywhere, he was stuck all over with jewels so huge, I'd not have believed in them, if he had not been a king.

I don't know how much pomp he'd expected of Alexander. I could see him pause a moment, wondering where he was, till he saw the face and knew. He offered willing fealty, in exchange for help against his enemy, a king called Poros. This Alexander promised, if the man did not offer allegiance. He put on a great feast for Omphis, and gave him gold. None is mined in those parts, so the princes greatly prize it. Omphis promised, in return, all twenty-five of his elephants, as soon as he'd got home on them. Alexander in turn was pleased. He never used them for war, thinking them uncertain, as indeed they are; but he valued them for their strength and wisdom. They carried the parts from which he set up his catapults. Once or twice he rode one; but said he liked to feel the beast that bore him, not sit on it in a chair.

Soon he held his war council, to plan the march on India. His sleeping-room at Alexandria was just behind the room of audience, so I heard it all.

Hephaistion got command of his own army. He was to cross Great Kaukasos by the good pass, which Sogdians call Khyber; when he reached the Indus, he was to bridge it for Alexander. Khyber being the easiest way (but for the men who live there) he was to take in his charge the followers and all the women, not leaving out the harem. Alexander, with his own army and the chief of the Companions, would take the hardest task; clearing the mountains which commanded the pass of anyone who threatened it.

As I listened, I thought, This is a crossroads in my life. Now or never.

I can't remember what he came in for after; to get a cloak or some such thing. "Alexander," I said, "I happened to overhear your war council."

"You always do. I only put up with it because you keep your mouth shut. Why tell me now?" He looked stern. He knew well enough what I was after.

"Don't send me with the followers. Take me with you."

"You should have listened better. Mine is a campaign, not a march. It may not be done by winter."

"My lord, I know. It's too long to leave you."

He frowned. He wanted to take me; but he believed in doing without comforts in the field. "You've never been trained to hardship."

"I come from the mountains that bred Kyros. Don't put me to shame."

He stood, still frowning, and looking about for what he'd come in for. I knew what it was without telling, and gave it him with a smile. "That's all very well," he said. "But war is war."

"You take tanners and carpenters and cooks and bakers. You take slaves. Am I worth less?"

"Too much. I wish you knew what you're asking for. And there won't be much time for love."

"For bed? I know. But for love, while I live, I shall always have time enough."

He looked into my eyes, then said, "I meant not to do this." He went to his coffer and took out a fistful of gold. "Get yourself more warm things, you'll need them. Pack away your dress-clothes and your tent-trimmings. Buy sheepskin horse-blankets. You may take one servant and one pack-mule."

In the passes it was already autumn. North of Khyber, the people were hunters and herders, whose second trade was robbery. They were reported fierce; Alexander wanted their submission.

Even up in the Parapamisos, I had not had mountain sickness. We were lower here than there; though Alexander climbed at first by slow stages, to temper our blood for the thin air. My childhood had not yet been lost in me; I went up without distress. Sometimes at evening I would count Alexander's breaths against mine, and they were faster; but he had more work to do. He never owned to fatigue.

Some say the Wise God's heaven is a rose garden. For me, it is in the heights. After all, he lives there. Watching the dawn on snows no bird had touched, I shivered with joy. We were invading a land of gods, whose cold hands would soon fall on us; there were wars to come; but I could feel no dread.

In the end, Alexander had let me take my Thracian

groom as well as my body-servant. I think he'd really feared I might die of hardship. At night in his campaign tent (made to his order; Darius had never owned anything so simple) he'd ask if I was well. At last, guessing what he'd never utter, I said, "Al'skander, you think eunuchs are different in too many ways. If we're shut up with women and live soft with them, then we grow like them; but so would any man. Just because we have women's voices, it doesn't mean we have women's strength."

He took my hand smiling. "You've not a woman's voice; it is too pure. It's like the aulos, the deep-toned flute." He was glad to be free of the harem.

In the night with its fierce white stars, before the snow-clouds had gathered, as I sat by my pine-wood fire the young squires would leave their own to squat beside me. "Bagoas, tell us about Susa, tell us about Persepolis, tell us about the court in Darius' day." Or I would watch the blaze where Alexander sat with Ptolemy and Leonnatos and his other officers. They would pass round the wine and talk and laugh; but there was no night when Alexander turned in with steps less steady than mine.

He never had me to bed. Always before hard tasks he would gather himself together, wasting nothing. Fire is divine. He was glad of me; that was enough.

Then the wars began. The tribesmen's forts clung to the crags, like martins' nests. The first we came to looked impossible to storm. Alexander sent an interpreter, to offer terms, but they defied him. The Persian kings had never brought these lands under law.

The forts had done well against the assaults of other tribesmen, who had stones and arrows. Alexander had light catapults, whose bolts must have seemed to them like the darts of demons. He had scaling-ladders too. When they saw his men coming over their walls, they left the fort and fled on the mountainside. The Macedonians ran after them, and killed all they could overtake, while the fort was burned. I watched it from the camp. Though a long way off, I felt concern for these little figures, caught in the rocks or on old snowfields. I had taken calmly the deaths of many, because I had not seen them as single men. It was folly, for they would have roused other tribes against us, if they'd got away.

When the fight was over, I learned what had made Alexander's troops so fierce. He had an arrow wound in the shoulder. He'd made light of it; the corselet had stopped it from sinking in its barb. No one ever made less of his wounds than he did in battle; but it was always the same, if he got one his men went nearly mad. It was part love, part dread of being left without him.

When the doctor had gone, I took off his bandage and sucked the place clear; who could say what such people put on their arrows? It was to do such things that I'd come, though I'd had too much sense to tell him so; the way to persuade him was always to beg a gift.

The camp was noisy; the soldiers had come without women, all but the hardiest who never left their men; now they had all those from the fort, tall broad-faced hillwomen with strong black hair and jewels stuck through their noses.

Alexander took a fancy for me that night. The wound opened and I was covered in blood; he just laughed, and made me wash in case the guard thought I'd murdered him. The wound felt easier, he said; no physician like love. It is true that when dry they often fester.

The next fort surrendered, having heard about the first; so everyone was spared, as his custom was. As we marched onward, the mountain gods sent winter. We pushed through thick driving snow like barley-grains; our clothes and our horses and the men's sheep-skin cloaks were frosted white; the beasts slithered and stumbled on the drifted tracks, which we needed native guides to find. Then the sky would clear, and the white would dazzle till we rode with eyes almost closed; that light can blind a man.

We were amply fed, Alexander saw to that; and not climbing higher than timber grows, we had warm blazing fires at night. If the wind pushed cold fingers through my furs, I just wrapped my scarf to keep my face from burning, and thought of my luck to be here with no Roxane; above all with no Hephaistion.

Alexander took the hill-forts one by one, except those that surrendered. I hardly remember one from another now, though King Ptolemy remembers each one. He did some notable deeds of arms up there, among them a duel hand to hand with an important chief, whose shield he's kept to this day. He has put them all in his book, and who shall blame him?

After many battles and sieges, we sighted Massaga, stretched across a hill-spur; no mere tribal fort, but a strong walled town.

It gave Alexander four days' work. On the first, when they made a sortie from their gates, he fled to lure them out, then whipped round on them and caught a good many, though the rest got back inside. Then, lest they still thought he was scared, he marched up to the walls, for which he got an arrow in his ankle. By luck no sinew was cut; the doctor told him to rest it, as one might tell a river to run back up the hills.

Next day he brought up rams and breached the wall; but the breach was stoutly held. At night, he limped now and then when he forgot, but stopped himself next moment.

The day after, he ran a bridge across to the breach from a wooden siege-tower (he'd brought engineers to make such things on the spot) and led the assault himself. Before he'd crossed, so many had pressed up to be fighting next him, that the bridge broke in the middle.

I died many deaths, before they scrambled out from the rubble below, and I saw his white-winged helmet. He limped back all grazed and bruised, but only said he was lucky not to have broken a leg; he'd just come from seeing the wounded.

Next day, with a stronger bridge, he tried again and got over. While they fought on the walls, the tribal chief fell to a catapult bolt; and the town sued for a truce, which Alexander granted.

Seven thousand of their best fighting men turned out to have been hired, from somewhere beyond the rivers; they were shorter and darker than the rest. Alexander had them called out apart; he wanted to hire them himself. They had a different tongue from the hillmen's, but the interpreter said he knew it. In the King's presence he addressed them; the officers replied; after some parley, he said they agreed to the offered terms. So they camped by themselves on a hill nearby, while the townspeople were treated with; and Alexander set scouts to watch them, they being strangers whose good faith he did not know, in a force that could be dangerous. He'd learned to take care, in Sogdiana.

"A good day's work," he said to me after supper. He had bathed, and I was dressing his ankle, which seemed to be healing clean in spite of everything.

A night-guard squire came in. "Sir. One of the outpost guards, asking to report." Alexander said, "I'll see him now."

The man was young, but looked steady. "Alexander. The Indians on the hill are getting ready to go."

He stood up, stepping on my clean bandage. "How do you know?"

"Well, King, the later it's grown, with everyone else asleep, the more they're stirring. It's not so dark you can't see them against the sky. Nobody's lying down; the whole camp's milling; the men are bearing arms, and I saw some leading pack-beasts. I've good eyes, Alexander, at night; I'm known for it. That's why the commander sent me to report."

Alexander's face set. He nodded slowly. Nothing was new, after two years in Sogdiana. "Yes, you did well. Stand by outside. Bagoas, I'll dress again." He called back the squire. "Fetch the interpreter. And hurry."

The man came, just out of bed. Alexander said, "The hired soldiers you treated with today; are you really fluent in their language?"

The man, looking scared, assured him that he was; he had gone to their country with the caravans, and bargained for the merchants.

"You are sure they agreed, and understood what they agreed to?"

"Great King, without any doubt."

"Very good. You can go. Menestas, have General Ptolemy waked, and ask him to see me now."

He came, looking as always alert, steady and tough as well-cured leather. Alexander said, "The Indian mercenaries are deserting. They must have sworn in to put us off guard. We can't have them joining with the tribes and falling on the column. If they can't be trusted they're a standing danger, held or let go."

"That's true. They're too many. And trained." He paused, and looked at Alexander. "Now? Tonight?"

"Yes. We'll take the whole force and do it quickly. Have the men turned out by word of mouth. No trumpets. While that's doing, I'll make the dispositions. There's clear ground all round that hill. We've enough men to ring it."

Ptolemy left. He called the squires to arm him. I heard the deep muttering stir as the camp was roused. The officers came for their orders. It seemed to take no time at all. His army was trained for swiftness, he only had to call for it. Soon the long files of men were stumbling and clanking off into the darkness.

After so much haste, the quiet seemed to last forever. Then the yells began. They seemed eternal, too. They crossed the valley like the sound of the last battle which, we are told, will end the world. But that will be between Light and Dark. Here all was night.

I thought I heard, in the din, shrill screams like women's. I was right. They had been with the Indians; had picked up the arms of fallen men and were killed in the darkness, fighting.

At last the yells grew less, then were few and broken. Then there was only, here and there, a death-cry. After that, night's silence.

Two hours before the late winter dawn, the camp sounded with men again. Alexander came back.

The squires unbuckled his blood-slimed armor, and took it out to clean. He looked drawn and grey; lines that had hardly showed, were cut across his forehead.

I took off his tunic; that was blood-soaked too, except where the armor had covered it. He seemed hardly aware of me, so that I looked at him as if myself unseen. Then his eyes turned to mine and knew them.

"It was necessary," he said.

I had the slaves get a bath ready. That too was necessary; even his face was splashed with blood, his arms and his knees were red with it. When he was in bed, I asked if he was hungry. He said, "No. Just a little wine." I brought him that, and the night-lamp, and was going away. "Bagoas," he said, looking up into my face. So I bent and kissed him. He received it like a gift, thanking me with his eyes.

I lay in my tent, in the cold before the dawn, with the fire dying outside, and thought, as I'd been thinking all night, that the interpreter was a Sogdian, and no Sogdian will own there is anything he cannot do. Still, if the Indians had believed they were free to go, they would have gone by day. Did they know they had broken faith, did they know they'd pledged it? Alexander had watched them. They must have looked as if they understood.

I thought of the heap of dead upon the hill, with the wolves and the jackals already tearing them; and I knew that other hands before his had sealed their death: the hand of Philotas; the hands of the dead squires; the hands of all those chiefs and satraps who had taken his right hand, sworn loyalty and been his welcome guests; then murdered his men whom he'd trusted to them, and fallen on his cities.

He had set out on his wars, as I knew while I still heard of him only from his enemies, looking for his own honor in all he met. Had he found it? Darius himself, if he'd lived to accept his mercy—would he have honored his given word unless from fear? I remembered the soldier's tale of the hospital at Issos. Truly, my lord had not received as he had given. One by one I had seen the wounds fall on his trust. Tonight I had seen the scars.

— And yet, I thought, this very grief I feel comes from him alone. Who else ever taught me mercy? While

I served Darius, I would have said of this night's work, Such things are always done.

Yes; if tonight he had wanted all from me, instead of only a kiss to pardon him, I would not have withheld even my heart; no, not with all those dead men's souls drifting upon the air. It is better to believe in men too rashly, and regret, than believe too meanly. Men could be more than they are, if they would try for it. He has shown them that. How many have tried, because of him? Not only those I have seen; there will be men to come. Those who look in mankind only for their own littleness, and make them believe in that, kill more than he ever will in all his wars.

May he never cease believing, even though he grows angry at wasted trust. He is more weary than he knows, his breath comes fast in the thin air of the heights, and his sleep is broken. Yes, souls of the dead, I would go to him if he asked me.

But he did not ask. He lay alone with his thoughts, and when I came at morning I found him with open eyes.

21

WE CAME down towards
the rivers, after more victories, the greatest being the
capture of the Aornos Rock, said to have baffled even
Herakles. Alexander added it to his chain of fortresses
which secured the homeward road.

And there was the city of Nysa, pleasant in the
spring air of the foothills, where the chief came out to
meet him, asking mercy for the place, since, so said
his interpreter, Dionysos himself had founded it; for
proof, his sacred ivy grew there, alone in all the region.
This interpreter was a Greek settler, who knew the
right names of everything. I myself, going about the
town, saw a shrine with the image of a beautiful youth
playing a flute. I pointed him out to a passing Indian,
saying, "Dionysos?" He answered, "Krishna"; but
doubtless it was the god.

Alexander and the chief got on well together, and
agreed on terms. Then, being a lover of marvels all
his life, Alexander had a longing to see the god's
sacred hill behind the city. Not to have it overtrampled,

he took only the Companions, the squires and me. Truly it was a paradise without art of man; green meadows and green shades, cedars and laurel groves; dark-leaved bushes with clusters of bright flowers like lilies; and the god's ivy on all the rocks. Indeed the place was divine, for a pure happiness seized us all there. Someone wove Alexander a crown of ivy; soon we were all garlanded and singing, or hailing Dionysos by his sacred cry. A flute piped somewhere and I followed it, but never found the musician. As I walked by a brook that plashed down ferny rocks, I met Ismenios, whom I'd scarcely seen since he left the squires for the Companions. He had grown still handsomer with manhood. He came up smiling, embraced and kissed me; then he went singing on his way, and I on mine.

Rejoicing in spring after the harshness of winter war, we went down towards the rivers. The tall shade-trees and banks of flowers we left behind with the hills. Round the Indus is barren sand, scoured at its flood-times. A little above that, stretching a mile over dunes and scrub, Hephaistion had pitched the camp of the Macedonians. Across the river was his bridge.

He rode out to meet Alexander. He had worked well, he and his engineers. The bridge was of pointed boats linked side to side, with a firm road laid across them. It was longer than the river's width, for that spreads quickly when the snows melt at its source; he had great cables stretched far inland, ready for this. Alexander said he'd done better than Xerxes had with the Hellespont.

Near the place reserved for Alexander's tent was the camp of Roxane's household. But, so I heard, after the King had greeted Hephaistion and commended him, his next words were, "How is Oxhead? Did the mountains tire him?"

He rode through the cheering soldiers, and then straight to the stables, hearing the old horse was short in the wind, and had been missing him. Then he held a war council. Sometime that day, he paid his respects in the harem.

Soon we crossed the river and were in real India, whose marvels I have been asked to recount so often that I could do it in my sleep. The first of them was King Omphis, waiting to receive Alexander with all his kingdom's splendors; his whole army drawn up on the plain, flashing and bright, with its scarlet standards, its painted bedizened elephants, its clashing cymbals and booming gongs.

They were all armed to the teeth. Alexander had seen enough of treachery; he had the trumpets sounded, and came on in order of battle. Luckily, King Omphis had sense, and guessed something was wrong. He rode out in front with a couple of sons and princes; Alexander, always glad once more to believe in men, at once rode out to meet him.

We were all splendidly entertained and banqueted. King Omphis' chief wife went in her curtained carriage drawn by pure white oxen, to fetch Roxane to a ladies' feast. The soldiers, laden with pay they'd had no chance to spend for a year, filled the bazaars, bargaining by signs. They needed cloth, their tunics being in tatters. It dismayed them to find no good strong wool for any money. Even the linen was flimsy, made not from flax but from Indian tree-fluff; being either white or gaudy, it caused much discontent. However, they had no lack of women; they could be had there even in the temples.

I looked everywhere for more of the heavy silk I had bought from the caravan at Marakanda; I fancied another suit of it, now we were in India whence it came. But I could not find any at all.

On the city outskirts, I came on one of the Indian marvels; the offspring tree, which lets down from its branches roots that turn into other trees. A phalanx could have camped within its shade; this one tree spread like a wood. Walking up to look, I saw sitting under it groups of men, some quite venerable, naked as they were born.

Even after the Macedonians, this astonished me; even they did not sit about in such a state. Yet these old men seemed full of dignity, and did not vouchsafe me a glance. One, who seemed the chief of them, with an unkempt beard down to his middle, had a ring of pupils, old and young, who listened with admiration; another had for audience a young child and a white-haired ancient; yet another sat cross-legged, still as a block, his eyes cast down to his belly, hardly seeming to breathe. A passing woman laid before him a garland of yellow flowers, showing no shame for his nakedness; nor did he, he did not so much as move his eyes.

These, as I now remembered, must be the naked philosophers, whom Alexander had said he wanted to see. They were not much like Anaxarchos or Kallisthenes.

Sure enough, here was Alexander himself approaching with some friends, escorted by one of King Omphis' sons. Neither teachers nor pupils rose, nor indeed paid any attention. The prince showed no anger, but seemed even to expect it. He called his interpreter, who addressed them, announcing Alexander; I heard his name.

At this, the chief man rose, followed by all the rest, except the cross-legged man still gazing at his belly. They stamped with their feet on the ground, two or three times, and then stood silent.

Alexander said, "Ask them why they did that."

At the sound of his voice, for the first time the cross-legged man looked up, and fixed his eyes on him.

The leader spoke to the interpreter, who said in Greek, "He asks, lord King, why you have come so far with so much trouble, when wherever you go, nothing of earth is yours but what is under your feet, till you come to die, when you will have a little more, enough to lie in."

Alexander looked at him earnestly for a while, then said, "Tell him I do not only travel the earth to possess it. I seek to know what it is, and what men are, also."

The philosopher bent down in silence, and held up a pinch of dust.

"But," said Alexander, "even the earth can be changed, and so can men."

"Men indeed you have changed. Through you they have known fear and anger, pride and desire, chains which will bind their souls through many lives. And you, who think yourself free because you have mastered fear and the body's greeds; the desires of the mind consume you like raging fire. Soon they will burn you all away."

Alexander thought a little. "That may be. So is the sculptor's wax consumed within the clay, and is gone forever. But in its room they cast the bronze."

When this was interpreted, the philosopher shook his head.

Alexander said, "Tell him I should like to talk further with him. If he will come with me, I will see he is treated with honor."

The old man's head lifted. Whatever he thought he was free of, I doubt he was free from pride. "No, King. Nor would I permit the least of my children here. What can you give me, or what can you take away? All I have is this naked body, and even that I do not need; by taking it you would lift from me my last burden. Why should I go with you?"

"Why indeed?" said Alexander. "We will trouble you no more."

All this time, the man with the garland had sat still, gazing at Alexander. Now he stood up and spoke. I could see his words disturbed the others; the leader for the first time looked angry. The interpreter motioned for silence.

"He says this, lord King. 'Even the gods grow weary of their godhead, and seek release at last. I will go with you till you are freed.' "

Alexander smiled at him and said he would be welcome. He took from a crotch of the tree an old breechcloth, which he wound on, and a wooden food-bowl, and followed barefoot after the King.

Later, I met a Greek who kept a shoeshop in the city and knew the sages; I asked him why they had been so angry with the man. He said it was not because they thought he had gone from greed of wealth, but because he had been drawn in love to a mortal creature. They held that even though his love was of the soul, it would be a chain to him, and cause him to be reborn after his death, which they think a punishment. This was all I could understand.

Certainly, all he would take from the King was food for his wooden bowl, and not much of that. Since no one could pronounce his name, we called him Kalanos, from the sound of a word he used in greeting. Soon we all grew used to him, sitting under some tree near the King's pavilion. Alexander asked him inside, and talked to him alone but for the interpreter. He said to me once that though people thought Kalanos did nothing, he had fought and won great battles to be what he was, and was magnanimous in victory.

He had even a little Greek, picked up from the settlers there. It was said he had been a scholar, before he joined the naked men. But Alexander did not have long to study with him; he had to make war upon King Poros.

This was King Omphis' enemy, against whom he'd asked for help. His land was beyond the next river, the Hydaspes. This too had been taken into the empire, under Darius the Great; its kings were still satraps in name, but had been let alone for generations, and were kings again. So King Poros told Alexander's envoys, when they came asking for fealty; he added that he would pay no homage to any ally of Omphis, descended as he was from lowborn slaves.

Alexander prepared for battle, but had first to rest his men, after the winter wars (Hephaistion's had had some hard fighting too, going through Khyber). He took his time, giving them games and festivals, though as it grew warm with spring, the rivers were rising. We were told that soon it would rain.

When we did march down to the Hydaspes along with King Omphis' troops, we were a vaster host than ever, in spite of the garrisons left in conquered strongholds. We made camp up above the river, while Alexander scouted for the best place to cross. It was brown and fierce already; one could tell it would never endure a bridge.

On one of these days, some person of consequence, whose name and race I forget, came to Alexander's tent for audience. He had been gone some time, so I said I would go and find him. I rode about the camp —no Persian will walk when he can ride—till I heard he had gone to the horse-lines. I went over to the endless rows of shelters, made from bamboo and grass and palm-leaves, which housed the cavalry mounts; a town in itself. At last a blue-tattooed Thracian slave, who was holding the King's charger, pointed me out a shelter standing alone, and handsomer than the rest. I dismounted and went inside.

After the Indian sun it seemed almost dark. Splinters of dazzle came through the chinks of the wall, making bars of light and shade. They fell on an old black horse, that lay in the straw with laboring sides; and on Alexander, sitting in the muck of the stable floor, with its head laid in his lap.

My shadow had darkened the doorway; he looked up.

I had no words. I just thought, I would do anything . . . As if I had had the words all along, I said, "Shall I fetch Hephaistion?"

He answered, "Thank you, Bagoas." I could just hear him. He'd not called the groom, because he could not command his voice. So I was not there for nothing.

I found Hephaistion by the river, among his engineers. They had brought his bridge-boats overland, in halves for cartage; he was seeing them put together. He stared at me in surprise; no doubt I looked out of place there. Besides, it was the first time I'd ever sought him out.

"Hephaistion," I said, "Oxhead is dying. Alexander wants you there."

He looked at me in silence. Maybe he would have expected me to send someone else. Then he said, "Thank you, Bagoas," in a voice he'd not used to me before, and called for his horse. I let him get well ahead, before I took the road.

Oxhead's funeral was held that evening; it has to be

quick, in India. Alexander had him burned on a pyre, so as to have his ashes for a proper tomb. He only told his friends; but it was wonderful how many old soldiers came quietly up, who had fought at Issos, and Granikos, and Gaugamela. There were bowls of incense to throw upon the pyre; we must have given old Oxhead a full talent's worth. Some of Omphis' Indians, who stood further off, uttered loud cries to their gods, thinking Alexander had sacrificed the horse for victory.

When the fire had sunk, he went about his work again. But at night, I saw he looked older. When he first had Peritas he had been a man; Oxhead, he had had since boyhood. That little horse (all Greek horses look little to a Persian) had known things of him I'd never known. That day some of them died, and I shall never know them.

At night it thundered; and the rain came down.

In the morning the dust was laid, the sun was out, and all smelled of growing greenness. But clouds soon gathered; next time, it was as if the river had poured down from the sky. And I heard it said this was only the beginning.

In the downpour, plodding through mud, without a dry stitch on them, Alexander marched his men to the riverbanks.

He would not take me. He said he could not tell where he'd be from hour to hour, let alone day to day, or when he would cross the river. He found time to bid me goodbye, but, as always, did not make much of it. He saw no cause. He would win, and soon be back. Tender farewells were for the losers.

Yet this was the greatest and most perilous of all his battles; and I did not see it.

The rain drummed down, turning the camp to quagmire. The wretched followers huddled in leaky booths; a good tent was riches. In the drenching storms I would give some wayfarer shelter; a half-drowned Baktrian child, a Greek ballad-singer; and, once, Kalanos the philosopher, whom I saw standing in a water-fall, in his single breechclout. When I beckoned him in, he signed a blessing; then crossed his feet upon his thighs, and sank into meditation. It was like being alone; but alone and happy.

At first, whenever the rain grew less, I would throw on a cloak and ride down to the river. There were troops along there for miles, but no one could tell me where the King was, nor what he meant to do. As it turned out, there was someone even more eager than I to know: King Poros, who had made his camp on the further shore, at the easiest point of crossing.

One night, in a lull of the roaring rain, we heard a great din of onset—trumpets, battle-yells, horses neighing. It had come at last. I lifted my hands to Mithra. The night was like pitch. All the camp was awake and listening. No word came back to us.

No wonder. No one had crossed the river. All that had happened was that Alexander had made a noise, and Poros had moved his whole army towards it, to stand by all night in the pouring rain.

Next night, the same. Now the great battle had really started; we held our breath. No battle. The next night, and the next, when we heard clamors we took it easily. So did King Poros, too.

Alexander never minded looking a fool, or even a poltroon, in the first part of a battle. He could afford it. By now, he had to find distant places to be believed in; but here he was far enough. He had fought no war with Omphis, to warn King Poros of what he was. Poros was seven feet tall, his only mount an elephant. It can't have been hard for him, to think the little pup across the river was all bark, no bite.

Alexander kept barking, and running back to his kennel. He had great convoys of stores brought to his camp, giving out, to whoever would listen and spread the news, that he would wait if he must till the rains were over and winter shrank the stream. So Poros could camp all that time on a mudbank in the wet, while Alexander worked up his courage.

It must have gone on a full quarter-month. One night came the worst storm yet; torrents of rain, lightning so frightful one could see it through the tent; I put my pillow over my head. At least, I thought, tonight there'll be no battle.

At dawn, the thunder rumbled away; and then we heard. It was the din of onset, greater than on all those nights before, but further. Above it rose a new sound, furious and high; the trumpeting of elephants.

Alexander had crossed the river.

He had planned it for that night in any case. The storm, though a hardship, was a general's gift. He had crossed a little way up river of Poros, where there were thick woods to screen his march, and a wooded island to screen his crossing. He had to get over before Poros knew and brought up his elephants. If the cavalry mounts saw them as they came to land, they would plunge off the rafts and drown.

Ptolemy has the whole battle in his book, and has shown Alexander's skill and daring for men to come. His first peril was perhaps his worst. He made the crossing, first leaping ashore himself; then, while the cavalry were being landed, found that the bank had been cut off by a new flood-channel, and was an island.

At last they found a ford, though it was deep. Ptolemy writes that the water was breast-high on the men, and the horses could just keep their heads above. (You see what I mean, when I say Greek horses look little to a Persian.)

Already Poros' son had been sent with a chariot squadron, to push them back in the river. Alexander formed his men up just in time. The prince fell; the chariots stuck in the mud; those who could, took flight. Poros had the news, chose a sandy stretch of firm land, and prepared for battle.

His front was unassailable; it had two hundred elephants spaced across. But he had an artist in war to deal with. To say much in little, Alexander lured out the cavalry by a show of weakness; attacked the front with mounted Scythian archers who shot and wheeled away; he himself charged the cavalry in front, Koinos at rear; he maddened Poros' elephants with arrows or thrown javelins, or by shooting down their mahouts, till they did more damage on their own side than on his.

It's all in King Ptolemy's book; he read it me. He has it just as I heard it at the time, except that more Macedonians fell than he has written. When he read me that part, I daresay I looked up; for he smiled, saying those numbers were in the royal archives, and old soldiers understand each other.

We on the further shore came down to the bank at first light to see. The rains had laid the dust which hides most battles. We could see clearly the elephants with their swaying howdahs, the wheeling horse, the milling foot; but what this confusion signified, we could not tell. I could not even pick out Alexander by his flashing arms, for the river had muddied him all over. The sun grew high. The dreadful din seemed unending. Then at last, the flight and pursuit began.

It grieves me more than all else I missed, that I did not see Alexander meet with Poros. It was a thing after his own heart; also a true one, which neither time nor man's deceit ever took from him.

Long after the fight was lost, the tall King fought on in the van. His elephant, brave even among that race, had never flinched. At last while he cast a javelin he was hit under his lifted arm, through the gap in his coat of mail. At this he turned his steed, and rode slowly after the rout. Alexander had watched him eagerly and longed to meet him; he thought so noble a man should be summoned only by another king, and asked Omphis to be his envoy. This did not do; Poros detested Omphis, and at the sight of him reached left-handed for a javelin. Alexander found someone more acceptable, and tried again. At this, Poros bade his elephant kneel; it put its trunk round him, and gently lifted him down. He asked for water— with the battle and his wound, he was parched with thirst—and went to meet Alexander.

"The finest-looking man I ever saw," Alexander said to me later. He spoke without envy. I expect it grieved him in his youth that he was not tall; but if so it had ceased to trouble him, now that his shadow stretched from east to west. "He is just like Homer's Ajax, but for his black skin and blue beard. He must have been in pain, but you'd never have known it. 'Ask what you wish of me,' I said. 'How shall I deal with you?' 'Like a king,' he said. Do you know, I knew it before it was interpreted? I said, 'That, I'd do for my own sake; ask something for yours.' He answered. 'There is no need, that is everything.' What a man! I hope his wound heals quickly. I'm going to give him more land than he had before. He will balance Omphis' power; but above all, I trust him."

He did not trust in vain. As long as he lived, no news of treachery came to him from there.

All that meant most to him was fulfilled in that river battle. He fought mightily against man and nature; did not his hero Achilles fight a river? Happier than Achilles, he had Patroklos by him to share his glory; Hephaistion was with him all that day. And he won with a welded army of all his peoples, just as Kyros fought with his welded Medes and Persians, though this was a greater thing. At the end, he found a brave enemy to make a friend of. Yes, that was my lord's last moment of perfect fortune.

Now it was done, his eyes were turned, as they always were, to the next horizon. What he lived for now was to make the march to Ganges, follow its shores, and reach the Encircling Ocean; his empire a finished work from sea to sea, crowned with a marvel. Thus his teacher Aristotle had told him the world was made, and I have not yet met a man who could deny it.

22

KING POROS' flesh wound
wound soon healed, and Alexander feasted him. He
was magnificent, still in his thirties though with sons
of fighting age, for the Indians marry young. I danced
for him, and he gave me some ruby earrings. To
Alexander's pleasure, the faithful elephant, scar-seamed
from earlier wars, recovered too.

There were victory games, and thank-offerings to
the gods. Just when the victims had been consumed,
the rain came down again and doused the fires. I had
never grown used to watching the divine flame pol-
luted with burning flesh; nor is any Persian easy when
he sees it quenched from the sky. But I said nothing.

The King founded two cities, one each side the
river. He named the right-bank one for Oxhead; his
tomb was to be in the public square, with his statue
cast in bronze.

After that, he and King Poros rode off to war
together. Roxane he left in the palace, where she could

have the company of King Poros' wives, and be in comfort out of the wet. Me he took with him.

They first had to fight Poros' cousin, a long-time enemy who'd declared war upon Alexander as soon as he learned that they were allies. His courage was not equal to his hate; he fled the test, and Alexander left Hephaistion's force to reduce the province, which he would give to Poros. He himself was for pushing on, drawn by the Encircling Ocean, making short work of anything in his way.

He offered peace to each town that surrendered; kept his word, and let them retain their laws. Those who fled their forts before him, he pursued without giving quarter, reckoning they would have made terms unless they meant to attack him in rear. It had often happened; yet, thinking how peasants will fly from the mere sight of soldiers, depending on what they've known of them before, I was sorry it had to be.

With Poros, he took the great fort of Sangala, despite its walls and its hill and its lake, and the triple wagon-wall drawn up all round them. Then he gave Poros leave to join Hephaistion in settling his new province. Himself, he pushed on towards the next river, the Beas; he would camp on its nearer shore, to rest his men. The rain came down.

We lumbered on, over ground trodden to mush by those before us. The elephants tugged their feet from the mud with sounds like great smacking kisses. The Scythians and Baktrians, to keep dry, wore in the wet swelter their hot felted clothes. The cavalry urged on footsore horses, each mile like three miles' work. The men of the phalanx trudged ankle-deep by the oxcarts which bore their gear; their boots warped with wetting and drying, now soaked again; the thin Indian stuff they'd had to buy for tunics plastered to their thighs; the edges of their cuirasses galled them through it as if they had been naked. The rain came down.

On rising ground above the river, they pitched the great tent of Darius; Alexander had brought it, to show himself as a king. It was green and fragrant here; we were coming towards hill country; from the east I could swear I smelled the breath of the mountains, but the clouds hid everything. The rain came down, steady, unwearied, sighing through the trees and the tall green canes; as if it had fallen since the world began, and would not cease till the world was washed away.

The tent was leaking. I had that seen to, and looked out for him a dry robe and shoes. When he came, he felt my clothes, and would accept no service till I had changed them. I was so used to being wet, I had hardly noticed.

He had his generals to supper. Listening inside, I could tell he was in good spirits. He said he'd heard that beyond the Beas the land was rich, the people were stout fighters, and the elephants bigger and stronger even than King Poros's. A last fine battle, before reaching the world's end.

But something odd had struck my ear. If he was a little drunk, his voice would always carry over the rest. But he was sober, and still it did. He was not loud; it was the others who were quiet.

He'd noticed, too. He bade them drink up, and chase the damp from their blood. They made a better show, till the meal was over and the servers gone. Then Ptolemy said, "Alexander, I don't think the men are happy."

He laughed. "Happy! If they were they'd be insane. This rain, it's like wading through Styx and on through Lethe. They've shown a fine spirit, and they've seen I know it. The wet season's due to finish; Poros told me it's overlong this year. As soon as it clears, we'll hold games and give good prizes, and have them fresh to go on."

They all said Yes, no doubt that would set them up.

At bedtime he said to me, "This rain would dispirit lions. If only I could have settled Baktria a half-year sooner, we'd have been here in winter." He did not say, "If I'd waited there half a year." He would have said it once. It was as if he felt, at last, the chariot of time pursuing him.

"After the rains," I said, "they say it's all fresh and

beautiful." I was glad he had made an early night of it. He'd been riding all day up and down the column, to see no one was bogged down. He looked tired, and the lines on his brow were back again.

Next day I came to his tent at dawn, to be first with good news. "Al'skander! It has stopped raining."

He jumped up, threw his blanket round him, and went to look. When first I'd known him he would have gone naked from his bed. He had grown more careful, from being often with Persians. A pale sun rose over the green leaves. Even its first rays had warmth; one could tell it was more than just a break in the rains.

"Thanks be to Zeus!" he said. "Now I can get my poor men in heart again. They deserve a holiday."

The riverbanks smelled of sap and young flowers. He gave orders for the games and invited entries. I took my horse Oryx (Lion was looking tired) and rode out to smell the breath of the mountains, before we turned for the plains.

I came back through the camp. Hundreds of times, all over Asia, I had ridden through it. Apart from land and weather, it was always much the same. But not today.

Even the camp-followers, whom I passed first, were restless. One noticed the carefree children, splashing in sunlit puddles, because the mothers had their backs to them chattering. In the quarter where the better-off lodged, such as artists and merchants, one of the actors whom I knew came running; when I drew rein, he said, "Bagoas. It is true the King's turning back?" "Back?" I said. "Why, it's only a few days' march to the Stream of Ocean. Of course he's not turning back." I rode on by the soldiers' camp. Then I knew something was wrong.

Soldiers in rest-camp have a thousand things to do; making good their kit and boots and weapons; buying things. There will be women, cockfights and dice-games; fortunetellers, jugglers and men with dancing dogs. Such people were all about, dejected, getting no trade. The men did nothing. Nothing, that is, but talk.

A dozen with heads together; a score, hearing one man; two or three arguing; they talked. And I never heard a laugh.

When officers passed, one might be called to, as a friend for counsel; another would be scowled at silently. Some glanced even at me, as if I might carry tales of them. I only wished I knew what to tell. It was then a memory knocked at my mind—of a night on the high moors, above Ekbatana.

No! I thought. It's not as bad as that, and with him it never could be. But it's bad. His generals must tell him. It would be insolence from me.

They began about noon, by ones and twos. I'd been right, that it was not like Ekbatana. No one wished Alexander harm. No one dreamed of another King. The men wanted one thing only: to go no further.

I had thought he'd make light of it, at least at first. But he'd always had the feel of his troops, and he knew his officers; those who made much of little never reached these men's rank. He was calm, but serious. At the end he said to Ptolemy and Perdikkas, "This must be taken in time. I shall speak myself. Give it out at once; every officer from brigade commander up, outside this tent an hour after sunrise tomorrow; allies and all. The rain's to blame for all this."

No more rain fell. I rode through the camp again a few hours later. The feeling had changed. Instead of sullenness there was purpose. Each senior officer's tent had a crowd of men outside it, quite orderly, waiting to speak.

Next morning he was up early, pacing about. He hardly knew I was dressing him. I saw his lips move with the words his mind was forming.

From first light, they had been gathering outside; Macedonians, Persians, Baktrians, Indians, Thracians. Together, they made up a biggish crowd; about as many as his voice would reach.

A trestle had been brought out for him to stand on. He wore his best battle armor, the winged silvery helmet, the jeweled belt from Rhodes. As he leaped on the rostrum, lithe as a boy, there was a breath like a sighing breeze. My actor friend had once said that he could have made his fortune in the theater.

I listened behind the tent-flap. This play had no part for me.

He said he grieved to hear the men had lost so much spirit; he had called them in council, to decide along with him whether to go on. He meant, of course, that he would persuade and not compel them. I don't think the notion of really turning back had entered his head.

He had a splendid style, eloquent without rhetoric, though he'd not written down a word. He spoke of their unbroken victories; why need they fear the men beyond the river? The end of their task was near. They were coming to the Encircling Ocean; the very same that washed Hyrkania in the north, and Persia southward; earth's utmost boundary. He could not believe— I could hear it in his voice—that they felt no touch of his burning eagerness. Had he not shared their dangers, he said, and had they not shared the spoils? Would they give up so near fulfillment? "Keep steadfastness!" he cried to them. "It is a lovely thing, to live with courage, and die leaving an everlasting fame."

His clear voice ceased. He waited. It was so quiet, you could hear a shrill-voiced bird, and the pi-dogs bickering.

After a while he said, "Come! I've said my say; I sent for you to hear yours." At this, there was a shifting and shuffling about. Suddenly I remembered the silence before Darius, at that last audience; and I felt the difference. *He* had been despised. Alexander had awed and shamed them; the words they'd come with had died before him. And yet, like Darius, he had not moved their minds.

"Someone speak out," he said. "You've nothing to fear from me. Isn't my word enough, do you want my oath on it?"

Someone muttered, "Yes, Koinos, go on."

A grizzled square man was shoved forward through the crowd. I'd known him well by sight, even before his great part in the river battle. He'd fought under Philip, but, a soldier first and last, never joined a faction. Where good sense and stubborn fortitude were called for, the King chose Koinos. They looked at each other. Koinos' face, the only one I could see, said, You'll not like this; but I trust you.

"Sir," he said, "you've called us here in free council, we all know that. But I'm not speaking for us commanders; I don't feel I've the right. With all we've had from you, we'd be overpaid already for going on. If you want to advance, it's for us to see it done; it's our duty, it's what we were promoted for. So, with permission, I'd like to speak for the men. Not that they come first with me, sir. You do. That's why I'm speaking."

Alexander said nothing. I could see his back taut as a bowstring.

"I'm the eldest here, I think. If I can claim a good name, I have you to thank, for giving me my chances. Well, sir. The men, as you said yourself, have done more than any army did before them. Thanks to you, again. But I put it to you, sir, that when they say it's enough, they deserve a hearing. Think how many of us Macedonians came out with you. How many of us are left?"

A good old man. A fine soldier. A Macedonian, speaking out to his King is his forthright way. What were my people to him, the Persian horsemen with their proud faces and slender strength? What were the strong Baktrians, the hawk-nosed Sogdians, the red-haired Thracians, the tall Indians in their jeweled turbans, the sharers in his victories? Chances along the way which led to home.

"We've died in the field; we've died of fever and the flux. There are the cripples who'll never fight again; and the men in your new cities; not all of them happy there, but there they are. And look at the rest of us, fit to scare the crows, dressed in Indian rags. When a soldier gets neither pride nor comfort from his turnout, it pulls down his spirits. The cavalry too, the horses' hooves are worn nearly down to the frogs. And, sir, we've wives and children at home. Already our children will be strangers; soon it will be our wives. Sir, the men want to get home with their loot, while they can still be somebody in their villages, looked up to. If they do that, you'll soon have a new army sprung up from the ground, asking to follow you. Go back, King. Your mother must be longing for a sight of you. Call up the young men who'll come out fresh. It's best, sir. Believe me, sir, it's best."

His voice cracked, and he dragged his fingers across his eyes. A raucous sound came from him, as if he were going to spit; but it was a sob.

As if it had released the others, cries broke out everywhere; not of anger or defiance, but sheer pleading. They almost moaned. They stretched out their arms. If well-picked officers felt like this, what about the men?

Alexander stood unmoving. The sounds faded; they waited his reply.

"Council dismissed." He turned his back, and went straight into his tent.

One or two senior generals, his friends, made a move to follow. He faced them in the entry and said again, "Council dismissed."

At Susa, I had learned how to be invisible. One picked that up quickly. While he paced about, I vanished in a corner. When he tugged at his helmet-strap, I came silently and disarmed him, and once more made myself nothing. It gave me time to think.

Did the soldiers share his faith in the Stream of Ocean? I wondered. I thought of the teeming camp with its wandering traders; the interpreters, waiting to earn their small hire when the language of signs broke down. Interpreters called to a king will translate what they are told to. Market interpreters, once paid, will gossip. Their work being all with travelers, they will talk of far places and the road ahead. Did the soldiers know more than we?

The great Aristotle, wisest of all the Greeks, had told Alexander how the world was made. But one thing was sure; he had never been to look.

Alexander was pacing the great tent, back and forth, back and forth. He must have covered a mile. I remained a nothing; to his need, I was nothing more. He needed faith in his dream, and my faith was gone.

Suddenly he fetched up before me, and cried aloud, "I *will* go on!"

I rose, being now visible. "My lord, you have surpassed Kyros. Herakles too, and Dionysos, and the Heavenly Twins. All the world knows it."

He searched my face. I concealed my faithlessness from him.

"I must see World's End. It is not to possess it. It is not even for the fame. It is to see it, to be there . . . and it is so near!"

I said, "They do not understand."

Later he called back Ptolemy and Perdikkas and the other generals, and said he was sorry he'd been short with them. He would speak to the commanders again next day; meantime they could be planning the new campaign, for when he had talked them round. The generals sat down at the table, busily making notes on the river-crossing and the march beyond. They were no better than I.

He felt that with his skin. All evening he was brooding. I doubt he slept. Next morning when the commanders came, he made no speech to them, just asked if they'd changed their minds.

A confusion of voices followed. I think a few things came out, rumors of distances and so on. Someone had heard such and such, from the interpreter of a caravan. Someone spoke of a half-month march through desert. After a time of this, Alexander called for silence.

"I have heard you. I told you, you had nothing to fear from me. I will order no Macedonian to follow me unwillingly. There are others who will go forward with their King. I shall advance without you. Go, as soon as you wish. Go home. Nothing more is asked of you."

He went in. I heard the voices outside, growing louder as they went off. Alexander said to the guard outside, "Admit no one at all."

But I was once more invisible. All day I came and went. Seeing me not dismissed at the outset, the guard let me back in. I would look through from the sleeping-place, lest he might have given way to distress, being alone. But he would be seated at the table, staring at his plans, or walking about. I saw he still clung to hope.

Whatever he had said, he would not go on without the Macedonians. This army, before which he had proved himself in boyhood, was part of his blood. It was like a lover. Why not? It had greatly loved him. He was shut up here, not in grief alone, but to bring the lover to his feet, asking for pardon.

No lover came. Over the great camp lay a heavy, brooding silence.

He did not send me away. I saw his solitude and did not trouble it. I brought him anything he seemed to need, went out if he looked restless, kindled the lamps at night. They brought him supper. He became aware of me, made me sit down and eat with him. Suddenly with the wine, though he did not take much, he began to talk. He said that all his life, now here or now there, some great longing had seized him, a certain deed to do, a certain wonder to reach and look at; longings so great, he knew that they came from a god. Always he had fulfilled them, always until now.

I hoped he would take me to bed. I could have done him good. But he was longing after another love than mine.

Next day, he stayed inside. The camp murmured sullenly. Everything was the same; except that this was the second day, and his hope was leaving him.

At evening I lit the lamp. Strange flying things threw themselves at the flame, shriveled and fell dead. He sat at the table, his fists propping his chin. I had nothing to give him. This time, I could not even bring Hephaistion to him. I would have done it, if I could.

After a while he took a book and opened it. He wants to compose his mind, I thought; and it put a thought in mine. I slipped away in the short Indian dusk, and went to the nearest shade-tree. There he was, his feet folded on his thighs and his hands laid in his lap. He knew enough Greek to converse in now, if one kept it simple.

"Kalanos," I said, "the King is in great grief."

"God is good to him," he answered; and, as I moved towards him, gently motioned me back. Right before me a great snake was coiled, in the dead leaves a yard away from him.

"Sit over there, and he will not be angry. He is the patient kind. He was angry when he was a man; now he is learning."

I mastered my fear and sat. The snake's coils stirred gently, and were still.

"Don't sorrow for the King, my child. He is paying part of his debt; he will return with a lighter burden."

I said, "To what god can I sacrifice, so that when he is born again, I may be born with him?"

"That *is* your sacrifice; to that you are bound. You will return, to receive his service."

"He is my lord and will always be. Can you lift his sorrow?"

"He is grasping his own wheel of fire. He has only to loose his hold. But it is hard for the gods to free themselves from godhead." He unfolded himself, and in one movement was on his feet. The snake hardly shifted.

Alexander was still at his book. I said, "Al'skander, Kalanos has been missing you. Will you see him, just for a little while?"

"Kalanos?" He gave me one of those looks that went right through one. "Kalanos misses nobody. You brought him." I cast down my eyes. "Yes, bring him in. Now I think of it, he's the only one, but you, I could bear to see."

When I had brought him past the guard, I went away. I did not try to listen. Healing magic is a sacred thing, and I feared to break it.

When at last I saw him leave, I entered. Alexander made me a sign of greeting, but was in thought, so I sat still. When supper came, he had me share it as before. Presently he said, "Have you ever heard of

Arjuna? No, nor I till tonight. He was an Indian king of times past and a great warrior. One day before a battle, he stood weeping in his chariot; not out of fear, but because honor bound him to fight his kindred. Then, just as you find in Homer, the shape of his charioteer was taken by a god, and the god addressed him."

He fell quiet, and I asked what the god had said.

"A good deal. They'd both have missed the battle." For a moment he grinned, then was grave again. "He told Arjuna he was a warrior born and must fulfill his destiny; but he must do it without regret or desire; he must not want the fruits of it."

"Could that be?" I asked. His seriousness surprised me.

"Almost, perhaps; by a man obeying orders. I've known men almost like that, and good men too, though they all valued a word of praise. But to lead men, to change their hearts, to make them brave—that, before anything can begin!—to see a new thing one must make, and not rest till one has made it—that needs a longing greater than for one's life."

"There are so many things, Al'skander, you want more than your life. And your life is all I have."

"Fire burns, dear Persian, and yet you worship it. I too. I have laid on it fear, and pain, and the body's needs, and the flames were beautiful."

"Truly," I said, "I have worshipped before that fire."

"But Kalanos, he wants me to lay on the fire all that the fire has given me—honor, fame among men now and men to come, the very breath of the god which says, Go further."

"Yet he himself left his friends to follow you."

"To free me, he says. But God gave us hands. If he'd meant them for folding in our laps, we should have no fingers." I laughed. He said, "Oh, he is a true philosopher. But . . . I was with him once when we passed a dying dog, kicked almost to death, its ribs staved in, panting with thirst. He rebuked me, because I drew my sword to end its pain. I should have let it complete its chosen path. Yet he himself would do no harm to any creature."

"A strange man. Yet there is something one must love in him."

"Yes. I enjoyed his company, I'm glad you brought him . . . Tomorrow, I shall have the omens taken for the river-crossing. If they're good, the men will think again." Even yet, he was grasping his wheel of fire.

"Yes, Al'skander. You will know then for sure what the god means for you." Something told me I was safe to say it.

It was done next morning. The Macedonians waited in muttering quiet. The victim struggled, itself an unlucky sign. When the liver was taken from the carcass, and laid in the hands of Aristander, the mutter died to a hush, as he turned the dark glossy flesh between his hands. Raising his voice for all to hear, he announced the signs were adverse in all their aspects.

Alexander inclined his head. He returned to his tent, taking the three generals with him. There he told them, quite calmly now, that he would not oppose the gods.

Soon after, he had in his friends and the eldest of the Companions, and told them they could give it out to the army. Nobody said much. They were thankful, but they knew what it was costing him. He sat down with the generals at his table, planning the march back; for a while, there was an everyday working calm. Then the sound began.

At that time, I had never heard a deep sea breaking; but it was like that. Then, as it came near, it was the noise of cheering. With grief I heard them rejoicing in his pain. Then there were voices close at hand, calling to the King. I asked if he would like the tent-flap opened.

"Yes," he said. "Yes, let's see how they're looking now."

They were Macedonians; a full thousand. As he stepped out they cried to him. Their voices were rough and ragged with tears of joy. Many flung up their hands, as Greeks do to the gods. They shouldered each other for a sight of him. One seamed veteran, pushing in front, fell on his knees. "Oh, King! Unconquered Alexander!" He was a man who had had some schooling. "Only by yourself you have been conquered, and that for love of us. The gods reward you! Long life to you, and undying glory!" He clasped and kissed the hand of Alexander, who raised him and gave him a pat on the shoulder. He stood a while longer, acknowledging their praises, and then went in.

The lover had returned, still deep in love. But one thing the first lovers' quarrel always leaves behind—the knowledge that it could be. In times past, I thought, he would have kissed that veteran.

Night came. He had a few friends to supper. On his working-table, the plans for the river-crossing still lay, the wax not yet smoothed out, just scored with great strokes of the stylos. He was quiet at bedtime; I could picture him tossing all night. I set the night-lamp in its place, and knelt down by him. "I would follow you to the last shores of the world, if it were a thousand miles."

He said, "Stay with me here instead."

He was readier for love than he had known; but I had known it. I used up some of the fire within him, that would have stayed sealed in its furnace, scorching his heart. Yes, though I could not bring him Hephaistion, that night he was glad of me. I saw him fast asleep, before I went away.

23

H E BUILT twelve altars, so tall they were like broad towers, for the twelve gods of the Greeks, to mark the end of his journey. Wide stairs wound round them for the priests and victims; the celebrants did their rites against the sky. If he had to turn back, at least he would do it with grandeur.

He rested the men as he had planned, with games and shows; they were festive now, having what they wanted. After that, we marched back across the rivers, to Hephaistion's province that he had settled for Poros. He had built a new city there, and was in it, waiting for Alexander.

They were alone a long time together. Having nothing much else to do, I sought out Kalanos, and asked him about the gods of India. He told me a little, then smiled and said I was advancing on the Way. Yet I had told him nothing.

Hephaistion was a worker, no doubt of that. The province was in good order, appointments made; he

was on the best of terms with Poros. He had a gift
for such things. Once before my time, Alexander having just conquered Sidon had even left him to choose
its King. Asking here and there, he learned that the
last of the old royal line, long since dispossessed by the
Persians, still lived in the city, poor as a rat, a day-
laborer in the gardens. But he had the name of a
good honest man, so Hephaistion enthroned him. The
rich nobles had nothing to fight each other for; and the
King ruled very well. He is only quite lately dead,
lamented by all. Oh, yes, Hephaistion had good sense.

Another boyhood friend of Alexander's had been
busy too; Niarchos, a lean-waisted, small wiry man, of
Kretan stock. He'd stuck firmly by Alexander in all
his quarrels with his father, and shared his exile. He
never forgot such things. Admiral of his fleet till he
left the Middle Sea, Niarchos had come all the way
east as a soldier, but now had again the water his race
loves best. He had been making a fleet on the Hydaspes.
Alexander meant to go down to the Indus, and on
down the Indus to the sea. If he had been kept from
going east to the Stream of Ocean, at least he would
strike it westward.

The men, who'd hoped to go straight back through
Khyber into Baktria, now learned they were to march
beside the fleet along the rivers. Tribes there had not
yet surrendered, and were reported fierce. The troops
were not delighted; Alexander told them he hoped they
would allow him to leave India, not run away from
it. His temper had shortened, since they had turned
him back. They looked at him and kept quiet. At least
they were headed homeward.

Alexander had supposed, till lately, that the Indus,
if followed far enough, would flow into the Nile. They
both had lotuses, and crocodiles too. He had lately
learned otherwise from some native rivermen; but, as
he said, there would still be things to see.

Old Koinos died here, of fever; he never saw Macedon after all. Alexander had kept his word, and never
held his plain speech against him; now he gave him a
fine funeral. Yet, within, something had altered. The

many-headed lover had flawed its faith. They had patched things up, from need of one another; they still loved, but did not quite forget.

The fleet, beached on the sandy banks broadened with early summer, was a fine sight; long war galleys, of thirty or twenty oars; light skiffs; round-sided tubs of all shapes and sizes; and the big flat horse-transports.

I kept my eyes on Alexander's galley, reckoning its space. Would he take me with him? It was a warship; would he think he should take only squires? On the land march, there was no knowing when I'd get back to him. And I would be under Hephaistion's command. He was to lead on the left bank the greater part of the army, the followers, the elephants and the harem. Not that he would deign to show me spite; but I felt I could not bear it. There was another small matter, too; I had never traveled before where Roxane was, and Alexander was not. From Hephaistion, I had nothing to fear but what was in myself. I felt no such assurance about *her*.

I had troubled myself for nothing. When I dared to ask him, Alexander said, "What, would you like it? Well, why not? They've told me so often I'm Persianized, no one should be surprised. Can you swim?"

"Oh, yes, Al'skander, I'm sure I could."

He laughed. "Neither can I."

We were seen off at dawn by King Poros and most of his subjects. The ships were strung out along the river as far as eye could see. Alexander's galley led; he stood in the prow, his hair wreathed from the embarkation sacrifice. He had invoked Ammon his father god, Poseidon of the Waters, Herakles and Dionysos; also the rivers of our passage, for the Greeks do worship the holy waters, though they pollute them (I was growing careless myself). With each libation, he threw in the gold cup along with the wine. In the ships around, everyone raised the paean; the armies on both banks took it up; the horses neighed, the elephants trumpeted. Then to the time of the chanteymen, with the light still cool and grey on the broad waters, we went downstream.

Of all the gifts Alexander gave me, which were many and rich, one of the best was his taking me on the river. I say it still, who have seen the festivals of the Nile. First came the thirty war galleys, their banks of oars beating like wings; then the motley fleet for miles; on either bank the long columns of the army, the heavy-armed phalanxes, the cavalry, the wagons, the painted elephants; and alongside, running to keep us in sight, thousands of Indians come for the marvel. Horses on ships were themselves a ten-years' wonder. The Indians ran amazed, joining their chants to our chanteys, till the river ran between cliffs and gorges; the land troops were lost to sight; for songs we had echoes from the cliffs, and the chatter of monkeys among their hanging green.

To me it was enchantment beyond all tales of the bazaar. In the galley's prow, Alexander grasped the figurehead's tall crest, gazing ahead. He gave off a flame of eagerness that caught us all. I ceased to care that all speech in a galley is public, that he had just a little shelter in the stern to sleep in, that we would barely touch hands till the voyage ended. Thrusting on into the unknown world, I entered a part of his soul that his men had known. Everything rang with him. One lost count of time, living in his wonder. Days of joy.

We were still some way from hostile country, and often put in on shore for the chiefs to do their homage. He would be set on a flower-decked throne; there would be horse-shows, dancing, often good; and singing, which seemed to me like the whine of market beggars. Then we would be off with the stream, waving to the troops on shore.

All good things must be paid for, Alexander always said. The river narrowed, the current tugged. Distant and faint at first, came a muffled roar, from the meeting of the waters, where the rapids are.

We had been warned that where the Hydaspes joined the Akisines between cliffs, the doubled waters boiled in whirlpools. Of the noise, no one had warned us. When we neared it, the rowers broke their beat from mere stunned fear; yet with the current we still plunged on. Onesikritos the chief pilot yelled out not to stop, but to row harder; they'd be dead men if the ships slewed round. They bent their backs to it. The pilot in the prow called back to the steersman, conning every yard. Near him stood Alexander, his eyes on the white water, his lips parted in half a smile.

In the giant hands of the river, I remember only wild motion, confusion, and deadly fear which luckily struck me dumb. Once thrown in that race, no one could save himself, nor Alexander. I found myself praying to an unknown god that when we'd been drowned we would be reborn together. Then we were through, still plunging and pitching, with the lower-bank oars all broken. In the tales, there is no enchantment without ordeal.

All the ships came through safe, but for two that collided, and some of their men were saved. Alexander made camp, as soon as we found good beaches.

That song was over.

We were nearing the Mallian country, whose cities had not submitted, and were preparing war. They were ruled by their priests; men quite unlike Kalanos, who indeed kept telling us he was just a god-seeker and not a priest at all. These priests were obeyed even by the warriors. They had proclaimed Alexander and all of us unclean barbarians. They abhor uncleanness, which is wherever they say it is. In Persia we own our slaves, but they are not unclean to us; here, the men of mean occupation, who come of a conquered race, though no one owns them, are so unclean that no priest nor warrior will eat food their shadows have fallen on. But these men lived humbly. Not so Alexander. If his shadow could pollute them, what would his rule do?

These were the last people on his westward way, before he turned towards Persia; only these stood between him and the mastery of all India from the Beas to the Indus mouth. He had been robbed of his dream; now the matter of India was work to finish, once for all. The spell of the river was broken; the wondering boy at the prow, setting foot on land, changed to a daimon who burned the air before him.

He sent Hephaistion's troops on five days ahead, to meet any Mallians who fled before him. Ptolemy's men he left three days behind, to catch those who fled back. When the trap was set, he stalked his prey.

We marched through desert, a night and a day, because it was quick and no one went there. It was cruel going, but short. We had most of a night to sleep in. At dawn, Alexander led out the cavalry against the first Mallian town.

It was no great way from camp, so I rode to watch.

There were the mud-brick walls, the peasant fields teeming with men. They had set outposts on the roads, to stop Alexander. No one had watched the desert, whence no one came.

The war-yell rose; the cavalry spurred into the fields. The men there were armed with farmers' tools, if they were armed at all. Sabers flashed in the dawn; the Mallians were reaped like barley.

I had thought he would call on them to surrender, as he'd always done. But they had refused already. He was giving no second chances.

He came back at evening, when they had stormed the citadel, covered with dust and blood. While the troops rested and ate, he was giving orders for a night march, to surprise the next city before warning reached them. Himself he scarcely rested. The light that had shone on the river had turned to heat.

So it went on. Even when the Indians all knew where he was, they refused surrender. He took a good many slaves, those who gave themselves up at last; but many fought to the death, or burned themselves in their houses. The soldiers too had hardened. They, even more than he, wanted to be done for good with India; no revolts breaking out behind them, to make him march them back. They would not have taken prisoners, if he had not ordered it.

War is war. If this had been Darius, I would just have been glad for him, that he went bravely into battle. I had wondered at Alexander, not that he killed, but that so often he did not. Even now, he was letting the women and children get away. But I grieved that his dream had turned to bitterness.

This campaign the Macedonians had not bargained for; and it made them sullen. When I got him ready for his brief night's rest, he looked dried and drawn. "The sappers brought down the wall," he said. "The men have always gone racing for a breach, before the dust could settle, to be in first. Today, I thought they'd never stop jostling about, waiting for each other. I went up and held the gap alone, till it put some shame in them." Of course they had followed him then, and taken the town. But the lines on his brow had deepened.

"Al'skander, it is a weariness of the spirit. When we are back in Persia, your land and mine, it will all be well."

"Yes, that will be good. But the frontiers must be secured, and well they know it. I've never asked them for blind obedience. We're Macedonians. I've always told them what we were about. They must sweat this through and make the best of it. As you do." He kissed me, just in kindness. He never needed desire, to make him grateful for love.

On our next day's march we passed the fallen city, screaming with kites, stinking with rotten flesh in the hot sun, with a filthy smell from the charred houses where Indians had burned themselves. In my heart I prayed the Wise God to free him from all this, and quickly.

One should take care with one's prayers. One should not presume before the gods.

The next city, when he drew near, turned out to have been forsaken. He sent word back that he would go straight on in pursuit, and the camp must follow.

When you follow an army, you have no need of guides. We came to a river, and a ford all churned with horse-hooves. On the far side, there had been a battle. The dead lay everywhere, like some strange fruit of the land, darkened with ripeness against the pale withered grass and scrub. A faint sweet stench was starting; it was hot. I was taking a drink from my flask, when I heard a moan close by. It was an Indian, a little younger than I, stretching his hand to the water. He was done for; his entrails spilled from his wound. Yet I dismounted, and gave him a drink. Those who rode near me asked if I was mad. Why indeed does one do such things? I suppose he only lived longer in his pain.

Soon we overtook some ox-wagons, sent by Alexander for his dead and wounded. The wounded had awnings over them, and the water-bearer with his donkey went beside. Alexander always looked well after his people.

The wagoners told us there had been fifty thousand Mallians in the field. Alexander had held them somehow, just with his cavalry, till the archers and the infantry came up; then the enemy fled to the walled town, which we would see beyond the palm grove. The King had it surrounded, and would rest his men for the night.

Before dusk we reached the round brown Mallian town, with its outer battlements, and the squat walls of its inner citadel. The tent-wagons trundled about with their slaves; the cooks unloaded their cauldrons and their sacks, set up their grids and earth-ovens, to give the men a good meal after the light midday ration. Alexander ate with his senior officers, Perdikkas, Peukestas and Leonnatos, planning the attack. "I shan't get the men up before dawn. The infantry's had a long hot march, and the cavalry's had a battle. A good sleep and a good breakfast, then up and at it."

At bedtime I looked at his splendid arms, which the squires had burnished, and his new corselet. He'd had it made in India, for the heat, lighter than his old one, with the plates quilted into Indian stuff. As if he had not shown up enough before, it was scarlet, with a gold lion worked on the breast.

"Al'skander," I said, "if you wore your old corselet tomorrow, I could get this cleaned. It's dirty from the battle."

He turned round with raised brows, and grinned.
"You Persian fox! I know what you're up to. Oh, no.
The men need to be shown, it's not enough to tell
them." He might have said that any time, but now it
had a touch of sourness. Then he laid his hand on
my shoulder. "Don't try to keep me from it, even in
love. I would rather end as I began . . . Come,
cheer up; won't you want to know tomorrow where
to look for me?"

He slept well, as always before a battle. He used to
say he left it then with the god.

Next day soon after sunup they closed in round the
town; the wagons moved up with the ladders and rams
and catapults, and the sappers' tools. For some time
we could see Alexander riding about, picked out, even
when small with distance, by his scarlet and his silver
helmet. Then he dismounted and was hidden in a mass
of men before the wall. Soon they vanished into it;
they must have forced a gate.

Troops poured in after them; ladders were carried
through. The walls above, which had been packed
with Indians, suddenly had emptied.

I rode forward to see better, on my own. There
were few followers here but slaves; the crowd was with
Hephaistion. No, there had been no surrender. The
Mallians had run back to their inner citadel, and
thronged its walls. Hidden by the town's low mud
houses, the Macedonians must be below.

A ladder reared in sight against the wall, and
settled. Then, mounting it, I saw a bright flash of
scarlet. It went steadily up till it reached the battlements; hung there shoving and struggling; then stood
upright on top, alone.

He was using the sword. One Indian fell; another
he pushed off with his shield. Then three men swarmed
up the ladder to fight beside him. The Indians fell
back from them. The ladder was packed with clam-
bering Macedonians. He had shown them once again.
Suddenly, like stones in a rock-fall, they tumbled down
out of sight. The ladder had broken under them.

I rode nearer, scarcely knowing what I did. The

four seemed to stand forever, pelted with missiles from the wall and the fort within. Then Alexander was gone. He had leaped down—on the inner side.

After the shortest pause, I expect of unbelief, the others followed him.

I don't know how long it really was before the next Macedonians scaled the wall; about as long perhaps as it takes to peel and eat an apple, or die ten times. They went up on each other's shoulders, or with ladders, or by making footholds with spears. They poured over and were gone. I mustn't expect, I kept saying to myself, to get a sight of him yet.

A group of men mounted the wall from within. They were carrying something scarlet. Very slowly, they lowered it down a ladder out of my sight. I could not see it move.

I slashed at my horse's rump, and galloped towards the city.

The lower town was empty, even of the dead, quite peaceful; pumpkins and gourds ripened on the flat roofs. Ahead, from the citadel, came battle-yells and death-screams, which I scarcely heard.

At the door of a poor house, in a street just outside the wall, three of the squires were standing, looking in. I pushed between them.

The shield they'd carried him on lay with a pool of blood in it. He was on a peasant's dirty bed, with Peukestas and Leonnatos standing over him. More squires were huddled in a far corner. There were chickens running about.

His face was like chalk, but his eyes were open. In his left side, where all the bright scarlet cloth was darkened, stood a long thick arrow. It moved, and paused, and moved again with his shallow breath.

His lips were parted, drawing in, through the pain, just enough air for life. The breath hissed softly; not from his mouth, but from the wound. The arrow was in his lung.

I knelt by his head. He was too far gone to know. Peukestas and Leonnatos looked up briefly. Alexander's hand unclenched and felt at the arrow. He said, "Pull it out."

Leonnatos, almost as white as he, said, "Yes, Alexander. We must just shift the corselet." I had handled it often. I knew how strong that quilting was. It was pierced, not torn. The arrow-flights would not pass through it.

"Don't be a fool," Alexander whispered. "Cut the shaft." He fumbled at his belt, got out his dagger, and sawed weakly. Then he coughed. Blood came from his mouth; the shaft jerked in his side. His face emptied of life. Faintly, still, the arrow moved in the wound.

"Quick," said Peukestas, "before he comes round again." He took the dagger, and scraped at the hard cane. While he whittled it, and Leonnatos held it steady, I undid the corselet-buckles. Alexander came round while Peukestas was still hard at it. He never stirred, as the barb ground in his side.

The shaft severed, leaving a handspan of pointed end. I slid the corselet from under him; we eased it off, hindered by the knots in the cane. Peukestas cut away the bloody chiton. The purple wound in the white flesh opened and closed, the air softly whistling through. Sometimes it paused; he was trying not to cough.

"In God's name," he whispered, "pull and have done."

"I'll have to cut for the barb," Peukestas said.

"Get on, then," said Alexander, and closed his eyes.

Peukestas took a deep breath. "Show me all your daggers." Mine had the finest point; I had bought it in Marakanda. He thrust it in close by the shaft, and worked it outward. I took Alexander's head between my hands. I don't suppose he even knew of it, through all that pain.

Peukestas withdrew the blade, moved the arrow sideways, set his teeth and pulled. The thick iron barb came out; then a dark stream of blood.

Alexander said, "Thank you, Peu–kes—" His head sagged; he lay like marble. Nothing moved but the blood; and even that soon ceased.

The doorway of the hut had been thronged with people. I heard the cry that the King was dead, spreading away.

In Persia, to bewail the dead comes without thought, like tears. But I offered him, as was his due, the gift of silence. Indeed, there was nothing else within me.

They were shouting up to the soldiers fighting in the citadel, that the King was dead. The clamor inside, which had gone on all this time, redoubled. You would have thought all the world's wicked had been flung at once into the Fiery River. It reached me without meaning.

"Wait," Leonnatos said. He picked up from the dirty floor a chicken feather, and laid it on Alexander's mouth. For a moment it was still; then the down by the quill moved faintly.

I helped them bind up the wound with whatever we could find. Tears streamed from my eyes. That time, I was not the only one.

At last, when they dared to move him, he was put upon a litter. The squires carried it, walking softly. As I followed, something flew over the citadel wall, and thudded in the dust beside me. It was a three-month Indian child, with its throat cut from ear to ear.

Up there, the soldiers still thought him dead. They were taking his blood-price, and washing out their shame. They left no living thing there.

For two days he lay in the open hand of death. He was drained of blood. The arrow had chipped a rib. Though almost too weak to lift his hand, he did that rather than speak. He spoke when the doctor would not leave him; he ordered him to see the wounded. I had understood his sign; he never had to open his mouth with *me*.

The squires helped with the nursing where they could; good lads, but nervous. I asked one, outside, "Why did he do it? Did the men hang back?"

"I'm not sure. Perhaps a little. They were clumsy bringing the ladders. He snatched one and set it himself, and went straight up."

The wound, though terribly torn and bruised, never went putrid. But as it healed, his sinews stuck to his ribs. Every breath caught him like a knife, then and long after. At first, a cough was such agony he had to press both hands to his side to hold it still. To the very end of his life, if his breath labored hard he was in pain. He hid it, but I always knew.

On the third day he could speak a little; they gave him a taste of wine. So the generals came then, to scold him for his recklessness.

Of course they were right. It was a wonder he'd lived till the arrow hit him. He fought on with it in, till he fell lifeless. In his tent was the old shield from Troy, with which Peukestas had çovered him; often I saw him look at it. He took the rebukes with patience; he had to, because of the men whom the ladder's breaking had trapped along with him. One had died, he owed his life to the others. But he had done as he'd meant, and forced the men to follow him. The lover was still true to the beloved; it was their eager rush that broke the ladder. He couldn't have foreseen that.

Leonnatos told him all about the massacre, to show him their devotion. He said, "The women and all the children?" and took a sharp breath and coughed up blood. Leonnatos was brave, but never quick in the head.

On the fourth day, when I was propping his pillows high to help him breathe, Perdikkas came in. He had been fighting on the far side of the town when Alexander was wounded. Having the highest rank, he was now in command; a tall man, dark-browed, both alert and steady. Alexander trusted him.

"Alexander, you're not fit to dictate a letter yet, so I've written one for you, with permission. It's for Hephaistion to give out to the army. Do you think you can just sign it?"

"Of course I can," said Alexander. "But I won't. Why disturb them? They'll start to say I'm dead. We've had enough of that."

"It's unfortunate; but that's what they're saying now. It seems someone carried the rumor. They believe we're keeping it dark."

Alexander pushed with his good arm (the left one dragged at his wound) and nearly sat up. I saw a stain of red on his clean bandage. "Does Hephaistion himself think this?"

"It may well be. I've sent a dispatch; but something from you would clinch it."

"Read me the letter." He heard it through, then said, "Add to that, before I sign, that I'll be coming in three days' time."

Perdikkas brought down his brows. "Better not. When you don't, it will make things worse."

Alexander's hand gripped the blanket. The red on the bandage spread. "Write down what I told you. If I say I'll go, I'll go."

He went, seven days from when he took his wound.

Once more I was with him on the river. He had a little tent in the stern. Though it was not far to the water, the litter's jogging had worn him out. He lay like the dead. I remembered him standing in the prow, with the wreath on his hair.

It took two nights and three days. For all I could do, a galley is short of comforts; and he felt the pull of the oars. He never complained. I sat by him, fanning off the water-flies, changing the dressings on his great half-scabbed wound, and thinking, It's for Hephaistion you are doing this.

Now, I can see he would have gone for the men alone. He had never named any deputy, in case he should be past choosing one, nor any successor if he fell. It was not that he would not think of death; he lived with it; but that he would not give one man such a place of power, or expose him to so much envy. He knew well enough how it would be at the camp, while they thought him dead. Three great generals were based there, Krateros, Ptolemy and Hephaistion, each with equal claim to the high command; the troops well knowing it; knowing too that if he were dead, the Indians would rise up behind them and before. Had I asked him why he was going, he would have answered, "It is necessary." But I remembered his voice saying, "Does Hephaistion think that?" and I nursed my grief.

It was late afternoon when the camp was sighted. He had dozed off. As he had ordered beforehand, the awning was furled up, to let him be seen. He was already among the army; the whole riverbank was thick with men awaiting the ship. When they saw him lie unmoving, a great wail broke out, spreading all along to the camp. It could not have been more if a Great King had died at Susa. But it was not custom that drew it from the Macedonians. Sheer grief wrung it out.

He woke. I saw him open his eyes. He knew what it meant; they had felt what it was to be without him. I don't blame him, if he let them feel it a little longer. The galley was almost at the quay, before he lifted his arm and waved.

They roared and cheered and yelled. The noise was deafening. As for me, I was watching the three generals waiting at the landing-quay. I saw whose eyes he met first.

A shaded litter was waiting. They put down his stretcher by it. He said something I could not hear, being still on board. It seemed he disliked the litter. Something always goes wrong, I thought, when I have to leave him to other people; what is it now?

When I came down the gangplank, a horse was being led up. "That's better," he said. "They can see now whether I'm dead."

Someone gave him a leg-up. He sat as straight as if on parade. The soldiers yelled. The generals walked beside him; I hoped they were watching in case he fell. He'd not even been on his feet till the day before, and then for long enough to make water.

Then the men came up.

They came in a great shouting wave, steaming with rank sweat in the Indian sun. The generals were shoved like nobodies. It was lucky they'd found him a quiet horse. The soldiers grasped at his feet, kissed the hem of his chiton, blessed him, or just got near and gazed.

At last some of the squires fought through to him, knowing, as no one did on shore, the state he was really in. They led his horse towards the tent prepared for him.

I squeezed through the crush like a cat under a gate. They were so carried away, they never even noticed it was a Persian pushing them. I'd heard enough by now from those who'd seen chest wounds in the field, of how a man would live till he tried to rise, then spew up a pool of blood and die in moments. About twenty paces from the tent, when I'd almost caught up, he drew rein. He knows he's going to fall, I thought, and I struggled nearer.

"The rest I'll walk," he said. "Just to let them know I'm alive."

He did it. They doubled the time for him, grasping his hands, wishing him health and joy. They tore flowers from the bushes, those waxen heavy-scented flowers of India, and flung them; some snatched wreaths from the shrines of Indians gods. He kept his feet, smiling. He never turned away love.

He went in. Kritodemos the doctor, who'd come by ship with him, hurried after. Coming out and seeing me outside—he knew me well by now—he said, "He's bleeding, but not much. What kind of stuff is he made of?"

"I'll see to him, as soon as the generals go." I'd brought along a bag with the things I needed. Ptolemy and Krateros came out fairly soon. So now, I thought, the real wait begins.

A crowd was milling before the tent. They seemed to think he would be giving audiences. The body-guard turned them off. I waited.

The palm trees were black against the sunset, when Hephaistion came out. "Is Bagoas there?" he asked the guard. I came forward. "The King's getting tired, he'd like to be settled down."

Getting tired! I thought. He should have been settled an hour ago.

It was hot inside. He'd been propped up, after a fashion. I did it again properly. A wine-cup was standing by him. "Oh, Al'skander!" I said. "You know the doctor said not, if you were bleeding."

"That's stopped, it was nothing." It was rest he'd needed to pick him up, not wine.

I'd already sent for water, to sponge him down. "Whatever have you been doing with this bandage?" I asked. "The dressing's slipped half off."

"It's nothing," he said. "Hephaistion wanted to see it."

I just said, "Lie over. It's stuck." I soaked it off, bathed him, put on the salve, bandaged him, sent for his supper. He could barely eat. He was tired almost beyond rest. When I'd settled him, I sat quiet in a corner; he'd grown used to having me there when he went to sleep.

A little later, as he was dropping off, he gave a great sigh. I came up softly. His lips moved. I thought, He wants me to fetch Hephaistion back to sit with him. But what he said was, "So much to do."

24

SLOWLY HE mended. The Mallians all sent envoys to surrender. He asked a thousand hostages, but, when they came, took that as proof of good faith and set them free.

Processions of honor came from his Indian lands, laden with gifts; gold bowls full of pearls, chests of rare wood filled with spices, embroidered awnings, gold necklaces thick with rubies, more elephants. Grandest of all were the tame tigers, hand-reared from cubs, pacing on silver chains. Alexander thought them more kingly even than lions, and said he'd have liked to hand-rear one himself, if he'd had time to care for it properly.

For each embassy he'd get out of bed, and be found enthroned as if he had nothing wrong with him. They always made long speeches, which had to be interpreted; he would reply, and be interpreted too. Then he would admire the gifts. I was afraid the tigers would smell his blood.

The wound dried up, though it still looked dreadful. One morning he said to me, pleased as a child who's pulled a loose milk-tooth, "Look what I got out," and showed a great splinter of rib. After that the pain was less sharp; but skin was still stuck to sinews, sinews to bone; and, so the doctor said, the lung inside to that. It hurt him to breathe deep, or use his arm; his strength was slow returning. This did not stop him from doing all the business which had heaped up while he was on campaign.

Soon after we arrived, Roxane came to his tent in her curtained litter, to greet her lord and ask how he did. She'd learned a little more Greek, as he told me after; it seemed she'd been gentle and meek and full of concern. I'd heard already that when the rumor came of his death, her screams had deafened the camp. Maybe it was true grief; on the other hand, she was still childless, and would have been no one at all, once he was gone.

After a month or so, he was on his feet; and we took to the river again, towards where it joins the Indus. It was a royal progress. The stream was broad and smooth; he took with him by water ten thousand foot alone, besides cavalry and their horses. The ships had colored sails and painted eyes on their prows, and high stern-ornaments carved and gilded; half Greece, half India. It was good to see him stand again at his galley's prow, looking ahead.

Where the rivers join, he saw a fine site for a city, and set up camp. He still needed rest. We were there most of the winter; pleasant enough, though I missed the hills.

Now he was settled somewhere, people were coming from as far as Greece. But one guest was unexpected; Oxyartes, Roxane's father, arrived with his eldest son, in a good deal of state, Oxyartes claiming he was concerned about some revolt in Baktria. My own belief is, he'd come to see if his grandson, the next Great King, was on the way.

There'd been little of Alexander's Indian campaigning on which he could have taken Roxane if he'd wished; but I suppose Oxyartes had thought that where there's a will, there's a way. Alexander now claimed to be quite well, and was even riding ("It's only a stitch, it just needs to be loosened up"), so could not blame his wound for slack attendance in the harem. For some weeks, in fact, he'd been well enough to make love—with someone who knew how to look after him. Therefore, I saw nothing of this state visit, having joined a pleasure-cruise up river, to view the crocodiles. One should always know when to vanish.

As a parting gift, Alexander gave his father-in-law a satrapy. It was under Parapamisos, about as far east as one could go and still be in Baktria; and a very long way from the royal cities of Persia. He was to have joint rule with a Macedonian general, who, I suspect, was asked to keep him busy there.

With spring, Alexander was ready to go west to Ocean. But between was all country of the ruler-priests, who gave him hard bloody wars. All peoples that acknowledged him, he welcomed in friendship; but if afterwards they rose up behind his back, he did not pardon easily. He could never bear with treachery.

At first, he left to his generals the strenuous sieges. But it ate at him like a sickness; he was short even with me. It was not for long. He was off into battle, coming back ready to drop; whether he used his left arm for shield or bridle, it dragged at the stiffened wound. The doctor gave me some tinctured oil to soften it; the nearest to pleasure my hands could give him then, he was too tired for anything more.

He now disposed his forces. Krateros was to go back to Persia through Khyber, and settle Baktria on his way; taking along the old and crippled soldiers, the elephants and the harem. I don't know how Roxane took it; better, I should think, when she learned where Alexander was going next. Over winter, he had not quite neglected her; but there was no sign of the next Great King.

Once on a time, I too would have been packed off by the easy way. Now it was never thought of. And even if I had foreseen what lay ahead, I would not have chosen it.

It was summer, before the frontier was settled, the new cities and ports were founded, and we were ready for the Ocean.

He did not embark an army; he went only to see the wonder; but we were still nearly a fleet. By now he'd rested from battle, to found a river-port, and was full of eagerness.

The Indus near its mouth makes even the Oxos look a rivulet. It seemed itself a sea, till we first felt the wind of Ocean. It nearly blew us under. The fleet just got to land with no one drowned. I thought that, all in all, Ocean might have treated Alexander more kindly.

The shipwrights made good; we set out with Indian pilots. Just as they said we'd almost reached the Ocean, it blew again; we ran for shore and moored the ships. And then the water went away.

It went out and out. The ships were left high and dry, some in mud, some tilted on sandbanks. No one knew what to make of it; it seemed a most dreadful portent. Our seamen and rowers from the Middle Sea had none of them seen such a thing in all their days. The storm was just wind; but this . . . !

Some men from Egypt said that if this was like the Nile, we might be stranded here half a year. No one could get much sense out of the Indians, who spoke some local dialect; they made signs that the water would come back, but we could not make out when. We made camp to wait.

It returned with the fall of dark. Wave by wave it came lapping up, lifting the stranded ships, knocking their sides together. We prepared to remove the camp out of its path, not knowing how far to fly. But at the place where we found them first, the waters halted. Next morning they had sunk again. And this, as we learned when we'd found an interpreter for the Indians, Ocean does twice a day.

Whatever they say in Alexandria, I promise this is no market-tale. Only last year, a Phoenician who'd sailed past the Pillars to Iberia told me that there it is just the same.

Once more the ships were mended; and there at last

stretched Ocean. At the land's end, Alexander sacrificed to his special gods; then we put to sea.

The breeze was light, the sky blue; the sea much darker, almost the color of slate. Small waves flung crystal spray. We passed two islands; then there was nothing between us and the very end of the world.

When Alexander had gazed his fill, he offered two bulls to Poseidon. Ocean had acted strangely on my belly; at the smell of the blood, I had to run to the side. And there I saw a silver fish, slender, about two spans long, rise from the water, fly skimming above, the full length of a spear-cast, and splash back again. No one saw it but I; and no one believed me after, except Alexander. Even he did not quite like to have it put in the Journal. But by Mithra, I swear it's true.

The bulls were flung overboard to the god. Alexander was not just thanking him for the sight of Ocean; he was asking favor for his old friend Niarchos, and all the fleet. They were to put out to sea, and go coastwise right from the Indus to the Tigris, looking for coastal towns or sites for ports. If a trade route could be founded direct from Persia to India, saving the long perilous caravan trail, Alexander thought it would be a great thing for mankind.

The coastal parts being reported harsh and barren, he would march the army alongside by land, to leave the fleet food-stores, and dig wells. Of course he chose the hardest part. We Persians all told him it was known for desert country, and Kyros himself had been in some trouble there. "The Indians claim," I said to him, "that he only came through with seven men left. But that may be their vanity, because he'd meant to invade them."

"Well," he said smiling, "he was a very great man. Still, we have gone a little further."

About midsummer, we set out.

In spite of Krateros' convoy, we were still a big force of many peoples. There was a crowd of the soldiers' women and all their children; and the Phoenicians stuck to us. They will bear much hardship in the way of trade; and there was no knowing what we might come upon in unknown land. They found it well worth their trouble; that is, at first.

Eastern Gedrosia is a land of spices. Spikenard with its furry clusters grew under our feet like grass, its bruised perfume filled the air. The gum on the little myrrh-trunks caught the sun like amber. Groves of tall trees dropped pale sweet petals on us. When the hills and vales of this pleasant land started to fall behind us, so did the Phoenicians. They stayed among the spices. They'd heard what was coming next.

Spice-bushes turned to scrub, and trees to thorns. For green valleys, we had scoured watercourses carving dry earth, their stony beds bone-dry, or with a trickle you could barely fill a cup from. Mazes of soft rock were sculpted by weather into weird shapes of ruined forts, toothed battlements, or monsters rearing upright. Over plains of boulders and round stones we had to bruise our feet to save our horses'; then there would be cracked mud-flats, white with salt. Nothing grew, but what will grow without rain in stone or dust.

At first there would be water not far off; by scouting inland the foragers got supplies. Alexander sent a load to the shore for Niarchos, with orders to find him water. The men came back saying they'd set up a sea-mark, but there was no place for a port. No one lived there, but wretched creatures shy and mute as beasts, wizened and hairy, with nails like claws. Their only food was fish, for the land bore nothing. For water there were little brack pools, not enough for a dog; it must be the wet in the raw fish that kept these people alive.

We marched on; and came to the sand.

Often in those two months I said to myself, If I live, I will wipe this time from my mind; I cannot even bear the memory. Yet now I turn to it. He is gone; and all times when he was there seem like lost riches. Yes, even that.

We marched by night. When the sun was high, no one could move and live for long. Scouts went ahead on camels, to find the next stream or water-hole, which we must reach wherever it was, or die. Sometimes

we came to it before sunup; more and more often
not, as our strength lessened and our horses failed.

The grim fretted rock we'd left seemed kindly, compared with the scalding sand. Even at night it held
the heat of the day. Its hills were too long to skirt;
going up one slid back one pace in two, going down
the men would glide. We horsemen must walk both
ways—as long as we had horses. They gave out before
the men; the wretched scrub and parched grass did not
give them strength to reach the water-stages. It was not
for long that the kites got them; after the foragers began to come back with nothing, a dead horse was a
feast.

My Lion dropped halfway up a sandhill. I tried to
get him up, but he just lay down. As if sprung from
the ground, a horde with swords and cleavers appeared.
"Give him time to die!" I cried; I'd seen a mule carved
up still breathing. They thought, when I showed my
dagger, it was to keep the meat for myself. I made
the sacrificer's cut into the neck-vein. I don't think it
hurt him much. I took a share for myself and my
servants; I gave them most of it. We in the King's
Household ate just like the King—the army ration,
but at least nobody stole it.

Mules died whenever no officer was in sight; men
would toss their own loot away, to get the beast of
burden. The cavalry took to sleeping with their horses.
I learned this trick too late; Oryx, who had held out
well, vanished while I slept. I never asked Alexander for
another; horses were for soldiers now.

Going on foot, I often came across Kalanos, making
his way like some lean long-legged bird. He had refused to go with Krateros and leave Alexander, from
whom he accepted a pair of sandals, when we came
to the stones. In the sunset hour, when everyone clung
to the last bit of rest before the march, I would see him
cross-legged, meditating with his gaze on the setting
sun. Alexander mastered or hid his weariness; Kalanos
seemed to feel none.

"Guess his age," Alexander said to me one day. I

guessed fifty-odd. "You're twenty years short. He says he's never been ill all his life."

"Wonderful," I answered. He was happy in having only his god to think of, while Alexander was working like a woodcutter's donkey, thinking about us all. I read his thoughts too well; that we were in this hell through his impatience, because he had not waited for winter to make the march.

About the third week out, when one no longer noticed whom one marched beside, but got along as one could, a soldier said to me, "Well, the King led us into this, but at least he sweats it out with us. Leading the column on foot, now."

"What?" I said. I wished I could not believe it. It was true.

We made camp two hours after sunrise, by a stream with real water running. I hurried with his drinking-jug before fools fouled it with their feet. I never trusted the slaves to bring it clean.

He came into the tent, bolt upright. I had his cup filled ready. He stood still in the entry, the first moment he'd not been on view, and pressed both hands to his side. His eyes were closed. I put down the cup and ran; I thought he'd fall. For a moment he leaned on me; then he straightened up and went to his chair, and I gave him water.

"Al'skander, how could you do it?"

"One can always do what one must." He took three breaths to that.

"Well, you did it. Promise me never again."

"Don't talk like a child. I must do it from now on. It is necessary."

"Let's see what the doctor says." I took the cup from him; it was spilling on his clothes.

"No." When he'd fetched more breath, he said, "It's good for me. It loosens the muscles up. That's enough, people are coming."

They came with their troubles and questions; he dealt with everything. Then Hephaistion came, carrying his rations, to sup with him in the hot morning. I hated trusting anyone else to see he ate. Still, I found later he had, and had taken a drop of wine. He had even been put to bed; he only half woke when I smoothed the doctor's oil on the red burning scar. I had hidden the oil, in case the slaves should eat it.

From then on, he led each day's march on foot and set the pace; long or short, sand or stones. He was in pain every step, in torture before morning. He lived on will.

The men knew it; the marks were stamped on him. They knew his pride; but they knew too that he was punishing himself for what he had made them suffer. They forgave him; their spirits fed on his.

When in the rising heat I got him out of his clothes, I found myself thinking, Will he ever win back all the life this is bleeding out of him? I suppose that already I knew the answer.

He was distressed for the fleet off his cruel coast. Even now he sent another food-store. The officer in charge came back to say the men had unsealed it on the way, and eaten it. Sitting up straight in his folding chair, Alexander said, "Tell them I reprimand their disobedience, and pardon their hunger. And if the mules have gone too, don't tell me. From now on"—he paused to get his breath—"missing mules are presumed foundered. Men can take so much; one must know when to hold one's hand."

Men had begun to die. A trifling sickness was mortal. They would fall out, in the dark of night, sometimes in silence, sometimes crying their own names, in hope that a friend would hear. There was much deafness in the night. What could anyone do, who was barely on his own feet? You would see a soldier with his child on his back, and know his woman had died; but the children mostly died first. I remember I heard one crying in the dark—perhaps it had been left for dead—but I just trudged on. I had one thing to do, there was no room for any other.

One day we came to a broad watercourse, with a fair stream in it, fresh and cold, good mountain water. It had been a shortish march; we were there before

dawn, to make camp in the cool. Alexander had his
tent pitched on the sands, where he could hear the
stream. He had just come in, half dead on his feet as
usual, and I was sponging his face before people arrived; when a strange sound approached, between a
rush and a roar. We listened, for an instant; Alexander
leaped to his feet, cried "Run!" and dragged me out
by the wrist. Then we ran indeed. A great surge of
brown water was bursting down the river-bed. The
roar we had heard was the grinding of the boulders.

Alexander shouted a warning. People were scrambling everywhere. As we reached higher ground, I
saw the tent tilt like a drunkard's hat, sink and go
swirling off in the wrack of flood. I thought, "The
oil's still in my wallet," and felt for it. Alexander
caught his breath from the run. Then, the screaming.

Others too had camped upon the shore. The soldiers'
women had put up their little awnings, and started to
make supper, while the children paddled. They were
swept away in hundreds, only a few score left.

That was the most dreadful day of that dreadful
march; men searching for the bodies, mostly in vain;
everyone else, dead tired already, making good under
the glaring sun. Alexander's tent was washed up somewhere, and spread to dry. All his things were lost.
After hours on his feet, he slept in Hephaistion's tent.
Meantime I'd gone begging among his friends; he'd not
a change of clothes to his name. Some of the things I
got were better than his own; he had traveled light. The
squires, who had his arms in keeping, had saved them
at least.

We made no march that night, from weariness, and
to give rites to the dead. Though if one had to die in
Gedrosia, it was something to die by water.

Young as I was, and lightly made, with a dancer's
muscles, I felt my strength ebbing now from night to
night. I lost count of time, just set foot before foot,
my mouth full of dust from the feet around me; the
nights began when I wanted only to lie down forever.
Then I would remember I had the oil, which helped
him a little; and that if I dropped out, the terrible sun

would rise and find me shelterless. So I flogged myself on, between love and fear.

All the marches were longer now; our pace was slower. Still he led, all night and in the heat of morning. At bedtime we scarcely spoke; it was our understanding he need waste no breath on me. Sometimes I had to stop him from lying down just as he was; he'd curse me, I would snap like a cross nurse at a child; it meant nothing, it rested him from keeping up a face; when he was refreshed he'd thank me.

According to the survey men, we had long passed the halfway of the march. He sent out the camel-scouts, to seek the first fertile land and find supplies. We heard no more of them; each march stretched longer into the heat of day, before we came to water. Once it was so long, Alexander called a halt even in the sun, to let the stragglers catch up. It was by an old stony watercourse, dried up. In last night's well there had been so little, none was left to carry along. He was sitting on a boulder, in his sun-hat of plaited grass. Ptolemy was by him, I expect asking how he felt, for he looked dreadful, drained and drawn and dripping with sweat. I could see him panting, even from where I was.

Someone said, "Where's the King?" I pointed; a Macedonian pushed past, followed by two Thracians, one of whom held a helmet upside down. It had water in it, not much, just enough to fill the crown. They must have scooped it from some crevice in the stream-bed, hidden by stones. God be thanked, I thought. I craved for it, but not so much as I craved to see him drink.

The tattooed Thracians shouldered along, guarding their treasure with drawn swords. Savage as they looked with their wild red hair, no troops had been more faithful. He'd had to wean them from bringing him severed heads and asking for a bounty; but they had not touched the water. They put up their weapons and ran to him; the first knelt down, with a grin all across his dusty blue-stained face, and held up the helmet.

Alexander took it. For a moment he looked inside. I don't think many felt envy, parched though we were. They could see his state for themselves.

He leaned forward, laid a hand on the Thracian's shoulder, said something in their language, and shook his head. Then he stood up, and, lifting the helmet, poured out the water, as Greeks do when they make libation to a god.

There was a deep hum, all along the column, as word went from man to man. As for me, sitting on a boulder in the empty channel, I put my face in my hands and wept. I expect people thought it was at the waste of water. Presently, finding my tears on my hands, I put out my tongue and licked them.

We no longer camped close to water when we reached it. The crush was too great; men would rush in and muddy it, or bloat themselves and die. It was good that morning. I made him lie on his bed while I sponged him over. He looked like a cheerful corpse. "Al'skander," I said, "there has never been anyone like you."

"Oh, that was necessary." He smiled at me. I saw it would still have been worth the price to him, if it had killed him.

"You needed it just as much," he said. "You look tired today."

Perhaps he saw more than I knew myself. For a few nights later, in the hour before dawn, I thought, as if another were speaking for me, "I can go no further."

After the hours of night, the sand had a little coolness. I stumbled along to a bit of scrub, which would shelter my head when the sun came up. Don't ask why I wished to spin out my death; it seems the nature of man. To rest was wonderful. I watched the long column dragging past. I did not call, as I had heard those others calling. I could only have said, Forgive me.

I lay there taking my ease, till a glimmer showed in the east. By then I had felt some good from resting, and began to think, What am I doing here? Was I mad? I could have gone on.

I got to my feet, and found the track of the column. For a while I felt almost fresh, and was sure I could catch up. I tipped my water-flask, in case a drop was left, though I knew I'd finished it. The sand was heavy and deep; it stank from the ordure of men and horses, buzzing with flies, which flew from it to drink my sweat. From the crest of a dune I saw the dust far ahead. The sun rose higher. My strength was done.

There was a piece of rock, baked red mud, eaten with weather. While the sun still slanted, it gave a patch of shade. My whole body was dry heat, my feet failed. I crawled there and lay face downward. This is my tomb, I thought. I have failed him. I have earned this death.

All was silent. The shadow began to shrink. I heard a horse's labored breathing, and thought, Madness comes first. A voice said, "Bagoas."

I turned over. Hephaistion stood looking down.

His face was white with dust, haggard with weariness. He looked like the dead. I said, "Why have you come for my soul? I did not kill you." But my throat was too dry to sound. He knelt and gave me water. "Not too much yet. More later."

"Your water," I whispered, ashamed. "No, I've come from camp," he said, "I've plenty. Get up, we haven't all day."

He heaved me to my feet, and onto his horse. "I'll walk him. He can't carry two, he'll die." I could feel the beast's bones through the saddlecloth; and it had had the day's march already. So had he. He dragged it along, hitting it when it stopped. My head was clearer. I said, "You came yourself."

"I couldn't have sent a man." Of course not, at the end of such a march. No one went back for stragglers. If you fell out, you fell out.

From the next dune we plodded up, I saw the growing stuff that fringed a stream, and the dark scatter of the camp. He shared more water between us, then handed me back the flask. "Finish it, it won't hurt you now."

Once more I strove for speech. At Susa, I had learned to express thanks gracefully. But all I could bring out was, "Now I understand."

"Keep up with the column, then," he said. "And look after him. I can't, I've my work to do."

Thanks to me, neither one of us had, that morning. The squires had done their best, but before them he always kept a face up. He was concerned for me, feeling my head to see if I had sunstroke. I said of my rescuer what was required by honor. He only answered, "That is Hephaistion; it always has been"; and it was as if he closed again the curtain guarding a shrine. It was my punishment. He had meant none; but I knew its fitness.

It was at the next day's halt, that the wind came.

We'd had none before, and now it brought no coolness; only sand, and sand, and sand; blowing under the tents, piling against them till each had its sloping sandhill. Grooms with muffled faces ran to muffle the horses' eyes. It was in our mouths and ears and clothes and hair. It lulled; we slept; and at evening, all shapes were changed, all the landmarks gone, which the scouts had plotted to lead us to next day's water. The waves of sand had swallowed a dead tree whole.

Our water-hole was nearly silted up. I thought this must truly be the end. At least this time, I thought, I shall be somewhere near him, even though it's with Hephaistion he will want to die.

I should have known it was not in him, to sit and wait for death. In the Mallian citadel, when he was lying with the arrow in him, he'd killed with his sword an Indian who came up to take his armor. So, now, he held a war council in his tent. "The guides have given up," he said. "We'll have to find our own landmark. There's only one we know which way to bear for, and that's the sea. We can steer for that by the sun. That's what we'll do."

In the hour before dawn, he set off with thirty horsemen; they had found just so many horses fit for the work. To see their course, they had to go by day.

They vanished beyond the dunes, carrying all our lives.

A score returned that night. Alexander had sent them back when he saw their horses failing. He himself had gone on with ten.

At next day's sunset, red in the sand-haze, we saw them black on the skyline. As they neared, Alexander looked leaner than ever, and the pain-lines were in his face; but he was smiling. We all drank his smile like life.

Five of the ten had fallen behind; with five he had pushed on. They crested a rise; there was the sea, and by the sea what no scouts had found before; green things growing which do not grow in brack. They jumped down and fell to digging, with daggers and bare hands, the thirsty horses nosing at their shoulders. Alexander was the first to strike water; and it was fresh.

The night after that we marched, Alexander leading to guide us. In sight of safety, he allowed himself to ride.

The sea was like polished iron; but it was wet, its mere sight refreshed us. Between it and the reeded dunes, was the strip of green where hidden streams seeped to the ocean.

For five days we followed it, cooled by sea breezes so that we marched by day; digging our wells, and drinking. At evening, we bathed in the sea. It was so delightful, that I forsook all my Persian modesty, and did not even care who saw what a eunuch looks like. We were all like children at play. The guides knew by the green that soon we should reach the road.

Then food began to arrive. The scouts had not died; they had reached the Gedrosian city to the northwest, and from there word had been sent round. The first camel-train came, well laden. It would have given us one spare meal all round, when the march began; now, fair shares made a feast. We were fewer now.

Going by easy stages, we felt strength return; and already faces looked less gaunt, when we came through the passes to the city of Gedrosia.

Here plenty welcomed us; corn and meat and fruit and wine, sent in from Karmania, the pleasant land ahead. We rested, ate and drank; our very skins seemed to drink in health from the green around us. Even Alexander began to gain some flesh, and have blood in his cheeks again. "They look fit now to enjoy themselves a little," he said, and led us on into Karmania, at strolling-pace.

There was a feast at every halt, and plenty of wine; he had sent ahead to have it ready. Someone, Ptolemy or Hephaistion, devised a plan for getting him to take a rest himself. Craftily, they didn't tell him he looked to need it, but said that after his conquests and ordeals, he should make the same progress Dionysos had done before him. They had two chariots lashed together, with a platform across, and couches, green wreaths and a handsome awning. With good horses from the city, it looked very fine, and he did not disdain it. There was room for him and a friend or two; and the troops cheered him along. A great deal has been made of this, with much nonsense about Bacchic revels; but that is what it comes down to. A good device; it gave him a ride on cushions.

In fresh meadows, by sweet waters, under shady trees, we made our camp. He said to me, "It's too long since I saw you dance."

Shockingly out of training as I was, I was young; the sap flowed back into me as into a watered vine; each day my practice moved from labor towards pleasure. Also it kept me from overeating; everyone's temptation then, and a dangerous one for eunuchs. Fat once put on is not shed so easily. Even since youth is past, I have managed to avoid it. I have him to think of. I've no wish to hear people saying, "Is *that* what the great Alexander chose to love?"

A racecourse was leveled, a square for trick-riding and such shows; and the carpenters ran up a very good theater. Singers and actors, dancers and acrobats were posting from everywhere in reach. All was gaiety, except for Alexander, who was getting news of what some of his satraps and governors had been up to, when they thought he was dying of his wound in India. In Gedrosia itself the satrap had been corrupt and slack. He was a Macedonian; Alexander put a Persian in his place. Meantime, the men must have rest and revelry; also he was awaiting Krateros and his army. Offenders elsewhere must wait.

His greatest trouble was getting no news of the fleet. Along that dreadful coast, he'd been able to leave them nothing. They were long overdue; if they perished, he would take it on himself forever.

Krateros and his throng arrived; our camp was once more a city. Roxane was in good health. Alexander paid his respects without delay, though he left again without much delay either.

I fell in with Ismenios, asking about for news of me. We took wine under a tavern awning, and exchanged our tales. "I always knew," he said, "that your bones were beautiful, but you must put a little more on them. But, Bagoas, the King! He looks—not older, I suppose —worn out."

"Oh, he's building up," I answered quickly. "You should have seen him a month ago." And I spoke of other things.

Just after, the governor of the district up the coast came posting by chariot, to say the fleet was safe, and Niarchos would be here directly.

Alexander lit up as if he'd slept for a week, and gave the governor presents. Nobody knew that this man, being as stupid as greedy, had offered them no help to lay up their ships, nor given them transport; just rushed off with his news lest anyone should get the reward before him. Days passed; Alexander sent out an escort but it found no seamen. The governor, still at court, was suspect and put under open arrest; Alexander looked more careworn than before, but sent out another escort. On the second day, it brought back two gnarled wizened men, their bodies like rawhide thongs, tanned almost black: Niarchos and his first officer. The escort had not known them, even when they asked for Alexander.

He came forward to embrace his boyhood friend, and

wept. Seeing their state, he supposed them the sole survivors. When Niarchos told him the whole fleet was
safe, he cried again for joy.

They'd had many hardships and adventures, which
are all in Niarchos' book. Kretans are tough; he lived to
campaign for years and write his memoirs. If you want
to hear of huge whales who flee from the sound of
trumpets, or the beastly lives of the Fish-Eaters, you
can go to him.

He and his men were feted; Alexander began to
look something like himself again. He entertained his
friends and honored the gods with festivals; and the
revels followed. A whole crowd of entertainers had
come in Krateros' convoy; things could be done in
style.

There were games, of course. The riding-events were
mostly won by Persians; the foot-races by Greeks, who
are fonder of using their legs. (Alexander had given
me two fine Karmanian horses.) Thracians won the
archery. All the allies got a chance to shine. But we
were almost in Persis now; when I saw him look with
liking on my people's graces, I knew he was one of
us.

The plays came next; all very Greek. Masks still
came strange to me. When I confessed to Alexander that
I'd sooner see the faces, he said he would agree if the
face was mine. In this last month, I'd been teaching
him once more to embrace delight, instead of pain. His
very body felt different, strained into a habit of endurance. A little tending was what he needed; he
looked years younger, when I'd loosened him up.

After the drama, the music contests. The day after
that, the dancing.

There were nine or ten of us, from everywhere between Greece and India; some very good. This won't be
my day, I thought; I'll just dance for him. If he likes it,
that's prize enough.

I had just come from where water stood for joy. I
wore white striped with green, and started with little
tinkling finger-bells for the mountain stream. Then the
river flashed and twisted, and took great leaps for the

rapids; flowed in slow bends; and sank down, stretching out its arms for the sea's embrace.

Well, it was as he liked it. But it seemed all the army had liked it too. Considering how good some of the rest had been, I was amazed at the noise.

The Indian, who came last, I thought a serious rival; he did Krishna with a flute; and the boy from Susa was very polished indeed. To tell the truth, I have never been too sure about that contest. If I was no better than the runners-up, I daresay I was no worse; and, as always, Alexander did not direct the judges. But the army did.

It was for him, of course. I don't think I was badly liked; I did not flaunt myself, nor intrigue, nor sell my influence. I'd been with him a long time now; I expect it touched them to see how his love endured. He had suffered; they wanted to see him happy; they had watched his face as I danced. They did it for him.

The crown was of gold olive-sprays with sheet-gold ribbons. He put it on me, and stroked the ribbons to fall into my hair, and said softly, "Beautiful. Don't go, sit here by me." I sat on the edge of the dais by his chair; we smiled at one another. The army clapped and stamped; a someone with a voice of Stentor yelled, "Go on! Give him a kiss!"

I looked down, confused. This was going too far, I wasn't sure how he'd take it. They were shouting it all round the theater now. I felt him touch my shoulder. They had been with him a long time, too; he could tell affection from insolence. He drew me up into his arms, and gave me two firm kisses. To judge from the applause, they liked it better than the dancing.

It is as well that Persian ladies do not attend public spectacles, as Greek ones do. I have always thought it a most immodest custom.

That night he said to me, "You've won back all your beauty from the desert, or even more." Well, that's not so hard, at twenty-two, when you have never had a wound. He meant that it was good at last to feel a little life left to spare in him, at the end of the day.

I made him happy, without putting too much tax on

it; how was my secret, he never knew the difference. He was content, which was all that mattered to me just then, and fell asleep straight after.

When I rose, the cover slipped away, but he did not stir. I lifted the lamp and looked at him. He lay on his side. His back was smooth as a boy's, his wounds were all in front. There was no weapon devised to cut, or pierce, or fling, that had not left its mark on him. His body was white against his sun-scorched limbs; it was long since he'd run in the ball-court naked with his friends, which had once so shocked me. In his side, the knotted scar dragged on his ribs; even now in his first sleep, his brow was not quite smooth. His eyelids were wrinkled, old in the face of a boy at rest. His hair shone paler than it used when lamplight fell on it; the threads of silver had turned to streaks, since we marched into Gedrosia. He was thirty-one.

I reached to pull up the cover. But I had to draw back, lest my tears should fall and wake him.

25

To REST the desert troops, he sent them under Hephaistion by the coast roads to Persia; it would be mild there when winter came. He himself, as always, had work to do. With a small force, mostly cavalry, he went straight up country, to Pasargadai and Persepolis.

Had I been with Darius in time of peace, I should have known these places, the royal heartland of my country. It was Alexander who knew them. When we were up in the hills, he took me for an early ride, to taste, as he said, the clean air of Persia once again. I breathed it and said, "Al'skander, we are home."

"Truly. I too." He looked towards the folded ranges, whose peaks had had the first snowfalls. "I'd say this only to you; shut it in your heart. Macedon was my father's country. This is mine."

I answered, "You never gave me a greater gift than that."

A fresh wind blew from the heights; the breath of our horses steamed in it. He said, "In Pasargadai, we shall lie in Kyros' own house. Strange that you're of his tribe, yet it will be I who'll show you his tomb. I've trouble to deal with thereabouts; but that's one thing I look forward to. Lucky we're both slim; the doorway's so narrow, even you will have to go sideways. They must have walled it half up against robbers, since they brought in that great gold coffin; it wouldn't go through now. His grave-offerings are still on the dais around it; you shall see his swords, the very clothes he wore, and his jeweled necklaces. They gifted him well, they must have loved him. I added something too; he taught me what it means to be a king." His horse fidgeted, tired of walking. "Behave," he said, "or Kyros shall have you . . . I left orders to sacrifice one horse a month to him; they said that was the ancient custom."

Then we gave them their heads and galloped. His face was glowing, his hair flicked in the wind, his eyes lit up. When he told me, after, that he'd felt no more than a stitch in his ribs, I half believed him. Persis had done him good. I thought, Happiness begins again.

Kyros' palace was fine and spacious in its old simple way; solid, of black and white stone. The white columns stood out a landmark. Next morning early, Alexander set out to revisit the hero's tomb.

It was a short ride, through the royal park. A few friends came too (many had gone on with Hephaistion) but he kept me by him. The park had run wild, but was lovely in the gold of autumn; the game, so long unhunted, hardly heeded our passing. The tomb stood in a grove of shade-trees. Alexander had had water channeled there last time he came, and the grass was green.

Kyros' little house stood on a stepped plinth, a simple colonnade around it. Persian words were engraved over the door, which I could not read. Alexander said "I asked about that last time. It says, MAN, I AM KYROS SON OF KAMBYSES, WHO FOUNDED THE EMPIRE OF PERSIA AND RULED OVER ASIA. DO NOT GRUDGE ME MY MEMORIAL." His voice shook a moment. "Well, let's go in."

He beckoned the guardian Magi of the precinct. When first they came to prostrate themselves, I had thought they looked unhappy; the place was ill-kept and overgrown. He motioned them to unlock the door. It was narrow, very old, and made of some dark wood clasped with bronze. One Magus brought on his shoulder the great wooden key. It moved the bolt quite easily. He opened the door, and withdrew into the distance.

"Come, Bagoas," said Alexander smiling. "You first; he was your King." He took my hand; we edged into the shadows. The only light was from the door; I stood by him, my eyes dulled from the sun outside, smelling ancient spices and mold. Suddenly he snatched away his hand and strode forward. "Who has done this?" Moving to follow him, I struck my foot on something. It was the thigh-bone of a man.

I could see now. There stood the dais, stripped bare. The gold coffin lay lidless on the floor, hacked with axes to break off pieces that would go through the doorway. Scattered beside it were the bones of Kyros the Great.

The entry darkened and lightened, as Peukestas, a biggish man, tried to get in and withdrew before he stuck. Alexander clambered fiercely into the sunshine. He was white with rage; the peak of his hair had risen. His eyes had looked less deadly when he struck down Kleitos. "Call the wardens," he said.

They were fetched from their house nearby, while anyone who could squeeze inside the tomb described the desecration to those without. Alexander stood with clenched hands. The wardens were flung at his feet, and groveled.

I interpreted, being the only other Persian there. Though of the priestly race, they seemed ignorant men, and terror made them foolish. They knew nothing, they had never entered the tomb, they had seen no one approach it, the thieves must have come by night (when their axes would have made a noise to wake the dead). They knew nothing, nothing at all.

"Take them to the prison," Alexander said. "I will have the truth."

He took me, to interpret their confessions. But neither fire nor pincers could change their story; nor could the rack; Alexander had it stopped before they were disjointed. "What do you think?" he said to me. "Are they lying or not?"

"I think, Alexander, they have just been negligent, and are afraid to tell you. Perhaps they got drunk, or left the precinct. Maybe someone planned it."

"Yes, perhaps. If so they have had their punishment. Let them go."

They hobbled off, glad to get away so lightly. Any Persian king would have had them impaled.

Alexander sent for the architect, Aristoboulos, who'd been with him at his first visit and inventoried Kyros' grave-goods. He was to repair the coffin, and rehouse the poor bones in proper state. So Kyros lies in gold again, and owns precious swords, though not those he fought with, and rich necklaces, though not the ones he wore. Alexander gave him a golden crown; then ordered the door walled up with a single slab, so that he should not be disturbed again. He was in there alone, before the masons started, saying farewell to his teacher.

A harsh welcome back to Persis. But harsher followed. Now he learned what had been done by men he'd left in trust, who had hoped he would never call them to account.

Some had been faithful; but some had set up like tyrants in the lands left to their charge; had plundered the rich, taxed the peasants to skin and bone, worked off old grudges on men who'd broken no law; enrolled themselves private armies. One Median lord had proclaimed himself Great King. One satrap had dragged from a lesser lord his maiden daughter, raped her, and passed her on to a slave.

I have heard it said that Alexander treated these people harshly. Tell that to someone who never saw what I did, when I was ten, and the soldiers came to my home.

True, he grew hard, as proof after proof came in. True, after some time of this he punished beginnings. He said he'd learned the look of a budding tyrant, and what came after; and would depose them for showing the early signs. Whoever complained, it was not the peasants, nor the small lords of my father's kind. That he would not let even his own race oppress our people was a wonder everywhere. He had been gone so long, they'd forgotten what he was like.

While he was away, one of the dearest friends of his childhood, a certain Harpalos, whom he'd left as treasurer at Babylon, had lived on the gold like a prince of India, set up his courtesans like queens, and fled with a load of money at the news of Alexander's return. This hurt him far more than the revolt of former enemies. "We all trusted him; Hephaistion too, who never trusted Philotas. In exile he could always make us laugh. Of course, I had nothing then for him to steal. Perhaps he didn't know himself what he really was."

All in all, he had enough to make him angry, before the new satrap of Persis obeyed his summons.

He was new because he had seized the satrapy. The Persian Alexander gave it to had died half a year before; of sickness it was said, though maybe of something he ate. Now envoys came with gifts, and a long letter, declaring the usurper had sent messages to Alexander, but getting no answer, had been looking after the province meanwhile, knowing of no one more fit to do it.

I was in his upper room with him when he read this letter, and threw it down. "Fit to do murder, robbery and worse. He has ruled this province like a wolf in winter; I've heard it everywhere. Any man who crossed him, put to death without trial. He's looted even the royal sepulchers." His brows came together; he was remembering Kyros. Perhaps indeed the Magi had kept silent because of someone they feared more than the King. "Well, I've witnesses enough already. Let him come; I shall like to see this Orxines . . . Bagoas, what's the matter?"

"Nothing, Al'skander. I don't know. I don't know where I've heard that name." It had been like some echo from a nightmare forgotten on waking.

"Was he cruel to you when you were with Darius? Let me know, if you remember anything."

"No," I said. "No one was cruel there." Of my life before, I'd only told him that I had been bought by a jeweler who ill-used me. The rest, he would only have pitied; but I'd wished to bury it, to forget forever. Now I asked myself if this Orxines could have been some hated client; but his rank was too high; and the horror was even deeper. Perhaps I just dreamed it, I thought; I had bad dreams when I was a slave.

That night, Alexander said to me, "Did they build this bed for elephants? Stay and keep me company." It was years since he'd slept in a Persian royal bed-chamber. We fell asleep quite soon. Dreams flung me into a terror long forgotten. My own scream woke me. It was the dead of night. Alexander was holding me to him. "See, you're with me, all's well. Whatever did you dream of?"

I clung to him wildly, like the child I had just been. "My father. My father without his nose." Suddenly I sat straight up in bed. "The name! I remember the name!"

"What name?" He looked up; he was always very serious about dreams.

"The name he told me, when they dragged him away to kill him. 'Orxines,' that was what he said. 'Remember the name. Orxines.'"

"Lie down, and be quiet a little. You know, I told you today Orxines was a villain. I expect that gave you the dream."

"No. I remember how he said it. His voice was different, because his nose was gone." I shivered. He covered me up and warmed me.

Presently he said, "It's not such a common name, but there may be others. Would you know this man again?"

"There was one lord from Persepolis. If that was he, I'll know him."

"Listen. Be near when I give him audience. I'll say to you, 'Bagoas, have you written that letter?' If it's not the man, say no, and go out. If it is, say yes, and stay; and I promise you, he shall know you before he dies. We owe it to your father's spirit."

"That was his last wish, that I'd avenge him."

"You loved him. In that, at least, you were fortunate . . . Come, sleep. He knows you have heard him now, he will not trouble you."

Next day the satrap came in state, as if confirmed in the rank already. He advanced to the throne, where Alexander sat in his Persian robes, and made the prostration gracefully. He had always had polished manners. His beard was grey now, and he'd grown a paunch. He made a tasteful speech about his seizure of the satrapy, all for the sake of good order and the King.

Alexander listened calmly, then beckoned me. "Bagoas, did you write that letter I spoke of?"

I answered, "Yes, lord King. You may be sure of it."

So I was there to hear him charged with his many murders. Strange that I only remembered him as my father's friend whom everyone trusted. He seemed the same man still, so amazed to hear such things about himself that I almost doubted them, till Alexander took him by surprise with something proven. Then his face grew horrible; I would not have known him.

He was tried soon after. The kin of his victims testified; many in rags, their fathers having been killed for their estates. Then came the guardians of the royal tombs of Persepolis, those who had not resisted; the rest were dead. Darius the Great had given him the most loot, but he'd done well with Xerxes, and had robbed my own dead master of his modest grave-goods; he seemed surprised at Alexander's minding that. Of stripping Kyros' bones he could not be convicted, since there were no witnesses; but it made no difference.

Alexander said at the end, "You chose yourself to be shepherd of your people. If you had been a good one, you would have left here with honor. You have been a beast of prey, and you shall die like one. Take him away ... Bagoas, speak to him if you wish."

As they were leading him off, I touched his arm. Even then, he had contempt to spare for a eunuch. I said, "Do you remember Artembares son of Araxis, your friend and host, whom you betrayed when King Arses died? I am his son."

I'd doubted it would mean much to him, after all the rest. But he had enough pride of birth to feel it. He flung off my hand; if he could, he would have stamped me underfoot. "Do I owe all this to you, then? I should have thought to buy your favor. Well, old times come round again. A eunuch rules."

Alexander said, "A eunuch shall hang you, since he is the better man. Bagoas, I leave it in your charge. See it done tomorrow."

I had nothing, really, to do; the captain whose usual work it was saw to it all, and only turned to me for the order to hoist him up. He kicked and writhed, on the high gallows against the wide sky of Pasargadai. I was ashamed to find it distasteful and take so little pleasure in it; it was disloyal to my father, and ungrateful to Alexander. I prayed in my heart, "Dear Father, forgive me that I am not a warrior, and have embraced my destiny. Accept this man through whom you died, and who robbed you of your son's sons. Give me your blessing." He must have given it; for he never again returned to me in dreams.

Ptolemy has only put in his book that Orxines was hanged "by certain persons, under Alexander's orders." I expect he thinks it showed some loss of dignity, to have brought me forward. Never mind. He does not know of the night, while I was still a boy, when my lord drew the story out of me. He was very true to his promises, as Ptolemy himself has written.

He gave the satrapy to Peukestas, who had saved his life in the Mallian city. After Orxines, no one blamed him for not appointing a Persian; but he did the nearest thing. Peukestas had come to love the land; he understood us, and liked our way of living, even our clothes, which he was well made to wear; he had often practiced his Persian on me. He ruled the province well, as much loved as Orxines had been hated.

We rode on to Persepolis. Alexander would have been there all this while, if there'd been a palace for him. Far off from the Royal Road we saw on the broad terrace the blackened ruins. He pitched his tent in open country outside; and I slipped away, to see what was left of the splendors Boubakes had wept for.

Already sand was drifted deep on the royal stairway, where the cavalcade of the lords had ridden. The sculptured warriors on the frieze marched up towards the roofless throne room, where only the sun held court between columns carved like flowers. Charred beams littered the harem; in its walled garden, a few tangled roses grew in a bed of cinders. I went back, and said nothing of where I'd been. A long time had gone by, since that feast of young men with torches.

At night he said, "Well, Bagoas, but for me we'd be better lodged tonight."

"Don't mourn for it now, Al'skander. You will build something better, and hold the feast as Kyros did."

He smiled. But he was brooding about Kyros' tomb; he was a great one for omens. Now these bones of grandeur, black and ragged against an angry sunset, revived his grief.

"Remember," I said to him, "how once you told me the blaze was godlike, an upward waterfall? How the tables were set with flame?" And I was going to add, "No fire without ash, Al'skander." But a shadow brushed me, and I closed my mouth on it.

We marched on towards Susa, where we were to meet Hephaistion's army. It grew cold in the passes, but the air was sweet and the great spaces stirred my heart. Alexander was happy too; he had some new plan, which he was not telling me yet. I felt him spark with it, and awaited his good time.

But one evening he came in looking troubled, and said, "Kalanos is sick."

"Kalanos? He's never ill. He was even well in the desert."

"I sent for him this evening; I felt like a talk with him. He sent back asking me to go to him."

"He sent for *you?"* I must admit, it shocked me.

"As a friend. I went, of course. He was sitting as he always does at his meditations, only propped against a tree. He usually gets up when I come, though he knows he needn't. But he asked me to sit down by him, because his legs had failed."

"I've not seen him since Persepolis. How did he march today?"

"Someone lent him a donkey. Bagoas, he looks his age. When first he came to me, I'd no notion how old he was, or I'd never have taken him from his home. A man of seventy can't change all his bodily habits without harm. He'd lived for years in peace, every day the same."

"He came for love of you. He says your fates were joined in some other life. He says . . ." I paused, having run on too fast. He looked up, saying, "Come, Bagoas." At last I answered, "He says you're a fallen god."

He was sitting naked for the bath, on the edge of his bed, with his hands on his sandal. Since first he was my lover, he'd never let me undo his shoes, unless he was wounded or dead tired, when any friend would do it. Now he sat still, his brows creased in thought. In the end he only said, as he took off his sandal, "I tried to get him to bed, but he said he must finish his meditation. I should have ordered it. But I left him there." I understood that; it was what he'd have wished himself. "I don't like his look. He's too old to force his strength. Tomorrow I'll send a doctor."

The doctor came back to report that Kalanos had a swelling in his entrails, and should travel in the sick-wagon. He refused, saying it would disturb his meditation, and that the foolish beast his body, if it would not obey, at least should not command him. Alexander gave him a soft-stepping horse to ride, and after each day's

march went to see how he was; which was always
thinner and weaker. Others went too; General Lysimachos for one was very fond of him; but sometimes
Alexander would stay alone. One evening he came
back so distressed that all his friends remarked it. It
was not till we were alone together that he said, "He
is resolved to die."

"Al'skander, I think he is in pain, though he does
not say so."

"Pain! He wants to die by burning."

I exclaimed in horror. It would have shocked me in
the execution place at Susa. Besides, it was a pollution
of holy fire.

"I felt the same. He says in his own country women
do it, rather than outlive their husbands."

"So say the men! I saw it done to a child of ten, and
she wished to live. They drowned her screams with
music."

"Some do consent. He says he will not outlive his
life."

"Could he get well?"

"The doctor won't answer for him. And he won't
accept a regimen . . . I didn't refuse him flat; he might
have done it himself at once, as best he could. With
every day's delay, there's just a chance he might take
a better turn. I don't think so now; I think I can see
the death-marks. But one thing I'm resolved on; when
he goes, he goes like a king. If it's true we live many
lives, he was that before." He paced about a little, then
said, "I will be there, as his friend. But I cannot
watch it."

So we reached Susa. Nothing was stranger to me
than that. The Palace was just the same; even some old
eunuchs, who had not marched with Darius, were still
bustling about. When they learned who I was, they
thought I must have been very clever.

Strangest of all was to stand again in the lamp-
shadows of the golden vine, and see that head on the
pillow. Even the inlaid casket was on the bed-table. I
found him looking at me. He held my eyes, and
stretched out his hand.

Afterwards he said, "Was it better?" He couldn't even wait to be told, supposing he'd needed telling. In some things, he was like a child.

The fountain court with its birds had been looked after. Alexander said it was just the place for Kalanos. He lay in the little room there; and each time I came to see him, he would ask me to open a cage. I hadn't the heart to tell him they were foreign birds, and might have trouble to make a living. It was his last pleasure, to watch them fly.

Hephaistion's army, with the elephants, had arrived before us. Alexander told his friends what Kalanos wanted, and ordered Ptolemy to prepare a royal pyre.

It was like a king's divan, decked with banners and garlands; underneath, it was filled with pitch and terebinth and tinder, and whatever would give the quickest and fiercest flame, mixed with Arabian incense.

In the square before the Palace, where all great ceremonies had been held since Darius the Great, the Companions stood drawn up, with the heralds and the trumpeters. On the fourth side were the elephants, newly painted, with sequinned draperies and gilded tusks. King Poros could have asked no more.

Alexander had chosen the cortege; the handsomest Persians and Macedonians on the tallest horses, in all their arms; then the offering-bearers, with grave-goods enough for a royal tomb, cloths sewn with gems and pearls, gold cups, vases of sweet oil and bowls of incense. They were to be laid on the pyre and burned with Kalanos. Alexander came in Darius' chariot, draped in white for mourning. His face looked drawn and set. I think he had devised all this magnificence, not just to honor Kalanos but to make it a little bearable.

Last of all came the living dead. Four big Macedonians carried his litter shoulder-high. The splendid Nisaian charger he had been meant to ride on, but was too weak to mount, was led beside him, to be sacrificed by the pyre.

He wore a thick wreath of flowers on his neck and

breast, as the Indians do on their wedding day. As he came near, we heard that he was singing.

He still sang to his god, as they laid him on the bier. Then, at this funeral of the living, his friends came up to take their leave.

All kinds of people came; generals and troopers, Indians, musicians, servants. The offering-bearers began to pile their gifts on the pyre. He smiled, and said to Alexander, "How like your kindness, to give me remembrances for my friends."

He gave away everything; the horse to Lysimachos, the cloths and the rest to all who'd known him well. To me, when I took his hand, he gave a Persian goblet worked with a lion, saying, "Do not fear, you shall drink to the very end, and no one shall take that from you."

Last came Alexander; we moved aside from respect, as he leaned over to embrace him. But Kalanos said quietly—only those nearest heard—"We need not say farewell. I will be with you in Babylon."

All now withdrew. The torch-bearers came up, a troop of them to make the kindling quicker. As the flames leaped, Alexander shouted for the battle-paean. The trumpets sounded; the soldiers yelled; the mahouts cried to the elephants, who lifted their trunks, and blared the salute they give to kings.

He was always tender to the pride of those he cared for. Feeling sure no old sick man could bear that searing pain without a cry, he'd ensured it should not be heard. He bowed his head as the fire rose roaring, and did not look. But I can witness that Kalanos lay with folded hands, while the flowers beneath them shriveled; he neither changed countenance nor opened his mouth. I only watched till he began to be disfigured; but all who watched to the end agreed that he did not stir.

He'd made Alexander promise to feast for him, not mourn; good healing wisdom, except that not touching wine himself, he'd never feasted with Macedonians. They were all rather mad that night, from horror or grief or both; someone proposed a drinking-contest by way of funeral games, and Alexander offered a prize. I think the winner downed two gallons. Many lay senseless until morning, on the couches or the floor; not the way to pass a cold winter night in Susa. The winner died of a chill, along with several more; so Kalanos got more than a horse for sacrifice.

Alexander had judged, not competed; he came to bed on his feet, already sobering and growing sad again.

"What did he mean," he said to me, "that he'd be with me in Babylon? Will he be reborn as a Babylonian? How shall I know the child?"

26

I T WAS next day that he asked me, "You have never seen Queen Sisygambis, have you?"

I heard the name as if in an ancient tale. She was the Queen Mother of Persia, whom Darius had left behind at Issos. "No," I said, "she was with you already, before I joined the Household here."

"Good. I want you to see her for me." I had quite forgotten that it was here at Susa he'd installed her and the young princesses, soon after the Queen had died. "If she would remember you at court, it might not quite do, you understand. But since she won't, I should like to send her someone charming, after so long with only letters and gifts. You remember, you chose me a chain of turquoises for her, at Marakanda? You'll find her well worth meeting. Give her my loving respects; say I've been impatient to see her, but business has held me back. Ask her if she'll do me the favor of receiving me in about an hour; and give her this." He showed me in its casket a necklace of Indian rubies.

390

I made my way to the Harem. When last I went, I had walked behind Darius, smelling the perfume from his robe.

At the Queen's entry, where I had never been, an old stately eunuch was fetched to sanction me. He was gracious, giving no sign of knowing what I had been, though of course such people know everything. I followed him down a corridor with sun-fretted lattices, and through an anteroom where matron ladies sat talking or playing chess. He scratched at a door beyond, announced me and who had sent me, then withdrew.

She sat straight in a tall straight chair, her arms along the chair-arms; over their ram-head ends, her fingers showed as fine as ivory spindles. She wore dark blue, with a dark blue veil over thin white hair. Her face was colorless, the face of an old white falcon brooding on its crag. Round her neck was the chain of turquoises from Marakanda.

I prostrated myself, with as much care as the first time before Darius. As I rose she spoke, in the high cracked voice of age.

"How is my son the King?"

It struck me dumb. How long had it been like this with her? She had had his body to deck for burial. Why had no one warned Alexander that her wits had gone? If I told the truth, she might fly into a frenzy, tear me with those long ivory nails, or dash her head on the wall.

Her old eyes stared at me fierce and bright, from their wrinkled lids. They blinked quickly once or twice, like an unhooded falcon's. They looked impatient. My tongue would not move. She struck one hand upon the chair-arm.

"I am asking you, boy, how is my son Alexander?" Her dark piercing gaze met mine, she had read my thought. She lifted her head against the chair-back. "I have only one son a King. There has never been any other."

Somehow I came to myself, remembered my training, gave her my message in proper form, and, kneeling, offered Alexander's gift. She lifted out the rubies in both hands, and called to two old waiting-ladies by the window. "See what my son has sent me."

They admired, were allowed to touch, while I knelt with the casket till someone should think to take it, and remembered the son she had thrown away.

He must have guessed, after he fled at Issos; who could have known her and not guessed? It had only remained for him to know that his place was filled. In the fountain court I had played my harp softly, to soothe a grief I only now understood. It was this had turned his rage on poor Tyriotes. Did he know she'd refused his rescue at Gaugamela? Perhaps they had kept that from him. Well that they had not met again; poor man, he'd had sorrow enough.

She noticed me in time, and motioned one of her ladies to take the casket. "Thank my lord the King for his gift, and say I shall receive him gladly." When I went out, she was still stroking the jewels on her lap.

"Did she like it?" said Alexander, as eager as if he'd been her lover. I told him she had shown great pleasure in it. "King Poros gave it me. I'm glad that she thought it worthy of her. *There* is the Great King who would have led your people, if God had made her a man. Both of us know it. We understand each other."

"It's as well God made her a woman; or you'd have had to kill her."

"Yes, there I was spared great grief. Did she look well? I've something important to say to her. I want to marry her granddaughter."

Through my first amazement, he still read my face. "That pleases you better than last time?"

"Alexander, it will please all the Persians." He had not set eyes on Stateira since she was a child at Issos, with her face in her mother's lap. This was a real state marriage, to honor our people and breed a royal line; it would have Sisygambis' blood, he'd remembered, as well as Darius's. As for Roxane, as second wife she'd still be above her station; Darius would never have made her more than a concubine. Keeping all these thoughts to myself, I hastened to wish him joy.

"Ah, and that's not all." We were in the fountain

court, a quiet retreat when the state rooms were full of envoys and officials. He cupped the fountain-fall in his palm and let it run out again. He was smiling.

"Now, Al'skander, tell me the secret. I've seen it in your face."

"Oh, I knew that! I can tell you now. This won't be only my wedding; it will be a marriage of both our peoples."

"Truly, Al'skander, yes."

"No, wait. All my own friends, my generals, and the best of my Companions will be marrying Persian ladies. I shall dower them all; and we shall all share the one wedding feast. What do you think of that?"

"Al'skander, no one else could have conceived it." Which was God's truth.

"I conceived it on the march, but it had to wait till I'd met the army. Most of them were serving there."

Well, I could see why he hadn't told me. He could hardly announce to me Hephaistion's wedding, before the bridegroom knew.

"I've been thinking," he said, "how many couples would make a handsome feast, without crowding the pavilion. I decided eighty." Getting back my breath, I said it sounded just right. "All my soldiers who've married Persian women will get dowries too. About ten thousand, I think."

He played smiling with the sunlit fountain-stream, which fell from his hand like gold.

"We'll make a new thing; two good wines blended to make a better, in a great loving-cup. Hephaistion will marry Stateira's sister. I should like his children to be my kin."

I suppose he felt my silence.

He looked in my face, came over and embraced me. "Dear one, forgive me. More than children are born of love. 'The sons of dreams'—do you remember? All this you begot; from loving you, I first learned to love your people."

After that, it was no pain to me to do my part; which was to call on the brides and their mothers, bring gifts, and tell them about procedure. I was well received in the harems; if they'd had plans of their own before Alexander had his, nobody said so. He had chosen, of course, for the greatest Macedonians the noblest brides; if these weren't always the best-favored, one can't have everything. The princesses, I did not see; but Drypetis would hardly disappoint Hephaistion; that was a handsome line. In all these years, I'd never heard he'd had a mistress; but if nephews and nieces were what Alexander asked him for, no doubt he would faithfully beget them.

Some silly man, whose name is not worth remembering, has written that Alexander slighted our people, because no Persian lord got a Macedonian wife. Where were these wives to come from? We were in Susa; there were only concubines or camp-followers. One can guess what the lady mothers of Macedon would have said, to dispatching their maiden daughters to the beds of unknown "barbarians." But why waste words on such folly?

Alexander meant this to be the greatest festival since his reign began. Already, weeks ahead, every weaver and carver and goldsmith in Susa was working into the night. I did not go to see if my old master prospered. One does not return to the midden one was flung in.

Since the King's return, artists in everything had been streaming over from Greece; news of the festival made them race. One of these, a flute-player of some fame called Evios, caused a trifling quarrel; or what should have been trifling, had the men concerned not been at odds already. So wars begin, with peoples as with men. So with Eumenes and Hephaistion.

Eumenes I knew only at a distance; but he'd been Chief Secretary all through Alexander's reign, and to his father before him. He was a Greek, who had had time to do some soldiering in India, and with success. He was about forty-five, grizzled and shrewd. I don't know why he and Hephaistion had always brushed up each other's fur. By my guess, it went back to Hephaistion's boyhood. Maybe Eumenes had envied him Alexander's love; maybe he just disapproved, as he did of me. I never took notice, knowing he could not harm me. It was different with Hephaistion. Since he led back the army, Alexander had made him Chiliarch, which is Greek for our Grand Vizier; he ranked next the King. He was incorruptible in office; but touchy about his dignity, among other things.

It had grown on him since India, where he'd had a jaundice fever. Doctors say you should not drink for a long time after; but try telling that to a Macedonian. Also he had a very constant nature; in love, and in resentment.

He was always polite to Persians; for Alexander's sake, and because our manners have civilized formality. It is impossible for Persians of decent breeding to brawl. We poison each other after consideration, or come to terms. Macedonians, who have no such restraints, are into it in a moment.

This flautist, Evios, was an old guest-friend of his from before my time; so he took charge of his entertainment. Susa was filling up; the lodging Hephaistion found for Evios had been taken by people of Eumenes' household; so Hephaistion turned them out.

Eumenes, a quiet man as a rule, went to him very angry. Whereas a Persian would have said it was all a dreadful mistake but too late for remedy, Hephaistion told Eumenes he must make room for guests of honor, like anyone else.

Eumenes, whose own rank was pretty high, went straight to Alexander, who had trouble to keep the peace. I know he had the flautist lodged elsewhere; I saw to that for him. What he said to Hephaistion, I could have overheard if I'd taken care; but I remembered that morning in the desert, and went away.

If, as I suspect, Hephaistion was asked to beg Eumenes' pardon, he thought it beneath him, and didn't do it. The enmity smoldered on. A petty squabble; why trouble to record it? Only because the end was to mix my lord's bitter grief with poison, and send him mad.

Meantime, being spared foreknowledge, I thought no more of it; nor I daresay did Alexander, who was busier still. He saw a good deal of the Queen Mother, and was shown his bride. He told me she had her mother's looks, and was a gentle modest maid. There was none of that kindling with which he had seen Roxane. I dared not ask him how *she* had taken the news.

The feast-day came. Darius the Great may have seen such splendors; no one living had. The whole Palace square was turned into a vast pavilion; in the center, the bridegrooms' tent, of fine cloth with bullion tassels, propped by gilt columns; all round it, awnings for the guests. The wedding would be by Persian rite; the bridal tent had gold chairs in couples. Our women being bred to modesty, the brides would only enter after the healths were drunk, when the grooms would take their hands, sit by them for the bridal song, and then retire.

Their fathers of course were present. Alexander asked me to help in their entertainment, because he wanted me to see the rite.

He wore the Mitra, and the royal robe of Persia, long sleeves and all. To tell the truth, his half-Greek dress suited him better; this called for Darius' height to set it off. But if there was one thing we'd learned in Persia, it was that a King is as tall as his soul.

For the crowd of lesser guests not to miss it all, he had heralds outside the tent, who would sound trumpets when the healths were drunk, give out the toasts, and announce the entry of the brides.

It all went perfectly. In the presence of the fathers-in-law, men of the noblest blood in Persia, the bridegrooms kept down their drinking, and did not even shout across the tent.

There were no prostrations. Alexander had given all the fathers the rank of Royal Kindred, which allowed them to kiss his cheek. There being no father-in-law for him, Oxathres took that place, and made a very fine figure, though he had to stoop for the kiss.

The King gave the bridal toast; the bridegrooms drank to the fathers, the fathers returned the honor, everyone drank to the King. The trumpets flourished for the entry of the brides. The fathers met them, took them by the hand and led them to the grooms.

Peasants apart, you seldom see the men and women of Persia walking together. Whatever Greeks may say, you won't find more beauty anywhere on earth than you do among our nobility, who have bred for it so choicely and so long. Handsomest of all was the foremost couple, Oxathres and his niece hand in hand. Alexander rose to meet them, and receive his bride. Yes, Darius had passed his good looks on to his children. Also his stature. She topped Alexander by a good half-foot.

He led her to her chair of honor by his throne; and the difference disappeared. He'd met her in the Queen Mother's rooms; and Alexander was nothing if not resourceful. He had had the legs of her chair cut down.

Of course they had to walk out together, when the bridal couples retired. I could almost hear his voice saying, "It is necessary." (Days later, I found pushed into some dark corner his wedding shoes. The soles had an inch of felt in them. He'd taken no such trouble when host to seven-foot Poros.)

Hephaistion and Drypetis matched up well. She was his height to an inch.

The feasting went on all night. I met old friends, and needed no pretense, to share the merriment. Years had gone by, since he spared Susa and first rode in there. He had gone far away and become a legend, while wrong was done in his name. Now they knew him. In that city Kyros is remembered; how he did not profane the sanctuaries of the conquered Medes, nor dishonor their nobility, nor enslave their peasants, but was a just King to us all. That a westerner should prove to be such another was a wonder everywhere. I saved up all I heard, to tell him later. He had done what he meant to do.

No doubt he did no less in the marriage bed. Stateira was installed in her royal rooms; but his visits turned to mere calls of courtesy, much sooner than with Roxane. A few days later, indeed, he visited the Sog-

dian. It may have been just to heal her wounded feel-
ings; but I'm not so sure. Stateira was, as he'd said,
a gentle modest girl; and he was a lover of fire. Roxane
had it, even if it smoked. He soon had enough of her;
yet from time to time she always drew him back.
Olympias his mother, that royal termagant, was still
berating his regent by every post. He would throw
down her letter in anger; yet with his answer would go
a gift, lovingly chosen. Perhaps there is something in
the proverb about how men choose their wives.

He had done what he meant to do. Yes—among *my*
people.

I was too happy. Once or twice, going about, I got
hard looks from Macedonians; but those whom kings
love are always envied; so was Hephaistion, and in
higher places than I. I never thought that all Persians
were more hated, till I saw Peukestas ride by in our
native dress. Our people, who'd already learned his
worth, saluted him; then, when he'd passed, I overheard some Macedonians. He had gone barbarian, it
was disgusting, how could the King encourage it? For
that matter, what was the King coming to himself?

I noted their faces and their regiment. I should not
have been sorry to do them harm with Alexander. But
it would only wound him, without doing him service. It
was hearts, not words, he had hoped to change.

Soon after this, he got to know that Macedonian
troops were waist-deep in debt, with creditors closing
in. With the loot they'd had, they should have been as
rich as princes; but they had no notion of bargaining,
as we Persians understand it; they'd pay double the
going price for all they bought, ate, drank or lay with.
Hearing of their distress, as if he'd not spent enough
upon their marriage dowers, Alexander gave out that
he'd settle up for them. Few came forward; and at last
the officers broke the truth to him; the men were saying he just wanted to know who was living beyond his
pay.

It hurt him more than anything since that day in
India, that they thought he'd lie to them. He could not

understand it. I could have told him. He was growing foreign to them, as he came closer to us.

So he had banking-tables set up in the camp, and told his paymasters to sit there without writing things. Any soldier who showed up a debtor's bond had it paid off, and no record made. It cost close on ten thousand talents, that piece of magnanimity. I thought that should shut their mouths awhile.

Spring was just breaking; along by the river one smelled the rising sap. The lilies would not be long. As I rode there one morning with Alexander, he looked at the hills and said, "Where was your home?"

"There, by that crag. The grey there, that looks like rock, that is the watchtower."

"A good place for a stronghold. Shall we ride up and see it?"

"Al'skander, I would see too much."

"Don't see it now. Listen to some news I've kept for you. Do you remember, five years ago, I said I was starting an army of Persian boys?"

"Yes. We were in Baktria. Is it only five years since then?"

"It does seem longer. We've put a good deal into it." Indeed, in thirty years he had filled three men's full lifetimes. "Well, five years is up. They're ready, and on their way here."

"That is wonderful, Al'skander." Six years since I came to him; thirteen since I left those walls, riding with my father's head.

"Yes, their instructors are very pleased with them. Race me to the trees." The gallop shook off my sadness, as he'd meant. As we breathed our horses, he said, "Thirty thousand, all eighteen years old. We'll see something, I think."

They reached Susa seven days later. He had a dais set up on the Palace terrace, for him and his generals to see the new corps parade. Presently, from their camp beyond the walls, came the Macedonian bugle-call, "Cavalry, march."

They came in squadrons, Macedonian-armed, but on

good Persian horses, not Greek scrubs. The Persians of Persis rode up first.

Macedonian dress or not, Persians are Persians. Their officers had not denied them those little touches that give an air; an embroidered saddlecloth, a cuirass with a device, a pennant on the Macedonian lance, a glittering bridle, a flower stuck in the helmet. And they had the Persian face.

I don't suppose they had all been recruited willingly; but they had pride in their training now. Each squadron pranced up to the square with lances poised; slowed down, pacing to music; wheeled before the royal dais, saluting with their spears; then did their show-tricks, saluted again, and cantered off while the next rode in.

All Susa watched, from the walls and rooftops. The sides of the square were crowded with Macedonians. No one denies they were the best-trained army the world has seen. All that these young men did, they could have done as briskly. But we do have more sense of style. So had Alexander.

When the long review was over, he came away glowing, and talking to the Persians of his bodyguard, Oxathres, and Roxane's brother, and one of Artabazos' sons. Right across the Great Hall, he caught my eye and smiled. He was late to bed, having sat up talking and drinking, as he did when he was pleased. "I never saw so much beauty in one day; but still I have picked the best." He pulled softly at my hair. "You know what I call these boys? I call them my Successors."

"Al'skander," I said lifting off his chiton, "did you call them that to the Macedonians?"

"Why not? They'll breed me successors too. What is it?"

"I don't know. You have taken nothing from them. But they don't like us to show excellence."

He stood up, clothed only in his many wounds, tossing back his hair; not dulled but lit by the wine. "To hate excellence is to hate the gods." He spoke so loudly, the squire on guard looked in to see all was well. "One must salute it everywhere, among unknown peoples, at the furthest ends of the earth; yet one must never cheapen it." He began pacing about. "I found it in Poros, though his black face was strange to me. And in Kalanos. I find it among your people. In respect for that, I hanged the Persian satraps along with the Macedonians. To excuse their crimes like something native to them, that would have been contempt."

"Yes. We are an ancient race. We understand such things."

"Those things and others," he said, leaving off his oration, and stretching out his arms.

The Greeks have written that at this time he grew short-tempered. I don't wonder. He wanted to be Great King in fact as well as name; and all he did for it, his own people hated. A few friends understood—Hephaistion did, I allow—for the rest, they'd sooner have seen him master of a race of slaves, with themselves as lesser masters. They didn't hide what they felt about the new cadets. And then, though the wound in his side had healed, he still tired more quickly than he used to do, though he'd have died sooner than own it.

They said we'd spoiled him with servility; maybe to such uncouth folk it seemed really so. *We* knew we'd made him used to decent manners, and a civilized court. *He* knew that it was necessary. Persians who were allowed to upbraid a king would think him a low barbarian without breeding or self-respect, whom it degraded them to serve. Any fool in Persia knows that. I set it down for the ignorant.

What did they lose through us? He'd given all those marriage dowers; he'd paid their debts; he'd held a parade of honor, with hosts of gifts and prizes for bravery and good service. Yet afterwards, when he took into the Companions some Persians of real distinction, it was resented. If his temper was sometimes harsh, they asked for it. It never was with me.

Spring was well on; he decided to spend summer at Ekbatana, like the kings before him. Most of the troops, led by Hephaistion, were to march up the Tigris valley to Opis, whence a good road leads through the passes; Alexander, to see something new which might prove useful, went to Opis by water. Down there the Tigris has lost its fierceness; it was a pleasant voyage up the ever-winding stream, past the palm groves and the margin of fruitful fields, with the oxen turning the water-wheels. The river was full of ancient useless weirs, which he caused to be cleared as he went; we dawdled along, sleeping ashore or aboard as his fancy took him. It was a rest from the court, from toil and anger. Green, peaceful days.

Near the end of the voyage, while they broke up one of these old weirs, we were moored in a shady creek; he reclined in the stern under a striped awning, with my head in his lap. Once he would have looked if there were Macedonians watching; now he did as he liked and they could make the best of it. In any case, there was no one about of much importance. He looked up at the waving palm-fronds, and played lazily with my hair. "At Opis, we'll be on the Royal Road to the west, and I can send the old veterans home. They've had work enough, since they told me in India how tired they were. It's true as Zenophon says, the commander may bear the same hardships, yet for him it's not the same. It was their tears that moved me. Stubborn old fools . . . still, stubborn in danger, too. When they go home, it won't be my fault if they ever want again."

The army arrived before us. It's a middle-sized city, with yellow mud-brick houses, and, like every town along the Royal Road, a stone lodging for the King. It was getting hot in the plain, but we were not staying. Nothing much had happened on the army's land march, except that Hephaistion and Eumenes had been quarreling all the way.

It had been building up before Susa. In Karmania, needing to repair the fleet, Alexander had asked a loan from his friends till he reached the capital. Their money, at least, had come through the desert safe, and he repaid with interest later. But Eumenes was close-fisted; when his offering came, Alexander said with irony that he would not rob the poor, and sent it back. "I wonder," he said to me that night, "what he'd

fetch out if his tent burned down." "Try it, Al'skander," I said. He was rather drunk; we were laughing;
I never thought he really would. The tent caught fire
next day. The trouble was that it burned so fast, the
Royal Journal and state letters went up along with it.
The money came out as ingots; sure enough, about a
thousand talents. Alexander asked for none; he'd had
his joke, if it came expensive for him. Whether
Eumenes thought it was Hephaistion who set him on to
it, I don't know. After Susa, if Eumenes had only
stepped in dog-shit, he'd have suspected Hephaistion
put it there.

On the march to Opis, being at open enmity, they
had picked up factions. I doubt they'd aimed at this.
Hephaistion had no need; Eumenes was a subtle
Greek, who knew better than to put himself in the
wrong. There had been no brawling; but those who
hated the King's Persian ways, and knew his friend sup-
ported them, were drawn to Hephaistion's enemy without urging.

By the time we got there, it was making Eumenes
anxious. He came to Alexander, said how much the
estrangement grieved him, and declared himself eager
to make it up. What he was chiefly eager for was not to
take the blame if it went on. Which it did; he had
lost his temper over the flautist's lodging, and what
he'd said, Hephaistion would not forget. It was seldom
indeed he disobliged Alexander. But he was a great
man now, and knew his dues. Alexander could not order him to swallow an insult. If he asked as a favor, it
was one he didn't get. Hephaistion, who had not
spoken to Eumenes for half a month, maintained his
silence. Soon after, we had other things to think of.

Alexander had a platform put up on the parade
ground, to address the troops. He was to discharge
the veterans, tell them their retirement bounty, and
give them their marching orders to the Middle Sea. A
simple business. I only went up on the roof to watch
because I was idle, and would always sooner look at
him than not.

The troops filled the ground, right up to the rostrum

with the Bodyguard around it. The generals rode up the lane that had been left, and took their places; last came the King, gave a squire his horse, went up and began to speak.

Before long, they started to wave their arms. The discharge bounty was wildly generous; I took it they were cheering.

Suddenly, he vaulted straight off the rostrum, and strode out through the Bodyguard among the soldiers. I saw him grab one with both hands, and shove him at the Guard, who took him in charge. The generals came scrambling after him. He moved about, pointing out some dozen men. They were marched away; he went round by the steps, came forward and spoke again.

There was no more arm-waving. He spoke for some time. Then he ran down the steps, jumped on his horse, and galloped towards his lodging. The generals followed as soon as they could get mounted.

I hurried down, to be in his room beforehand and hear what it was all about. The door opened; he said to the bodyguard outside, "No one. On any business whatever. Do you understand?"

He flung in, slamming the door before the guard could close it. He didn't see me at first; I took one look and kept quiet. He was in a white-hot fury; his worn, brilliant face was blazing with outrage. His lips were moving, going over whatever he'd said out there. I just caught the end. "Yes, tell them at home how you forsook me, and left me to the care of the foreigners you conquered. No doubt it will bring you glory among men, and heaven's blessings. Get out."

He sent his helmet crashing into a corner, and started on his cuirass. I came forward to unbuckle it.

"I can do it." He shoved away my fingers. "I said nobody here."

"I was inside. Alexander, whatever is it?"

"Go and find out. You'd better go, I don't trust myself with anyone. I'll send for you later. Go."

I left him tugging at the straps, and cursing under his breath.

After a moment's thought, I went along to the

squires' room. The one who had held the King's horse had just arrived. I joined the crowd around him.

"It was mutiny," he said. "They'd have killed any other man. Oh, Bagoas! Have you seen the King?"

"He won't talk. I only saw from the roof. What did he say to them?"

"Nothing! I mean, he gave the veterans their discharge, thanked them for their courage and their loyalty; all proper and nicely put. He was just getting on to their bounties, when some of the serving troops started shouting out, 'Discharge us all!' When he asked them what they meant by it, they all took it up. 'You don't want us now, it's all mother-fucking barbarians . . . Oh, I'm sorry, Bagoas."

"Just get on," I said. "What then?"

"Somebody yelled, 'Go marching with your father. The one with horns.' He couldn't make himself heard. So he jumped straight down, right into the middle of them, and started arresting the ones who'd started it."

"What?" someone said. "Not on his own?"

"No one laid a finger on him. It was uncanny. As if he were really a god. He had on his sword, but he never touched it. The men just submitted like oxen; the first, he handled himself. You know why? I know. It's his eyes."

"But then he spoke again," I said.

"You saw that? He saw the prisoners taken off, then he went up and told them their fortune. He started by saying Philip brought them up from nothing, wearing sheepskins he said—is that really true?"

The squire from the noblest house said, "My granddad told us only the lords wore cloaks. He said it showed who you were."

"And the Illyrians came raiding right into Macedon?"

"He said all the peasants came up to the fort at night."

"Well, the King said Philip had made them masters of all the people who used to kill them with fright, and when he died there were sixty talents in the treasury, a few gold and silver cups, and five hundred talents in debts. Alexander borrowed eight hundred more, and that's what he crossed to Asia with. Did you know that? Well, he reminded them of all the rest since then, and he said, I'll always remember this, 'While I have led you, not one of you has ever been killed in flight.' He said if they wanted to go home they could go today, and boast of it when they get there, and good luck to them. That's what he said."

A young one called out, "Let's go and see him, and tell him how *we* feel." They often talked as if they owned him. I found it endearing.

"He won't have anyone in," I said. "He won't have me."

"Is he weeping?" said the one with the softest heart.

"Weeping! He's as angry as a hit lion. Keep your heads out of his mouth."

I kept mine out till evening. All his friends had been turned away, even Hephaistion. His quarrel with Eumenes was still on; I don't think Alexander had quite forgiven that. Servants with food were shut out like the rest. The wounded lion had no wish to see a doctor.

At night I went to see if he'd take a bath. The squires would have let me in, but I feared it might earn them a mauling from the cave, and made them announce me. The growl from within said, "Thank him and tell him no." I noted the thanks, which I'd not had earlier; presented myself next morning, and was admitted.

He was still licking his wounds. Last night's anger had set into deep resentment. It was all he could talk about. I got him shaved and bathed and fed. Everyone else was still being kept out. He gave me most of his address to the army; fine fiery stuff, too good to keep to himself. He was like a woman reliving her quarrel with her lover, word by word.

Just after, the guard scratched at the door. "King, there are some Macedonians from the camp, asking leave to speak with you."

His face altered. You could not quite say his eye lit

up. He just tilted his head to one side a little. "Ask them," he said, "what they are still doing here, when they discharged themselves yesterday. Tell them I am seeing no one; I am busy with their replacements. They can draw their pay and go. Bagoas, will you fetch me my writing-things?"

He was at his table all day. At bedtime, he was deep in thought; there was a kind of sparkle in his eye, but he kept his counsel. Next morning he sent for the generals. From then on, the place teemed with officers, mostly Persian; and Opis seethed like an anthill with the top knocked off.

The Macedonian camp was still full of soldiers. Not wishing to be torn asunder, I sought in friendlier places the cause of all this stir. I soon found out. Alexander was forming an all-Persian army.

It was not just a new corps, like the young Successors. All the great Macedonian regiments, the Silver Shields, the Infantry Companions, were being made up from Persians. Only the chief Macedonian generals, and his most loyal friends, were left holding commands. The Companions themselves would be half Persian, at least.

The first day, orders went out. On the second, the commanders started work. On that day also, Alexander gave the rank of Royal Kin to the whole Persian nobility who'd had it under Darius; all could kiss his cheek instead of making the prostration. He added to these just eighty Macedonians, those who had shared his wedding.

The dust outside was enough to choke you. Inside, Alexander in his Persian robe was being kissed in greeting by Persians assuming their new appointments. I watched in the shadows, thinking, He is all ours, now.

It was quiet; we know how to behave in the Presence. So the noise from the terrace sounded clearly; a heavy clatter, like ironwork being unloaded; and Macedonian voices, unhushed as they always are, but very sorrowful.

The sounds increased. The Macedonian generals looked at each other, and at Alexander. He tilted his head a little, and went on with what he was saying. I slipped off to an upper window.

The terrace was full of them, overflowing into the square. They were all unarmed; they had stacked their weapons. They stood before the Palace doors, with a lost murmuring; for all the world like dogs who've run truant to the woods, and come back to find the house locked for the night. Soon, I thought, they will put back their heads and howl.

Sure enough, with a noise to split your ears, they began to cry out like souls in ordeal, "Alexander! Alexander! Alexander, let us come in!"

He came out. With one great cry, they fell upon their knees. The one nearest him clung weeping to the skirt of his Persian robe. He said nothing; just stood where he was and looked at them.

They implored his pardon. They would never do it again. They would condemn their ringleaders. They would stay on this spot night and day, just as they were, till he forgave and pitied them.

"So you say now." He spoke sternly; but I thought his voice had a shake in it. "Then what got into you all at the Assembly?"

There was another chorus. The one who had grasped his robe—I saw he was an officer—said, "Alexander, you call Persians your kin. You let them kiss you; and which of us has done it?" Those were his words, I swear.

Alexander said, "Get up." He raised the man and embraced him. The poor fellow, knowing no etiquette, made a clumsy botch of the kiss; but you should have heard the cheering. "You are all my kindred, every one of you from now on." His voice, without disguise, had broken. He came forward with outstretched hands.

I stopped counting how many pressed up to kiss him. His cheeks were glistening. They must have tasted his tears.

All the rest of the day, he spent rearranging the new commands, under Persian names, alongside the Macedonian, without any Persian commander losing face. It did not seem to give him very much trouble. My belief is, he'd had it all in his head before.

He came to bed dead tired; but his smile was a smile of triumph. Well, he had earned it. "They changed their minds," he said. "I thought they might. We have been a long time together."

"Al'skander," I said. He turned his smile on me. It was so close to the tip of my tongue, I almost said it: "I have seen the great courtesans of Babylon and Susa. I have seen the cream from Corinth. I used to think I was not so mean in the art myself. But the crown is yours."

However, one could not be quite sure he would understand; so I said instead, "Kyros would have been proud to accomplish that."

"Kyros . . . ? You've given me a thought. What would he do now? He would hold a Feast of Reconcilement."

He held it before the veterans left for home. It was as grand as the wedding, except that we'd left the awnings at Susa. In the midst of the Palace square was an enormous dais, where all the nine thousand guests could see the royal table, at which sat around him the chief Macedonians and Persians, with the leaders of the allies. Greek seers and Magi invoked the gods together. All those at the feast had equal honors; except that the Macedonians sat next him. He couldn't deny that to the old, forgiven lover, after all those kisses and tears.

To me, of course, it made a certain difference. At a real Persian court, a royal favorite, even though he takes no bribes, is treated with much respect. No one offends him. Still, it would have been a shadow of the substance I had already. I did not grieve that Hephaistion sat beside him; it was the Chiliarch's formal right. He had not used the great Reconcilement to make his peace with Eumenes. I thought to myself, Al'skander knows he'd not have asked *me* in vain.

So, when he lifted the great loving-cup to the sound of trumpets, and begged the gods to give us all kinds of blessings, but harmony between Macedonians and

Persians above all, I drank with a whole heart, and drank again to the hope reborn in his face.

All is well, I thought. And soon we go to the hills. Once more, after so long, I shall see the sevenfold walls of beautiful Ekbatana.

27

THE VETERANS were sent off with love and money. Krateros was leading them. In Macedon, he was to take the regency; Antipatros would come out in his place.

This was high politics. Alexander just said that Krateros needed sick-leave. Some said he wanted sick-leave himself from his mother's and regent's endless intrigues and bickerings, which might end in civil war; others, that he thought Antipatros had ruled like a king so long, he might start to think he was one. He had been faithful; but all this while he'd expected Alexander to be coming back. He was getting rather too purple, was what Alexander said.

In his parting speech to the veterans, he said, "I honor you by trusting you to Krateros, my most loyal follower, whom I love you as my own life." *Most* loyal . . .? It passed well enough, in a speech of thanks and farewell.

To shake hands with Eumenes may well have been the first thing Hephaistion had refused to Alexander.

Now every day made it harder. Eumenes had humbled himself to come forward first; no man of his standing, once rebuffed, was going to do it twice. Meeting they exchanged cold stares; apart, each said what he thought of the other to whoever would pass it on.

You may say that here was my chance. Anyone used to courts will say so. I would have said it once; I knew better now. Alexander, of whom men tell many legends, lived by his own. Achilles must have Patroklos. He might love his Briseis; but Patroklos was the friend till death. At their tombs in Troy, Alexander and Hephaistion had sacrificed together. Wound Patroklos, and Achilles will have your blood. Eumenes knew; he'd known them since they were boys.

So, instead of telling tales and making mischief, I gave no sign that I even knew of trouble. That legend was a limb of Alexander. His very blood flowed into it. If anyone bruised it, let it be Hephaistion himself, not I. Besides, there was that morning in the desert.

The court set out for Ekbatana. Stateira was left with her grandmother at Susa. Roxane was brought along.

We had a diversion on the way. Atropates satrap of Media, who'd heard of Alexander's dealings with other satraps, planned a little treat for him. The first time he'd passed that way, he'd asked whether the race of Amazons, mentioned by Herodotos, was still alive. Atropates had had none to offer, and must have been brooding on it ever since.

One morning, a silvery bugle-call echoed back and forth along the pass we'd camped in. Up pranced a troop of cavalry, daintily armed with round shields and little axes. The leader leaped from her horse, saluted Alexander, and told him they had been sent by Atropates. She had the right breast bare, as in all the legends, and small enough. As the left was covered, there was no knowing if that one was any bigger.

Having rejoined her troop, the lady put them through a very dashing display. The soldiers, eyeing all those bare breasts, nearly cheered their heads off. Alexander said to Ptolemy, "Atropates must be out of

his mind. Warriors? Those are just girls. Do they look
to you like whores?"

"No," Ptolemy said. "They've been picked for their
looks and riding."

"What kind of fool does he take me for? Well, we
must have them out of camp before the men get at
them. Bagoas, do something for me. Tell them their
show was so delightful, I'd like to see the musical ride
again. Hydarnes, can you raise me an escort of sober,
middle-aged Medes? And quickly?"

They looked prettier still, flushed from their riding;
the men were licking their chops like dogs at a kitchen
door. There were whistles and calls when the ride began again. In a great hurry, Alexander collected
presents. He chose jewelry, not weaponry, but it was
well received. The grizzled Medes led off their charges
to a sound of groans.

We camped in the upland pastures of Nysa, the
royal horselands. The brood-mares were still about
fifty thousand, though so many had been lifted in the
years of war. They were a delight to Alexander, who
established a guard for them, and chose out some likely
colts. He gave one to Eumenes. If it was by way of
thanks for his thankless offer to Hephaistion, and a
salve for pride, none of that was said; but Hephaistion,
who had done the first wrong in the quarrel, may have
read that into it. Certainly Eumenes' faction did, and
were saying that pride went before a fall.

I know, having seen the list, that Alexander had
planned asking Hephaistion to dinner that night with
some old friends. He'd have been charming to him before everyone, smoothed down his feathers, shown that
Patroklos was Patroklos still.

That day, he came face to face with Eumenes in the
camp.

I don't know if it was design or chance. I had
ridden out to see the horse-herds, and was coming
back; they were well away by the time I heard the
shouting. Hephaistion was saying that Greeks had
been played out for a hundred years, that Philip had
thrashed them everywhere, and Alexander had found

them with only tongues for weapons; *those* they knew how to use. Eumenes said that swaggering braggarts needed no talebearers; their own noise told enough.

Each faction booed and cheered; the crowds were growing. It would be blood before long. I began to edge out. Already I heard the rasp of swords in scabbards; when there was a drumming of violent hooves, brought to a clattering halt. A high fierce voice shouted, once. All other sounds failed. Alexander, his bodyguard behind him, sat staring down, his mouth shut, his nostrils flaring. In the hush, one heard the shake of the horses' bridles.

The long pause ended. Hephaistion and Eumenes stepped towards him, each starting to blame the other.

"Be silent!"

I jumped down and held my horse, making myself small in the crowd. I did not want my face ever remembered, along with what was coming.

"Not a word. Either of you." His speed had flicked back the hair from his brow; he had it rather short, for the summer heat. His eyes had paled, anger furrowed his brow like pain. "I demand discipline from men I appoint to keep it. You are to lead my soldiers in battle, not in brawls. Both of you deserve to be put on a charge of mutiny. Hephaistion, I made you what you are. And not for this."

Their eyes met. It was as if I saw them bleeding, letting the blood run down unheeding with faces of stone.

"I order you to renounce this quarrel. Under pain of death. If it breaks out again, you will both be on trial for treason. The proved aggressor will suffer the usual penalty. I shall not commute it."

The crowd held its breath. It was not just the public reprimand of two such men, in itself a thing unheard of. They were Macedonians. They knew the legend.

The factions were sheathing their swords in furtive quiet. "At noon," he said, "you will both report to me. You will shake hands before me and swear a reconcilement, which you will keep to in look, and word, and deed. Is that understood?"

He wheeled his horse and rode off. I slipped away in the crowd. I dared not look at Hephaistion's face, in case he saw me there. I did not see it either when he took the oath before Alexander.

That night he had them both to supper. A gesture of forgiveness; but to both alike. That special kindness to Patroklos must be for another day.

I'd barely seen him, till it was time to dress. It was worse than I'd thought. He looked haggard, and hardly spoke. I dared say nothing. But when I was doing his hair, I took his head in my hands and laid my cheek on it. He gave a deep sigh and closed his eyes. "I had to do it. Nothing else was possible."

"There are wounds that only kings must suffer, for the sake of all." I had been a long time thinking what to say, that he'd forgive me after.

"Yes. That is the thing."

I longed to embrace him, and tell him I would never have made him suffer it. But, I thought, they will make it up; what then? Besides, there was always the desert. So I just kissed him once, and went on with what I was doing.

Supper broke up early. I thought he'd just been afraid of their getting drunk and starting again. But he loitered in his tent instead of coming to bed; then put a dark cloak on and went out. I saw him throw a fold about his head; he didn't want it seen where he was going, though he must have known I'd guess.

He was not very long away. They must have patched it up, after a fashion; one could tell that after. But if it had gone as he wished, he'd not have finished the night as he did with me. Nothing was said in words; much was said all the same, perhaps too much. I loved him, and could not help it.

Time passes, edges wear down. We camped three or four days more among the tall glossy horse-herds. Hephaistion and Eumenes addressed each other with quiet courtesy. Alexander went riding with Hephaistion, to choose him a horse. They came back laughing, much as they used, except that one knew it had been worked for. Time alone will not heal it, I thought; only the will to forget. "I shall not commute it." The one knows those words were forced from him, the other that they were said. None of it can be undone, or talked away. But they have been bound so long, they will agree to forget; it is necessary, nothing else is possible.

We went up the passes, eastward to Ekbatana.

No snow, now, on the sevenfold ramparts; they glowed like jeweled necklaces on the mountain's breast. Not sleet, but cool delightful breezes blew through the high airy rooms. The make-shift shutters were cleared away; it was a summer palace, with the King expected. Beautiful carpets covered the royal floors. Lamps of fretted silver and gilded bronze hung from the gold-leafed rafters, in the Bedchamber where Darius had struck my face, and I had stumbled out weeping into Nabarzanes' arms.

The hills were green and full of streams; one could smell the heights. I would ride in them at last; we were to stay all summer.

At night he walked out on his balcony, to cool his head from the wine. I stood beside him. The plant-tubs smelled of lemon flowers and roses; the breeze came pure from the mountains. He said, "When first I came here, chasing Darius, though it was full winter, I said to myself, Someday I must come back."

"I too. When I was with Darius, being chased by you, I said the same."

"And here we are. Longing performs all things." He gazed at the brilliant stars, conceiving new longings, as a poet conceives a song.

I knew the signs. He was absent and exalted, and would pace with brows creased in thought, which I always knew from trouble. One must never ask till he was ready. He would come out with it of a sudden, as if he'd given birth.

He was delivered one morning, so early that I was the first to hear. I found him up and walking about stark naked, as he must have been doing since before dawn. "It's Arabia," he said the moment he saw me. "Not the inland parts, that's just a matter of seeing the tribesmen don't raid the ports. It's the coast we need;

and no one knows how far it runs south or west. Just think. We can make harbors along Gedrosia, now we know where there's water. From Karmania up the Persian Sea, that's easy sailing. But we need to round Arabia. Once up the Arabian Gulf—*that* end's well charted—you're in Egypt. And from there, do you know this, there's a channel right through to the Middle Sea? Their King Neko started it; and Darius the Great carried it through. It needs clearing and widening, that's all. Once we round Arabia, if we can, ships can go all the way from the Indus, not just to Susa—to Alexandria, Piraeus, Ephesos. Cities made from small towns, villages where there was nothing; poor savages like Niarchos' Fish-Eaters brought into the world of men; and all the great peoples sending their best to one another, sharing their thought. The sea's the great road. Man has hardly set his foot on it."

I was nearly running, to keep up and listen. "Italy, now. My sister's husband died making war there, he should have waited for me. They'll have to be brought into order before long, or that western tribe, the Romans, will have it all. Good fighters, I've heard. I should let them keep their own form of government; and I could use their troops to push the empire westward, along north Africa. I long to see the Pillars of Herakles; who knows what may lie beyond?"

There was much more. Sometimes snatches come back to me, and then I lose them; seeing only his face in the cool early light, worn and shining, worn fine like much-used gold; his deep eyes bright as a fire-altar; his tousled hair, faded yet still a boy's; and the strong obedient body forgetful of its wounds, ready to face the tasks of another life-span, pacing as if already on its way.

"So Babylon must be the capital, at the center. The harbor should have slips for a thousand galleys. I shall go straight from here, to get started, and prepare the fleet for Arabia . . . Why are you looking sad?"

"Only at leaving Ekbatana. When do we go?"

"Oh, not till the cold begins. We will have our summer." He turned his eyes to the mountains, and would have walked naked to the balcony, if I'd not put a robe on him. "What a place for a festival! We'll have one before we go. It's time I offered something to the immortals."

We had our summer.

On the hills with the hounds crying, racing the clouds; in the rose garden with its lotus pools; in the high hall whose columns were sheathed with gold and silver, as I did my Dance of the River to the sound of flutes; in the great Bedchamber where I had been shamed and now was cherished, each day and night, I used to say to myself, I will miss nothing; I will never let my eye or my ear or my soul or my senses sleep, never forget to know that I am happy. For it will be a long campaign; who knows when we shall come back?

Thus the Wise God gives us prophecy enough, but not too much; as he does to birds, who foresee the winter, but not the night of ice that will drop them from the bough.

Alexander started at once to put in train his plans for the fleet, and the great harbor at Babylon, sending orders ahead. He wanted the north of the Hyrkanian Sea explored, to see how the coast led round to India. He also did much state business Darius would have handed to someone else; it was the custom for the King to take a holiday at Ekbatana. When I told Alexander so, he looked surprised, and said he was taking one; he had never been so idle in his life.

The summer before, we had been in Gedrosia. I would dabble my hand in the lotus pool, and think, I am happy. Let never a moment flow by me unthanked, unkissed.

One night I said, "Are you happy, Al'skander?"

He said smiling, "Couldn't you tell?"

"Oh, yes, that. I mean here, in Ekbatana."

"Happy?" he said, turning it over. "What is happiness?" He stroked me, so that I should know him grateful. "To have achieved one's longing, yes. But also, when all one's mind and body are stretched to breaking, when one hasn't a thought beyond what to do next moment; one looks back after, and there it was."

"You will never settle down, will you, Al'skander? Not even here."

"Settle down? With all I have to do? I should hope not."

He was already planning the autumn festival, and sent word of it to Greece. Hordes of actors and poets, singers and kitharists would be on the way. He was not inviting athletes. In the old days, he said, they had been all-round men, the heroes of their cities in war; now they had trained themselves into mere machines for winning one event. "A catapult can throw further than any soldier, but it can't do anything else. It's not good for the men to have such people beat them. Nor for the boys to see it."

"The boys" now meant one thing to him. When the veterans left, returning to their wives and leaving, as soldiers do, the women who'd followed them with so much hardship, he had made the children his wards. He would not have them suffer in Macedon as unwanted foreign bastards; they should be reared for what they were, half Persian, half Macedonian, part of the harmony he'd prayed for at the Susa love-feast. Boys old enough to leave their mothers were at school already, and had come up here with the court. There were to be events for them at the games; he went sometimes to watch them training.

He went sometimes, too, along the latticed walk to the Harem. Roxane was like a sharp sauce to him; nauseous if one fills one's plate with it, yet a little now and then will make one crave for the taste again. It did not trouble me.

Summer fled by in the cool sweet hills; the roses rested before their autumn flowering. There came a day of change. His face was smoothed with joy; he could talk about nothing long without, "Hephaistion thinks . . ." or "Hephaistion was saying . . ." Somewhere, perhaps up in the mountains riding alone, they had broken the wall, cast themselves into each other's arms, were once again Achilles and Patroklos; they would begin forgetting.

In the wisdom of my hard schooling, I'd done nothing to delay it; no malice could be remembered against me now. I had shut in my silent heart, as always, "Say that you love me best of all." So I kept what I had. He'd no need to forget the nights when he'd turned to me, and known that I understood. I had not defaced the legend.

Now that it was restored, polished and shining, I was aware of a relief. He'd not been himself without it. He had lived so long at stretch, in labors and wounds and sickness and endurance, it did not do for him to have the roots of his life disturbed.

Hephaistion must have known it; he was not a fool. I expect, indeed, in his heart he was still a lover. He'd felt he should be upheld against Eumenes, right or wrong. Just so the Macedonians felt about the Persians. Just so I felt, but had the sense to keep it quiet. Alexander attracted jealousy. He was much beloved; and he never turned love away.

Even in the cool air of Ekbatana, and doing no more than two men's work, he still tired sooner than he'd done before his wound. I was glad this other wound was healing. He'd go more rested to Babylon, where the real work would begin.

Banners went up on gilded poles with sculptured finials. A city of tents arose, for the artists at the festival. The racecourse and the stadium were cleared and leveled. The architects made a theater, with a crane to fly on the gods, and a machine for wheeling in murdered corpses, which Greek poets set such store by. Thettalos, Alexander's favorite actor, a handsome Thessalian in his fifties, was welcomed with open arms and given the best tent. They came pouring in, flute-players, chorus-boys, scene-painters, singers and dancers, rhapsodists, acrobats; high-class courtesans and low-class whores, among them some eunuchs so shameless and bedizened, I was ashamed to see them about. Traders swarmed everywhere, selling food and gewgaws and cloth and spices, and, of course, wine.

The Palace flowed with it. There was a party every night, for the artists, or for Alexander's friends. Patroklos was back; he gave himself up to gaiety. For nights on end, I didn't get him sober to bed. He was never dead drunk, knowing he couldn't sleep it off next day; he had to be at the contests. His friends, not restrained by duty, often left the hall feet first. One gets used to this, when living among Macedonians.

While I was getting him into his state robe for the contest of choral odes, he said to me, "Hephaistion's not well. He's running a fever."

Once he used never to talk of him to me; now he often would, after all our unspoken secrets. I said I was sorry, and hoped it was nothing much.

"He must have had it on him last night, if he'd only known it. I wish I'd kept down the drinking." He went off, and the trumpets sounded.

Hephaistion was worse next day, and had cramps in his belly. Busy as he was, Alexander spent all his spare time with him. Achilles had always bound Patroklos' wounds. He got him the most noted doctor in Ekbatana, a Greek called Glaukias; to whom he gave advice, as he told me after. But he really had some knowledge; Aristotle had taught it him, and he had kept it up. It was agreed the patient should take no solid food. The priests were told to sacrifice for his healing.

The third day he was lower; weak as a babe, rambling in his talk, and full of fever, so Alexander said. It was the day for the comedies and farces; he did not sit them out, just came from the sickroom in time to give the prizes. When I asked the news at evening, he said, "He's better, I think. Restless and crotchety, a good sign. He's strong, he'll throw it off . . . I was sorry to disappoint the artists, but that was necessary."

There was a party that night, but he left it early to see how Hephaistion was; reporting him asleep, and looking easier. Next day, though still with some fever, he was much better. Alexander attended all the contests; his absence had much upset the comedians. In the evening he found Hephaistion sitting up, and asking for food.

"I wish," he said to me later, "I could have sent him something good from supper." He was still fond of this pleasant custom. "But the belly-cramps leave a weakness in the entrails; I saw that often in the Oxos country. I told the doctor to be sure and keep him on slops."

He still kept his bed, much better, but with a little fever at night, when the artists' contest ended, and the games began.

Alexander loved the arts; but the games were his close concern. He presided over everything; always remembered the victor's record in battle and in earlier games, when he gave the crowns. For such things the army loved him. After two or three days of this, came the day for the boys.

I'd played truant from the men's events, finding better pastime in the artists' quarter; but I went to the stadium for the boys' race, to see the breed Alexander was rearing up. He was sure to want to talk about it after.

They looked healthy, having been well fed since he took them over; with features from nearly everywhere, all crossed with Macedonian; no doubt there'd be half-Indians too, when they were old enough. The half-Persians were far the handsomest. I sat just across the track from Alexander. At the march-past, they went off with their faces lit from his smile.

They lined up; the trumpet sounded; they sped from the marks. They wore little breechcloths from respect for Persian modesty, no more. A pretty sight, I was thinking; when I was aware of a stir about the throne. Some messenger was standing by Alexander. He had jumped to his feet. The steps behind had closed up with people; he shoved them aside before they could make way, he nearly stepped on them. He was gone, with those nearest him scrambling after.

I clambered from my place. I must know what it was; I might be needed. Being on the far side of the stadium delayed me. When I reached the Palace, the royal rooms were deserted. It was then I guessed.

I went up the stairs, turned a crooked passage; I had no need to ask the way. I had heard from the stairway the dreadful sound of grief, which lifted the hair on my head.

No one was guarding the door. A knot of men stood outside. I slipped in among them, unnoticed as a household dog. I had never been before in Hephaistion's room. It was handsome, with red wall-hangings and a stand of silver vessels. A smell of sickness hung in the air. He lay on the bed, his face turned up, his mouth fallen open. Someone had closed his eyes. Grasping the body with both fists, lying across it, his mouth pressed to its face, was Alexander. He lifted his head, and gave again that dreadful cry; then buried his head in the dead hair.

After a while Perdikkas, awkward with shame and pity (yes, and already fear), said, "Alexander."

He looked up. I stepped forward, caring for none of them. He had turned to me before, and knew that I understood. His gaze passed over me, empty. It seemed at that moment that for him I had never been. Lost, gone, possessed.

I looked at this strange room, never forgotten, where I stood like a dead thing unmourned, unburied, tossed naked into the night; at the bed with its burden, the wall-hangings of stags and archers, the silver ewers; the bed-table shoved askew, with something on it: an empty wine-jar tumbled on its side, and a platter with the picked carcass of a chicken.

Suddenly Alexander flung himself to his feet and stared at us, as if he might kill any one of us without caring which. "Where is the doctor?"

Ptolemy looked round to ask the servants, but they had long since fled. He said, "He must have gone to the games."

I had withdrawn near the door, and was aware of something behind me. It was the man himself, slower than I had been to take alarm; just come, just aware of what he saw. Alexander sprang across like a beast of prey, fastened on him, and shook him to and fro. "You murderer! Why did you leave him? Why did you let him eat?"

The man, almost past words, stammered that he had seemed to be out of danger, that he had ordered him chicken broth.

Alexander said, "Hang him. Take him away and hang him. Do it now."

Perdikkas looked at Ptolemy. His eyes were on Alexander; without moving them, he nodded. The man was dragged away, under Seleukos' escort. Alexander went back to the bed, stared down at it, and lay where he had been before. The corpse moved, shaken with his sobbing.

More people were at the door, men of rank who'd just had the news. Those within all looked at one another helplessly. Peukestas touched my shoulder, and said softly in Persian, "You speak to him."

I shook my head. Only one thing was wanting to my heart's death, that he should hate me for being the one who was left alive.

So I ran away; through the city, through the stink and litter of the fair, through the street of the women, unseeing till I heard their laughter; into the country, I don't know where. A cold stream I stumbled in waked my mind. I looked back at the city; the sun was sinking, the colored ramparts glowed. Did I run off, I thought, when his flesh was wounded? Now he is stricken in his mind and might hurt me in his madness, now I forsake him, a thing no dog would do.

Dusk was falling. My clothes were torn, my hands bleeding, from thorns I could not recall. Without even thinking to make myself presentable, I went straight back. There was much the same knot about the door. Within, dead silence.

Two or three men came out to talk apart. Ptolemy said softly, "We must get him out before it starts to stink, or he'll lose his reason. Maybe for good."

"By force then?" said Perdikkas. "He won't come else. It must be all of us; it's no time to be singled out."

I slipped away. Nothing should get me in there, to

see him look from that dead face to mine. I went to his room and waited.

He was quiet when they brought him in, no one was handling him. They all stood round him expressing grief and praising the dead, I daresay the first chance they'd had. His eyes moved from face to face, as if he were at bay among their spears. Suddenly he cried, "Liars! You all hated and envied him, all of you. Go, leave me alone."

They exchanged looks and went. He stood in the state robe he'd worn for the games, white upon purple, all creased from being lain on. A groan burst from him, as if all the wounds he had borne in silence found voice at once. Then he turned and saw me.

I could not read his face. He had no weapon; but his hands were very strong. I went and knelt, and reached for his hand and kissed it.

He stared down at me and said, "You have mourned for him."

It took me a moment to remember my brier-torn clothes, my scratched face and hands. I grasped a tear in my coat, and ripped it top to bottom.

He took me by the hair, and pulled back my face to look in it. I said to him with my eyes, When you come back I will be waiting, if I am alive. If not, it was my destiny. It seemed he would search me forever with his mad eyes, grasping my hair. Then he said, "You fetched him when Oxhead died. You honored him when he saved you from the desert. *You* never desired his death."

I praised the dead to him, kneeling, grasping his hand. It was my confession, though he did not know it. I had welcomed my rival's faults, hated his virtues. Now I drew them out with pain from where my wishes had buried them, and offered them, his trophies, wet with my blood. He was the victor forever, now.

Alexander's eyes had wandered. He had not heard half I'd said. He let me go, returning to his solitude. Presently he lay down, and covered his face.

All next day he lay there, accepting no consolation.

Though he let me take no care of him, he did not send me out; he seldom knew I was there. The generals acted on their own, canceling the games, getting the banners changed to wreaths of mourning. Seleukos, who had kept the doctor unhanged lest the King should change his mind, dared not ask, and hanged him. The embalmers, summoned in time, did their work upon Hephaistion. There were many Egyptians with the camp.

At night, without really seeing me, he let me give him water. Without his leave, I brought in cushions and slept there. At morning I saw him wake from a brief sleep, and endure remembrance. That day he wept, as if he had only now learned how. It was as if he had been stunned, and began to stir. Once he even thanked me. But his face was strange, and I dared not embrace him.

Next morning he was awake before me. He was standing with a dagger in his hand, hacking off his hair.

For a moment I thought his senses were quite gone, that he might next cut his throat or mine. Greeks in our day only lay one lock on the funeral pyre. Then I remembered Achilles, shearing his hair for Patroklos. So I found the trimming-knife, and said, "Let me do it. I'll do it just as you want."

"No," he said, hacking away. "No, I must do it myself." But he grew impatient with the back, and let me finish it, so that he could be off. Roused from his living death, staring wide awake, he went like a trail of fire.

He asked where was Hephaistion; but the embalmers had him, steeped in niter. He asked if the doctor had been hanged (Seleukos had been prudent there) and commanded the body to be nailed on a cross. He ordered the manes of all army horses to be cropped in mourning. He ordered the gold and the silver to be stripped from the battlements of Ekbatana, and the colors painted over black.

I followed where I could, in case he should lose the sense of where he was, or become a child. I knew that he was mad. But he could tell where and with whom he was. He was obeyed in everything; Glaukias the doctor was black with crows.

I was trailing him, not too near in case he saw me, when he happened on Eumenes, who had seen his swift course too late. His face I couldn't see; but I saw the terror in Eumenes'. He knew he was suspect of wishing Hephaistion dead.

Soon after, a rich catafalque appeared in the square before the Palace, hung with mourning wreaths. A message reached Alexander that friends of the dead had reared it, to dedicate their offerings. He came to see it. Eumenes was first; he dedicated his whole panoply of arms and armor, which were very costly. A whole procession followed him. Everyone came, who'd had a cross word with Hephaistion any time in the last five years.

Alexander watched calmly, like a child who is lied to and not deceived. He spared them not for their pretenses, but for their penitence and their fear.

When they had done, all who had really liked Hephaistion came and made offerings. I was surprised how many there were.

Next day Alexander planned the funeral. It was to be in Babylon, the new empire's center, where his memorial would stand forever. When Darius sued for peace after the fall of Tyre, he'd offered as ransom for his mother and wife and children ten thousand talents. On Hephaistion, Alexander was spending twelve.

It quietened his mind, making these dispositions, choosing an architect for a royal pyre two hundred feet high, planning the funeral games, which were to have three thousand competitors. He was clear and precise in everything.

At bedtime, he would talk to me of Hephaistion as if memory could give him life; what they did as boys, what he'd said of this or that, how he trained his dogs. Yet I felt something unsaid; I felt his eyes when I turned away. I knew; he was thinking that his taking me had grieved Hephaistion; that he should make amends. Quietly he would put me aside, punishing himself not me, making his gift to the dead. He would do it, if once his resolve was set.

My mind ran like the hunted stag that scarcely knows it runs. I said, "It's good that Eumenes and the rest made their dedications. He is at peace with them now. He has forgotten mortal anger. Of all men on earth he is only concerned with you, set as he is now among the immortals."

He stepped away, leaving the towel in my hands, and pressed the heels of his hands against his eyes, till I feared he'd harm them. I don't know what he saw in that sparkling darkness. Coming out of it, he said, "Yes. Yes. Yes. So it must be, nothing else is possible."

I got him to bed and was going out, when he said, as briskly as he'd planned the games, "I shall send to Ammon's oracle, tomorrow."

I made some soft answer and crept off. What new turn had I given his madness? I had been thinking in Persian, when I spoke of the immortals; the souls of faithful men, safe through the River into Paradise. But Alexander, he had thought in Greek. He would ask the oracle for Hephaistion to be a god.

I tossed on my bed and wept. His resolve had set, he would do it. I thought of the Egyptians, the oldest people, scornful in their long history. They will mock him, I thought; they will mock him. Then I remembered; he is a deity himself already; Ammon acknowledged him. Without Hephaistion, he cannot bear even immortality.

So perfect was my grief, it made my mind white and empty, and I slept.

Next day he chose priests and envoys, and offerings for the god. The embassy left the day after.

After this he was much calmer; his madness healed a little from day to day, though all lived in fear of it. His friends made donations towards the funeral. Eumenes gave the most, no doubt remembering when his tent burned down; he would still walk a mile to avoid crossing Alexander's path.

To throw off sorrow, I rode out to the hills. From there I looked back, and saw the sevenfold walls stripped of their glories, seven rings of black; and I wept again.

28

IME PASSES, all things pass. He ate, and began to sleep, and to meet his friends. He even gave one or two audiences. His shorn hair began to grow. He would talk to me, sometimes, of daily things. But he did not recall the embassy on its way to Siwah.

Autumn drew to winter. It was past the time when the kings had been used to leave for Babylon. There were embassies from half over the empire and beyond, on their way to meet him there.

The Egyptians had worked their skill upon Hephaistion. He lay in a gilded coffin, on a dais hung with precious cloths, in one of the state rooms. The trophies of arms, the dedications, were set up around him. They had not swaddled and cased and masked him, as they do it here in Egypt. A body they have treated, even unwrapped, will keep the features of life for many ages. Alexander often went to visit him. Once he took me, because I had worthily praised the dead, and lifted the lid for me to see him. He lay upon cloth

429

of gold, in the pungent smell of spices and of niter; he would blaze like a torch, when they came to burn him in Babylon. His face was handsome and stern, the color of darkened ivory. His hands were crossed on his breast; they rested on the shorn locks of Alexander's hair.

Time passed; he could talk to his friends now; and then his generals in their soldiers' wisdom, doing what I could not, brought him the medicine that had power to do him good. Ptolemy came to him, to say that the Kossaians had sent to demand their tribute.

They were a tribe of famous brigands, who lived about the passes between Ekbatana and Babylon. Caravans which took that road would wait till they were big enough to hire a regiment of guards. Every year, it seems, even the kings had been raided, till they'd agreed to pay a sackful of gold darics before the autumn progress, to buy the Kossaians off. This toll was overdue, and they had sent to ask for it.

Alexander's *"What?"* was almost like old times. "Tribute?" he said. "Let them wait. I'll give them tribute."

"It's very difficult country," said clever Ptolemy, rubbing his chin. "Those forts are eagles' nests. Ochos could never reduce them."

"You and I will, though," said Alexander.

He set out within seven days. Any Kossaians he killed, he said, he would dedicate to Hephaistion, as Achilles had done the Trojans on Patroklos' pyre.

I packed my things without asking. He had given me no more of those hidden looks; he took me for granted, all that I asked just now. I had accepted in my heart that he might never take me to bed again, lest it grieve Hephaistion's spirit. That mourning had become an accustomed thing. I would live, if I could be near him.

In the passes, Alexander split his force between himself and Ptolemy. Up here it was already winter. We were an army camp, as in Great Kaukasos, moving light as the forts fell one by one. Each night he turned in, no longer brooding, but full of the day's campaign. On the seventh day, for the first time he laughed.

Though the Kossaians were robbers and murderers, without whom mankind is better, I had dreaded for his sake some sick-brained, furious slaughter. But he'd been brought to himself. Certainly he killed when battle called for it; perhaps Hephaistion was pleased, if the dead like blood as much as Homer says. But he took prisoners as his custom was, and held the chiefs for bargaining. His mind was as clear as ever. He saw every goat-track to the eagles' nests; his ruses and surprises were an artist's work. Artists are healed by their art.

After one such triumph, he gave supper in his tent to his chief officers. I said beforehand, easily, "Your hair wants trimming, Al'skander," and he let me take off the ragged ends. That night he got rather drunk. He had never done it since the death; it would have been base to drown that grief. Now he did it in victory, and as I helped him to bed my heart was lighter.

We moved on to the next stronghold. He set the siege-lines. The first snow whitened the tops, and the men drew close round the fires. He came in glowing from frost and flame, and greeted the guardian squires as he used to do. When I brought the night-lamp, he reached out and drew me by the hand.

I offered no art that night, or no more than had become my nature; only the tenderness from which pleasure springs of itself like flowers from rain. I had to rub my eyes on the pillow to hide my tears of joy. I saw on his sleeping face the marks of madness and pain and sleeplessness; but they were wounds turning to scars. He lay at peace.

I thought, He has rebuilt the legend in everlasting bronze. He will keep faith with it, if he lives to three-score and ten. Hephaistion's regiment is always to bear his name whoever may command it, just so he will be forever Alexander's lover; no one else will ever hear, "I love you best." But in that shrine will be only the legend dwelling; the man will be hissing blue flames,

then dust. Let his place be in Olympos, with the immortals, so long as my place is here.

I stole off softly, before he woke. He was attacking
the fort at daybreak; he would not have time to think
of it overlong.

The Kossaians had never been hunted in midwinter,
in all their wicked history. The last forts, starved out,
surrendered in return for the captives' freedom. It had
all taken forty days. Alexander garrisoned the strongpoints along the pass, pulled down the rest, and the
war was over. The caravans poured through. The Royal
Household was sent for, to come down to Babylon.
Already hard red buds gemmed the bare bushes shedding their snow.

But for his madness, he could have wintered down
there, in the mild season, planning the new harbor and
the Arabian fleet. Now he'd be there when the Persian
kings would have been thinking of Persepolis. All
through the Kossaian war, the troops of embassies had
been kicking their heels, awaiting him.

They met him when he pitched camp beyond the
Tigris. He had made ready for them in state; but no
one had been prepared for what really came.

They were not just from the empire, but from most
of the known world; from Libya, with a crown of
African gold; from Ethiopia, with the teeth of hippo-
camps and the tusks of enormous elephants; from
Carthage, with lapis and pearls and spices; from
Scythia, with Hyperborean amber. Huge blond Kelts
came from the northwest, russet Etruscans from Italy;
even Iberians from beyond the Pillars. They hailed him
as King of Asia; they brought disputes from far beyond
his frontiers, begging his wise judgment. They came
with dedications, asking oracles, as Greeks go to the
greatest shrines of their gods.

Most of these distant folk must have looked for a
man of towering stature; some of the Kelts were as tall
as Poros; yet none left his presence wondering why he
was what he was. He was equal even to having the
earth laid in his hands.

Indeed, in our time his face has changed the very

faces of the gods. Look where you like, at the statues
and the paintings. All the world remembers his eyes.

It helped his sickness, to be seen for what he was.
After all he'd suffered, the Greeks were muttering that
he'd reached a fortune above the human lot, and the
gods are envious. To one such I said, "Speak for your
own. Ours is Great King and envies no one; he re-
joices in light and glory. That's why we offer him fire."
No wonder the Greeks have envious gods, being full of
envy themselves.

For three days he had no time for grieving. He went
on exalted in his mind, remembering Siwah, and thinking of the west, whose peoples he'd now first seen. But
sometimes his face would change, as if sorrow touched
his shoulder, saying, "Had you forgotten me?"

In the river plains, already the corn pricked the
rich earth with green. Babylon's black walls lay along
the flat horizon, when to our last camp on the road a
man came riding. It was Niarchos, from the city.
Though his hardships had left their mark, you could
now see he was only forty; yet he looked care-ridden, to
me. Oh no, I thought; don't bring new troubles just
when he is better. So I stayed to listen.

Alexander welcomed him, asked after his welfare
and the fleet's; then said, "And now tell me what's
wrong."

"Alexander, it's the Chaldean priests, the astrolo-
gers."

"What's amiss with them? I gave them a fortune to
rebuild the Zeus-Bel temple. What are they after
now?"

"It's not that," Niarchos said.

Though I could not see him from where I was, I felt
a sinking. It was not his seaman's way, to beat about.

"Well, what, then?" said Alexander. "What's the
matter?"

"Alexander, they read me my stars before we
marched to India. It all came true. So just now I went
again. They told me something that . . . upset me.
Alexander, I knew you when you were so high. I know
your birthday, the place, hour, everything they need. I

asked them to read the stars for you. They say Babylon's in a bad aspect for you now. They were coming out on their own account, to warn you off. It's a lee shore for you, they say. Unlucky."

There was a little pause. Alexander said, quietly, "How unlucky?"

"Very. That's why I came."

A shorter pause. "Well, I'm glad to see you. Tell me, have they finished building the temple?"

"They're barely past the foundations. I don't know why."

He laughed. "I do. They've been drawing the sacred tax for the temple upkeep, ever since Xerxes pulled it down. For generations. They must be the richest priests on earth. They thought I'd never be back, and it could go on forever. No wonder they don't want me through the gates."

Niarchos cleared his throat. "I didn't know that. But . . . they told me I'd be in ordeal by water, and live to be honored by a king, and marry well with a foreign woman. I told you at the wedding feast."

"They knew you were an admiral and my friend. Wonderful! Come to supper."

He arranged for Niarchos' lodging, and finished his day's work.

At bedtime, he looked up at me leaning over him, and said, "Eavesdropper! Don't look so woebegone. It serves you right."

"Al'skander!" I fell on my knees beside him. "Do as they say. Never mind if they keep the money. They're not seers, they don't need to be pure of heart; it's a learning they have. Everyone says so."

He reached and ran a lock of my hair between his finger and thumb. "So? Kallisthenes had learning, too."

"They'd be afraid to lie. All their honor's in true predictions. I've lived in Babylon, I've talked to all sorts of people in the dancing-houses—"

"Have you indeed?" He tugged at the lock softly. "Tell me more."

"Al'skander, don't go into the city."

"What's to be done with you? Get in, you're not fit to sleep alone."

The Chaldeans met him next day.

They came in their sacred robes of a shape unchanged for centuries. Incense was burned before them; their wands bore the emblems of the stars. Alexander met them in his parade armor, all Macedonian. Somehow they persuaded him to come apart among them, with only the interpreter. Chaldeans have almost their own language, and Babylonians don't speak good Persian either; but I hoped enough would reach him to move his mind.

He came back looking serious. He was not one of those who think God has no name but the one they heard in childhood.

They had begged him to march east; which would have taken him to Susa. But all his dearest concerns were fixed in Babylon; the new harbor, the Arabian voyage, Hephaistion's funeral rites. He was still in doubt of their good faith. Old Aristander was dead, whom he could have asked to take the omens.

At all events, he said that since the west was unpropitious, he would go round the city on the eastward side, and reach the South Gate that way.

There is no Eastern Gate, and we soon knew why. That side, we came to a great stretch of marsh, treacherous and full of pools. The Euphrates seeped round into it. He could still have made a greater circuit, even if it crossed and recrossed the Tigris, and come back up the Euphrates. But he said impatiently, "That settles it. I'm not squatting like a frog in a swamp to please the Chaldeans." Since the embassies, he knew the world's eyes were on him. Perhaps that really settled it. At all events he turned back, by north and west.

Still he did not enter the gates, but camped up river. Then he heard more embassies were coming, this time from Greece. Anaxarchos, ever officious, reminded him that Greek thinkers no longer believe in omens. It touched his pride.

The Palace had been long prepared for him. As he drove through the gates in Darius' chariot, ravens fought overhead, and one fell dead before his horses.

However, as if to confound the auguries, the first news that met him was of life and fortune. Roxane had traveled straight down from Ekbatana to the Palace Harem. When he visited her there, it was to hear that she was with child.

She had known already, at Ekbatana; she told him she had waited to make quite sure. The truth, as I have no doubt, was that it was at the time of his madness, and she'd been afraid to give him news that would bring him near her.

He made her all the accustomed gifts of honor, and sent her father the news. He himself took it quietly. Perhaps he'd given up the thought that she would conceive by him, and had meant, in due time, to breed an heir from Stateira. Perhaps his mind was on other things.

When he gave me the news, I cried, "Oh, Al'skander! May you live to see him victorious at your side!"

I grasped him in both hands, as if I had power to defy the heavens. We stood in silence, understanding each other. At last he said, "If I'd married in Macedon, as my mother wanted, before I crossed to Asia, the boy would have been twelve by now. But there was never time. There is never time enough." He kissed me and went away.

It was torment to me to have him out of my sight. I watched him move among the half-forgotten splendors known to my boyhood. Then, I had come here light of heart. Now fear and grief hung on me like a sickness. Why had he listened to the Chaldeans, obeyed their warning and then defied it? It is Hephaistion, I thought, reaching out to him from the dead.

One must live, he'd said to me long ago, as if it would be forever, and as if each moment might be the last. He began at once to have the great harbor dug, and the fleet built for Arabia, which Niarchos would command. It was spring now, as warm as a Susa summer. He would ride back from the new harbor, and make for the royal bath. Nothing in the Palace gave him so much pleasure. He loved the cool walls, the fretted screens glimpsing the river, the great bath with its lapis-blue tiles and their golden fish. He would float there with the water lifting his hair.

But there was always Hephaistion. He was due now for his rite of burning.

The fleet and the new harbor were both in hand. Alexander had time; and soon he had time only for this. He returned a little into his madness. If one woke him, he was sensible; but he would drift back into dreams. Alexander's dreams were daimons. He conjured them, and they obeyed him.

He had ten furlongs of the city wall knocked half down, and leveled out to a square. Within this he had a platform made of fine tiles, each side a furlong. That was the base of the pyre. From that it tapered up, story upon story; each tier with carved sculptures, as fine in wood as if they'd been meant to last forever. At the bottom, ships' prows with archers and warriors, larger than life; then torches twenty feet long, adorned with eagles and serpents; then a scene of wild beasts and hunters, gilded. Next above, trophies of arms, both Macedonian and Persian, to show both races had held the dead in honor. Above that I don't know what, elephants, lions, garlands. Near the top were figures of winged sirens, hollow behind, in which singers would lament before the pyre was kindled. Great crimson flags hung down between the stages. There was room inside for a stairway, to bring him up with dignity.

I thought, No king has gone like this since the world began. He has dreamed it as if it were for himself. I watched his face, his eyes lifted to the pyre in his quiet madness, and dared do nothing, not even touch him.

The funeral car had been escorted by Perdikkas from Ekbatana. Hephaistion lay in state in the Palace, here as there. Alexander went oftener to see him now; he would soon be gone. Medios of Larissa, who had been his friend, had a little bronze likeness of him made, by a sculptor who'd seen him often, to give Alexander. He received it so gladly, that one friend after another, vying in affection or for favor, had small statues made in gold or ivory or alabaster. Soon the room was full of them; he was there wherever I looked. And I had thought that when the pyre was kindled, that would be the end of him.

One day, being alone, I took the best likeness into my hand, thinking, Who were you, what are you, that you can do this to my lord? He came in behind me, and said, "Put that down!" with such anger that I nearly dropped it. I put it back somehow, shaking with fear of exile. He said more quietly, "What were you doing?" I answered, "He was dear to you. I wanted to understand him."

He took a turn across the room, then said, "He knew me."

No more. I was pardoned, he meant no hurt. I had asked, he answered.

They had been born in the same month, in the same hills, of the same race, with the same gods; had lived under one roof from their fourteenth year. Truly, when to me we had seemed like one, to how much I had been a stranger.

Time will pass, I thought. They could bear to be parted on campaign; it will come to seem only like that. If there is time.

The day came. In the dusk before dawn, they lined the square about the platform; generals, princes, satraps, priests; standard-bearers, heralds, musicians; the painted elephants. By the steps were the braziers and the torches.

The bearers took up the coffin by the hidden stairs. As they reached the topmost deck, looking small as toys, and laid it on its stand, the hidden sirens sang, faint in the sky. They came down, still singing. The torches were kindled at the braziers.

The pyre stood on palm-wood columns; the space between was piled up with tinder and dry straw. Alexander came forward with his torch, alone.

He was exalted above his madness, into ecstasy. Peukestas, who'd seen him fight on with the Mallian arrow in him, said later that then he looked just the same. The elephants curled back their trunks and trumpeted.

He flung in his torch; flames leaped from it. The friends followed; the brands pelted in; the fire jumped through the gratings, into the tier of ships. It began to roar.

The pyre was tinder-filled up its center, through all its two hundred feet. The blaze spired upward, past ships and archers and lions and eagles and shields and garlands. At the top it enwrapped the coffin, and burst in a great peak of flame, against the green sky of sunrise.

Once at Persepolis, that feast of fire, they had looked up side by side.

For a while the high tower stood in its fearful beauty; then tier after tier caved in. An eagle crashed to the platform with flaming wings; the sirens toppled inwards; the coffin vanished. The timbers, the heavy carvings, began to hurtle down, throwing up spark-clouds tall as trees. The pyre was a single torch burning to its socket, by whose light I saw his face alone.

The sun came up. The whole parade stood stupefied in the heat. When nothing was left but red embers and white ash, he gave the order to dismiss. He gave it himself. I had thought they would have to wake him.

As he was leaving, a crowd of priests approached him, robed from all kinds of temples. He answered briefly and passed on. They looked unhappy. I overtook one of the squires who had been near, and asked what it had been about.

He said, "They asked if they could rekindle the sacred fires now. He said not till sundown."

I stared at him, unbelieving. "The temple fires? He ordered them put out?"

"Yes, for the mourning. Bagoas, you look bad, it was all that heat. Come in the shade here. Does it mean something in Babylon?"

"They do it when the King is dead."

Silence fell between us. At last he said, "But when he ordered it, they must have told him that."

I hurried to the Palace, hoping to get him alone. Even to light them now might avert the omen. Had there not been enough, that he must make his own?

But already he had summoned a score of people, and was finishing off plans for the funeral contests. Grave Persian faces showed me that others had tried to warn him. Old Palace eunuchs who had lived to see the fires three times doused were whispering, and rolled their eyes my way. I did not join them. The temples were dark till sunset. Alexander worked on the games all day. There had been nothing much left to do, but it seemed that he could not stop.

They lasted near half a month. All the best artists from all the Greek lands were there. I went to the plays, mostly to watch his face. Only one of them stays with me, *The Myrmidons,* which Thettalos had done before for Alexander; it's about Achilles, and Patroklos' death. Thettalos himself had just lost a dear friend, a fellow actor who had died on the journey down from Ekbatana. He carried it through; he was a professional. Alexander sat as if his mind were far away. I knew the look. He had had it when Peukestas cut out the arrow.

The music seemed to do him good; he looked released from himself when the kitharists were playing. Afterwards he entertained all the winners, saying just the right things to each. Perhaps, I thought, the last of the madness had been seared out of him by so much burning.

He began to go down again to the river, to watch the seamen training; he held races for the rowers, and offered prizes. Then the embassies from Greece arrived.

They were envoys of compliment, to honor his safe return from the world's end. They brought gold crowns, exquisite wreaths of jewelers' work, and scrolls of honor. Even the envious Athenians came, full of lying compliments. He knew they lied. But he gave them in return the statues of the Liberators, fetched from Susa, to put back on their citadel. When he made the presentation, he pointed as if by chance to the daggers, and caught my eye.

The last embassy was from Macedon.

It was not like the rest. The regent, Antipatros, whom Krateros was to supersede, had sent his son to speak for him.

During all his years of regency, which went back to King Philip's day, Queen Olympias had hated him, my belief being that she wished to govern instead. Knowing of all her slanders, it was perhaps no wonder if he thought they had made their mark, and he'd been sent for to go on trial; for ten years he'd not set eyes on Alexander, to know him better. Even so, one would have thought he'd have had more sense than to send his son Kassandros. That is, if his faith was good.

Whenever Alexander had told me about his boyhood, he'd mentioned this youth, as then he'd been, with detestation. They had disliked each other at sight, and on all through their schooldays; once they had come to blows. The reason he had been left behind in Macedon was simply that Alexander would not have him in the army.

However, he had helped his father put down a rising in southern Greece, and done quite well there; no doubt both had hoped that this would recommend him now. He arrived, after so long, almost a stranger; only this stranger and Alexander hated each other on sight, as they'd done before.

He was an arrogant, freckled, red-haired man, with the old-time Macedonian beard. He was also, of course, a perfect stranger to court life in Persia. One had forgotten such people existed.

No doubt he was mad with envy. The Throne Room had been refurnished, to receive the embassies; about the throne was a great half-circle of couches with silver feet, where the King's chief friends, Persian and Macedonian, had a right to sit when he gave audience. All the Household would stand behind him. My own place, now we were back among real procedure, was near the throne. I was there to watch Kassandros when he came. While he awaited Alexander, I saw him look at us eunuchs as if we were noxious vermin.

The audience did not go well. There had been petitioners out from Macedon to plead causes against the regent. Kassandros was too hasty, in saying they had come to be well away from all the evidence; I think one, at least, had been sent by Queen Olympias. Only one man had ever been allowed to speak against her to Alexander, and he was dead. Alexander broke the audience off, and asked Kassandros to wait while he saw some Persians.

Barbarians before *him!* I could see his fury. He stepped back, and the Persians, who were below the rank of Royal Kin, made the prostration.

Kassandros sneered. It is not true, as some say, that he laughed aloud. He was an envoy with work to do. Nor is it true that Alexander knocked his head on the wall. He had no need.

It is true the sneer was open; I suppose anger made him reckless. He turned to some companion he'd brought with him, pointing a finger. Alexander let the Persians rise, spoke to them, dismissed them; then stepped down from the throne, grasped Kassandros in one hand by the hair, and stared into his face.

I thought, He is going to kill him. So did Kassandros I daresay. But it was more than that. It was more than the kingly power, more even than the word of Ammon's oracle. He had been through fire and darkness. All he needed was to lay it bare. Kassandros stared as the bird does at the serpent, white with pure naked terror of man for man.

"You have leave to go," said Alexander.

It was a good way to the doors. He must have known his fear had marked him like a brand, and all we creatures of his scorn had seen it.

Later on, when I had Alexander alone, I said to him, "Hate like that is dangerous. Why don't you pack him off home?" He answered, "Oh, no. He'd go back and tell Antipatros I'm his enemy; urge him to revolt, kill Krateros when he gets there, and seize Macedon.

Antipatros might do it, if he was put in fear of his life. Let alone, he has more sense. If I meant him harm, I'd hardly have his other son as cupbearer. He's been where he is too long, that's all. No, till Krateros is in Macedon and Antipatros leaves it, Kassandros stays here under my eye . . . Hephaistion could never stand him, either."

In earlier days, I'd have begged him to have the man put quietly out of the way. I knew that what he would not own to, he would not do. It is my life's regret I did not take it on myself in secret. It torments me, to think that with one little phial I might have quenched that murderous hate that has pursued my lord even beyond the tomb; his mother, his wife, the son I never saw, who would have given us something more of him than memory.

Summer came on. All Persian kings would have been at Ekbatana. I knew he would never ride through those gates again; I was only glad he had the fleet and harbor to keep him busy. It was four months since the Chaldeans' prophecy. Except when I saw the new Bel temple going up, I could almost forget them.

Soon we left the city for a while. Down river, there were floods every year when the snows at its source were melting, and the people there, who were of old Assyrian stock, lived poor because of it. Alexander wanted to plan dams and canals against it, and make new farmlands. It was only a river cruise, but it cheered me to have him outside the walls.

He always loved rivers. The ships wound among man-tall reed-beds, the Assyrian pilots conning the channels. Sometimes great shade-trees met above, and we glided through green caves; sometimes we pushed through lily-pads in open pools; the river has many branches there. Alexander would stand in the prow, and sometimes take the helm. He had on the same old sun-hat he used to wear in Gedrosia.

The stream broadened between drooping willows which tossed in a flaw of wind. Among them stood blockish ancient stonework; with figures, worn by time and flooding, of winged lions and bulls, man-headed. When Alexander asked about them, the Babylonian shipmaster said, "Great King, those are the tombs of the old-time kings, when the Assyrians ruled here. This was their burial ground."

On the words, a gust plucked off Alexander's sunhat, and whirled it overboard. Its purple ribbon, the symbol of royalty, was loosened and carried away. It whipped itself round the rushes beside a tomb.

The ship glided on by its own way; the rowers had shipped their oars. All along the craft passed a murmur of awe and dread.

A rower, a young quick swarthy man, dived off, struck for the bank, and unwound the ribbon. He paused with it in his hand, thought of the muddy water, and wound it round his head to keep it dry. Alexander took it with a word of thanks. He was quiet. I had all I could do not to cry aloud. The diadem had gone to a tomb, and passed to another head.

When his work was done, he went back to Babylon. I could have beaten my breast, at the sight of those black walls.

When he told the seers about the omen, they all said that the head which had worn the diadem ought to be struck off. "No," he said. "He meant well and did what anyone might. You can give him a beating, if the gods demand some expiation. Don't lay on too hard, and send him to me after." When the man came he gave him a talent of silver.

We returned to nothing but prosperity. Peukestas proudly paraded a well-trained army of twenty thousand Persians. His province was in first-class order; he was better liked than ever. Alexander gave public commendations; and began a scheme for a new Persian-Macedonian force. No one mutinied; even Macedonians had started to think that Persians might be men. Some of our words were passing into their speech.

The day came, long waited for, when the embassy returned from Siwah.

Alexander received it in the Throne Room, his Companions round him on the silver couches. Ceremoniously, the chief envoy unrolled Ammon's papyrus. He had refused to share his godhead; but Hephaistion still had his place with the immortals. He had been proclaimed a divine hero.

Alexander was content. After his first madness, he must have guessed it was as far as the god would go. Hephaistion could still be worshipped.

Commands went out to all the cities, to build him a temple or a shrine. (Here in Alexandria, I often pass the empty site near the Pharos. I expect Kleomenes, who was satrap then, took all the money.) Prayers and sacrifices were to be offered him, as an averter of evil. All solemn contracts must be sworn in his name, beside the names of the gods.

(The temple he should have had in Babylon was in the Greek style, with a frieze of lapiths and centaurs. That place is empty too. I don't suppose one stone of all those sacred places was ever set on another. Well, he should still be satisfied. He had his sacrifice.)

Alexander feasted the envoys, in honor of Hephaistion's immortality. The other guests were friends who would understand. He was lighthearted, almost radiant. One would have thought the omens all forgotten.

He was some days happy and busy, having done drawings for the shrines. He called on Roxane, whom he found healthy and strong; Sogdian women don't make much of pregnancy. Then he pressed on with plans for the new mixed army.

It meant changes in all the forces. When he was ready to reassign commands, he sent for the officers, to appoint them. He was in the Throne Room; he knew well by now what proper ceremony means to Persians. The Household was assembled behind the throne.

It was now full summer and very hot. He broke off halfway through, to take his friends to the inner room for a drink of cold citron-water mixed with wine. They would not be long; it was not worth going away; we waited behind the empty throne and the couches, and talked of trifles.

We never saw the man, till he was among us. A man in shabby clothes, a common man among thousands, but for his face. To his crazed intentness, all of us were invisible. Before we had time to move, he had sat down on the throne.

We stared appalled, hardly believing. It is the most dreadful of all omens; that is why, through all our people's history, it has been a capital crime. Some of us leaped forward to drag him off, but the old ones cried out in warning. It would unman the kingdom, for eunuchs to free the throne. They began to wail and to beat their breasts, and we joined their lamentation. For a while it lulls the mind, and one need not think.

The officers down in the hall, aroused by the noise, ran up in horror, seized the man and had him down from the dais. He stared about, as if bewildered by this concern. Alexander came out from the inner room, his friends behind him, and asked what was going on.

One of the officers told him, and showed the man. He was a common soldier, unarmed, an Uxian if I remember. Of us the King asked nothing. I suppose our outcry had told enough.

He walked over and said, "Why did you do this?" The man stood and blinked, without mark of respect, as if at any stranger. Alexander said, "If he was sent for this, then I must know who sent him. Don't question him till I am there."

To us he said, "Quiet. That is enough. The audience is open." He finished the assignments, without carelessness, without haste.

At sundown, he came up to change his clothes. Now we were at Babylon, we had the whole ceremonial. It was I who handled the Mitra. Reading my eyes, as soon as was proper he sent out the rest. Before I could ask, he said, "Yes, we questioned him. I had it stopped. He knew nothing, not even what brought him there. He could only say he saw a fine chair and sat in it. He was due for court-martial, for repeated disobedience; of course he had not understood his orders. I am satisfied he was out of his mind."

He spoke coolly and firmly. All my blood stood still. I had longed to know that the man had confessed to deceit and a human plot, though one look at his face had told me. It is the true omens that come without intent.

"Al'skander," I said, "this one you will have to kill."

"That has been done. It is the law; and the seers said it was necessary." He walked to the flagon-stand, filled a wine-cup and made me drink. "Come, make a better face for me. The gods will do what they will. Meantime we live, and they will that too."

I swallowed the wine like medicine, and tried to smile. He was wearing a thin white robe of Indian stuff, for the summer heat, which showed his body like the robes the sculptors carve. I set down the cup and threw my arms round him. He seemed to glow from within, as always. He felt unquenchable as the sun.

When he was gone, I looked about at the images of gold and bronze and ivory, watching gravely from their stands. "Leave hold of him!" I said. "Are you not yet content? You died through your own fault, through disobedience, impatience, greed. Could you not love him enough to spare him that? Then leave him to me, who love him more." They all looked back at me and answered, "Ah, but I knew him."

More embassies came from the Greeks, garlanded as they come before their gods. Once more they crowned him; with gold fruiting olive, gold barley-ears, gold laurel, gold summer flowers. I can see him still, wearing each crown.

A few days later, his friends said that with all these triumphs, he himself had not yet celebrated his victory over the Kossaians. (They were now so much won over, he had taken some thousands into the army.) It was long, they said, since he'd held a komos; and the feast of Herakles was coming.

They meant no harm. Even the worst sought only favor; the best wanted in kindness to give him a care-free evening, make him remember his glory and forget his grief. The gods can do with anything what they will.

He proclaimed the feast, ordered sacrifices to Herakles, and gave the troops a free wine-issue all round. The komos began at sundown.

It was a sweltering Babylon night. They had soon done with the food. I had planned, with his friends, a small surprise for him; a dance of Macedonians and Persians, four a side, mock-war first and then friendship. We were bare, but for helmets and kilts or trousers. Alexander was very pleased with it, called me to sit by him on his supper couch, and shared his gold cup with me.

His face was flushed; no wonder, with the heat and wine, but there was a brightness about his eyes I didn't like. I had had a quick rubdown to take off the sweat, but was of course still warm. When he put his arm round me, I felt that he was hotter.

"Al'skander," I said under the noise, "you feel like fever."

"No more than a touch. It's nothing. I'll turn in after the torch-song."

Soon they took up the torches, and walked singing into the gardens, to get the night's first cool. I slipped off to the Bedchamber, to see everything was ready. I was glad to hear the chant returning and tailing off. He came in. If we'd been alone, I'd have said, "To bed with you now, and quick about it." But before the Household I always observed the forms. I stepped forward to take the diadem. His robe came off damp with sweat, and I saw him shiver. He said, "Just rub me down, and find me something a little warmer."

"My lord," I said, "you are not going out again?"

"Yes, Medios has a little party, just old friends. I promised to look in."

I gazed at him in entreaty. He smiled and shook his head. He was Great King, not to be disputed with before the Household. It is in our blood, that such things must not be done; therefore we cannot do them, without the air of insolence. As I rubbed him down, my eye caught the stands of images. Why are *you* not here, I thought, now when you could be useful, to say, "Don't be a fool; you are going to bed if I have to push you in. Bagoas, go and tell Medios the King can't come"?

But the images held their hero poses; and Alexander in a Greek robe of fine wool went with his torchbearers down the great corridor with its lion frieze.

I said to the rest, "You may all retire. I will wait up for the King. I will have you called, if he needs attendance."

There was a divan I slept on, if he was going to be late; his coming always woke me. The moon climbed the sky before my open eyes. When he came, the cocks were crowing.

He looked flushed and tired, and walked unsteadily; he'd been drinking, on and off, from sunset till dawn; but he was very sweet-tempered, and praised my war-dance. "Al'skander," I said, "I could be angry with you. You know wine's bad for a fever."

"Oh, it's gone off. I told you it was nothing. I'll make up my sleep today. Come to the bath with me, you've been all night in your clothes."

The first light shone through the screens, and the birds were singing. The bath left me refreshed and drowsy; when I'd put him to bed, I turned in myself and slept till nearly evening.

I went softly into the Bedchamber. He was just awake, turning restlessly. I went up and felt his brow. "Al'skander, it has come back."

"Nothing much," he said. "Cool hands. Don't take them away."

"I'll have supper brought here. The river fish is good. And what about a doctor?"

His face hardened, and he moved his head from my hands. "No doctors. I've seen enough of *them*. No, I'll get up. I'm having supper with Medios."

I argued, implored; but he had woken cross and impatient. "I tell you it's nothing. The swamp-fever, I expect. It's over in three days."

"Maybe for the Babylonians; they're seasoned. It can be bad. Why can't you take care of yourself? You're not at war."

"With you I will be, if you go on like a wet-nurse. I've been sicker than this, riding all day over mountains. Give out that I want to dress."

I wished he'd been going to anyone but Medios, who would take no care of him, or notice anything wrong. He'd been a great supporter of Hephaistion in his quarrel with Eumenes; making it worse, I'd heard, for he had a biting tongue, and some of his gibes had gone abroad in Hephaistion's name. No doubt his mourning had been sincere; but he'd not been slow to use the favor it brought him. He could speak honey as well as vinegar, knew how to amuse Alexander and make him laugh. Not a bad man; but not a good one either.

I was dozing, when Alexander returned. By the sky, it was not long past midnight. I was glad to get him back so early. "I left them at it," he said. "The fever's up a little. I'll cool down in the bath, and get to bed."

His breath shuddered as I disrobed him. He felt burning hot. "Let me just sponge you," I said. "You ought not to bathe like this."

"It will do me good." He would hear no sense, but walked through in his bath-robe. He did not stay in the water long. I· dried him, and had just put on his robe, when he said, "I'll sleep here, I think," and made for the couch by the pool. I went quickly over. He was shaking with ague in every limb; his teeth were chattering. He said, "Get me a good warm blanket."

In Babylon, in midsummer, at midnight! I ran off and fetched his winter cloak. "This will do till the cold fit's over. I'll keep you warm."

I covered him with it, and threw my own clothes on top, then got under and held him in my arms. He was shivering worse than ever, yet his skin was scorching. He said, "Closer," as if we were naked in a snowstorm. As I wrapped myself round him, the prophetic voice was silent, which had said at Ekbatana, "Carve this upon your heart." It spared me; it did not say, "Never again."

The shivering stopped, he began to feel hot and to sweat, and I let him be. He said he would sleep here where it was fresher. I dressed and waked the Keeper of the Bedchamber, to send what he would need, and a pallet for me. Before morning the fever lessened, he slept, and I closed my eyes.

I woke to his voice. The bathhouse was full of people tiptoeing about. He had just waked, and was ordering Niarchos to be summoned. Niarchos? I thought; whatever does he want *him* for? I had forgotten, in my concern, that it was getting near time for the Arabian voyage. Alexander was planning a morning's work.

He walked to the Bedchamber to be dressed; then, since he could hardly stand, lay on the divan. When Niarchos came, he asked if the propitiation sacrifice for the fleet was ready. Niarchos, who I could see was disturbed by his looks, said yes, and asked who he would like to make the offering-prayer for him. "What?" he said. "I'll make it myself, of course. I'll go by litter, I'm a little shaky today; I expect this is the last of it." He brushed off Niarchos' protests. "It was the favor of the gods that brought you safe from Ocean. I sacrificed for you then, and they heard me. I shall do it now."

They bore him off, under an awning against the crushing Babylonian sun, in which he stepped out and stood to pour the libations. When he came back he could scarcely touch the light meal I'd ordered; but he had in Niarchos and all his chief officers, with a clerk to take notes, and was four full hours talking of supply ships, water and stores.

Days passed. The fever did not leave him. He meant, when the fleet sailed, himself to lead a supporting coast march, looking out for harbor sites; so he had to delay the sailing. Each morning he declared that he was better; each day he was carried to the household altar, to offer the morning prayer; each time he was weaker; each evening the fever began to mount.

The Bedchamber was full of people coming and going; the Palace, of officers awaiting orders. Though its thick walls kept out the sun, he craved for green shade and the sight of water, and had himself ferried across the river to the royal gardens. There he would lie under the trees, his eyes half closed, near a fountain that splashed into a basin of porphyry. Sometimes he sent for Niarchos and Perdikkas, to plan the voyage and the march, sometimes for Medios to gossip and play at knucklebones. Medios tired him, too proud of being chosen, staying too long.

Other times he chose the bathhouse, and had his bed set by the edge where he could step down easily; he liked to cool himself in the tepid water, to be dried sitting on the blue-tiled verge, and get back into clean sheets. He slept there too, for the cool, and the sound of the river lapping outside.

I did not leave him, for Medios, or the generals, or anyone else. I had put off easily my Palace dignities; the old man I had displaced gladly resumed them. I changed my court dress for serviceable linens. As Chief Eunuch of the Bedchamber, I would have had my daily offices, my occasions to withdraw. Now those who came saw only the Persian boy, holding a fan or drinking-cup, bringing blankets when an ague took him, sponging him and putting on dry sheets after a sweat, or sitting quiet on a cushion against the wall. I was safe, my place aroused no envy. Only one man would have taken it from me, and he was white ash on the winds of heaven.

When my lord sent the great men away, it was to me that he turned his eyes. I had one or two quiet slaves to fetch and carry; all the needs of his person I saw to myself. Thus people ceased to see me, more than the pillows or the water-ewer. They still sent to the Palace, by old custom, the pure spring water which had always been the drink of the Persian kings. It refreshed him; I kept it by him on the bed-table, in an earthen cooler.

At night I had my pallet set beside him. He could reach the water; if he wanted anything more, I always knew. Sometimes if the fever kept him restless he liked to talk to me, recalling old hardships and old wounds, to prove he would soon be victor of his sickness. He never spoke of the death-omens, any more than in the midst of battle he would have spoken of surrender. When he'd been ill a week, he still talked of marching in three days. "I can begin by litter, as soon as the fever's down. This is nothing, to things I've thrown off before."

They had given up asking him to have a doctor. "I don't need the same lesson twice. Bagoas looks after me better than any doctor."

"I would if you let me," I said when they had gone. "A doctor would make you rest. But you think it's only Bagoas, and do just what you like." He had been carried out that day to sacrifice for the army. For the first time, he had poured the libation lying down.

"To honor the gods is necessary. You should be praising my obedience, gentle tyrant. I should like some wine, but I know better than to ask."

"Not yet. You've the best water in Asia, here." One reason I never went out when Medios came, was for fear the fool would give him wine.

"Yes, it's good." He emptied his cup; he'd only been teasing. When he grew lively, I knew the fever was coming up. But that evening it seemed less. I renewed my vows to the gods of what I'd given them for his recovery. When he rode out against the Scythians, the omens had been bad, but had been fulfilled by sickness only. I slept with my hopes reviving.

His voice woke me. It was still dark, the watch after midnight.

"Why have you not reported sooner? We have wasted half the night march. It will be noon, before we come to water. Why have you let me sleep?"

"Al'skander," I said, "you were dreaming. This is not the desert."

"Put a guard on the horses. Never mind the mules. Is Oxhead safe?"

His eyes wandered past me. I wrung out a sponge in mint-water and wiped his face. "See, it's Bagoas. Is that better?" He pushed at my hand, saying, "Water? Are you mad? There's not enough for the men to drink."

His fever had mounted, at the time when it had

always sunk. I tilted the cooler over the cup. It was half empty; and the stream was not clear but dark. It was wine. Someone had come while I slept.

Mastering my voice, I said softly, "Al'skander. Who brought the wine?"

"Has Menedas had water? Give it him first, he has fever."

"We all have water, truly." I emptied the cooler and filled it from the great jar. He drank thirstily. "Tell me, who gave you wine?"

"Iollas." He had only named the King's cupbearer. Disordered as he was, this may have been all he meant. Yet Iollas was Kassandros' brother.

I went over to ask the night-slave, and found him sleeping. I had asked none of them to serve night and day, as I was doing. I left him as he was, lest being forewarned he should escape his punishment.

Alexander dozed restlessly till morning. The fever had not remitted, as it had at this time before. When they carried him to the household altar and put the libation cup in his hand, it shook so much that half the offering spilled before he could pour it. This change was from when he had the wine. Before, I could have sworn that he was mending.

The night-slave, when I questioned him, had known nothing; he must have slept for hours. I sent orders to the Household, that he should be flogged with the leaded whip. The night-guard squires knew nothing either, or so they said; it was not in my power to have them questioned. The bathhouse was harder than the Bedchamber to guard; someone might have slipped in from the river.

It was a grilling hot day. Alexander asked to be carried over to the shady place by the porphyry fountain. If a breath of breeze was stirring, one caught it there. I had stocked the summerhouse with everything he might need. As I settled him on the bed, I heard his breathing. It had a harshness which was new.

"Bagoas, can you prop me up a little? It catches me here." He put his hand to his side.

He was naked but for the sheet. He had his hand to the wound from the Mallian arrow. This, I think, was the moment when first I knew.

I fetched pillows and eased him up on them. Despair was treachery while he fought on. He must not feel it in my voice, in my hands' tenderness.

"I shouldn't have had the wine. My own fault, I asked you." He panted even from so few words, and pressed his hand to his side again.

"Al'skander, I never gave it you. Can you remember who did?"

"No. No, it was there. I woke and drank it."

"Did Iollas bring it?"

"I don't know." He closed his eyes. I let him rest, and sat on the grass close by him. But he was resting to speak again. Presently he asked for the Captain of the Bodyguard. I went and beckoned him up.

Alexander said, "General order. All officers from commander up, assemble—in the inner courtyard— to await orders."

I knew, then, that he began to guess.

There will be no farewell, I thought as I waved the palm-leaf fan to cool him and keep off the flies. He will not surrender. And nor must I.

A ferryload of his friends came over, to see how he was. I met them, to warn them he was short of breath. When they came up, he said, "I had—better—go back."

The bearers were called. People crowded with him onto the ferry. He looked round and whispered, "Bagoas." So one got out, and made room for me.

They took him to the Bedchamber, where winged gilded daimons guarded the great bed. Long ago, in another life, I had prepared it for another king.

We propped him on high pillows, but still heard the rasp of his breath. If he wanted anything, he spoke to me without voice, as he used when his wound was fresh. He knew I would understand him.

After a while, Perdikkas came in, to tell him the officers were still in the courtyard awaiting orders. He signed to bring them in. They crowded into the

Bedchamber. He made a gesture of greeting; I saw him draw breath to speak, but he coughed instead and brought up blood. He motioned them to dismiss, and they went away. Not till the last had gone, did he press his hand to his side.

After this, the generals brought the doctors without his leave. Three came. Weak as he was, they feared him because of Glaukias; but he suffered quietly their fingers on his wrist, their ears laid to his chest. He watched them, as they looked at one another. When they brought a draught he took it and slept awhile. One of them stayed with him, so I rested an hour or two. He would need me there at night, with my wits about me.

At night he was in high fever. They would no longer leave him to me alone; three of the Companions watched with him. One of the doctors would have sat by his pillow; but he put out his hand and held my arm, so the doctor went.

It was a long night. The Companions dozed in their chairs. He coughed blood and then slept a little. About midnight his lips moved. I bent to hear. He said, "Don't drive it away." I looked about but saw nothing. "The snake," he whispered, pointing to a shadowy corner. "Nobody harm him. He is sent."

"No one shall harm him," I said, "upon pain of death."

He slept again. Then he said, "Hephaistion."

His eyes were closed. I kissed his forehead and did not speak. He smiled, and was quiet.

In the morning he knew me, and where he was. The generals came in and stood about his bed. All over the room one could hear his labored breathing. He looked from one to the other. He knew well enough what it meant.

Perdikkas came forward and bent towards him. "Alexander. We all pray the gods will spare you for many years. But if their will is otherwise, to whom do you leave your kingdom?"

He forced his voice, so as to speak aloud. He began, this I have always believed, to pronounce the name of Krateros. But his breath caught, and he finished with a gasp. Perdikkas murmured to the others, "He says, To the strongest."

Krateros, kratistos. The sounds so much alike, the meaning, even, of the name. Krateros, whom he had always trusted, was on his way to Macedon; I am persuaded he meant to leave him regent for the unborn child; King even, if it should be a girl, or die. But Krateros was a long way off; his cause was no one's here.

Nor was it mine. What was Macedon to me, what did I care who ruled it? I looked only at my lord, to see if he was troubled; but he had not heard. While he was at peace, it was all one to me. If I gave offense to the others, they might take me from him. I held my tongue.

Presently he beckoned Perdikkas back; then drew from his finger the royal signet carved with Zeus enthroned, and gave it him. He had chosen a deputy, while he was too sick to rule. It need have meant no more than that.

Sitting quiet by the bed, only the Persian boy, I saw the faces begin to watch each other, reckoning policy and power, looking sideways at the ring.

He saw them. His eyes had been on the distance; but they moved, and I know he saw. I bent over him with the sponge; I thought he had seen enough. He looked at me as if we shared a secret. I laid my hand on his; there was a white band on his finger, where the ring had kept off the sun.

All was silent, but for his quick rough breath. In the quiet, I heard outside a deep stir, a many-voiced murmur. Ptolemy went out to see. When he did not return, Peukestas followed, then the others. Soon after, they all came in again.

Perdikkas said, "Alexander. It's the Macedonians outside; all the men. They—they want to see you. I've told them it's impossible, that you're too ill. Do you think if I let in just a few, a score or so, to represent the others, do you think you could bear with that?"

His eyes opened wide. He began to cough. While I

held the towel for the blood, he made a gesture of command, meaning, Wait till I am ready. Then he said, "All. Every man."

Wherever the ring might be, the King was here. Perdikkas went out.

Alexander pushed himself a little sideways, and looked at me. I moved the pillows, to prop him there. Someone opened the private postern, for the men to leave by when they had passed the bed. Their muttering voices approached. Peukestas looked at me with kindness, and made a little motion with his head. He had always shown me courtesy; so I understood him. I said to Alexander, "I will come back after," and went out by the postern door.

As soldiers to their general, as Macedonians to their King, they had come to bid him farewell. Now at the last they must find him all their own, not with his Persian boy closer to him then they.

From the alcove where I stood unseen, I watched them leaving, a stream of men I thought would never end, one after one. They wept, or spoke in husky whispers; or just looked dazed, as if they had learned that the sun would not rise tomorrow.

They took hours to go by. The day wore towards noon. I heard one say, "He greeted me with his eyes. He knew me." Another said, "He recognized me right away. He tried to smile." A young one said, "He gave me a look, and I thought, The world is breaking." A veteran answered, "No, lad, the world goes on. But the gods alone know where."

At last, no more came. I went in. He lay as I'd left him; all that time, he had held himself eyes-front to them, not letting one pass without a look of greeting. Now he lay like the dead, but for his panting breath. I thought, They have drained the last life from him, and left me nothing. May the dogs eat them.

I lifted him on one arm, and changed the pillows so that he lay easier. He opened his eyes, and smiled. I understood that this gift of theirs, whatever it had cost him, was what he would have asked of his guardian god. How could I grudge it him? I put away my anger.

The generals had stood aside while the men passed by. Ptolemy wiped his eyes. Perdikkas stepped over to the bed. "Alexander. When you are received among the gods, at what times shall we offer you worship?"

I don't think he expected any answer; just wanted, if he could still be heard, to make a gift of honor, as he felt it due. He was heard. Alexander came back to us, as if out of deep water. The smile still hung about him. He whispered, "When you are happy." Then he closed his eyes, and returned where he had been.

All day he lay on the high pillows, between the gilded daimons with spread wings. All day the great men came and went. Towards evening, they brought Roxane. The child was big in her. She flung herself on him, beating her breast and tearing her hair, wailing as if he were already dead. I saw his eyelids creasing. Her I dared not speak to, for I had seen her look of hate; but I whispered to Peukestas, "He can hear, it troubles him," and they made her eunuchs lead her out.

Sometimes I could rouse him to take a drink of water; sometimes he seemed already in the death-sleep and would not stir for me; yet I felt his presence, and thought that he felt mine. I thought, I will not ask heaven for any sign from him; let him not be troubled by my love, only know of it if God pleases; for love is life to him, he has never turned it away.

Night fell and the lamps were kindled. Ptolemy stood by the bed, looking down, remembering him, I suppose, in Macedon as a child. Peukestas came up and said that he and a few friends were going to keep vigil for him at the shrine of Serapis. Alexander had brought the god's cult from Egypt; he is a form of the risen Osiris; they would ask his oracle whether he would heal Alexander, if he were carried to the shrine.

It is man's nature to hope even in extremity. As

the flickering lamplight moved on his quiet face, mocking me with false shadows of life, I awaited some promise from the god. But my body knew. My body weighed with his death, as heavy as clay.

The night passed for me in starts and stretches. It was long since I had slept; sometimes I found myself with my head leaned on his pillow, and looked if he had stirred; but he slept on, with quick shallow breaths, broken with deep sighs. The lamps faded, the first pallor of dawn showed the shapes of the tall windows. His breathing had changed its sound, and something said to me, He is here.

I drew close and whispered, "I love you, Alexander," and kissed him. Never mind, I thought, from whom his heart accepts it. Let it be according to his wish.

My hair had fallen on his breast. His eyes opened; his hand moved, and touched a strand, and ran it between his fingers.

He knew me. To that I will take my oath before the gods. It was to me that he bade farewell.

The others, who had seen him move, rose to their feet. But he had gone away. He was on the threshold of his journey.

Someone was at the door. Peukestas stood there. Ptolemy and Perdikkas went to meet him. He said, "We watched all night, and at dawn we went to the oracle. The god said it would be better for him here."

When his breath ceased, the eunuchs all bewailed him. I suppose that I did too. Outside the Palace it was heard, and the sound spread through the city; there was no need to give out that the King was dead. As we took the high pillows from behind him, and laid him straight, the squires on guard came in and stood there bewildered, and walked out crying.

He had died with closed eyes and mouth, as seemly as in sleep. His hair was tousled from the tossing of his fever, and I combed it; I could not keep from doing it as if he could still feel. Then I looked for the great men who had half filled the Bedchamber, for someone to order how he was to be cared for. But they had all gone. The world had broken; the pieces lay like shattered gold, spoil for the strongest. They had gone to gather them up.

After a while the Palace eunuchs grew uneasy, not knowing who was King. One after another went off, to see how things stood; the lesser followed the greater. I did not notice at first that I was there alone.

I stayed, for I could not think of anywhere else to be. Someone will come, I thought; he is mine until they claim him. I uncovered his body, and looked at his wounds which I had known by touch in the dark, and covered him again. Then I sat down by the bed, and leaned my head on it, and I think that I fell asleep.

I woke to the slanting light of evening. No one had come. The air was heavy with heat. I thought, They must come soon, his body will not withstand it. But no breath of corruption came from him; he seemed no more than sleeping.

Always the life in him was stronger than in other men. I felt at his heart in vain; his breath did not mist the mirror; yet somewhere deep within him the soul might still remain, preparing to depart, but not yet gone. I spoke to that; not to his ears, I knew they would not hear me, but to whatever of him might hear.

"Go to the gods, unconquered Alexander. May the River of Ordeal be mild as milk to you, and bathe you in light, not fire. May your dead forgive you; you have given more life to men than you brought death. God made the bull to eat grass, but the lion not; and God alone will judge between them. You were never without love; where you go, may you find it waiting."

At this, the memory came to me of Kalanos singing on his flower-wreathed bier. I thought, He has kept his word; he has put off for his sake being born again; himself having passed in peace through fire, he is here to lead him across the River. It eased my heart, to know he was not alone.

Suddenly, in this stillness, a great clamor approached the room. Ptolemy and Perdikkas rushed in with a band of soldiers, and the royal squires. Perdikkas shouted, "Bolt the doors!" and they crashed them to. There were shouts and hammerings; those outside broke in the doors. Perdikkas and Ptolemy called to their men to defend the King's body from traitors and pretenders. I was almost crushed as they backed around the bed. The wars for the world had started; these people were fighting to possess him, as if he were a thing, a symbol, like the Mitra or the throne. I turned to him. When I saw him still lie calm, bearing all this without resentment, then I knew he was truly dead.

They had begun to fight, and were throwing javelins. I stood to shield him, and one of them grazed my arm. I have the scar to this day, the only wound I ever took for him.

Presently they parleyed, and went away to go on with their dispute outside. I bound up my arm with a bit of towel, and waited, for it was not proper he should be without attendance. I lit the night-lamp and set it by the bed, and watched with him, till at morning the embalmers came to take him from me, and fill him with everlasting myrrh.

AUTHOR'S NOTE

ALL PUBLIC acts of Alexander here recounted are based upon the sources, the most dramatic being the most authentic. It has been impossible to find room for all the major events, even, of his crowded life, or to demonstrate the full scope of his genius. This book attempts only an angle shot, with certain highlights.

Source histories all commend the "moderation" of his sex life. None suggest that he was celibate; had he been, it would of course have been assumed that he was impotent; the Christian ideal of chastity was still unborn. A general pattern emerges of a fairly low physical drive—unsurprising, when such immense energies were spent elsewhere—coupled with a passionate capacity for affection. We know as little as we do of his love affairs, partly because they were few, partly because he was a good picker; none of his partners involved him in scandal.

That Hephaistion was his lover seems, on the evidence, probable to the verge of certainty, but is nowhere actually stated. Plutarch's account of a child by Memnon's widow after the fall of Damascus is, for sound reasons, doubted by modern historians, and there is no other record of his having had a mistress. Bagoas is the only person explicitly named in the sources as Alexander's *eromenos*.

He first appears in Curtius: *Nabarzanes, having received a safe-conduct, met him* [Alexander] *bringing great gifts. Among these was Bagoas, a eunuch of remarkable beauty and in the very flower of boyhood, who had been loved by Darius, and was afterwards to be loved by Alexander; and it was especially because of the boy's pleadings that he was led to pardon*

Nabarzanes. This last is typical Curtius embroidery; the safe-conduct shows that Alexander was willing to hear Nabarzanes' account of himself, and no doubt this decided the issue. How Bagoas came into his hands, when none of Darius' suite was allowed with him after his arrest, and Nabarzanes himself escaped with only six hundred horsemen, is not explained.

There is a widespread modern delusion that all eunuchs became gross and flabby. To correct it one need go no further back than the eighteenth century and its famous operatic *castrati,* whose romantic looks caused them to be much pursued by women of fashion. A portrait of the greatest, Farinelli, done in early middle age, shows a handsome sensitive face, and a figure many modern tenors might envy. The diarist Dr. Burney, writing of him still later, said, "He is tall and thin, but looks very well for his time of life, is lively and well bred."

The story of Darius' last days occurs only in Curtius. It is vivid and detailed; is irrelevant to the bias for which Curtius is notorious, and is probably authentic. If so, the final scenes can only have been supplied to some early chronicler by one of Darius' eunuchs, who were the only witnesses; it is reasonable to suppose by Bagoas himself. With his favored place at court he must have been known to all Alexander's contemporary historians.

History next knows Bagoas some six years later, when the anecdote of the kiss in the theater is given both by Plutarch and Athenaeus. The location in Karmania is highly significant; there Alexander still had with him only those who had followed him through India and the desert march. After all these vicissitudes, Bagoas was not only still high in his affection, but evidently well liked even by the xenophobe Macedonian troops, in itself surprising. Alexander always repaid with lifelong loyalty a personal devotion, and this seems the likeliest explanation of such a long attachment.

The young eunuch's origins are unknown; but the conjecture that he was of good birth is not fanciful.

Such boys, whose looks had been taken care of and not spoiled by malnutrition or hardship, once enslaved were always at the highest risk of prostitution. Sokrates' disciple Phaidon (Phaedo) is the best-known case.

Bagoas' last appearance has been irretrievably garbled by Curtius; one can only do one's best with it. Luckily for Bagoas' reputation, we have the first-class evidence of Aristoboulos the architect, who actually restored Kyros' tomb for Alexander, that he went there when first at Persepolis, saw for himself the valuable grave-goods, and had them inventoried by Aristoboulos, whose description is preserved by Arrian, along with his account of the desecration. In Curtius, Alexander only goes to the tomb on his return from India, and finds it bare because Kyros has been buried only with his simple weapons; a notion which would no doubt delight Roman sentiment but surprise an archaeologist. Bagoas, who has a spite against Orxines for not having sent him a bribe, invents a nonexistent treasure and accuses him of its theft. None of the crimes for which Orxines was in fact punished are mentioned; he is supposed an innocent victim. When the impossible is discarded from this tale not much is left. I have assumed that Bagoas did some-how enter the scene, having some grievance against the satrap with which Alexander sympathized. In view of Orxines' murderous record, I have supplied the com-monest grudge of the ancient world, a family blood-feud.

Muddled sensationalism is typical of Curtius, an unbearably silly man with access to priceless sources now lost to us, which he frittered away in the cause of a tedious literary concept about the goddess Fortune, and many florid exercises in Roman rhetoric. (Alex-ander, exhorting his friends kindly to remove the ar-row stuck in his lung, is impressively eloquent.) The favors of Fortune being conducive to hubris and nemesis, Alexander's story is bent that way by re-course to Athenian anti-Macedonian agitprop, written by men who never set eyes on him, and bearing about as much relation to objective truth as one would

expect to find in a *History of the Jewish People* com-
missioned by Adolf Hitler. This had been revived in
Augustus' time by Trogus and Diodorus, who found
in a king three centuries dead a safe whipping-boy
for the divine pretensions of the living ruler. No at-
tempt is made at consistency with the undisputed facts.
A corrupted tyrant would have been cut down by the
Opis mutineers the moment he stepped down among
them; they could have done it with perfect impunity
(the fate of more than one Roman emperor) and elected
a new King, as was their right. That instead they
complained to Alexander of not being allowed to kiss
him is not fiction but history.

As regards the ancient world, the political motives
of these unconvincing attempts to show Alexander
corrupted by success are clear enough. More puzzling
is a present-day outbreak of what one may call black-
washing, since it goes far beyond a one-sided interpreta-
tion of facts to their actual misrepresentation. A re-
cent popularization says only of Philotas' execution
that it was "on a trumped-up charge," though his con-
cealment of the assassination plot is agreed on by all
the sources. (What would be the position of a modern
security guard who, informed there was a bomb on
the royal plane, decided not to mention it?) Hephaistion is "fundamentally stupid," though in not one of
his highly responsible independent missions, diploma-
tic as well as military, was he ever unsuccessful. Alexander is baldly accused of compassing his father's
death, though not only is the evidence, literally, nil;
Philip had not even a viable alternative heir to supply
a motive. "Severe alcoholism" is said to have hastened
Alexander's end; any general practitioner could explain
what a severe alcoholic's work capacity is, and what
his chance of surviving lung perforation, unanaes-
thetized field surgery, and a desert march. After the
gesture of the troops at Alexander's deathbed, an event
unique in history, it is somewhat surprising to be told
that few people mourned him. That there are fash-
ions in admiration and denigration is inevitable; they

should not however be followed at the expense of truth.

In the same spirit, the most sinister motives have been sought for his policies of racial fusion. Yet no one took less trouble to conceal his aversions than he; it is staringly obvious that, once among Persians, he simply found he liked them. Surely in our day it takes a somewhat insular mind to find this either discreditable or strange.

Though accounts of Alexander's general deterioration do not hold water, there seems little doubt that he did suffer some severe mental disturbance just after Hephaistion's death. Whether such a breakdown could have recurred cannot be known. Alexander's nature was a kind of self-winding spring. The tensions of his childhood demanded compensation in achievement; achievement accumulated responsibilities, at the same time suggesting further achievements; the spiral was inexorably ascending, and one cannot be sure this process could have continued through a normal life-span without disaster. Perhaps Kalanos' parting words were more promise than warning.

Bury and other historians have pointed out the connection between a tainted water supply and heavier wine-drinking in the army. Aristoboulos, who was at court through Alexander's reign, says his usual habit was to sit over his wine talking into the night, but without getting drunk. According to Plutarch he got rather euphoric towards the end of the session; a phenomenon which can be observed today in persons not given to excess. Occasional drinking-bouts were however characteristically Macedonian, as we already find before Alexander's accession.

Rumors that he was poisoned, rife for centuries after his death, do not tally with the detailed case history of his last illness. His loss of voice points to the most common fatal complication right up to the discovery of antibiotics—pneumonia. Pleurisy would be a certain sequel in view of his Mallian wound. Aristoboulos says that when in high fever he drank wine and became delirious; he is not said to have demanded it. If it was conveyed to him in malice then he was, morally speaking, poisoned, and the presence of a mortal enemy like Kassandros should not be overlooked.

Curtius has preserved a story that his body was found uncorrupted, in spite of the summer heat and of a long delay in fetching the embalmers, due to the chaos following his death. The period given, six days, is of course absurd; but it is quite possible that a deep coma deceived the watchers a good many hours before clinical death occurred. The embalmers did their work with skill. Augustus Caesar, visiting his tomb at Alexandria, admired the beauty of his features after three hundred years.

The account of Hephaistion's end suggests he had typhoid, where, though appetite often returns before the lesions in the gut have healed, solid food causes perforation and swift collapse. In our own century typhoid patients have been killed in hospital by misguided relatives smuggling them food. Hephaistion's boiled fowl, about the size of a modern bantam, would be more than enough.

Arrian has been followed for the squires' conspiracy, except for my own guess that letters from Aristotle were found among Kallisthenes' papers. Alexander's friendly correspondence with his tutor ceased from this time.

The romantic figure of Roxane has not been treated with a groundless skepticism. There is no need to dismiss the marriage as political; her rank was middling and her beauty famous. But about two months later, the squires could count upon finding Alexander in bed without her; and we know what she did when he died. She can have wasted no time in mourning. She sent, with such speed that it outstripped the news, a letter to his royal wife Stateira, written in his name, summoning her at once to Babylon; and had her murdered as soon as she arrived.

Sisygambis, the Queen Mother of Persia, when told of Alexander's death, bade her family farewell, shut herself up without food, and died five days later.

Events this book has no room for, or which Bagoas would not have known of, have been taken into account in the portrayal of Alexander. It needs to be borne in mind today that not till more than a century later did a handful of philosophers even start to question the morality of war. In his time the issue was not whether, but how one made it. It is noteworthy that the historians most favorable to him, Ptolemy and Aristoboulos, were those who knew him in life. They wrote when he was dead, with no incentive but to do him justice.

When his faults (those his own times did not account as virtues) have been considered, we are left with the fact that no other human being has attracted in his lifetime, from so many men, so fervent a devotion. Their reasons are worth examining.

Sources for the General Reader

The best is Arrian, who drew mainly on the lost memoirs of Ptolemy and Aristoboulos, and wrote with a high sense of responsibility. His *Life of Alexander* is available in the Penguin Classics (as *The Campaigns of Alexander*), or in the Loeb Classical Library with Greek and translation interleaved, and notes. Plutarch, whose *Lives* is published by Everyman, is colorful, but made little effort to evaluate his evidence, and should not be swallowed whole.

Proper Names

It is of course implausible to have a Persian using Persian names in their Greek forms; but since in the Persian they would be unrecognizable and unpronounceable to almost all general readers (Darius for example is Darayavaush) I have retained the usual convention.

Roxane is pronounced with the accent on the first syllable.

ABOUT THE AUTHOR

MARY RENAULT was born in London, where her father was a doctor. She first went to Oxford with the idea of teaching, but decided that she wanted to be a writer instead, and that after taking her degree she should broaden her knowledge of human life. She then trained for three years as a nurse, and wrote her first published novel, *Promise of Love*. Her next three novels were written during off-duty time when serving in the war. One of them, *Return to Night*, received the M.G.M. award. After the war, she went to South Africa and settled at the Cape. She has traveled considerably in Africa and has gone up the east coast to Zanzibar and Mombasa. But it was her trip to Greece, her visits to Corinth, Samos, Crete, Delos, Aegina and other islands, as well as to Athens, Sounion and Marathon, that resulted in her previous brilliant historical reconstructions of ancient Greece, *The Last of the Wine, The King Must Die, The Bull from the Sea, The Mask of Apollo* and *Fire from Heaven*.